KU-542-873

Shortliste...

Shortlisted for the *Guardian* First Bo...

**Winner of the FT/Oppenheimer Fund
Emerging Voices Award**

**Longlisted for the
International Dylan Thomas Prize**

**An *Observer, Economist, Financial Times,
Herald* and *New York Times* Book of the Year**

'The best debut of the year by some distance'

Alex Preston, *Observer* Books of the Year

'A striking, controlled and masterfully taut debut…The
tale has a timeless quality that renders it almost allegorical
and it is the more powerful for it'

FT

'It's like being in a Zola or Theodore Dreiser novel…
The Fishermen is an elegy to lost promise […] and yet it
remains hopeful about the redemptive possibilities of a
new generation'

Guardian

'Chigozie Obioma truly is the heir to Chinua Achebe'

Times

'Full of deceptive simplicity, lyrical language and playful Igbo mythology and humour... an impressive and beautifully imagined work'

Economist

'A mighty fry-up of pop culture, fable and verbal invention'

New Statesman

'Suffused with an air of legend and the supernatural... *The Fishermen* establishes Obioma as a writer to be taken seriously... ingenious, subtle, ambitious and intriguing'

TLS

'Obioma's long-limbed and elegant writing is shot through with strikingly elevated phrasings... rich with ancient themes of filial love, fratricide, vengeance and fate... its power is unmistakable'

Wall Street Journal

'[A] confident début novel... frank and lyrical'

New Yorker

'Mythic... a truly magnificent debut'

Eleanor Catton, Man Booker Prize Winner

CHIGOZIE OBIOMA was born in 1986 in Akure, Nigeria, and currently lives in the United States. He graduated from the University of Michigan with an MFA in Creative Writing, and is now an assistant professor of Literature and Creative Writing at the University of Nebraska-Lincoln. *The Fishermen* is his first novel.

THE
FISHERMEN

CHIGOZIE OBIOMA

AN IMPRINT OF PUSHKIN PRESS

ONE

an imprint of Pushkin Press

71–75 Shelton Street, London WC2H 9JQ

First published in Great Britain by ONE in 2015
This edition first published in 2016

3 5 7 9 8 6 4 2

ISBN 978 0 957548 86 2

Text designed and typeset by Tetragon, London
Printed and bound by CPI Group (UK) Ltd, Croydon, CR0 4YY

www.pushkinpress.com/one

For my brothers (and sisters),
the "battalion",
a tribute.

The footsteps of one man cannot create a stampede.

IGBO PROVERB

The madman has entered our house with violence
Defiling our sacred grounds
Claiming the single truth of the universe
Bending down our high priests with iron
Ah! yes the children,
Who walked on our Forefathers' graves
Shall be stricken with madness.
They shall grow the fangs of the lizard
They shall devour each other before our eyes
And by ancient command
It is forbidden to stop them!

MAZISI KUNENE

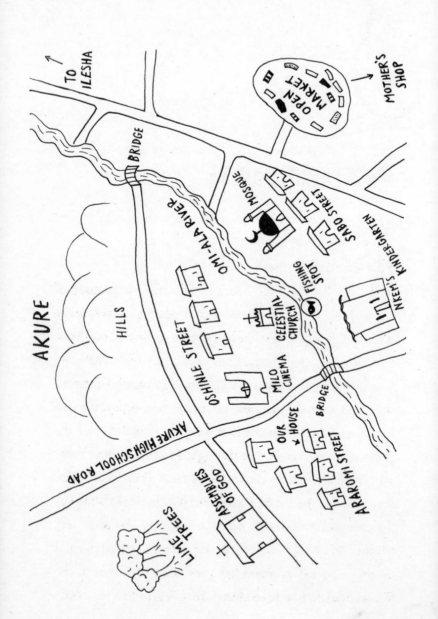

1

FISHERMEN

We were fishermen:

My brothers and I became fishermen in January of 1996 after our father moved out of Akure, a town in the west of Nigeria, where we had lived together all our lives. His employer, the Central Bank of Nigeria, had transferred him to a branch of the bank in Yola—a town in the north that was a camel distance of more than one thousand kilometres away—in the first week of November of the previous year. I remember the night Father returned home with his transfer letter; it was on a Friday. From that Friday through that Saturday, Father and Mother held whispering consultations like shrine priests. By Sunday morning, Mother emerged a different being. She'd acquired the gait of a wet mouse, averting her eyes as she went about the house. She did not go to church that day, but stayed home and washed and ironed a stack of Father's clothes, wearing an impenetrable gloom on her face. Neither of them said a word to my brothers and me, and we did not ask. My brothers—Ikenna, Boja, Obembe—and I had come to understand that when the two ventricles of our home— our father and our mother—held silence as the ventricles of the heart retain blood, we could flood the house if we poked them. So, at times like these, we avoided the television in the eight-columned shelf in our sitting room. We sat in our rooms, studying or feigning to study, anxious but not asking questions. While there, we stuck out our antennae to gather whatever we could of the situation.

By nightfall on Sunday, crumbs of information began to fall from Mother's soliloquy like tots of feathers from a richly plumed bird: "What kind of job takes a man away from bringing up his growing sons? Even if I were born with seven hands, how would I be able to care for these children alone?"

Although these feverish questions were directed to no one in particular, they were certainly intended for Father's ears. He was seated alone on a lounge chair in the sitting room, his face veiled with a copy of his favourite newspaper, the *Guardian,* half reading and half listening to Mother. And although he heard everything she said, Father always turned deaf ears to words not directly addressed to him, the kind he often referred to as "cowardly words." He would simply read on, sometimes breaking off to loudly rebuke or applaud something he'd seen in the newspaper—"If there is any justice in this world, Abacha should soon be mourned by his witch of a wife." "Wow, Fela is a god! Good gracious!" "Reuben Abati should be sacked!"—anything just to create the impression that Mother's lamentations were futile; whimpers to which no one was paying attention.

Before we slept that night, Ikenna, who was nearly fifteen and on whom we relied for the interpretation of most things, had suggested Father was being transferred. Boja, a year his junior, who would have felt unwise if he didn't appear to have any idea about the situation, had said it must be that Father was travelling abroad to a "Western world" just as we often feared he someday would. Obembe who, at eleven, was two years my senior, did not have an opinion. Me neither. But we did not have to wait much longer.

The answer came the following morning when Father suddenly appeared in the room I shared with Obembe. He was dressed in a brown T-shirt. He placed his spectacles on the table, a gesture requesting our attention. "I will start living in Yola from today onwards, and I don't want you boys to give your mother any troubles." His face contorted when he said this, the way it did whenever he wanted to drive the hounds of fear into us. He spoke slowly, his voice deeper and louder, every word tacked nine inches deep into the beams of our minds. So that, if we went ahead and disobeyed, he would make us conjure the exact moment he gave us the instruction in its complete detail with the simple phrase "I told you."

"I will call her regularly, and if I hear any bad news"—he struck his forefinger aloft to fortify his words—"I mean, any funny acts at all, I'll give you the Guerdon for them."

He'd said the word "Guerdon"—a word with which he emphasized a warning or highlighted the retribution for a wrong act—with so much vigour that veins bulged at both sides of his face. This word, once pronounced, often completed the message. He brought out two twenty-naira notes from the breast pocket of his coat and dropped them on our study table.

"For both of you," he said, and left the room.

Obembe and I were still sitting in our bed trying to make sense of all that when we heard Mother speaking to him outside the house in a voice so loud it seemed he was already far away.

"Eme, remember you have growing boys back here," she'd said. "I'm telling you, oh."

She was still speaking when Father started his Peugeot 504. At the sound of it, Obembe and I hurried from our room, but Father was already driving out of the gate. He was gone.

Whenever I think of our story, how that morning would mark the last time we'd live together, all of us, as the family we'd always been, I begin—even these two decades later—to wish he hadn't left, that he had never received that transfer letter. Before that letter came, everything was in place: Father went to work every morning and Mother, who ran a fresh food store in the open market, tended to my five siblings and me who, like the children of most families in Akure, went to school. Everything followed its natural course. We gave little thought to past events. Time meant nothing back then. The days came with clouds hanging in the sky filled with cupfuls of dust in the dry seasons, and the sun lasting into the night. It was as if a hand drew hazy pictures in the sky during the rainy seasons, when rain fell in deluges pulsating with spasms of thunderstorms for six uninterrupted months. Because things followed this known and structured pattern, no day was worthy of remembrance. All that mattered was the present and the foreseeable future. Glimpses of it mostly came like a locomotive train treading tracks of hope, with black coal in its heart and a loud elephantine toot. Sometimes these glimpses came through dreams or flights of fanciful thoughts that whispered in your head—*I will be a pilot, or the president of Nigeria, rich man, own helicopters*—for the future was what we made of it. It was a blank canvas on which anything could be imagined. But Father's move to Yola changed the equation of things: time and seasons and the past began to matter, and we started to yearn and crave for it even more than the present and the future.

He began to live in Yola from that morning. The green table telephone, which had been used mainly for receiving calls from Mr Bayo, Father's childhood friend who lived in Canada, became the only way we reached him. Mother waited restlessly for his calls and marked the days he phoned on the calendar in her room. Whenever Father missed a day in the schedule, and Mother had exhausted her patience waiting, usually long into midnight, she would unfasten the knot at the hem of her *wrappa*, bring out the crumpled paper on which she'd scribbled his phone number, and dial endlessly until he answered. If we were still awake, we'd throng around her to hear Father's voice, urging her to pressure him to take us with him to the new city. But Father persistently refused. Yola, he reiterated, was a volatile city with a history of frequent large-scale violence especially against people of our tribe—the Igbo. We continued to push him until the bloody sectarian riots of March 1996 erupted. When finally Father got on the phone, he recounted—with the sound of sporadic shooting audible in the background—how he narrowly escaped death when rioters attacked his district and how an entire family was butchered in their house across the street from his. "Little children killed like fowls!" he'd said, placing a weighty emphasis on the phrase "little children" in such a way that no sane person could have dared mention moving to him again, and that was it.

Father made it a tradition to visit every other weekend, in his Peugeot 504 saloon, dusty, exhausted from the fifteen-hour drive. We looked forward to those Saturdays when his car honked at the gate, and we rushed to open it, all of us anxious to see what snack or gift he had brought for us this time. Then, as we slowly became accustomed to seeing him every few weeks or so, things changed. His mammoth frame that commandeered decorum and calm, gradually shrunk into the size of a pea. His established routine of composure, obedience, study, and compulsory siesta—long a pattern of our daily existence—gradually lost its grip. A veil spooled over his all-seeing eyes, which we believed were capable of noticing even the slightest wrong thing we did in secret. At the beginning of the third month, his long arm that often wielded the whip, the instrument of caution, snapped like a tired tree branch. Then we broke free.

We shelved our books and set out to explore the sacred world outside the one we were used to. We ventured to the municipality football pitch where most of the boys of the street played football every afternoon. But these boys were a pack of wolves; they did not welcome us. Although we did not know any of them except for one, Kayode, who lived a few blocks from us, these boys knew our family and us down to the names of our parents, and they constantly taunted us and flogged us daily with verbal whips. Despite Ikenna's stunning dribbling skills, and Obembe's goalkeeping wonders, they branded us "amateurs." They frequently joked, too, that our father, "Mr Agwu," was a rich man who worked in the Central Bank of Nigeria, and that we were privileged kids. They adopted a curious moniker for Father: Baba Onile, after the principal character of a popular Yoruba soap who had six wives and twenty-one children. Hence, the name was intended to mock Father whose desire to have many children had become a legend in our district. It was also the Yoruba name for the Praying Mantis, a green ugly skeletal insect. We could not stand for these insults. Ikenna, seeing that we were outnumbered and would not have won a fight against the boys, begged them repeatedly in the custom of Christian children to refrain from insulting our parents who had done nothing wrong to them. Yet they continued, until one evening when Ikenna, maddened at the mention of the moniker, head-butted a boy. In one quick flash, the boy kicked Ikenna in the stomach and closed in on him. For a brief moment, their feet drew an imperfect gyre around the sand-covered pitch as they swirled together. But in the end, the boy threw Ikenna and poured a handful of dirt on his face. The rest of the kids cheered and lifted the boy up, their voices melding into a chorus of victory complete with boos and *uuh uuhs*. We went home that evening feeling beaten, and never returned there.

After this fight, we got tired of going outdoors. At my suggestion, we begged Mother to convince Father to release the console game set to play *Mortal Kombat*, which he seized and hid somewhere the previous year after Boja—who was known for his usual first position in his class—came home with *24th* scribbled in red ink on his report card and the warning *Likely to repeat*. Ikenna did not fare any better; his was sixteenth out of forty and it came with a personal letter to Father from his teacher, Mrs Bukky. Father read out the letter in such a fit of anger that the only words I heard were "Gracious me! Gracious me!" which he repeated like a refrain. He would confiscate the games and forever cut off the moments that often sent us swirling with excitement, screaming and howling when the invisible commentator in the game ordered, "Finish him," and the conquering sprite would inflict serious blows on the vanquished sprite by either kicking it up to the sky or by slicing it into a grotesque explosion of bones and blood. The screen would then go abuzz with "fatality" inscribed in strobe letters of flame. Once, Obembe—in the midst of relieving himself—ran out of the toilet just to be there so he could join in and cry "That is fatal!" in an American accent that mimicked the console's voice-over. Mother would punish him later when she discovered he'd unknowingly dropped excreta on the rug.

Frustrated, we tried yet again to find a physical activity to fill up our after-school hours now that we were free from Father's strict regulations. So, we gathered neighbourhood friends to play football at the clearing behind our compound. We brought Kayode, the only boy we'd known among the pack of wolves we played with at the municipality football pitch. He had an androgynous face and a permanent gentle smile. Igbafe, our neighbour, and his cousin, Tobi—a half-deaf boy who strained your vocal chords only to ask *Jo, kini o nso?*—Please, what did you say?—also joined us. Tobi had large ears that did not appear to be part of his body. He was hardly offended—perhaps because he couldn't hear sometimes, for we often whispered it—when we called him *Eleti Ehoro*—One With a Hare's Ears. We'd run up the length and breadth of this pitch, dressed in cheap football jerseys and T-shirts on which we'd printed our football nicknames. We played as if unhinged, frequently volleying the balls into neighbouring houses, and embarking on botched attempts to retrieve them. Many times, we arrived at some of the places just in time to witness the neighbours puncturing the balls, paying no heed to our pleas to give them back because the ball had either hit someone or destroyed something. Once, the ball flew over a neighbour's fence and hit a crippled man on the head and knocked him off his chair. At another time, the ball shattered a glass window.

Every time they destroyed a ball, we contributed money and bought a new one, except for Kayode, who, having come from the town's sprawling population of the acutely poor, could not afford even a kobo. He often dressed in worn-out, torn shorts, and lived with his aged parents, the spiritual heads of the small Christ Apostolic Church, in an unfinished two-storeyed building just down the bend of the road to our school. Because he couldn't contribute, he prayed for each ball, asking God to help us keep this one for much longer by preventing it from crossing the clearing.

One day, we bought a new fine white ball with the logo of the Atlanta 1996 Olympic Games. After Kayode prayed, we set out to play, but barely an hour into the game, Boja struck a kick that landed in a fenced compound owned by a medical doctor. The ball smashed one of the windows of the lush house with a din, sending two pigeons asleep on the roof to a frantic flight. We waited at some distance so we could have sufficient space to flee should someone come out in pursuit. After a long while, Ikenna and Boja started for the house while Kayode knelt and prayed for God's intervention. When the emissaries reached the compound, the doctor, as if already waiting for them, gave chase, sending us all running ankle-to-head to escape. We knew, once we got home that evening, panting and perspiring, that we'd had it with football.

* * *

We became fishermen when Ikenna came home from school the following week bursting with the novel idea. It was at the end of January because I remember that Boja's fourteenth birthday, which was on January 18th, 1996, had been celebrated that weekend with the home-baked cake and soft drinks that replaced dinner. His birthdays marked the "age-mate month," a period of one month in which he temporarily locked age with Ikenna, who was born on February 10th, one year before him. Ikenna's classmate, Solomon, had told him about the pleasures of fishing. Ikenna described how Solomon had called the sport a thrilling experience that was also rewarding since he could sell some of the fish and earn a bit of income. Ikenna was even more intrigued because the idea had awakened the possibility of resurrecting Yoyodon, the fish. The aquarium, which once sat beside the television, had housed a preternaturally beautiful Symphysodon fish that was a colony of colours—brown, violet, purple and even pale green. Father called the fish Yoyodon after Obembe came up with a similar sounding word while trying to pronounce Symphysodon: the name of the fish's specie. Father took the aquarium away after Ikenna and Boja, on a compassionate quest to free the fish from its "dirty water," removed and replaced it with clean drinking water. They would return later to notice the fish could no longer rise from among the row of glistening pebbles and corals.

Once Solomon told Ikenna about fishing, our brother vowed he would capture a new Yoyodon. He went with Boja to Solomon's house the next day and returned raving about *this* fish and *that* fish. They bought two hooked fishing lines from somewhere Solomon had showed them. Ikenna set them on the table in their room and explained how they were used. The hooked fishing lines were long wooden staffs with a threadlike rope attached to the tip of the staff. The ropes carried iron hooks on their ends, and it was on these hooks, Ikenna said, that baits—earthworms, cockroaches, food crumbs, whatever—were attached to lure the fish and trap them. From the following day onwards, for a whole week, they rushed off every day after school and trekked the long tortuous path to the Omi-Ala River at the end of our district to fish, passing through a clearing behind our compound that stank in the rainy season and served as a home for a clan of swine. They went in the company of Solomon and other boys of the street, and returned with cans filled with fish. At first, they did not allow Obembe and me to go with them although our interests were piqued when we saw the small, coloured fish they caught. Then one day, Ikenna said to Obembe and me: "Follow us, and we will make you fishermen!"—and we followed.

We began going to the river every day after school in the company of other children of the street in a procession led by Solomon, Ikenna and Boja. These three often concealed hooked fishing lines in rags or old *wrappas*. The rest of us—Kayode, Igbafe, Tobi, Obembe and I—carried things that ranged from rucksacks with fishing clothes in them to nylon bags containing earthworms and dead roaches we used as baits, and empty beverage cans in which we kept the fish and tadpoles we caught. Together we trod to the river, wading through bushy tracks that were populated with schools of prickly dead nettles that flogged our bare legs and left white welts on our skin. The flogging the nettles inflicted on us matched the strange botanical name for the predominant grass in the area, *esan*, the Yoruba word for retribution or vengeance. We'd walk this trail single file and once we'd passed these grasses, we'd rush off to the river like madmen. The older ones among us, Solomon, Ikenna and Boja, would change into their dirty fishing clothes. They would then stand close to the river, and hold their lines up above the water so the baited hooks would disappear down into it. But although they fished like men of yore who'd known the river from its cradle, they mostly only harvested a few palm-sized smelts, or some brown cods that were much more difficult to catch, and, rarely, some tilapias. The rest of us just scooped tadpoles with beverage cans. I loved the tadpoles, their slick bodies, exaggerated heads and how they appeared nearly shape-less as if they were the miniature version of whales. So I would watch with awe as they hung suspended below the water and my fingers would blacken from rubbing off the grey glop that glossed their skins. Sometimes we picked up coral shells or empty shells of long-dead arthropods. We caught rounded snails the shape of primal whorls, the teeth of some beast—which we came to believe belonged to a bygone era because Boja argued vehemently that it was that of a dinosaur and took it home with him—pieces of the moulted skin of a cobra shed just by the bank of the river, and anything of interest we could find.

Only once did we catch a fish that was big enough to sell, and I often think of that day. Solomon had pulled this humongous fish that was bigger than anything we'd ever seen in Omi-Ala. Then Ikenna and Solomon went off to the nearby food market, and returned to the river after a little more than half an hour with fifteen naira. My brothers and I went home with the six naira that was our share of the sale, our joy boundless. We began to fish more in earnest from then on, staying awake long into the nights to discuss the experience.

Our fishing was carried out with great zeal, as though a faithful audience gathered daily by the bank of the river to watch and cheer us. We did not mind the smell of the bracken waters, the winged insects that gathered in blobs around the banks every evening and the nauseating sight of algae and leaves that formed the shape of a map of troubled nations at the far end of the riverbank where varicose trees dipped into the waters. We went every single day with corroding tins, dead insects, melting worms, dressed mostly in rags and old clothing. For we derived great joy from this fishing, despite the difficulties and meagre returns.

When I look back today, as I find myself doing more often now that I have sons of my own, I realize that it was during one of these trips to the river that our lives and our world changed. For it was here that time began to matter, at that river where we became fishermen.

2

THE RIVER

Omi-Ala was a dreadful river:

Long forsaken by the inhabitants of Akure town like a mother abandoned by her children. But it was once a pure river that supplied the earliest settlers with fish and clean drinking water. It surrounded Akure and snaked through its length and breadth. Like many such rivers in Africa, Omi-Ala was once believed to be a god; people worshipped it. They erected shrines in its name, and courted the intercession and guidance of Iyemoja, Osha, mermaids, and other spirits and gods that dwelt in water bodies. This changed when the colonialists came from Europe, and introduced the Bible, which then prised Omi-Ala's adherents from it, and the people, now largely Christians, began to see it as an evil place. A cradle besmeared.

It became the source of dark rumours. One such rumour

was that people committed all sorts of fetish rituals at its banks. This was supported by accounts of corpses, animal carcasses and other ritualistic materials floating on the surface of the river or lying on its banks. Then early in 1995, the mutilated body of a woman was found in the river, her vital body parts dismembered. When her remains were discovered, the town council placed a dusk-to-dawn curfew on the river from 6 p.m. to 6 a.m., and the river was abandoned. Incident after incident accumulated over many years, tainting the history of the river and corrupting its name so much so that—in time—the mere mention of it triggered disdain. It did not help that a religious sect with a bad reputation in the country was located close to it. Known as the Celestial Church or the white garment church, its believers worshipped water spirits and walked about barefoot. We knew our parents would severely punish us if they ever found out we were going to the river. Yet we did not give it a thought until one of our neighbours—a petty trader who walked the town hawking fried groundnuts on a tray she carried on her head—caught us on the path to the river and reported us to Mother. This was in late February and we had been fishing for nearly six weeks. On that day, Solomon had angled a big fish. We jumped up at the sight of it wriggling against the dripping hook, and burst into the fishermen song, which Solomon had invented. We always sang it at peak moments, such as the fish's death spiral.

The song was a variation of the well-known ditty performed by the adulterous wife of Pastor Ishawuru, the main character of the most popular Christian soap in Akure at the time, *The Ultimate Power*, during her recall to church after she was banished for her sin. Although Solomon came up with the idea, most of the suggestions that eventually made up the lyrics came from nearly every one of us. It was Boja's suggestion, for instance, that we put "the fishermen have caught you" in place of "we have caught you." We replaced her testimony to God's ability to hold her up against the power of Satan's temptations with our ability to hold the fish firm once caught and not let it escape. We so greatly delighted in this song that we sometimes hummed it at home or in school.

Bi otiwu o ki o Jo,	Dance all you want,
ki o ja,	fight all you will,
Ati mu o,	We've caught you,
o male lo mo.	you cannot escape.
She bi ati mu o?	Haven't we caught you?
O male le lo mo o.	You certainly can't escape.
Awa, Apeja, ti mu o.	We, the fishermen, have caught you.
Awa, Apeja,	We, the fishermen,
ti mu o, o ma le lo mo o	have caught you, you can't escape!

We sang the song so loudly after Solomon's catch that evening that an elderly man, a priest of the Celestial Church, came to the river barefoot, his feet as noiseless as a phantom's. When we began visiting the river and found this church within our ambit, we immediately included it in our adventures. We'd peek at the worshippers through the open mahogany windows of the small church hall with peeling blue paint, and mimic their frenzied actions and dances. Only Ikenna deemed it insensitive to the sacred practice of a religious body. I was closest to the path from which the old man came, and was the first to see him. Boja was on the other side of the river, and when he spotted the man, he dropped his line and hurried ashore. The part of the river where we fished was hidden from the rest of the street by long stretches of bushes on both sides and you could not see the waters until you took the rutted path carved out of the bush from the adjoining street. After the old man had entered the path and drawn near, he stopped, having noticed two of our beverage cans sitting in shallow holes we'd dug with our hands. He peered down to see the contents of the cans, around which flies were hovering, and turned away, shaking his head.

"What is this?" he asked in a Yoruba whose accent was foreign to me. "Why were you shouting like a pack of drunks? Don't you know that the house of God is just on the other side?" He pointed in the direction of the church, turning his body fully to the pathway. "Don't you have any respect for God, eh?"

We'd all been taught that it was rude to answer an older person's question meant to indict us, even if we could readily provide an answer. So instead of replying, Solomon apologized.

"We are sorry, baba," he said, rubbing his palms together. "We will refrain from shouting."

"What are you fishing from these waters?" asked the old man, ignoring Solomon and pointing to the river whose waters had now become a bed of darkening grey. "Tadpoles, smelts, what? Why don't you all go home?" He blinked his eyes, his gaze roving from one person to the other. Igbafe stifled laughter, but Ikenna chewed him out by mumbling "Idiot" under his breath; too late.

"You think it's funny?" the man said, staring at Igbafe. "Well, it's your parents I pity. I'm sure they do not know you come here and will be sorry if they ever find out. Haven't you heard the government has banned people from coming here? Oh, kids of this generation." He glanced around again with a look of astonishment and then said: "Whether you leave or not, do not raise your voices like that again. You hear?"

With a long-drawn sigh and shaking of the head, the

priest turned and walked away. We burst into laughter, mocking the white robe flapping against his thin frame, which had given him the appearance of a child in an over-sized coat. We laughed at the fearful man who could not stand the sight of fish and tadpoles (because he peered at the fish with terror in his eyes), and at the imagined odour of his mouth (even though none of us had been close enough to smell his breath).

"This man is just like Iya Olode, the madwoman who people say is even worse," Kayode said. He'd carried a tin of fish and tadpoles and it tilted in his hand now, so he covered its top to prevent it from spilling over. His nose was running but he seemed not to be conscious of it, so that the milky white secretion hung just beneath his nos-trils. "She is always dancing around the town—mostly dancing Makosa. The other day, she was chased out of the big open-market bazaar at Oja-Oba because they said she crouched at the very centre of the market, just beside a meat seller's shed and shat."

We laughed at this. Boja quivered as he laughed, and then as if the laughter had drained him of all energy, he dropped his hands on both knees, panting. We were still laughing when we noticed that Ikenna, who had not uttered a single word since the priest interrupted our fishing, had emerged from the water on the far side of the banks where wilted esan grass prostrated into the river. He'd started to unbuckle his wet shorts when our attention was drawn to him. We watched as he removed his dripping fishing clothes, too, and began drying himself.

"Ike, what are you doing?" Solomon said.

"I'm going home," Ikenna replied curtly as if he'd been impatiently waiting to be asked. "I want to go and study. I'm a student, not a fisherman."

"Now?" said Solomon. "Isn't it too early and we have—"

Solomon did not complete his sentence; he'd understood. For the seed of what Ikenna had now begun to act out—a lack of interest in fishing—was sown the previous week. He'd had to be persuaded to come with us to the river that day. So, when he said: "I want to go and study. I'm a student, not a fisherman," no one questioned him any further. Boja, Obembe and I—left with no choice but to follow him since we never did anything Ikenna did not approve of—began dressing for home, too. Obembe was packing up the lines into the worn-out *wrappas* we had stolen from one of Mother's old boxes. I picked up the cans and small polythene bag in which the rest of the unused worms wriggled, struggled and slowly died.

"Are you all really leaving?" Kayode asked as we followed Ikenna, who did not seem keen on waiting for us, his brothers.

"Why are you all going now?" Solomon said. "Is it because of the priest or because of that day you met Abulu? Did I not ask you not to wait? Did I not tell you not to listen to him? Did I not tell you that he was just an evil, crazy, madman?"

But none of us said a word in reply, nor did we turn to him. We simply walked on, Ikenna ahead, holding only the black polythene bag in which he kept his fishing shorts. He had left his hooked fishing line at the bank, but Boja had picked it up and carried it in his own *wrappa*.

"Let them go," I heard Igbafe say behind us. "We don't need them; we can fish by ourselves."

They started to mock us, but the distance soon cut them off, and we began to walk through the tracks in silence. As we went I wondered what had come over Ikenna. There were times when I could not understand his actions, or his decisions. I depended mostly on Obembe to help me clarify things. After the encounter with Abulu the previous week, which Solomon had just referred to, Obembe had told me a story he said was responsible for Ikenna's sudden change. I was pondering this story when Boja cried: "My God, Ikenna, look, Mama Iyabo!" He'd seen one of our neighbours, who hawked groundnuts about on foot, seated on the bench in front of the church with the priest who'd come to the river earlier. By the time

Boja raised the alarm, it was already too late; the woman had seen us.

"Ah, ah, Ike," she called out at us as we passed, calm as prisoners. "What have you come to do here?"

"Nothing!" Ikenna answered, quickening his pace.

She'd risen to her feet, a tiger of a woman, arms raised as if about to pounce on us.

"And the thing in your hand? Ikenna, Ikenna! I'm talking to you."

In defiance, Ikenna hurried down the path, and we followed suit. We took the short turn behind a compound where the branch of a banana tree, snapped in a storm, bowed like the blunt snout of a porpoise. Once there, Ikenna faced us and said: "Have you all seen it? Have you seen what your folly has caused? Didn't I say we should stop going to this stupid river, but none of you listened?" He piled both hands on his head: "You will see that she will certainly blow the whistle to Mama. *You want to bet it?*" He slapped his forehead. "You want to?"

No one replied. "You see?" he said. "Your eyes have now opened, right? You *will* see."

These words throbbed in my ears as we went, driving home the fear that she would definitely report us to Mother. The woman was Mother's friend, a widow whose husband had died in Sierra Leone while fighting for the

African Union forces. He left her with only a gratuity that was sawn in half by her husband's family members, two malnourished sons Ikenna's age, and a sea of endless wants that prompted Mother to step in to help from time to time. Mama Iyabo would definitely sound the alarm to Mother as payback that she'd found us playing at the dangerous river. We were very afraid.

* * *

We did not go to the river after school the following day. We sat in our rooms instead, waiting for Mother to return. Solomon and the others had gone there hoping we'd come, but after waiting a while and suspecting we were not coming, they came to check on us. Ikenna advised them, especially Solomon, that it was best they stopped fishing, too. But when Solomon rejected his advice, Ikenna offered him his hooked fishing line. Solomon laughed at him and left with the air of one immune to all the dangers Ikenna had enumerated as lurking like shadows around Omi-Ala. Ikenna watched as they went, shaking his head with pity for these boys who seemed determined to continue down this doomed path.

When Mother came home that afternoon, much earlier than her usual closing time, we saw at once that the neighbour had reported us. Mother was deeply shaken by the weight of her ignorance despite living with us in the same house. True, we'd concealed our trade for so long, hiding the fish and tadpoles under the bunk bed in Ikenna and Boja's shared room because we knew about the mysteries that surrounded Omi-Ala. We'd covered up the smell of the bracken water, even the nauseating smell of the fish when they died, for the fish we caught were usually insignificant, weak, and barely ever survived beyond the day of their catch. Even though we kept them in the water we fetched from the river, they soon died in the beverage cans. We'd return from school every day to find Ikenna and Boja's room filled with the smell of dead fish and tadpoles. We'd throw them with the tin into the dump behind our compound's fence, sad because empty tins were hard to get.

We'd kept the many wounds and injuries we sustained during those trips secret, too. Ikenna and Boja had ensured Mother did not find out. She once accosted Ikenna for beating Obembe after he heard him singing the fishermen's song in the bathroom, and Obembe swiftly covered for him by saying that Ikenna had hit him because he'd called Ikenna a pig-head, therefore deserving Ikenna's wrath. But Ikenna had hit him because he thought it foolish for Obembe to be singing that song at home when Mother was in the house, at the risk of blowing our cover. Then

Ikenna had warned that if he ever made that same mistake, Obembe would never see the river again. It was this threat, and not the slight blow, that had caused Obembe to weep. Even when, in the second week of our adventure, Boja popped his toe into the blade of a crab's claw near the bank of the river and his sandal became awash in his own blood, we lied to Mother that he was injured in a football match. But in truth, Solomon had had to pull the crab's claw out of his flesh while every one of us, except Ikenna, was asked to look away. And Ikenna, enraged at the sight of Boja's profuse bleeding and the fear that he might bleed to death despite Solomon's solid assurances that he would not, had smashed the crab to pieces, cursing it a thousand times for causing such grievous harm to Boja. It pained Mother that we had succeeded in keeping it secret for such a long time—over six weeks, although we lied that it was only three—within which she did not even suspect that we were fishermen.

Mother paced about that night with heavy footsteps, wounded. She did not give us dinner.

"You don't deserve to eat anything in this house," she said as she moved around, from the kitchen to her room and back, her hands unsteady, her spirit broken. "Go and eat the fish you caught from that dangerous river and be stuffed by it."

She shut the kitchen door and padlocked it to prevent us from getting in to find food after she'd gone to bed, but she was so troubled she kept up her characteristic monologue when aggrieved long into the night. And every word that fell from her mouth that night, every sound she made, penetrated our minds like poison to the bone.

"I will tell Eme what you have done. I'm certain that if he hears it, he'll leave everything else and return here. I know him, I know Eme. You. Will. See." She snapped her fingers, and afterwards, we heard the sound of her blowing her nose into the edge of her *wrappa*. "You think I would have ceased to exist if something bad had happened to you or if one of you had drowned in that river? I will not cease to live because you chose to harm yourselves. No. *"Anya nke na' akwa nna ya emo, nke neleda ina nne ya nti, ugulu-oma nke ndagwurugwu ga'ghuputa ya, umu-ugo ga'eri kwa ya*—The eye that mocks a father, that scorns an aged mother, will be pecked out by the ravens of the valley, will be eaten by the vultures."

Mother ended the night with this passage from Proverbs—the most frightening I knew of in the entire Bible. Looking back, I realize it must have been the way she quoted it, in Igbo—imbuing the words with venoms—that made it so damning. Aside from this, Mother said all else in English instead of Igbo, the language with which our parents communicated with us; while between us, we spoke Yoruba, the language in Akure. English, although the official language of Nigeria, was a formal language with which strangers and non-relatives addressed you. It had the potency of digging craters between you and your friends or relatives if one of you switched to using it. So, our parents hardly spoke English, except in moments like this, when the words were intended to pull the ground from beneath our feet. Our parents were adept at this, and so Mother succeeded. For, the words "drowned," "everything," "exist," "dangerous" came out heavy, measured, charged and indicting, and lingered and tormented us long into the night.

3

THE EAGLE

F ather was an eagle:
 The mighty bird that planted his nest high above the rest of his peers, hovering and watching over his young eagles, the way a king guards his throne. Our home— the three-bedroom bungalow he bought the year Ikenna was born—was his cupped eyrie; a place he ruled with a clenched fist. This is why everyone has come to believe that had he not left Akure, our home would not have become vulnerable in the first place, and that the kind of adversity that befell us would not have happened.

Father was an unusual man. When everyone was taking up the gospel of birth control, he—an only child who had grown up with his mother longing for siblings—had a dream of a house full of children, a clan from his body. This dream fetched him much ridicule in the biting economy of

1990s Nigeria, but he swatted off the insults as if they were mere mosquitoes. He sketched a pattern for our future—a map of dreams. Ikenna was to be a doctor, although later, after Ikenna showed much fascination with planes at an early age, and encouraged by the fact that there were aviation schools in Enugu, Makurdi and Onitsha where Ikenna could learn to fly, Father changed it to pilot. Boja was to be a lawyer, and Obembe the family's medical doctor. Although I had opted to be a veterinarian, to work in a forest or to tend animals at a zoo, anything that involved animals, Father decided I would be a professor. David, our younger brother, who was barely three in the year Father moved to Yola, was to be an engineer. A career was not readily chosen for Nkem, our one-year-old sister. Father said there was no need to decide such things for women.

Although we knew from the very beginning that fishing was nowhere on Father's list, we did not think of it at the time. It became a concern from that night when Mother threatened to tell Father about our fishing, thereby kindling the fire of fear of Father's wrath in us. She believed that we'd been pushed into doing it by bad spirits that must be exorcised by strokes of the whip. She knew we would rather wish the sun fell down and burned the earth with us on it than receive Father's wracking Guerdon on the flesh of our buttocks. She said we'd forgotten that our father was not the kind of man who would dip his foot in another shoe because his own was damp; he would rather trek the earth on bare feet.

When she went to the store with David and Nkem the following day, a Saturday, we attempted to destroy every evidence of our trade. Boja hurriedly concealed his hooked fishing lines and the extra one we had under rusting roofing sheets—leftovers from when the house was built in 1974—piled against the fence at our mother's backyard tomato garden. Ikenna destroyed his fishing lines, and threw the broken pieces into the dump behind our fence.

Father visited that Saturday, precisely five days after we were caught fishing the river. Obembe and I made an exigent prayer on the eve of his visit, after I'd suggested that God could touch Father's heart and make him refrain from whipping us. Together we knelt on the floor and prayed: "Lord Jesus, if you say you love us—Ikenna, Boja, Ben and me," he began. "Don't allow Father to visit again. Let him stay in Yola, please Jesus. Please listen to me: you know how hard he would whip us? Don't you even know? Listen, he has cowhides, *kobokos* he bought from the meat-roasting mallam—that one is very painful! Listen, Jesus, if you let him come back and he whips us, we won't go to Sunday school again, and we won't sing and clap in church ever again! Amen."

"Amen," I repeated after him.

When Father arrived that afternoon the way he'd often done, honking at the gate, driving into the compound amidst joyful acclaim, my brothers and I did not go out to greet him. Ikenna had suggested we remain in the room and feign sleep because we could annoy Father the more if we went out to welcome him "just like that, as if we'd done nothing wrong." So we gathered in Ikenna's room, listening attentively to Father's movements, waiting for the moment Mother would begin her report, for Mother was a patient storyteller. Each time Father returned, she would sit by him on the big lounge in the sitting room and detail how the house had fared in his absence—a breakdown of home needs and how they were met, whom she had borrowed from; of our school reports; of the church. She would particularly bring to his notice acts of disobedience she found intolerable or believed were deserving of his punishment.

I remember how she once fed him, over two nights, with news of our church member who gave birth to a baby that weighed so-and-so pounds. She told about the deacon who accidentally farted while on the church podium the previous Sunday, describing how the microphones had amplified the embarrassing sound. I particularly liked how she recounted an incident about a robber who was lynched in our district, how the mob knocked down the fleeing thief with a hail of stones, and how they got a car tyre and placed it around his neck. She'd emphasized the mystery behind how the mob got petrol within that fleeting moment, and how, within coughing minutes, the thief had been set ablaze. I as well as Father had listened intently as she described how the fire had engulfed the thief, the blaze prospering at the hairiest parts of the thief's body—especially his pubic area—as it slowly consumed him. Mother described the kaleidoscope of the fire as it enveloped the thief in an aureole of flame and his jolting cry with so much vivid detail that the image of a man on fire stayed in my memory. Ikenna used to say that if Mother had been schooled, she would have made a great historian. He was right; for Mother hardly ever missed a detail of anything that happened in Father's absence. She told him every single story.

So, they first talked about tangential matters: Father's job; his view about the depletion of the naira under the "rotten polity that is this current administration." Although my brothers and I had always wished we knew the kind of vocabulary Father knew, there were times when we resented it and other times when it just felt necessary, like when he discussed politics, which could not be discussed in Igbo because the words for it would be lacking.

"Aministation," as I believed it was called at the time, was one of those words. The Central Bank was heading for doom, and the subject he most dwelt on that day was the possible demise of Nnamdi Azikiwe, Nigeria's first president, whom Father loved and saw as a mentor. Zik, as he was called, was at a hospital in Enugu. Father was bitter. He bemoaned the poor health facilities in the country. He swore at Abacha, the dictator, and railed on about the marginalization of Igbos in Nigeria. Then he complained about the monster the British had created by forming Nigeria as a whole, until his food was ready. When he began to eat, Mother took the baton. Did he know that all of the teachers at the kindergarten where Nkem had been enrolled loved her? When he said, "*Ezi okwu*—Is it true?" she chronicled little Nkem's journey so far. What about the Oba, the King of Akure? Father wanted to know, so she filled him in on the Oba's fight with the Military Governor of the state whose capital Akure was. Mother went on and on until, just when we were not expecting it, she said: "Dim, there is something I want to tell you."

"I'm all ears," Father replied.

"Dim, your sons Ikenna, Boja, Obembe, and Benjamin, have done the worst, the very, unimaginable worst."

"What have they done?" Father asked as the sound of his silverware on his plate rose sharply.

"*Heh*, okay, Dim. Do you know Mama Iyabo, Yusuf's wife, the one who sells groundnuts—"

"Yes, yes I know her, go straight to what they did, *my friend*," he shouted. Father often referred to anyone as "my friend" if that person annoyed him.

"*Ehen*, that woman was selling groundnuts to that old priest of the Celestial Church close to the Omi-Ala when the boys emerged from the path leading to the river. She recognized them at once. She called to them but they ignored her. When she told the priest she knew them, he told her the boys had been fishing the river for a long time, and that he had tried to warn them several times, but they wouldn't listen. And what is more tragic?"—Mother clapped her hands to prepare his mind for the grim answer to the question—"Mama Iyabo recognized the boys were your sons: Ikenna, Boja, Obembe, and Benjamin."

A moment of silence followed in which Father fixed his eyes on one object—the floor, the ceiling, curtain, anything, as if asking these things to be witnesses of the despicable thing he'd just heard. While the silence lasted, I let my eyes wander around the room. I looked from Boja's football jersey that hung beside the door, to the wardrobe, to the single calendar on the wall. We named it M.K.O. calendar because it had four of us and M.K.O. Abiola, Nigeria's former presidential contestant, in it. I spotted a dead cockroach—possibly killed in a rage—whose maxillae were now flattened against the worn yellow carpet. This reminded me of the effort we'd made to find the video game Father hid from us, something that would have kept us from fishing. We'd searched our parents' room one day to find the game while Mother was out with the little ones, but it was nowhere—not in Father's cabinet, not in any of the uncountable chests of drawers in the room. Then we brought down Father's old metal box, the one he said our grandmother bought for him the first time he left the village for Lagos in 1966. Ikenna was sure it'd be there. We carried the iron box out, which was heavy as a casket, to Ikenna and Boja's room. Then Boja diligently tried all the keys until, creaking, the lid snapped open. As they were carrying it, a cockroach who had crawled out from the box, scampered atop the rusting metal and flew off. When Ikenna opened it, the dark-red insects invaded the room. In the twinkling of an eye, a cockroach was on the louvres, one was creeping head-down at the door of the wardrobe, and another was crawling into Obembe's sneaker. With a cry, my brothers and I made a stampede on the thousand cockroaches for nearly thirty minutes, trying to chase them as they scurried about. Then we carried the box out. After we swept the room clean of the cockroaches, and Obembe lay back on the bed, I saw under his feet the charred bits of cockroaches: a stray hind, a mashed flattened head with jarred eyes, and fragments of detached wings, some even in the space between his toes and a yellow paste that must have been squeezed out from the thorax of the insects. One lay whole under his left foot, flattened to the thickness of paper, its wings doubled and flared.

My mind, like a spinning coin, stilled when Father, in an unusually calm voice, said, "So, Adaku, you sit here and tell me in all truth that my boys—Ikenna, Bojanonimeokpu, Obembe, Benjamin—were the ones she saw at that river; that dangerous river under a curfew, where even adults are known to have disappeared?"

"Indeed, Dim, it was your sons she saw," she replied in English because Father had suddenly begun speaking in English, and had emphasized the last syllable of the word "disappeared" by a high pitch.

"Gracious me!" Father cried repeatedly in quick succession so that the syllables split and the two words came out as Gra-cious-me, like the sound produced when one taps on a metal surface.

"What is he doing?" Obembe asked, teetering on the brink of tears.

"Will you shut up?" Ikenna raged in a low voice. "Didn't I warn you to stop fishing? But you all chose to listen to Solomon. Now here's the result."

Father had said, "So you really mean it was my boys she saw?" while Ikenna was speaking, and now, we heard Mother say "Yes."

"Gracious me!" Father cried even louder now.

"They are all inside," said Mother, "just ask them, and you will see for yourself. To think they actually bought fishing equipment, hooks, lines, and sinkers with the pocket money you gave them, makes it all the more devastating."

Mother's emphatic knock on the phrase "with the pocket money you gave them" stung deep into Father's flesh. He must have coiled up like a prodded worm.

"How long did they do this?" he asked. Mother, trying to shield herself from blame, hesitated at first, until Father barked, "Am I talking to a deaf and mute?"

"Three weeks," she submitted in a voice that was defeated.

"Good gracious! Adaku. Three weeks. With you under the same roof?"

That was a lie, though. We had told Mother that it was three weeks only with hopes that that would minimize the weight of our offense. But even that inaccurate information was enough to thaw Father's wrath.

"Ikenna!" he bellowed, "Ike-nna!"

Ikenna sprang to his feet from the floor where he'd sat when Mother began to give Father the report. At first, he made for the door, then stopped, stepped back and felt his buttocks. He'd doubled his pair of shorts to reduce the impact of what was to come, although he, like the rest of us, knew it was most likely Father would give us the blows on our bare skin. He now raised his head and cried, "Sir!"

"Come out here at once!"

With freckles scattered over his face like buboes, Ikenna moved forward again, stopped as if an invisible barrier had suddenly massed in his way, then rushed out.

"Before I count to three," Father shouted, "all of you come out here. Now!"

We hared out of the room at once, and formed a back-cloth behind Ikenna.

"I suppose you all heard what your mother told me," Father said, a long line of veins gathered on his forehead. "Is it true?"

"It is true, sir," Ikenna answered.

"So—it is true?" Father said, his eyes momentarily pinned to Ikenna's sunken face.

He did not wait for an answer; he went to his room in a rage. My eyes had fallen on David, who'd sat in one of the lounges gazing at us, a packet of biscuits in his hand as he braced to watch us getting whipped, when Father returned with two cowhides, one flung across his shoulder, and the other clenched in his grip. He pulled the small table, on which he'd had his meal, to the centre of the room. Mother, who had just cleared and cleaned it with a rag, fastened her *wrappa* around her bosom as she waited for that moment when she would feel Father had taken his punishment too far.

"Each of you will spread like a mat on this table," Father said. "You will each receive your Guerdon on your bare flesh, the way you came into this sinful world. I sweat and suffer to send you to school to receive *a Western education* as civilized men, but you chose instead to be fishermen. Fish-a-men!" He shouted the word repeatedly as if it were anathema to him, and when he'd said it the umpteenth time, he ordered Ikenna to spread out on the table.

The beating was severe. Father made us number the blows as they landed. Ikenna and Boja, sprawled across the table with their shorts rolled down, counted twenty and fifteen each, while Obembe and I counted eight apiece. Mother tried to intervene, but was deterred by Father's stern warning that if she interfered, she would receive the beating with us. And perhaps, given the weight of his anger, he may have meant it. Father had gone on, unmoved by our screams and shouts and cries and Mother's pleas, railing about how he worked to make money and spitting the word "fishermen" with fury until he retired to his room, his cowhide slung on his shoulder, and we held the seats of our pants, wailing.

* * *

The night of the Guerdon was a cruel night. Like my brothers, I had refused to have dinner despite being hungry and lured by the aroma of fried turkey and plantains—a rarity which Mother, knowing pride would not allow us to eat and hoping to punish us the more, had made. In fact, dodo (fried plantains) had not been made in our house in a long time before then. Mother had banned it a year or so earlier after Obembe and I stole pieces from Mother's cooler, and lied that we'd seen rats eating the dodos. I'd yearned desperately to sneak out of the room to pick one of the four plates on which Mother had dished out our portions from the kitchen, but I would not for fear I would betray what my brothers intended to be a hunger strike. This unsatisfied hunger had intensified my pain so that I had cried late into the night, until I drifted off into sleep.

Mother woke me the following morning, tapping me and saying, "Ben, wake, wake; your father wants you, Ben."

Every node in my body seemed afire with pain. It seemed my buttocks had acquired surplus flesh. I was, however, relieved that our hunger strike, which I'd feared might extend into the next day, would not linger after all. For we always nursed grudges against our parents in the aftermath of such severe punishment and avoided them and food for a period of time to get back at them and to—at best—have them apologize and pacify us. But we could not do that this time, as Father himself had summoned us.

To leave the bed, I first crawled to its end, and then stepped down slowly, my buttocks filled with tacks of pain. When I entered the sitting room, it was still dim. Electricity had been cut since the previous night and the sitting room was lit by a kerosene lantern placed on the centre table. Boja, the last person to sit, came with a slight limp in his gait, cringing with every move. After we all settled into our seats, Father stared at us for a long time, his hands on his chin. Mother, seated facing us just a stretch away from me, untied the side of the swaddling *wrappa* fastened into a knot under her armpit, and lifted her brassiere. Her rounded, milk-filled breast disappeared at once into Nkem's tiny grip. The infant greedily covered the round, dark, and stiff nipple with her mouth like an animal taking in its prey. Father seemed to have watched the nipple with interest, and when it had gone from sight, he removed his eyeglasses and placed them on the table. Whenever he removed his eyeglasses, the great resemblance Boja and I bore to him—dark skin and a bean-shaped head—often became clearer. Ikenna and Obembe were cloaked in Mother's anthill-coloured skin.

"Now, listen, all of you," Father said in English. "I was hurt by what you did for many reasons. First, *I told you* before I left here not to give your mother any troubles. But what did you do? You gave her—and me—the mother of all troubles." He glanced from face to face.

"Listen, what you did was truly bad. Bad. Just how could kids receiving Western education engage in such a barbaric endeavour?" I did not know what the word "endeavour" was at the time, but because Father had shouted it, I knew it was a grim word. "And secondly, your mother and I are appalled by the dangerous risks you took. This was not the school I sent you to. Nowhere around that deadly river will you find books to read. Despite the fact that I have always *told* you to read your books, you no longer have eyes for your books." Then, with a dead-serious frown on his face and his hand raised in an awe-inspiring gesture, he said, "Let me warn you *my friends*, I will send anyone who comes to this house with a bad school grade to the village to farm or tap palm wine—*Ogbu-akwu*."

"God forbid!" Mother retorted, snapping her fingers over her head to swat away Father's spiritually toxic words. "None of my kids will be this."

Father glanced angrily at her. "Yes, *God forbid*," he said, imitating Mother's tender tone of voice. "How will God forbid when under your nose, Adaku, they went to that river for six weeks; Six. Good. Weeks." He shook his head as he counted six weeks with his fingers. "Now listen, *my friend*, from now on, you must make sure they read their books. Do you hear me? And your closing time for work from now on is five, no longer seven; and no work on Saturdays. I can't have these kids sliding into the pits under your nose."

"I have heard," Mother replied in Igbo, tsking.

"In all," Father continued, gazing round at us in a broken semicircle, "cut your fads from now. Try to be good children. No one enjoys whipping his kids—no one."

Fads, we'd come to understand from Father's frequent usage of the word, meant useless indulgences. He was about to speak on, but was interrupted by the sudden swirl of the ceiling fan, signalling the abrupt restoration of erratic power. Mother switched on the bulb and wound down the wick of the kerosene lantern. In the lull that the occasion gave and because the bulb's glow rested on it, my eyes fell on the year's calendar: although it was now March, the calendar was still turned to the page of February, which had the painting of the eagle captured in flight, wings spread, legs stretched, claws curved, and the bird's prominent sapphire eyes staring into the camera. His grandeur spread over the vista in the background as though the world were his and he was the creator of all—a god with wings and feathers. I thought then, with a certain crippling fear that something would change in a fleeting moment and disrupt that interminable stillness. I feared that the bird's frozen wings would be suddenly thawed and begin to flutter. I feared that its bulging eyes would blink, its legs would move. I feared that when that happened—when the eagle left that space, that portion of the sky in which it'd been caught since February 2nd, when Ikenna flipped the pages of the calendar to this one—this world and everything in it would change beyond reckoning.

"On the other hand, I want you all to know that even though what you did was wrong, it reflected once again that you have the courage to indulge in something adventurous. Such adventurous spirit is the spirit of men. So, from now onwards, I want you all to channel that spirit into something more fruitful. I want you to be a different kind of fishermen."

We glanced at each other with surprise, except Ikenna, who kept his eyes on the floor. He'd been hurt most of all by the whipping, especially because Father had put much of the blame on him and had whipped him the hardest without knowing that Ikenna had tried to make us stop.

"What I want you to be is a group of fishermen who will be fishers of good dreams, who will not relent until they have caught the biggest catch. I want you to be juggernauts, menacing and unstoppable fishermen."

This surprised me deeply. I'd thought that he disdained that word. Grasping for meaning, I looked at Obembe. He was nodding his head at everything Father said, his brow tinged with the hint of a smile.

"Good boys," Father muttered, a wide smile smoothening the rough creases that anger and fury had strewn over the yarn of his face. "Listen, in keeping with what I have always taught you, that in every bad thing, you can always dig up some good things, I will tell you that you could be a different kind of fishermen. Not the kind that fish at a *filthy swamp* like the Omi-Ala, but fishermen of the mind. Go-getters. Children who will dip their hands into rivers, seas, oceans of this life and become successful: doctors, pilots, professors, lawyers. Eh?"

He gazed round again. "Those are the kinds of fishermen I want to have as children. Now, would you be willing to recite an anthem?"

Obembe and I nodded immediately. He glanced at the pair whose eyes were focused on the floor.

"Boja, you?"

"Yes," Boja mumbled reluctantly.

"Ike?"

"Yes," Ikenna said after a prolonged pause.

"Very good, now all of you say 'ju-gger-nauts.'"

"Ju-gger-nauts," we all repeated.

"Me-*na*-cing. M-e-n-a-c-i-n-g. Me-nacing."

"Unstopp-able."

"Fishermen of good things."

Father laughed a deep, throaty laugh, adjusted his tie, and gazed closely at us. With his voice ascending a new crescendo and thrusting his fist aloft so that his tie flung upward, he yelled: "We are fishermen."

"We are fishermen!" we chorused at the top of our lungs, each one of us surprised at how suddenly—and nearly effortlessly—we'd broken into this excitement.

"We trail behind our hooks, lines and sinkers."

We repeated, but he heard someone say "tail" instead of "trail," so he made us pronounce the word in isolation before continuing. Before he did that, he bemoaned that we did not know the word because we spoke Yoruba all the time instead of English—the language of "Western education."

"We are unstoppable," he continued, and we repeated after him.

"We are menacing."

"We are juggernauts."

"We will never fail."

"That's my boys," he said, our voices settling like sediment. "Can I have the new fishermen embrace me?"

Feeling robbed by Father's magical overturn of what had been a deep revulsion to appreciation, we rose to our feet one after the other and placed our heads between the flaps of his unbuttoned coat. We embraced him for seconds during which he patted and kissed our heads, and the next person in line repeated the ritual. Afterwards, he took up his briefcase and brought out clean twenty-naira notes, bound by a paper tape with the stamp of the Central Bank of Nigeria. He gave Ikenna and Boja four pieces each, Obembe and me, two apiece. He gave one piece each for David, who was asleep in the room, and Nkem.

"Don't forget anything I've told you."

We all nodded and he began to leave, but as if called back by something, he turned and walked to Ikenna. He put his hands on Ikenna's shoulders and said, "Ike, do you know why I flogged you the most?"

Ikenna, whose face was fixed on the floor as if there was a movie screen on it, mumbled "Yes."

"Why?" Father asked.

"Because I'm the first born, their leader."

"Good, bear that in mind. From now on, before you take any action, look at them; they do whatever you do and go wherever you go. That's to their credit, the way all of you follow each other. So, Ikenna, don't lead your brothers astray."

"Yes, Daddy," Ikenna replied.

"Guide them well."

"Yes, Daddy."

"Lead them well."

Ikenna hesitated a bit, then mumbled: "Yes, Daddy."

"Always remember that a coconut that falls into a cistern will need a good washing before it can be eaten. What I mean is if you do wrong, you will have to be corrected."

Our parents often found the need to explain such expressions containing concealed meanings because we sometimes took them literally, but it was the way they learned to speak; the way our language—Igbo—was structured. For although the vocabulary for literal construction for cautionary expressions such as "be careful" was available, they said "*Jiri ire gi guo eze onu*—Count your teeth with your tongue." To which, once, while scolding Obembe for a wrong act, Father had burst out laughing when he saw Obembe moving his tongue over the ridge of his mouth, his cheeks furrowed, saliva drooling down his jaws as he attempted to take a census of his dentition. It was why our parents most often reverted to English when angry, because being angry, they didn't want to have to explain whatever they said. Yet even in English, Father often transgressed in both the use of heavy vocabularies and English idioms. For Ikenna once told us how as a child, before I was born, Father asked him in a very serious tone to "take time," and in obedience, he'd climbed the dining table and removed the wall clock from its hook.

"I hear, sir," Ikenna said.

"And you have been corrected," Father said.

Ikenna nodded and Father—in a moment unlike any I'd ever witnessed—asked him to promise. I could tell that even Ikenna was surprised. For Father demanded obedience to his words from his children; he did not ask for mutual agreements or promises. When Ikenna said "I promise," Father turned and stepped out and we followed to watch his car steer down the dusty road, feeling sore that he was leaving yet again.

THE PYTHON

Ikenna was a python:

A wild snake that became a monstrous serpent living on trees, on plains above other snakes. Ikenna turned into a python after the whipping. It changed him. The Ikenna I knew became a different one: a mercurial and hot-tempered person constantly on the prowl. This transformation had started much earlier, gradually, internally, long before the whipping. But it was after the punishment that the manifestations first began, causing him to do the things that we didn't think he was capable of doing, the first of which was to harm an adult.

About an hour after Father left for Yola that morning, Ikenna gathered Boja, Obembe and me in his room just after Mother went to church with our younger siblings, and declared that we must punish Iya Iyabo, the woman who told on us. We had not gone to church that day because we claimed we were ill from the beating, so we sat on the bed in his room to listen to him.

"I must have my pound of flesh and you must all join me in this because you caused it," he said. "Had you listened to me, she would not have caused Father to beat me so much. Look, just look—"

He turned and pulled down his shorts. Although Obembe closed his eyes, I didn't. I saw red stripes on the plump cheeks of his buttocks. They appeared as those on the back of Jesus of Nazareth—some long, some short, some crossed each other to make a red X, while some stood out from the rest like lines on the palms of an ill-fortuned individual.

"That was what you and that idiotic woman caused me. So, you all should come up with ideas on how to punish her." Ikenna snapped his fingers. "We must do that today. That way, she will come to know that she cannot mess with us and go scot-free."

While he was speaking, a goat bleated from behind the window. *Mmbreeeeheheeeh!*

This riled Boja. "That crazy goat again, that goat!" he cried, rising to his feet.

"Sit down," Ikenna yelled. "Let it alone now, and give me ideas on that woman before Mama returns from church."

"Okay," Boja said, sitting back. "You know Iya Iyabo has

lots of hens?" For a while Boja sat, his face turned in the direction of the window where the goat's bleating could still be heard. Even though it was clear his mind was fixed on the bleating goat, he said: "Yes, she keeps a whole lot."

"Mostly roosters," I put in, wanting to make him know that it was roosters, not hens that crowed.

Boja cast a sneery look at me, sighed, and said, "Yes, but must you tell us the gender of the hen? I have told you many times to stop bringing this stupid animal fascination into important—"

Ikenna chewed him out. "Ooh, Boja, when will you learn to face what is important, which is telling us what your ideas are. You are wasting time getting angry at the bleating of a foolish goat, and rebuking Ben for something as trivial as the difference between a rooster and a hen."

"Okay, I suggest we get one of them and kill and fry it."

"That is fatal!" Ikenna exclaimed, making an irritated face, as if on the cusp of vomiting. "But I don't think it's proper to eat that woman's chicken. How are we even going to fry it? Mama will know we fried something here; she will smell it. She will suspect we stole it, and stealing will earn us even more severe strokes of the whip. None of us wants that."

Ikenna never dismissed Boja's ideas without giving them a proper thought. They had a mutual respect for each other.

I hardly ever saw them argue, unlike the way they would answer my questions with an outright "no" or "wrong" or "incorrect." Boja agreed that it was true, nodding repeatedly. Next, Obembe suggested we throw stones into the woman's compound and pray they hit either her or one of her sons, and then take to our heels before anyone comes out of the compound.

"Wrong idea," Boja said. "What if those sons of hers, those big hungry boys who always dress in tattered clothing with biceps like Arnold Schwarzenegger, catch and beat us?" He demonstrated the bulge of their brawny biceps.

"They will beat us even worse than Father," Ikenna noted.

"Yes," said Boja, "we can only imagine it."

Ikenna nodded in agreement. I was now the only one who hadn't made a suggestion.

"Ben, what do you have to say?" Boja said.

I gulped, my heart beating faster. My confidence often wilted when my older brothers urged me to make a decision rather than make one for me. I was still thinking when my voice, as if autonomous of the rest of me, said: "I have an idea."

"Then say it!" Ikenna ordered.

"Okay, Ike, okay, I suggest we get hold of one of the roosters and," I fastened my eyes to his face, "and—"

"Yes?" Ikenna said. Their eyes were all fixed on me as if I'd just become a wonder.

"Behead it," I concluded.

I had barely said those words when Ikenna cried, "That is really fatal!" and Boja, suddenly wild-eyed, started clapping.

My brothers gave me credit for an idea whose source was a folktale my Yoruba language teacher had told my class at the beginning of the term, about a vicious boy who goes on a rampage decapitating all the cocks and hens in the land. We hurried out of our compound with a covert path to the woman's house in our minds, passing small bushes and a carpenter's shop, where we had to close our ears with our hands to shield them against the deafening sound of the filling machines as they sawed wood. The woman, Iya Iyabo, lived in a small bungalow whose exterior was identical to ours: a small balcony, two windows with louvres and nettings, an electric meter box clamped to the wall, and a storm door, except that her fence was not made of bricks and cement but of mud and clay. The fence was cracked in places from long exposure to the sun, and was littered with spots and smears. An overhead electric cable reached through the branches of one of the trees and stretched out of the compound to connect to a high power pole.

We listened at first for sounds of life, but Ikenna and Boja soon concluded the compound was empty. At Ikenna's command, Obembe climbed over the fence, using Ikenna's shoulder as a ledge. Boja joined him while I stayed with Ikenna to keep watch. Just after the two of them climbed in, the sound of a rooster squawking and frantically flapping its wings came ever closer, as did the sounds of my brothers' feet chasing the cock. It happened repeatedly until we heard Boja say "Hold it still, hold it still, and don't let it go" the way we used to speak when our hooks angled a fish when we were still fishing the Omi-Ala.

At the shout, Ikenna tried to climb the fence quickly to see if they'd caught it, but stopped short of that. From behind the wall, he echoed Boja's words. "Don't let it go, don't let it go." His buttocks slipped up above the waistline of his pants as he planted his foot in a hole on the fence. Old coatings rained down below him like dust. With one foot secured, he pulled himself upwards, holding on to the top of the wall. From behind his hand, a skink rose and journeyed away in agitation, its multi-coloured body smooth and shiny. Half of him stretched into the compound, and half outside, Ikenna took the rooster from Boja, crying, "That's my boy! That's my boy!"

We returned to our own compound and went straight to the garden in the backyard, the size of a quarter of a football field. It was fenced around with cement bricks on all three corners, two of them marking off the boundaries with our neighbours—Igbafe's family on one side, and the Agbatis on the other. The third, which faced our bungalow directly, marked off a boundary with the landfill where a colony of swine lived. A pawpaw tree stretched out of the landfill, just over the fence, while a tangerine tree—usually extremely leafy in the rainy season—stood agelessly between the fence and the well in the compound. This tree sat just about fifty metres further inside the compound from the well—a big hole in the ground, with a neck made of concrete around it. Attached to the concrete was a metal lid that Father locked with a padlock in dry seasons when wells dried up in Akure and people stole into our compound to fetch water. On the other side of the backyard, patched to a corner of the fence bordering Igbafe's family's compound was the small garden in which Mother planted tomatoes, corn and okra.

Boja set the petrified cock down on the chosen spot, and took the knife that Obembe had brought from our kitchen. Ikenna joined him and together they held the chicken in place, unshaken by its loud squawks. Then we all watched as the knife moved in Boja's hand with unaccustomed ease, a downward slit through the rooster's wrinkled neck as if he'd handled the knife several times before, and as if he were destined to handle it yet again. The cock twitched and made aggravating movements that were restrained by all our hands holding it firmly. I looked over our fence to the top floor of the two-storeyed building overlooking our compound and saw Igbafe's grandfather, a small man who had stopped speaking after an accident a few years earlier, seated on the large veranda in front of the door of the house. He had the habit of sitting there all day and he used to be the butt of our jokes.

Boja severed the cock's head, leaving a jolting outpouring of blood in its wake. I turned away and returned my eyes to the old mute man. He appeared like a moment's vision of a faraway warning angel whose warnings we could not hear owing to the distance. I did not see the rooster's head fall into the small hole Ikenna had dug in the dirt, but I watched as its trunk palpitated violently, spurting blood about, its wings raising dust. My brothers held it down even more firmly until it gradually quieted. Then we set off with the headless corpse in Boja's grip, the blood marking our trail, unshaken by the few people who looked on in awe. Boja flung the dead rooster over the fence, blood spitting around as it careered in the air. Once it was out of sight, we felt satisfied we had had our revenge.

* * *

Ikenna's frightening metamorphosis did not, however, begin then; it began long before Father's Guerdon, and even before the neighbour caught us fishing at the river. It first showed itself in an attempt to make us hate fishing, but this was fruitless, for the love of fishing had been wired into the arteries of our hearts at the time. In his frail effort, he dug up everything he deemed bad about the river, things we had never before observed. He complained, just a few days before the neighbour caught us, that the bush around the river was filled with excreta. Although we had never seen anyone do this, nor even perceived the odour he so painstakingly described to us, Boja, Obembe and I did not argue with him. He said at one point that Omi-Ala's fish were polluted, and stopped us from bringing the fish into his room. Hence, we began keeping them in the room I shared with Obembe. He even complained he had seen a human skeleton floating underneath the waters of the Omi-Ala while fishing, and that Solomon was a bad influence. He said these things as if they were undeniable truths newly discovered, but the passion we'd developed for fishing had become like liquid frozen in a bottle and could not be easily thawed. It was not that we did not have reservations about the enterprise; we all did. Boja hated that the river was small and only contained "useless" fish; Obembe had troubles with what the fish did at night since there's no light under the water, in the river. How, he frequently wondered, did the fish move about—since they did not have electricity or lanterns—in the pitch black darkness that covered the river like a sheet at night; and I detested the weakness of the smelts and tadpoles, how they died so easily even when you stored them in the river's water! This frailty sometimes made me want to cry. When Solomon came knocking the following day, the day the neighbour caught us, Ikenna had insisted at first that he would not go to the river with him. But when he saw that we, his brothers, were leaving without him, he joined in, taking his fishing line from Boja. Solomon and the rest of us cheered him, hailing him a most valiant "Fisherman."

The thing that was consuming Ikenna was like a tireless enemy, hiding inside him, biding its time while we plotted and carried out our revenge on Iya Iyabo. It began to control him from the day Ikenna severed ties with Obembe and me, keeping only Boja with him. They barred Obembe and me from their room, and excluded us from joining in at the new football place they discovered a week after the whipping. Obembe and I longed for their companionship, and waited in vain for their return every evening, yearning for our kinship that seemed to be slipping away. But as days went by, it began to seem as if Ikenna had got rid of an infection in his throat by finally coughing us out, like a man who'd simply cleared his stuffed passages.

At around the same time, Ikenna and Boja hassled one of Mr Agbati's children, our cross-wall neighbours who owned a rickety lorry that was known as "Argentina" because of the legend "Born and raised in Argentina" inscribed around its frescoed body. Owing to its feebleness, the lorry made deafening noises when starting, often rattling the neighbourhood and waking people from sleep in the early hours of the day. This engendered several complaints and quarrels. In one of the fights, Mr Agbati came off with a perpetual swelling on his head after a female neighbour hit him with the heel of her shoe. From then on, Mr Agbati began sending one of his children to inform the neighbours whenever he wanted to start the lorry. The children would knock on every neighbour's door or gate a couple of times, announcing that "Papa wan start Argentina, oh." Then they would run off to the next house. That morning, Ikenna—who had begun to grow more belligerent and irascible—fought the oldest of the children after accusing the boy of being a *nuzance*, a word Father often used to describe someone who made unnecessary noise.

Later that same day, after we had returned from school and eaten, he and Boja went to play football at the pitch while Obembe and I stayed home, sad that we could not go with them. We were watching television, and were still on the same programme, one about a man who settled family disputes, when they returned. They had only been gone for half an hour. As they hurried into their room, I saw that Ikenna's face was covered with dirt, his upper lip was swollen into a pulp and there were bloodstains on his jersey which had the sobriquet "Okocha" and the figure 10 inscribed on its back. Once they shut their door, Obembe and I ran to our room and stood beside the wall to eavesdrop on their conversation to find out what had happened. At first, we only heard the closet doors opening and closing, and the sound their feet made as they walked on the worn carpet. It was long before we caught the words "If I hadn't thought Nathan and Segun would come in if I did and outnumber us, I would have joined in the fight." This was Boja's voice and he was not finished yet. "If only I had known they wouldn't join, if only I had known."

The sound of feet rapping on the carpet followed this declaration, after which Boja continued: "But he did not even really beat you, that frog; he was only lucky to have," he paused as if searching for the right words, "to have... done this."

"You didn't fight for me," Ikenna burst out suddenly. "No! You stood by and watched. Don't even try to deny it."

"I could have—" Boja began to say after a brief pause, breaking the silence.

"No you didn't!" Ikenna cried. "You stood by!"

This was loud enough for Mother to hear from her room; she had not gone to work that day because Nkem was having diarrhoea. She scrambled to her feet, slapped the floor a few times with her flip-flops and started knocking on their door.

"What is going on there, why are you shouting?"

"Mama, we want to sleep," said Boja.

"Is that why you won't answer the door?" she asked, and when no one answered back, she said: "What was the shouting in that room about?"

"Nothing," Ikenna replied sharply.

"It better be nothing," said Mother. "It better be."

Her flip-flops slapped the floor again in rhythm as she returned to her room.

* * *

Ikenna and Boja did not go out to play after school the following day; they stayed in their room. Wanting to take advantage of the situation to communicate with them again, Obembe seized on the opportunity of a television show Ikenna particularly liked to bring them to the sitting room. Both of them had not watched television since the neighbour caught us at the Omi-Ala, and Obembe continually ached for the days when we all saw our favourite programmes together with riotous glee—*Agbala Owe*, the Yoruba soap opera, and *Skippy the Bush Kangaroo*, an Australian drama. Obembe always wanted to reach out to them whenever any of the programmes was on, but the fear that he might annoy them often stopped him. On this day, however, having grown desperate and because *Skippy the Bush Kangaroo* was Ikenna's favourite, first he craned his neck to look through the keyhole of their room's door so he could see our brothers through it. Then making the sign of the cross, his lips moving inaudibly with the rhythm of the words "The Father, the Son and the Holy Spirit," he started pacing about the room singing the theme song of the show:

> *Skippy, Skippy, Skippy the bush kangaroo*
> *Skippy, Skippy, Skippy our friend ever true.*

Obembe had told me many times over those dark days of separation from our brothers that he wanted to put an end to the rift, but I'd always warned he'd incur their wrath. I'd managed to dissuade him every single time. So when he began to sing that song, I began to fear for him again. "Don't, Obe, they'll beat you," I said, gesturing that he stop.

The effect of my entreaty was like a sudden pinch on the skin that attracted only a minute response. He'd stopped and cast a lingering stare at me as though unsure of what he had heard. Then shaking his head, continued, "Skippy, Skippy, Skippy the bush kangaroo—"

He stopped singing when the handle of the door of my brothers' room twitched. Ikenna appeared, walked to the lounge beside me, and sat in it. Obembe froze like a statue and remained by the wall, under a framed photo of Nnene, Father's mother, holding the newly born Ikenna in 1981. He would maintain this posture for very long as if pinned to the wall. Boja came out after Ikenna and sat down.

Skippy, the kangaroo, had just fought with a rattlesnake, making prodigious leaps every time the serpent lunged to sting him with its venomous tongue, and the kangaroo was now licking its paws.

"Oh, I hate when this stupid Skippy does this annoying paw-licking!" Ikenna fumed.

"He just fought with a snake," Obembe said. "You should have seen—"

"Who asked you?" Ikenna snarled, jumping to his feet. "I said who asked you?"

In anger, he kicked Nkem's mobile plastic chair so that it plunged into the big shelf which held the television, VHS player and telephone. A glass-covered framed photo of Father as a young clerk of the Central Bank of Nigeria crashed behind the cupboard, shattering into pieces.

"Who asked you?" Ikenna, ignoring the fate of Father's treasured portrait, repeated for the third time. He pressed the red button on the television and it went dead.

"*Oya*, all of you to your rooms!" he cried.

Obembe and I ran there, panting. Then, from our room, I heard Ikenna say "Boja, why are you still waiting there? I said, all of you."

"What, Ike, me, too?" Boja asked in astonishment.

"Yes, I said all—all!"

The silence was broken by the sound of Boja's feet as he walked to his room, and then the sound of their door slamming. After we'd all gone, Ikenna turned on the television and settled to watch—alone.

I have come to believe that it was here that the first mark of the line between Ikenna and Boja—where not even a dot had ever been drawn before—first appeared. It altered the shape of our lives and ushered in a transition of time when craniums raged and voids exploded. They stopped speaking. Boja came descending like a fallen angel, and landed where Obembe and I had long been confined.

* * *

In those early days of Ikenna's metamorphosis, we all hoped the hand that held his heart, having clenched into a fist, would unclench in no time. But days rolled past and Ikenna moved farther and farther from us. He hit Boja after a heated argument a week or so later. Obembe and I were in our room when this happened because we'd started to avoid the living room whenever Ikenna was there, but Boja often stayed put. It must have been Ikenna's anger at his persistence that caused the argument. All I heard was blows and their voices as they argued and swore at each other. It was on a Saturday and Mother, who no longer went to work on Saturdays, was at home taking a nap. But when she heard the noise, she ran out to the living room, swaddled from bosom to knee because she'd breastfed Nkem who had been crying earlier. Mother first tried to break up the fight by calling on them to stop, but they paid no heed. She plunged in and pulled them apart until she was stretched between them, but Boja held on to Ikenna's T-shirt in defiance. When Ikenna tried to wrest himself free, he did it with such a ferocious jerk of Boja's arm that he mistakenly pulled off the *wrappa* Mother was swaddled in, stripping her to her underpants.

"*Ewooh!*" Mother cried. "Do you want to bring a curse on yourselves? Look what you have done; you have stripped me naked. Do you know what it means—to see my nakedness? Do you know it is a sacrilege—*alu*?" She fastened the *wrappa* around her bosom again. "I will tell Eme everything you have done from A to Z, don't you worry."

She snapped her fingers at both of them, now standing apart, still trying to catch their breath.

"Now tell me, Ikenna, what did he do to you? Why were you fighting?"

Ikenna threw off his shirt and hissed in reply. I was stupefied. Hissing at an older person in Igbo culture was considered an insufferable act of insubordination.

"What, Ikenna?"

"*Eh*, Mama," Ikenna said.

"Did you hiss at me?" Mother said in English first, then placing her hands on her bosom, she said, "*Obu mu ka ighi na'a ma lu osu?*"

Ikenna did not answer. He moved back to the lounge where he'd sat before the fight, picked up his shirt and walked to his room. He slammed the door so hard that the louvres in the sitting room rattled. Mother, astounded at the brazen insult in his act of walking out on her, stood with mouth agape, her eyes fixed on the door, and her wrath piqued. She was about to head to the door to discipline Ikenna when she noticed Boja's broken lip. He was dabbing the shirt now covered with crimson stains against his bloodied lips.

"He did that to you?" Mother asked.

Boja nodded. His eyes were red, full of bottled tears that were held back from pouring out only because it would have meant he'd been beaten. My brothers and I hardly ever cried when we fought, even if we'd suffered severe blows or had been hit in the most sensitive places. We always tried to stifle tears until we went out of everyone's sight. Only then did we let it out, and sometimes, in spades.

"Answer me," Mother shouted. "Have you turned deaf?"

"Yes, Mama, he did it."

"*Onye*—Who? Ike-*nna* did this?"

Boja nodded in reply, his eyes on the stained shirt in his hands. Mother walked closer to him and tried to touch the wounded lip, but Boja squirmed in pain. She stepped back, still gazing at the wound.

"Did you say Ikenna did it?" she asked again as if Boja had not replied before.

"Yes, Mama," Boja said.

She fastened her *wrappa* again, this time tighter. Then she walked briskly to Ikenna's door and began banging on it, calling on Ikenna to open it. When there was no response, she began threatening aloud, punctuating her words with tsks to give them resolve. "Ikenna, if you don't open that door now, I will show you that I'm your mother, and that you came out from between my legs."

Now that she threatened with tsks, she did not wait too long before the door opened. She pounced on him and an exchange of blows and tantrums followed. Ikenna was unusually defiant. He received every slap with protests and even threatened to hit back, further aggravating her. Mother struck more blows. He cried freely and complained aloud that she hated him because she did not reprimand Boja for the provocation that led to the fight in the first place. In the end, he pushed her to the floor and ran out. Mother chased after him, her *wrappa* falling again as she did. But by the time she got to the sitting room, he was gone. She raised her *wrappa* to cover her bosom as before. "Heaven and earth hear me," she swore, touching her tongue with the tip of her index finger. "Ikenna, you will not eat anything in this house again until your father comes back. I don't care how you do it, but not in this house." Her words clogged with tears. "Not in this house, not until Eme returns from wherever he is. You will not eat here."

She was speaking to those of us now gathered in the sitting room and to others, perhaps our neighbours who were probably listening from the other side of the lizard-infested fence. For Ikenna had vanished. He'd probably crossed the road to the other side of the street, walked northwards to Sabo, along the dirt road that led further into the part of the city where old hills rose above three schools, a cinema in a crumbling building and a big mosque, from where the muezzin called for prayers through mighty loudspeakers at dawn every day. He did not return that day. He slept somewhere he never disclosed.

Mother paced the house all that night, anxiously waiting for Ikenna to knock on the storm door. When, at midnight, she was compelled to lock up the gate for safety—armed robbery occurred frequently in Akure in those days—she sat with the keys near the main door, waiting. She'd driven the rest of us to our rooms to sleep and only Boja remained in the sitting room because he could not enter his room for fear of Ikenna. Obembe and I did not sleep, either; we listened to Mother from our beds. She went out many times that night, thinking she'd heard a knock at the gate, but returned all those times alone. She barely sat down. When a deluge began later, she telephoned Father, but the repeated rings went unanswered. As the *pon-pon*, *pon-pon* sound of the phone repeated itself again and again I tried to imagine Father seated in the new house in the dangerous city, his spectacles on, reading the *Guardian* or the *Tribune*. That image of him was torpedoed by the static on the line, which made Mother hang up.

I did not know when I eventually slept, but I soon found myself and my brothers in our village, Amano, near Umuahia. We were playing football—two-a-side—near the bank of the river when Boja suddenly kicked the ball to a footbridge that was once used as the only crossing over the river. Biafran soldiers had hastily constructed it, after blowing up the main bridge during the Nigerian civil war, as an alternate bridge by which they could cross in the event of an invasion by Nigerian troops. It was hidden away in the forest. The footbridge was made of slats of wood held together by rusting metal loops, and thick ropes. It had no handrails one could support oneself with while crossing it. The portion of the river that flowed under the bridge was bedded underneath with rocks. Rocks and stones, reaching out of a hilly part of the forest, were visible just below the waters. Ikenna ran to the bridge without thinking, and was at the centre of it in no time. But the moment he picked up the ball, he suddenly realized he was in danger. As he gazed with trepidation at the chasm beneath him, the chasm fed his eyes with visions of his death by a fall that would end in a fatal contact with the stones. Suddenly engulfed in fear, he began crying "Help! Help!" Just as scared as he was, we began calling on him: "Ike, come, come." In obedience to our entreaty, he spread his hands, and letting the ball fall into the gash, began walking towards us, slowly, his gait like that of someone wading through a pool of mud. As he came, tottering dangerously, the slats—made fragile with age and decay—cracked, and the bridge snapped,

84

breaking in two. Ikenna descended at once with planks of broken wood, metals and a loud jolting cry for help. He was still falling when, abruptly waking, I heard Mother's voice scolding Ikenna for having endangered his life by sleeping out and returning wet and ill. I once heard that the heart of an angered man will not beat with verve, it will inhale and bloat like a balloon, but eventually deflate. This was the case with my brother. For by morning, when I heard his voice, I ran out to the sitting room to see with my own eyes that he had returned drenched, helpless, an afflicted man.

* * *

With every day that passed, Ikenna became more distant from us. I hardly saw him in those days. His existence was reduced to these minimal movements around the house, the noise of his often exaggerated coughing and of the transistor radio whose volume he'd often raise so high Mother would ask him to turn it down if she was at home. Sometimes I saw him briefly leave the house, in haste mostly, not once seeing his face. I saw him again later that same week when he came out to see a football match on television. David had taken ill the previous night and vomited his dinner. Mother did not go to her store at the town bazaar that day, but sat at home to nurse David. After school, while Mother looked after David in her room, my brothers and I watched the match. Ikenna—who could not resist seeing the match, but also could not send the rest of us out of the room because Mother was there—sat aloft at the dining table as mute as a deer. It was almost at the end of the half-time when Mother came into the sitting room with a ten-naira bill in her hand and said: "I want both of you to go and get David some medicine." Although she did not mention names, she'd apparently addressed Ikenna and Boja; they ran errands outside the house because they were older. For a moment after Mother spoke, none of them moved an inch. This staggered Mother.

"Mama, am I your only child?" Ikenna replied rubbing his chin where Obembe had told me he'd seen some beard earlier. Although I had not noticed it at the time, I did not dispute it. Ikenna had just turned fifteen, and to my eyes, he was now a full adult able to grow beards. Yet, the thought that he was old came with the strong fear that once he grew into an adult, he would disconnect from us, go to higher college or just leave home. That thought never fully formed at the time though. It hung in my mind like a television acrobat, who, having just made a prodigious leap remained—after a click of the pause button—in mid-air, unable to complete the jump.

"What?" Mother asked.

"Can't you send someone else? Must it always be me? I'm tired and don't want to go anywhere."

"You and Boja will go and get it whether you like it or not. *Inugo*—Do you hear?"

Ikenna dropped his eyes, in a moment of wild contemplation and then, shaking his head, said: "Okay, if you insist it must be me, I will go, but I must go alone."

He stood and made forward to take the money, but Mother retracted the bill into her fist, concealing it. This shocked Ikenna. He stepped back, aghast. "Won't you give me the money and let me go?" he asked.

"Wait, let me ask you. What has your brother done to you? I really want to know, *really*."

"Nothing!" Ikenna cried. "Nothing, Mama, I'm okay. Just give me the money and let me go."

"I'm not talking about you but about your relationship with your brother. Look at Boja's lip." She pointed to Boja's injury that was now almost fully healed. "Look at what you did to him; what you did to your blood brother—"

"Just give me the money and let me go!" Ikenna bellowed and stretched out his hand.

But Mother, unruffled, continued while he was speaking, so that they competed for the same moment, giving way to a rush of words that came out from both of them as: "*Nwanne gi ye mu n hulu ego nwa anra ih nhulu ka mu ga ba*—Your brother *give me* who suckled *the money* the same breasts *and let me* as you did *go*!"

"Give it to me and let me go!" Ikenna cried now, louder, as if enraged even more by every word Mother had said that'd climbed on his own words, but Mother responded with soft tsks and monotonous shaking of her head.

"Just give me the money, I want to go alone," Ikenna said in a more restrained voice. "I beg you; please, just give me the money."

"May thunder strike your mouth, Ikenna! *Chinekem eh!* My God! When did you start challenging me, eh, Ikenna?"

"What did I do to you now?" Ikenna shouted and began stamping mad on the floor in protest. "What is this? Why are you always nit-picking on me? What have I done to you, this woman? Why don't you let me alone?"

Seated there, we all—like Mother—were shocked by Ikenna's address of Mother, *our mother*, as "this woman."

"Ikenna, is that you?" she asked in a subdued voice, pointing her forefinger at him. "Is that you, a duck that flutters its wings like a cock does? Is that you?" But as she was speaking, Ikenna made for the door. Mother watched as he opened it, then snapping her fingers, raised her voice after him, "Just wait until your father calls, I'll tell him what you have become. Don't worry, just let him return."

Ikenna hissed and then—in a show of brazen defiance unprecedented in our house—stormed out of the house, forcefully slamming the door behind him. As if to enunciate what had just happened, a car honked insanely for a length of time, and when it finally stopped, it left the din to echo in my head, thickening the enormity of Ikenna's defiance. Mother settled into one of the lounges, shock and anger tightening their grip around her heart, as she mumbled despairingly to herself, her hands clutched around her bosom.

"He has grown, Ikenna has grown horns."

I was moved to see her in such despair. It seemed a part of her body, which she had got accustomed to touching, had suddenly sprouted thorns and every effort made to touch that part merely resulted in bleeding.

"Mama," Obembe called to her.

"Eh, Nnam—my father," she replied.

"Give me the money," Obembe said. "I could go to get the medicine, and Ben could come with me. I'm not afraid."

She looked up at him and nodded, her eyes lightening up with a smile.

"Thank you, Obe," she said. "But it is dark, so Boja will go with you. You both should be careful."

"I will go too," I said, rising to get my clothes.

"No, Ben," Mother said. "Stay here with me. Two is enough."

In the state of mind I have come to develop after the breakdown of our lives, I often remember that phrase, "Two is enough," as a foreboding of the things that would befall our family a few weeks after that day. I sat down beside Mother and Obembe and pondered about how much Ikenna had changed. I'd never seen him act rude to Mother; for he loved her greatly. Of all of us, he looked the most like her. He took her colour of the tropical anthills. In this part of Africa, married women often went by the name of their first child. Hence, Mother was commonly known as Mama Ike or Adaku. Ikenna enjoyed most of the earliest cares that she ever gave her kids. It was in his cot we all laid years later. We all inherited his baskets of medicines and baby-care things. He had stood on Mother's side against anyone in the past—even Father. Sometimes when we disobeyed Mother, he punished us before she took any action. Their partnership was what gave Father the satisfaction that we could be well reared, even in his absence. The small depression on the fourth finger of Father's right hand was a scar from Ikenna's bite. Years before I was born, Father hit Mother in a fit of rage. Ikenna swooped in on him and bit him on his finger, naturally ending the fight.

5

THE METAMORPHOSIS

I kenna was undergoing a metamorphosis:

A life-changing experience that continued with each passing day. He closed himself off from the rest of us. But though he was no longer accessible, he began to leave shattering traces of himself around the house in actions that left lasting impacts on our lives. One such incident occurred at the beginning of the week following that altercation with Mother. It was a parents-teacher day, so school let out early. Ikenna remained alone in his room, while Boja, Obembe and I sat in our room playing a game of cards. It was a particularly hot day and we were all naked to the waist, seated on the carpet. Our wooden shutter was wide open, wedged with a small stone to let in air. Upon hearing the door of his room open and close, Boja said: "That is Ike going out."

And then, after a little pause, we heard the opening and closing of the sitting room's storm door, too. We had not seen Ikenna in two days because he'd hardly been at home, and when he was, he stayed in his room, and whenever he was there, no one, not even Boja with whom he shared the room, entered it. Boja had remained cautious of Ikenna since their last fight because Mother had asked him to stay away from Ikenna until Father returned to exorcise the evil spirits that had possessed him. So Boja mostly stayed with us, accessing the room only at times like this when he was sure Ikenna was not there. He rose to go to the room to take a few things he needed quickly while Obembe and I waited for him to return and continue the game. He'd barely gone out when Obembe and I heard him cry "*Mogbe!*"—a cry of lamentation in Yoruba. As we ran out, Boja began shouting "Calendar M.K.O.! Calendar M.K.O.!"

"What, what?" Obembe and I asked him as we rushed towards the room. Then we saw for ourselves.

Our prized M.K.O. calendar was charred to pieces, and meticulously destroyed. I could not believe it at first, so I glanced at the wall where it had always hung, but what I saw was a cleaner, shinier, and almost glossy, blank square surface of the wall, its edges slightly smeared with spots where it had been taped. The sight horrified me; my mind could not grasp it, for the M.K.O. calendar was a special calendar.

The tale of how we obtained the calendar had been our greatest achievement. We always retold ourselves this story with great pride. It was in the middle of March 1993, in the heat of the presidential election campaigns. We'd arrived at school one morning while the assembly bell was ringing its dying chimes, and quickly merged into the group of chatting pupils, steadily forming lines and columns according to class on the assembly ground. I stood in the nursery line, Obembe in the first grade's line, Boja in the fourth grade's line, and Ikenna in the fifth grade's line—just second to the last one near the fence. Once all the lines had formed, the morning assembly began. The pupils sang the morning hymns, said the Lord's Prayer, and sang the Nigerian anthem. Afterwards, Mr Lawrence, the head teacher, stood on the podium and opened the large school attendance register. Then, with a microphone, he began calling out the names. When he called a pupil's name and surname, we cried out "Present, sir!" and simultaneously raised our hands. In this manner, he took a roll call of all the four hundred pupils of the school. When Mr Lawrence got to the fourth grade's line, and called the first name on the list, "Bojanonimeokpu Alfred Agwu," the pupils burst into laughter.

"In all of your fathers' faces!" Boja cried out, raising his two hands, his fingers spread apart, to *waka* at the pupils—a gesture of cursing.

That wiped out all laughter from the crowd of pupils, and still they stood, no one moving, no one saying a word except for a few murmurs that swiftly tapered off. Even the dreaded Mr Lawrence, the only person I knew who whipped sorer than Father and who was almost never seen without a whip, appeared dazed and momentarily incapacitated. Boja had been angered that morning even before we got to school. He had been embarrassed when Father asked him to take out the mattress he had wetted when he woke. What he did when Mr Lawrence called his name might have been caused by that; for it was usual for the pupils to laugh whenever Mr Lawrence, a Yoruba man, struggled to accurately pronounce Boja's full Igbo names. Knowing Mr Lawrence's deficiency, Boja had become used to his employment of approximate homophones, which, depending on his mood, ranged from the utterly jarring—"Bojanonokwu"—to the utterly funny—"Bojanolooku"—which Boja himself often recalled, and even sometimes boasted that he was such a menacing figure that his name could not be pronounced by just anybody—like the name of a god. Boja had often revelled in those moments and until that morning, had never complained.

The headmistress walked to the podium and Mr Lawrence, dumbfounded, stepped back. The megaphone made a prolonged shriek as it was passed from his hand to hers.

"Who said those words on the grounds of Omotayo Nursery and Primary School, a renowned Christian school built and founded on the word of God?" the head-mistress said.

I was seized with the fear of an imminent severe punishment Boja would receive for this act—perhaps he would be whipped on the podium or asked to do "labour," which entailed sweeping the entire school compound or weeding the bush in front of the school with bare hands. I tried to catch Obembe's eyes because he was in a line two rows from me, but he would not turn away from Boja.

"I asked who?" the headmistress's voice bellowed again.

"Me, ma," a familiar voice replied.

"Who are you?" she asked, her voice lower than it was before.

"Boja."

There was a brief pause, after which the headmistress's distinct voice beamed "Come here" into the megaphone. As Boja made to go out to the podium, Ikenna ran forward, stood in front of him and cried out aloud "No, ma, this is unfair! What has he done? What? If you are going to punish him, you have to punish all of these people who laughed at him, too. Why should they laugh at him and mock him?"

The silence that followed these bold words, Ikenna's and Boja's defiance, was for a moment spiritual. The megaphone in the headmistress's hands shook unsteadily and then fell to the ground with a loud shriek. She picked up the megaphone, dropped it on the podium, and stepped back.

"In fact," Ikenna's voice rose again, above the noise of a colony of birds sailing towards the hills, "this is unfair. We'd rather leave your school than be punished unjustly. My brothers and I will all leave. Now. There are better schools out there where we can get better Western education; Daddy will no longer pay the big money to you."

I remember, in sparkling mirror memory, the unsure movements of Mr Lawrence's legs as he reached for the long cane, and the headmistress's gesture that stopped him. Yet, even if she had let him, he would not have been able to catch up with Ikenna and Boja who'd begun to walk through the lines that gently parted for them among the pupils, who, like the teachers, seemed to have frozen with fear. Then, our older brothers grabbing my hand and Obembe's, we ran out of the school.

We could not go home directly because Mama had just given birth to David and was convalescing. Ikenna said we'd get her worried if we returned home less than an hour after we'd left for school. We walked about in an end street that was mostly empty grassland, with signposts saying

This land is owned by so and so, do not trespass. We stopped at the façade of a half-finished, abandoned house. Fallen bricks and crumbling pyramids of sand were scattered all over with what appeared to be dog shit. We entered the structure and sat on a slab of paved floor with a roof— something Obembe suggested would become the house's sitting room. "You should have seen the headmistress's daughter's face," Boja said. We mocked the teachers and pupils and raved about what we'd done, exaggerating the scenes to make them movie-like.

We'd sat there for about thirty minutes talking about what had happened at school when our attention was suddenly drawn to a distant rising noise. We saw a Bedford truck slowly approaching in the distance. It was covered with posters bearing the portraits of Chief M.K.O. Abiola, the presidential aspirant of the Social Democratic Party (SDP). The truck was loaded with people on top of its open back, and was abuzz with voices singing a song that appeared on state television frequently during those days: the song that held up M.K.O. as "the man." The people were singing, drumming, with two of them—men dressed in white T-shirts with a photograph of M.K.O.—also blowing trumpets. All around the street, onlookers reared out of houses, sheds, shops, some peeping from windows. As the group went, some of them disengaged from the truck and distributed posters. They gave Ikenna, who stepped forward to meet them while the rest of us stayed back, a small one that had M.K.O.'s smiling face, a white horse beside him, and the words *Hope '93: Farewell to Poverty* cascading downwards at the right-hand corner of the poster.

"Why don't we follow this group and see M.K.O.?" Boja said suddenly. "If he becomes the president after the election, we'd be able to always brag that we've met the president of Nigeria!"

"Ah—true, but if we go along with them in our uniform," Ikenna reflected, "they might probably send us away. They know full well that it is still early in the day and school couldn't have let us out by now."

"If they say so, we can tell them we left because we saw them," Boja replied.

"Yes, yes," Ikenna agreed, "they will respect us even more."

"What if we follow them from a distance, through corner-corner?" Boja said. He met Ikenna's nod of approval; encouraged, he continued: "That way, we can stay clear of trouble and still see M.K.O."

This idea stuck. We walked through the corners of the street, rounding off a large church and an area where northerners lived. A pungent odour hung around the bend in the alley where the big abattoir was located. As we passed, we heard knives knapping on slabs and boards as the butchers chopped meat, the mob voices of patrons and butchers rising steadily, shoulder-to-shoulder, with the knapping. Outside the gate of the abattoir, two men knelt on a mat and bowed in prayers. A third, standing a few metres from the two, was doing ablutions with water from a small plastic kettle he held in his hand. We crossed the road, passed our neighbourhood and saw a man and a woman standing outside our gate. Their eyes were fastened to a book the woman had in her hand. We hurried past, casting furtive glances around to make sure none of our neighbours had spotted us, but the street seemed deserted. We passed a small church constructed out of teak and zinc roofing on whose wall was an elaborate painting of Jesus with a nimbus around his crown of thorns. From a hole in his chest, drops of blood dripped down, but held, below his visible ribs. A lizard crossed the line of trailing drops of blood with its tail erect, its vile shape obliterating the punctured chest. Clothes hung on the open doors of the shops in front of which were rickety tables crammed with tomatoes, canned beverages, packets of cornflakes, tins of milk and various effects. Just across from the church was a bazaar sprawled over a large expanse of land. The procession had zipped through the thin path between boulders of humans, stalls, and shops, their trucks plodding ponderously to attract the market people. All over the bazaar, the congested mass of humanity seethed like a tribe of maggots. As we plodded through the bazaar, Obembe's sandal came loose. A man had placed his heavy shoe on the sandal's strap and Obembe had to force it from under the man's foot, in the process of which the strap had snapped, leaving the sandal with only a front cover strap like a flip-flop. He began dragging his feet as we made out of the bazaar down a wheel road with declivities.

We'd barely set on this path when Obembe stopped, cupped his hand over his ear and began crying, "Listen, listen" frantically.

"Listen to what?" Ikenna said.

Just then, I heard a noise similar to that of the convoy, closer and more palpable this time.

"Listen," Obembe curtly said, gazing skywards. Then suddenly, he burst out: "*Helicot! Helicota!*"

"He-li-copter," Boja said in a voice that sounded nasal because his eyes were still focused on the sky.

The complete picture of the helicopter had now appeared, gradually dropping to the level of the two-storeyed buildings in the neighbourhood. It was painted green and white, the colours of the Nigerian flag, with the portrait of a white horse poised to sprint engraved in an oblong circle in the centre of the single partition. Two men holding small flags sat on the threshold of one of its doors, shading out a man in police uniform and another in sparkling ocean-blue *agbada*, Yoruba traditional attire. The entire area was abuzz with cries of "M.K.O. Abiola." Vehicles honked on the roads, motorcycles revved their engines to deafening wails as the gathering of a massive mob began somewhere in the distance.

"M.K.O!" Ikenna cried breathlessly, wailing. "M.K.O. is in that helicopter!"

He grabbed my hand and we ran in the direction where we thought the helicopter might be landing. We found it landing just outside a magnificent building that was surrounded by a league of trees, and a nine-foot barbed-wire fence, apparently owned by an influential politician. It was much closer than we'd imagined and we were surprised that, besides the aides and a chief who was outside the gate waiting for M.K.O., we were the first to reach the spot. We arrived singing one of M.K.O.'s campaign songs but stopped to watch the helicopter land, its fast swirling blades summoning a dust cloud that shielded M.K.O. and Kudirat, his wife, from sight as they stepped out. When it cleared, we saw that M.K.O. and his wife both wore shiny traditional attire. As a mob gathered, uniformed guards and guards in plain clothes formed a wall to edge it away. The people were cooing, cheering and calling his name aloud, and the Chief waved to acknowledge them. As this scene unfolded, Ikenna started singing a church song we'd hijacked, remixed, and constantly sang for Mother to soothe her whenever she was mad at us. We'd put "Mama" in place of "God." But now, Ikenna replaced "Mama" with "M.K.O.," and we had all joined in, singing at the top of our lungs:

> *M.K.O., you are beautiful beyond description.*
> *Too marvellous for words.*
> *The most wonderful of all creatures,*
> *Like nothing never seen nor heard.*
> *Who can touch your infinite wisdom?*
> *Who can fathom the depths of your love?*
> *M.K.O., you are beautiful beyond description.*
> *Your majesty is enthroned above.*

We'd started a repeat when M.K.O. signalled that the aides bring us closer. Frantic, we made our way over and stood in his presence. Up close, his face was round and his head conical. When he smiled, his eyes lent his features abundant grace. He became a real person: no longer a figure that existed exclusively in the realm of television screens and newspaper pages, but suddenly as normal as Father or Boja, or even Igbafe and my classmates. This epiphany filled me with sudden fear. I stopped singing, dropped my eyes from the bright face of M.K.O., and planted them on his shoes that glistened from polishing. On one side of the shoes was the iron sculpture of the head of a being that appeared like Medusa in Boja's favourite movie, *Clash of the Titans*. Ikenna would tell me later, after I mentioned the head, that he'd polished one of Father's shoes with the same embossment. He spelt out the name because he could not pronounce it: V-e-r-s-a-c-e.

"What are your names?" M.K.O. asked.

"I'm Ikenna Agwu," Ikenna said. "These are my brothers: Benjamin, Boja and Obembe."

"Ah, Benjamin," Chief Abiola said, smiling widely. "That's my grandfather's name."

His wife, who was dressed in an identical robe as M.K.O. and carried a shiny handbag, bent down towards me and stroked my head as one would stroke a densely furred dog. I felt metal scratch lightly against my short-haired scalp. When she withdrew her hand, I noticed that what had touched my scalp was a ring; she wore one on almost every finger. M.K.O. raised his hand to cheer the massive crowd that had now gathered all around the vicinity, chanting the theme of his campaign: "Hope '93! Hope '93!" For a while, he repeated the word *awon*—"these" in Yoruba—in different tones as he tried to get the crowd to hear him.

When the chant ebbed and a fair silence ensued, M.K.O. thrust his fist in the air and shouted, "*Awon omo yi nipe M.K.O. lewa ju gbogbo nkan lo.*"

The crowd responded with wild shouts of acclaim, some of them whistled with fingers curved on both sides of their mouths. He gazed down on us as he waited for them to quiet, then he continued in English.

"In all my life in politics to date, I've never ever been told this, not even by my own wives—" The crowd interrupted him with a roar of laughter. "No one, I mean, has ever told me that I'm beautiful beyond description—*pe mo le wa ju gbogbo nka lo.*"

The throng of voices cheered again as he rubbed my shoulder with his hand.

"They say I'm too marvellous for words."

The crowd mauled his words with a tumult of applause, the tooting louder.

"They say I'm like nothing they've ever seen before."

The mob waged in again, and once they calmed, M.K.O.—in the most aggressive cry possible—exploded: "Like nothing the Federal Republic of Nigeria has ever seen before!"

The crowd took the air for almost a limitless measure of time, after which they let him speak again, but this time to us and not to them.

"You will do something for me. You all," he said, his index finger making a circle in the air above us. "You will stand with me and take a photograph. We will use it for our campaign."

We nodded, and Ikenna said, "Yes, sir."

"*Oya*, stand with me."

He signalled one of his aides, an able-bodied man in a tight brown suit and a red tie, to come forward. The man bent towards him and whispered something in his ear from which the word camera was only just audible. In no time, a smartly dressed man in a blue shirt and tie approached, with a camera hanging on his chest by a black strap with *NIKON* crested all over it. A few more aides tried to push back the crowd as M.K.O. broke off from us now for a minute to shake hands with his host, the politician who stood close, waiting to receive his attention. Then M.K.O. turned back to us. "Are you ready now?"

"Yes, sir," we chorused.

"Good," he said. "I will come to the centre and both of you,"—he gestured to Ikenna and me, "move here." We stood to his right and Obembe with Boja to his left. "Good, good," he muttered.

The photographer, one knee on the ground, and the other bent now, aimed his camera until a bright flash lit our faces in a heartbeat second. M.K.O. clapped and the crowd clapped and cheered. "Thank you, Benjamin, Obembe, Ikenna," M.K.O. said, pointing at each of us as he said our names. When he got to Boja, he paused in confusion, prompting him to say his name. M.K.O. repeated it in slanting syllables: "Bo-*ja*".

"Wow!" M.K.O. exclaimed, laughing. "It sounds like *Mo ja*," ("I fought" in Yoruba). "Do you fight?"

Boja shook his head.

"Good," M.K.O. muttered, "don't ever." He wagged his finger. "Fighting is not good. What is the name of your school?"

"Omotayo Nursery and Primary School, Akure," I said in the singsong manner that we had been taught we should use to answer the question whenever it was asked.

"Okay, good, Ben," M.K.O. said. He raised his head towards the crowd. "Ladies and gentlemen, these four boys of one family will now be awarded scholarships by the Moshood Kashimawo Olawale Abiola campaign organization."

As the crowd applauded, he dipped his hand into the large side pocket of his *agbada* and gave Ikenna a bunch of naira notes. "Take this," he said, pulling one of his aides closer. "Richard, here, will take you to your home, and deliver it to your parents. He will also take down your names and address."

"Thank you, sir!" we cried almost in unison, but he did not seem to have heard us. He'd already begun walking towards the big house with his aides and hosts, turning every now and then to wave at the crowd.

We followed the aide to a black Mercedes parked across the road, and he drove us home in it. And from that day, we began to pride ourselves on being M.K.O. boys. The four of us were called out to the podium during the school's assembly one morning and applauded after the headmistress, who seemed to have forgotten and forgiven the circumstances that had led to our accidental encounter with M.K.O., made a long speech about the importance of making good impressions on people—of being "good ambassadors of the school." Then she announced, even to greater applause, that our father, Mr Agwu, would no longer have to pay our school fees.

Despite these obvious profits, the fame it brought us in and around our district, and Father's financial relief and joy, the M.K.O. calendar embodied bigger things. It was a badge to us, a testimonial of our affiliation with a man almost everyone in the west of Nigeria believed would be Nigeria's next president. In that calendar was a strong hope for the future, for we'd believed we were children of Hope '93, M.K.O.'s allies. Ikenna was convinced that when M.K.O. became president, we could go to Abuja,

Nigeria's seat of government, and we would be let in by just showing the calendar. That M.K.O. would put us in big positions and probably make one of us the president of Nigeria someday. We had all believed this would happen, and put our hope in this calendar, which Ikenna had now destroyed.

★ ★ ★

Once Ikenna's metamorphosis became cataclysmic and began to threaten the repose we had been living in, Mother became desperate for a solution. She asked questions. She prayed. She warned. But all to no avail. It seemed increasingly obvious that the Ikenna who was once our brother had been bottled in a tightly sealed jar and thrown into an ocean. But on the day the special calendar was destroyed, Mother was shaken beyond words. She'd returned from work that evening and Boja, who'd sat in the midst of the charred bits and pieces, weeping for long, gave her the remains of the calendar which he'd swept into a plain sheet of paper, and said: "That, Mama, is what our M.K.O. calendar has become."

Mother, disbelieving, first went to the room to see the blank wall before unwrapping the paper in her hand. She sat on the chair that rested against the buzzing refrigerator. She knew, like us, that we did not have more than two copies and Father had gladly given one copy to the headmistress of our school who hung it in her office after the aides of Chief M.K.O. Abiola opened the scholarship there.

"What has come over Ikenna?" she said. "Isn't this the calendar he would have killed to protect; the one for which he beat Obembe?" She spat "*Tufia!*" the Igbo word for "God forbid," repeatedly, snapping her fingers over her head—a superstitious gesture meant to swish away the evil she had seen in Ikenna's action. She was referring to when Ikenna beat Obembe for smashing a mosquito on the calendar, leaving an indelible stain—caused by the mosquito's blood—on M.K.O.'s left eye.

She sat there wondering what had happened to Ikenna. She was worried because Ikenna was, until recently, our beloved brother, the forerunner who shot into the world ahead of all of us and opened every door for us. He guided us, protected us and led us with a full-lit torch. Even though he sometimes punished Obembe and me or disagreed with Boja on certain issues, he became a prowling lion when an outsider rattled any of us. I did not know what it was to live without contact with him, without seeing him. But this was exactly what began to happen, and as the days passed, it seemed he deliberately sought to hurt us.

After seeing the blank wall that night, Mother said nothing. She merely cooked eba, and warmed up the pot of ogbono soup she had prepared the previous day. After we'd eaten, she went into her room, and I thought she had gone to sleep. But at what must have been midnight, she came into the room I shared with Obembe.

"Wake up, wake up," she called, tapping us.

I screamed upon her touch. When I opened my eyes, all I saw was two distinct eyes blinking in the stark darkness.

"It is *me*," Mother said, "do you hear? It is me."

"Yes, Mama," I said.

"Shhhhhhh… don't shout; you will wake Nkem."

I nodded, and although Obembe had not shouted as I did, he nodded, too.

"I want to ask both of you something," Mother whispered. "Are you awake?"

She tapped my leg again. In a jolt, I let out a loud "Yes!" and Obembe followed.

"*Ehen*," Mother muttered. It appeared as if she'd had a long session of praying or crying or, just as likely, both. Not long before that day—when Ikenna refused to go to the pharmacy with Boja to be precise—I'd asked Obembe why Mother cried so often when she was not a child, and thus past the age of frequent crying. Obembe had replied that he did not know either, but that he thought women were prone to crying.

"Listen," Mother, now seated on the bed with us,

said. "I want both of you to tell me what caused the rift between Ikenna and Boja. I'm sure you both know, so, tell me—quickly, quickly."

"I don't know, Mama," I said.

"No, you know," she countered. "There must be something that happened—a fight or quarrel I do not know of; just something. Think."

I nodded and started to think, to try to understand what she wanted.

"Obembe," Mother called after only a wall of silence greeted her query.

"Mama."

"Tell me, your mother, what caused the rift between your brothers," she said, this time, in English. She knotted her *wrappa* around her chest as if it had come loose, something she often did when agitated. "Did they have a fight?"

"No," Obembe replied.

"Is it true, Ben?"

"Yes, it is, Mama."

"*Fa lu ru ogu?*—Did they quarrel?" she asked, returning to Igbo.

We both replied "No," Obembe's coming much later after mine.

"So, what happened?" she asked after a short pause. "Tell me, *eh*, my princes, Obembe Igwe, Azikiwe, *gwa nu mu ife me lu nu, biko* my husbands," she pleaded, employing the heart-melting endearments she bestowed on us in times like this when she wanted to obtain some information from us. She'd bestow royalty on Obembe, ascribing him the title of an *igwe*, a traditional king. She'd confer the name of Nigeria's first indigenous president, Dr Nnamdi Azikiwe, on me. Once she called us these names, Obembe began staring at me—an indication that there was something he did not want to say, but which—nudged by Mother's entreaties—he was now wholly ready to say. Hence, Mother only needed to repeat the endearments just once more before Obembe spilled it, for she had already won. Both she and Father were good at digging into our minds. They knew how to burrow so deep into our psyche when they wanted to find things out that it was sometimes difficult to think they didn't already know what they were asking about, but were merely seeking to confirm it.

"Mama, it began the day we met Abulu at Omi-Ala," Obembe said once Mother repeated the endearment.

"Eh? Abulu the madman?" Mother cried, springing to her feet in terror.

Obembe, it seemed, had not expected this reaction. Perhaps frightened, Obembe cast his eyes on the bare mattress spread out in front of him and said nothing. For this was a metal-lidded secret, one that Boja had warned us never to reveal to anyone after Ikenna first started drawing a line between us and him. "You have both seen what it has done to Ikenna," he'd said, "so keep your mouths shut." We had agreed, and promised to wipe it out of our memory by committing a lobotomy on our minds.

"I asked you a question," Mother said. "Which Abulu did they meet? The madman?"

"Yes," Obembe affirmed in a whisper, and quickly glanced at the wall that partitioned our room from our elder brothers' room, suspecting that they might have heard he'd revealed the secret.

"*Chi-neke!*" Mother cried. Then she sat back on the bed slowly, her hands on her head. She remained in that strange silence for a moment, grinding her teeth and tsking. "Now," she said suddenly, "tell me at once, what happened when you met him? Did you hear me, Obembe? I said, and I'm saying for the last time, tell me what happened at that river."

Obembe hesitated for a while longer, too afraid to begin the story he'd partly told in that one revealing sentence. But it was too late, for Mother had already started to wait anxiously, her feet suddenly set on the hill as if she'd seen a raptor advancing towards her fold, and she, the falconer, was ready for a confrontation. Hence, it was now impossible for Obembe, even if he'd wanted to, to resist her.

*   *   *

A little more than a week before the neighbour caught us, my brothers and I were returning from the Omi-Ala River with the other boys when we met Abulu along the sandy pathway. We had just completed a fishing session at the river and were walking home, discussing the two big tilapias we'd caught that day (one of which Ikenna had fiercely argued was a Symphysodon) when, upon reaching the clearing where the mango tree and the Celestial Church were located, Kayode cried: "Look, there's a dead man under the tree! A dead man! A dead man!"

We all turned at once to the spot and saw a man lying on a mat of fallen leaves at the foot of the mango tree, his head pillowed on a small broken branch still foliated with leaves. Mangoes of different sizes, colours—yellow, green, red—and ones in different stages of decomposition lay about everywhere. Some were squashed, some rotten from bird bites. The soles of the man's feet, which laid plain before our eyes, were so ugly that it seemed that athlete's foot had carved sinewy lines all over them, giving them the resemblance of a complex map, coloured with dead leaves that clung to every line.

"That's not a dead man; he is the one humming this tune," Ikenna said calmly. "He must be a madman; this is how mad people behave."

Although I'd not heard the tune before, I did now that Ikenna called our attention to it.

"Ikenna is right," Solomon said. "This is Abulu, the vision-seeing madman." Then snapping his fingers, he said, "I detest this man."

"Ah!" Ikenna cried. "Is it him?"

"It is him—Abulu," Solomon said.

"I didn't even recognize him," said Ikenna.

I looked at the madman, whom Ikenna and Solomon had revealed they knew, but I could not remember having ever seen him before. A great number of mad people, derelicts and beggars roamed the streets of Akure, and there was nothing noteworthy or distinct about any of them. It was thus strange to me that this one not only had a distinct identity, but also a name—a name people seemed to know. As we looked on, the madman raised his hands and held them strangely in the air, still, with a sublimity that struck me with awe.

"Look at that!" Boja said.

Abulu sat up now, as if glued to the spot, peering straight into the distance.

"Let's leave him alone and go on our way," Solomon

said at that point. "Let's not talk to him, let's just go; leave him alone—"

"No, no, we should rattle him a bit," Boja, who'd moved towards the man, suggested. "We shouldn't just leave like that, this could be fun. Listen, we could frighten him, and—"

"No!" Solomon said forcefully. "Are you mad? Don't you know this man is evil? Don't you know him?"

While Solomon was still speaking, the madman burst into a sudden roar of laughter. In fear, Boja swiftly skipped backwards and rejoined the rest of us. Just then, Abulu sprang acrobatically to his feet with one prodigious leap. He put both hands together to his side, clasped his legs, and without a part of his body moving, fell back into his former position. Thrilled by this callisthenic display, we clapped and cheered in admiration.

"He is a giant—Superman!" Kayode cried and the others laughed.

We'd forgotten that we had been going home, darkness was slowly covering the surface of the horizon and our mother might soon begin looking for us. I was thrilled and fascinated by this strange man. I cupped my hand around my mouth and said: "He is like a lion!"

"You compare everything to animals, Ben," Ikenna said, shaking his head as if the comparison had annoyed him.

"He is not like anything, you hear? He is just a madman—
a madman."

Lost in the moment, I watched this awesome creature
with all the concentration I could gather until details of
him filled my mind. He was robed from head to foot in
filth. As he rose spryly to stand, some of the filth rose with
him, while some was left in patches on the ground. He had
a fresh scar on his face just below his chin, and his back was
caked with a dripping mess from some dead mango in a
state of putrefaction. His lips were dried and cracked. His
hair was unkempt; it stretched like tendrils, giving him
the appearance of a Rastafarian. His teeth, most of which
were blackened as if singed, reminded me of fire-blowing
gypsies and circus players who blew fire from their mouths
and probably, I thought, burned their teeth. The man lay
bare before our eyes, stark naked except for a shred of rag
which hung loosely from his shoulder down to his waist;
his pubic region was covered with a dense foliage of hair in
the midst of which his veiny penis hung limply like trouser
rope. His legs were bursting with taut varicose veins.

Kayode picked a mango and threw it in the direction
of Abulu, and at once, as if expecting it, the madman
caught the mango in the air. Holding out the fruit as if it
was an acrid substance he could not bring close to himself,
he slowly rose to his feet. With a loud, piercing cry, he

hurled the mango so high it might have landed at the town centre, some twenty miles away. This swept the ground from beneath our feet.

In silence, we stood there, frozen, watching this man until Solomon moved forward and said: "You see? Do you see what I tell you? Can an ordinary human being do this?" he pointed in the direction of the projectile that was the mango. "This man is evil. Let us go home and leave him. Haven't you heard how he killed his brother, eh? What can be worse than a man who killed his own brother?" He put his hand to hold the lobe of his ear in the manner of an older person giving instruction to a child. "We must all go home, now!"

"He is right," Ikenna said after a moment's thought. "We should all go home. See, it is getting late."

We started on our way, but once we began, Abulu burst out in laughter. "Ignore him," Solomon urged, waving us on. The rest marched on, but I couldn't. I'd become suddenly afraid, on account of Solomon's description of him, that this man was so dangerous he could jump on us and kill us. I turned, and when I saw that he was coming after us, my fear was inflamed.

"Let us run," I cried, "he will kill us!"

"No, he can't kill us," Ikenna said and turned rapidly to face the madman. "He can see we are armed."

"With what?" asked Boja.

"Our fishing hooks," Ikenna replied curtly. "If he comes any closer, we will tear his flesh with the hooks, just like we kill fish, and throw his body in the river."

As if deterred by this threat, the madman stopped and stood still, his hands masking his face, making strange sounds. We continued and had walked a fair distance away when we heard a loud cry of Ikenna's name. We pulled to an immediate halt in shock.

"*Ikena*," the voice called again with a Yoruba accent that lengthened the *e* sound of the first letter and obliterated the second *n* so that it sounded as *Ikena*.

We glanced around in bewilderment to see who'd said the name, but Abulu was the only person within sight. He now stood a few metres from us, his arms folded across his chest.

"*Ikena*," Abulu repeated aloud, inching closer towards us.

"Let's not listen to Abulu's prophecies. *O le wu*—it is dangerous," Solomon shouted at us, his Yoruba thickening with a twang of his Oyo dialect. "Let's go home now, let's go." He pushed Ikenna forward. "It's not good to listen to Abulu's prophecies, Ike. Let us go!"

"Yes, Ike," Kayode said, "he is of the devil, but we are Christians."

For a moment, we all waited for Ikenna, whose eyes now stayed on the madman. Without turning to the rest of us, he shook his head and cried, "No!"

"What no? Don't you know Abulu?" Solomon asked. He caught Ikenna by the shirt, but Ikenna pulled away from him, leaving a piece of his old Bahamas resort T-shirt in Solomon's hand.

"Leave me," Ikenna said. "I'm not going away. He is calling my name. *He is calling my name.* How did he know my name? How—how is he calling my name?"

"Maybe he heard it from one of us," Solomon said, matching Ikenna's forceful tone.

"No, he didn't," Ikenna shouted. "He didn't hear it from anyone."

He had just said that when—in a softer, subtler voice— Abulu called again, "*Ikena.*" Then raising his hands, the madman burst into a song I'd heard people sing in our neighbourhood without knowing where it came from or what it meant, and the song was titled: "The Sower of Green Things."

We all listened to his rapturous singing for a while, even Solomon. Then, shaking his head, Solomon picked up his fishing hook, tossed the piece of Ikenna's shirt to the ground and said: "You and your brothers may stay, but I won't stay."

Solomon turned and Kayode followed him. Igbafe, conspicuously indeterminate, threw glances back and forth between us and the vanishing duo. Then slowly, he began walking away until, after about a hundred metres, he began to run.

Abulu had stopped singing by the time I had lost sight of those who had left us, and he had resumed calling Ikenna's name. When it seemed he'd called it for the thousandth time, he cast his eyes above, lifted his hands and shouted: "*Ikena*, you will be bound like a bird on the day you shall die," he cried, covering his eyes with his hands to demonstrate blindness.

"*Ikena,* you will be mute," he said, and closed his ears with both hands.

"*Ikena*, you will be crippled," he said, and moved his legs apart, folding his palms together in the way of spiritual supplications. Then he knocked his knees together and fell backwards into the dirt as though the bones of his knees had suddenly been broken.

When he said: "Your tongue will stick out of your mouth like a hungry beast, and will not return back into your mouth," he thrust out his tongue, and curled it to one side of his mouth.

"*Ikena*, you shall lift your hands to grasp air, but you will not be able to. *Ikena*, you shall open your mouth to speak on that day"—the madman opened his mouth and made a loud gasping sound of *ah, ah*—"but words will freeze in your mouth."

As he spoke, the din of an aircraft flying overhead mopped his voice into a desperate whimper at first, and then—when the plane had drawn much closer—it swallowed the rest of his words like a boa. The last statement we heard him make, "*Ikena*, you will swim in a river of red but shall never rise from it again. Your life—" was barely audible. The din and the voices of children cheering at the plane from around the neighbourhood threw the evening into a cacophonous haze. Abulu cast a frenzied gaze upwards in confusion. Then, as if in a fury, he continued in a louder voice that was whipped into faint whispers by the sound of the aircraft. As the noise tapered off, we all heard him say "*Ikena*, you shall die like a cock dies."

Abulu fell silent and his face lit up with relief. Then he moved one of his hands in the air as if scribbling something on an invisible hanging paper or book with a pen no one else but he could see. When it seemed he was done, he started to go, singing and clapping along.

We watched the forward-and-backwards swing of his backbone as he sang and danced, the song's charged lyrics falling back on us like wind-borne dust.

A fe f ko le fe ko	As the wind cannot blow
ma kan igi oko	without touching the trees
Osupa ko le hon ki	As no one can block the light
enikan fi aso di	of the moon with a sheet
Oh, Olu Orun,	Oh, father of the host for
eni ti mo je Ojise fun	whom I'm an oracle
E fa orun ya,	I implore you to tear the
e je ki ojo ro	firmaments and give rain
Ki oro ti mo to	That the green things
gbin ba le gbo	I have sown will live
E ba igba orun je,	Mutilate the seasons so my
ki oro mi bale mi	words can breathe,
Ki won ba le gbo.	That they yield fruit.

The madman sang on as he went away from us until his voice petered out, along with all of his corporeal convoy—his presence, his smell, his shadow that clung to the tree and the ground, his body. And once he was out of sight, I noticed that the night had descended heavily around us, covering the roof of the world with a crepuscular awning, and—in what seemed like the blink of an eye—had turned the birds nesting in the mango tree and the sprawling esan bush around it into black objects that were imperceptible to the eyes as they flew past us. Even the Nigerian flag that hovered over the police station two hundred metres away had darkened and the distant hills had merged with the dark sky as if there was no partition between the sky and the earth.

My brothers and I went home afterwards, bruised as if we'd been beaten in an easy fight, while the world around us continued to run with the machinery of things unaltered, with nothing suggesting that something of portentous significance had happened to us. For the street was alive, bustling with the night-time cacophony of roadside sellers with lanterns and candles on tables and people walking around whose shadows were scattered on the ground, walls, against trees, on buildings like life-sized murals. A Hausa man in northern garment stood behind a wooden shed covered with tarpaulins, turning a pile of skewered meat on a charcoal hearth set in a metal bowl from which thick black smoke was rising. Separated from this man by a running sewer were two women who sat on a bench, bent over an actual hearth, roasting corn.

We were only a stone's throw from our house when Ikenna stopped walking, forcing the rest of us to a halt, so that he stood in front of the three of us, now a mere silhouette. "Did any of you hear what he said when the plane was flying past?" he said in a voice that was unsteady yet measured. "Abulu kept speaking, but I did not hear."

I had not heard the madman; the plane had caught my attention so much that, for the time it was visible, I had watched it closely, my hand shaded over my eyes to try to catch a glimpse of its most likely foreign passengers heading, perhaps, somewhere in the Western world. But it seemed neither Boja nor Obembe had heard him, for neither said a word. Ikenna had turned and was about to start walking when Obembe said: "I did."

"What then are you waiting for?" Ikenna thundered loudly. All three of us stepped back a few metres.

Obembe steeled himself, afraid that Ikenna would hit him.

"Were you deaf?" Ikenna shouted.

The rage in Ikenna's voice frightened me. I dropped my head to avoid looking straight at him and focused, instead, on his shadow that was sprawled on the dirt. As I watched the actions of his actual body by the movement of his shadow on the dirt, I saw it throw what it held in its hand to the ground. Then his shadow flowed towards Obembe, its head elongating at first and then retracting back into shape. When it steadied, its arms flailed briefly and then I heard the sound of Obembe's tin fall and felt a splash of its content on my leg. Two small fish—one of which Ikenna had argued was a Symphysodon—shot out of the tin, and began writhing and thrashing about in the dirt, muddied by the spilled water as the tin swung from side to side, spurting out more water and tadpoles until it stilled. For a moment, the shadows did not move. Then a hand that elongated and stretched across the other side of the street was followed by a cry from Ikenna's voice: "Tell me!"

"Didn't you hear him?" Boja asked menacingly even though Obembe—frozen in a posture of his hand shielding himself from an expected assault from Ikenna—had begun to speak.

"He said," Obembe stammered, but stopped when Boja spoke. Now he began afresh again: "He said—he said that a fisherman will kill you, Ike."

"What, a fisherman?" Boja said aloud.

"A fisherman?" Ikenna repeated.

"Yes, a fisher—" Obembe did not complete this, he was trembling.

"Are you sure?" Boja said. When Obembe nodded, Boja said: "How did he say it?"

"He said '*Ikena*, you shall—'" He stopped, his lips shaking as he gazed from face to face and then to the ground. It was with his eyes cast down to the ground that he continued: "He said Ikenna, you shall die by the hands of a fisherman."

It is hard to forget the black cloud that covered Ikenna's face after Obembe said those words. He glanced up as if in search of something, then he turned in the direction where the madman had gone, but there was nothing to be seen but a sky turned to orange.

We were almost at our gate when Ikenna faced us, but with his eyes cast on no one in particular. "He saw a vision that one of you will kill me," he said.

More words dangled feverishly on his lips, but didn't spill out. They seemed to retract inside as if they were fastened to a rope that was pulled back from within him by an unseen hand. Then, as if unsure of what to say or do, and without waiting for any of us to speak—for Boja was starting to say something now—he turned and walked on through our gate, and we followed him.

THE MADMAN

Those the gods have chosen to destroy, they inflict with madness.

IGBO PROVERB

A bulu was a madman:

His brain, Obembe said, dissolved into blood after the near-fatal accident that left him insane. Obembe, through whom I came to the understanding of most things, knew Abulu's history from God-knows-where and he told it to me one night. He said Abulu, like us, had a brother. His name was Abana. Some people in our street remember him as one of the two brothers who attended Aquinas College, the premier boys' high school in the town, with a white plain shirt and white khaki shorts that were always spotlessly clean. Obembe said Abulu loved his brother; that they were inseparable.

Abulu and his brother grew up without their father.

When they were kids, their father went on a Christian pilgrimage to Israel and never returned. Most people believed he was killed by a bomb in Jerusalem, while one of his friends who'd gone on the same pilgrimage said he had made his way to Austria with an Austrian woman and settled there. So Abulu and Abana lived with their mother and their elder sister who, by the time she was fifteen, took up whoring and moved to Lagos to practise her trade.

Their mother operated a small restaurant. Constructed with wood and zinc materials, it was popular in our street in the eighties. Obembe said even Father ate there a couple of times when Mother was pregnant and became too heavy to make food. Abulu and his brother used to serve at the restaurant after school, washing the plates and cleaning the rickety tables after every meal, supplying toothpicks, sweeping the floor that became darker with soot and grime each year until it looked like a mechanic's workshop, and keeping the flies out in the rainy seasons, waving raffia-plaited hand fans. Yet, despite all they did, the restaurant brought little return, and they still could not afford proper education.

Want and lack exploded in their minds like a grenade and left shrapnel of desperation in its wake, so that—in time—the boys began to steal. But when they robbed a rich widow's house with knives and toy guns, carrying away a briefcase full of money, the widow raised alarm once they set out running, and a mob took chase. A fast-moving car knocked Abulu down, as he attempted to cross a long road in haste to escape his pursuers, and sped away. At the sight, the mob hurriedly dispersed, leaving Abana alone with his injured brother. Alone, he picked up Abulu and managed to get him to the hospital where doctors rushed in to contain a damage already done. Abulu's brain cells, Obembe said, had floated out of their compartments into foreign zones in his head, changing his mental configurations and completing the awful process.

When Abulu was discharged, he returned home a changed being—like a newborn whose mind is a clean slate, without a single dot on it. In those days, all he did was stare—blankly, concentratedly—as if his eyes were the only organ in his body and it could perform the functions of all the others, or as if every organ was dead except the eye. Then, as time passed, the insanity fledged, and while it still sometimes lay dormant, it could be roused when triggered—like a tiger merely asleep. The things that roused his insanity to life were diverse and numerous—a sight, a spectacle, a word, anything. The din of a plane flying over the house was what first did it. Abulu had cried out in a rage and ripped his clothes as the plane flew past. Were it not for Abana's timely intervention, he would have got out of the house. Abana wrestled him to the floor and held him there until his strength diminished. Then he sprawled on the floor, asleep. The next time the insanity was stirred by the sight of his mother's nakedness. He was seated in one of the chairs in the sitting room when he saw her going into the bathroom unclothed. He sprang from his chair as if he'd seen an apparition, hid behind the door and watched her bathe through the keyhole, the sight tossing many strange dice about in his brain. He brought out his erect penis and began fondling. Then when he saw she was about to exit, he hid himself and quietly stripped. He then slunk into her room, knocked her to the bed and raped her.

Abulu did not leave his mother's bedside afterwards; he held her as if she was his wife, while she cried and grieved in his arms until his brother returned. Furious at what Abulu had done, Abana beat Abulu with his leather belt, refusing to yield to his mother's pleadings until Abulu fled from the room in great pain. He pulled out the television aerial from its weak ballast, rushed back into the room and pinned his brother to the wall with it. Then, letting out a horrendous yelp, he ran out of the house. His madness had fully set in.

For the first years Abulu walked and slept in market-places, unfinished buildings, refuse dumps, open sewers, under parked cars—anywhere, everywhere the night met him, until he came upon a decrepit truck a few metres from our house. The truck had crashed into an electric pole in 1985, killing an entire family. Abandoned because of its bloody history, the truck gradually atrophied into a kingdom of wild cactus and elephant grass. Once he found it, he set to work, dislodging nations of spiders, exorcising untamed spirits of the dead, whose bloodstains had left perpetual smears on the seats. He removed spattered glass fragments, weeding out wild tiny islands of moss that clung to the bare moth-eaten furniture of the truck, and annihilated the helpless race of cockroaches. He then stored his belongings—materials picked from garbage, discarded objects of various kinds, and almost anything that piqued his curiosity—in the truck. Then he made it his home.

Abulu's insanity was of two kinds—as though twin devils constantly played competing tunes in his mind. When one played the tune that passed for regular or ordinary madness, Abulu wandered about naked, dirty, smelling, awash with filth, trailed by a sea of flies, dancing in the streets, picking up waste from bins and eating it, soliloquizing aloud or conversing with invisible people in languages not of this world, screaming at objects, dancing on street corners, picking his teeth with sticks found in dirt, excreting on roadsides, and doing all the things that stray derelicts do. He went about with his head forested with long hair, his face patched with boils, and his skin greasy with dirt. At times he talked with a league of doppelgangers and invisible friends whose presence was fogged from ordinary eyes. When in this sphere of insanity, he became a man on the move—he walked almost perpetually. And he did his walking mostly barefoot, treading on unpaved roads from season to season, month to month and year to year. He trod on dumpsites, on rickety bridges with splintered woods, and even on industrial sites that were often littered with nails, metals, broken tools, glasses, and various sharp objects. Once, when two cars collided on the road, Abulu—unaware there had been a car accident—walked through the shattered glass and bled so much he fainted and sprawled in the dirt until the police came and took him away. Many who saw what happened thought he'd died and were shocked to see him walking towards his truck six days later, his scarred body covered in hospital clothes, his varicose-veined legs concealed in socks.

When in the realm of insanity, Abulu went about completely naked, dangling his enormous penis—sometimes in a state of erection—unabashedly as if it was a million-naira engagement ring. His penis once bred a popular scandal, one that people told stories about all over the town. A widow who had badly wanted a child had once seduced Abulu: she took him by the hand one night to her house, washed him and had sex with him. Abulu's insanity, it was rumoured, temporarily vanished while with that woman.

When the affair became known and public, and people began calling her Abulu's wife, the woman left the town, leaving the madman with a crushing obsession for women and sex. Not long after, rumours of his nightly visits to La Room Motel began to spread. It was said that a few of the prostitutes regularly smuggled him into their rooms under a thick cover of darkness. Almost as rampant as those rumours was the legend of Abulu's open masturbations. Solomon once told us of a madman whom he and a few people had watched masturbate under the mango tree near the Celestial Church by the river. But I did not know Abulu at the time, nor did I know what he meant by masturbation. Solomon then went on to tell us how, in 1993, Abulu was caught clinging to the colourful statue of the Madonna in front of the big St. Andrew's Cathedral. Perhaps thinking it was a beautiful woman, who, unlike the other women he leered at, did not make any move to resist him, he held the statue and began humping against it, moaning, while people gathered, laughing at him until some devotees wrested him off it. The Catholic Council would eventually pull down the desecrated statue and erect one in the compound of the church, within its fence. Then, as if still unsatisfied, they surrounded the statue with an iron gate.

Despite all of these stirrings he caused, when in this mode Abulu harmed no one.

Abulu's second realm of insanity was extraordinary; a state he entered in sudden gusts as if while in this world—picking from a bin or dancing to inaudible music or any of the things he did—he'd find himself raptured into a dream world. But whenever in that state, he never completely left our world; he occupied both—one leg here, one leg there as if he were a mediator between two domains, an uninvited intermediary. His messages were for the people of this world. He subpoenaed tranquil spirits, fanned the violence of small flames, and rattled the lives of many. He entered this realm mostly in the evenings when the sun had shed all of its light. Having transformed into Abulu the Prophet, he'd go about singing, clapping and prophesying. He would slink into compounds with unbarred gates like a thief if he had prophecies for anyone there. He would disrupt anything to declare his visions—even funerals. He became a Prophet, a scarecrow, a deity, even an oracle. Often, though, he shattered both realms or moved between both as though the partition between them was only hymen-thin. Sometimes, when he came across people he needed to prophesy to, he would temporarily delve into the other state and tell them the prediction. He would chase after a moving vehicle, crying out his prophecy if it was for someone in it. People sometimes turned violent when he tried to make them hear a vision; they sometimes harmed him, piling curses, tears and jeremiads—like a heap of soiled clothes—on his head.

The reason they hated him was because they believed his tongue harboured a catalogue of catastrophes. His tongue was a scorpion. The prophecies he gave to people bred fear of the dark fate awaiting them. At first, no one heeded his words until event after event buried the possibility of the things he saw being taken as mere pockets of coincidences. The earliest, most prominent one was when he predicted the ghastly motor accident that claimed an entire family. Their car had plunged into a bigger portion of the Omi-Ala close to the city of Owo, drowning them—exactly the way Abulu had said it would happen. Then there was the man he said would die from "pleasure"; that man would be carried out of a whorehouse a few days later, having died while having sex with one of the prostitutes. These strings of occurrences engraved themselves in flaming letters on the memories of people and carved a fear of Abulu's prophesies in their minds. People began to see his visions as ineluctable, and they believed he was the oracle of the scribbler of the telegraph of fate. From then on, whenever he gave a prediction to someone, they went about believing in its inevitability so much that in many cases, people attempted to prevent it from happening. One very memorable instance was the case of the fifteen-year-old daughter of the man who owned the big theatre hall in the town. Abulu predicted she would suffer brutal rape by the child she would bear. Gravely shaken by this grim future awaiting her, the girl took her own life and left a note saying she'd rather not wait to face that future.

In the fullness of time, the madman became a menace, a terror in the town. The song he sang after every prophecy became known by almost every inhabitant of the town, and they dreaded it.

Most bothersome was Abulu's tendency to peek into people's pasts the way he could into the future, so that he often dismantled vain kingdoms of people's thoughts and lifted shrouds from the swaddled corpses of buried secrets. And the results were always very dire. He once revealed, upon sighting a woman and her husband getting out of their car, that she was a "whore." "*Tufia!*" the madman had cried, spitting. "You keep sleeping with Matthew, your husband's friend, even in your matrimonial bed? You have no shame! No shame!!" Then the madman, having set that marriage on fire—for, after a string of denials, the husband would find out about the affair and divorce his wife—walked away, totally oblivious of what he'd done.

Yet in spite of all this, a fraction of Akure's population liked Abulu and wanted him alive, for he frequently helped people, too. An armed robbery attack was botched when, foreseeing it, Abulu went about announcing that four men "clothed in masks and dark clothes" would attack the district that night. The police were called in to watch over the street, and when the robbers appeared, the police stopped them. Just about the same time he predicted the robbery, he also revealed the hideout of certain men who had kidnapped a little girl for ransom. The girl was the daughter of one of the state politicians. Following Abulu's accurate directions one night, the police arrested the men and rescued the girl. Again, Abulu earned appreciation and people said the politician loaded the madman's truck with gifts. It was said that the politician even contemplated taking him back to a psychiatric hospital for healing, but others countered, arguing if his insanity left him, he would be of no use to them. Abulu had always escaped psychiatry. After the incident in which he'd walked on a pool of shattered glass, he was taken to a psychiatric hospital. But while there, he challenged the doctors, threatening that he was sane and claiming that he was being incarcerated there illegally. When that did not help, he set himself on a suicidal hunger strike, refusing—no matter how he was pressured—to drink even water. Fearing he would die from the strike and because he'd begun to demand a lawyer, they let him go.

7

THE FALCONER

Turning and turning in the widening gyre,
the falcon cannot hear the falconer.

W. B. YEATS

Mother was a falconer:
The one who stood on the hills and watched, trying to stave off whatever ill she perceived was coming to her children. She owned copies of our minds in the pockets of her own mind and so could easily sniff troubles early in their forming, the same way sailors discern the forming foetus of a coming storm. She occasionally eavesdropped on us in attempts to catch snippets of our conversations even before Father moved out of Akure. There were times when we gathered at my brothers' room, and one of us would slink to the door to detect if she stood behind it. We'd pull the door open and expose her in the act. But,

like a falconer who knew her birds deeply, Mother often succeeded in tracking us. Perhaps she'd already begun to sense that something was wrong with Ikenna, but when she saw the M.K.O. calendar ruined, she smelt, she saw, she felt and she knew that Ikenna was undergoing a metamorphosis. It was thus in an attempt to find out what had started it that she'd coaxed Obembe into divulging the details of the encounter with Abulu.

Although Obembe had left out what happened after Abulu went away, the part about how he'd told us all what Abulu had said while the plane flew past, a monstrous grief seized Mother nonetheless. She had punctuated every point of the account with a trembling cry of "My God, My God," but after Obembe finished, she stood up, biting her lips and fidgeting, visibly ripped from inside-out. She went out of our room afterwards without saying a word, shaking from head to foot as if she'd caught a cold while Obembe and I sat pondering what our brothers would do if they knew we'd divulged the secret to her. Just about then, I heard her voice and theirs as she confronted them on why they never told her such a thing had happened. Mother had barely left their room when Ikenna stormed into ours in a rage, demanding to know which idiot had revealed the secret to her. Obembe pleaded that she forced it out of him, in a voice that was deliberately loud so Mother could hear and intervene. She did. Ikenna left us with a vow to punish us when she was not around.

An hour or so later, when it seemed she'd slightly recovered, Mother gathered us in the living room. She wore a headscarf that was knotted behind her head into the shape of a bird's tail—a sign she'd been praying.

"When I go to the stream," Mother said with a voice that was husky and broken, "I carry my *udu*. I stoop at the brook and fill my *udu*. I walk from the stream—" Ikenna gave a wild yawn at this time and heaved a sigh. Mother paused, stared at him for a while and continued. "I walk—to my home, to my home. When I get there I set my pot down only to find it empty."

She let the words sink in, rounding us up with her eyes. I had imagined her walking down a river with an *udu*—an earthen jar—balanced on her head with the help of a wrappa formed into many layered rings. I'd been so drawn and moved by this simple story, by the tone in which she told it that I hardly wanted to know what it meant because I knew that such stories, told just like that after we'd done something wrong, always had kernelled meanings; for Mother spoke and thought in parables.

"You, my children," she continued, "have leaked out of my *udu*. I thought I had you, that I carried you in my *udu*, that my life was full of you"—she stretched her hands and carved them into a convex—"but I was wrong. Under my nose, you went to that river and fished for weeks. Now, for even longer, you have harboured a deadly secret when I thought you were safe, that I would know if you faced any dangers."

She shook her head.

"You have to be cleansed from every evil spell Abulu has cast on you. We are all going to the service at the church this evening. So, no one goes anywhere else today," Mother said. "Once it's four, we will all go to the church."

David's playful laughter came from Mother's room, where she'd left him with Nkem, and occupied the silence created after Mother delivered her speech and watched us to make sure her words had sunk into our heads.

She rose and was heading to her room, when she stopped abruptly because of something Ikenna said. She turned back sharply: "*Eh?*" she said. "Ikenna, *isi gini*?—What did you say?"

"I said I'm not going to church with you today for any cleansing," Ikenna replied, switching back to Igbo. "I can't bear to stand in front of that congregation and have people looming over me, trying to cast out some spell." He stood up briskly from the lounge. "I mean, I just don't want it. I don't have any demon; I'm fine."

"Ikenna, have you lost your mind?" said Mother.

"No, Mama, but I just don't want to go there."

"What?" Mother shouted. "Ike-nna?"

"It's the truth, Mama," he replied. "I just don't want"—he shook his head—"I just don't, Mama, *biko*—please, I don't want to go to any church."

Boja, who had not spoken to Ikenna since their altercation concerning the television programme, rose to his feet and said: "Me neither, Mama. I won't go for any cleansing. I don't feel I or anyone needs deliverance from anything. I'm not going there."

Mother was about to say something, but the words tripped backwards in her throat like a man falling from the top of a ladder. She gazed back and forth between Ikenna and Boja with an expression of shock.

"Ikenna, Bojanonimeokpu, have we taught you nothing? Do you want that madman's prophecy to come true?" Spittle formed a weak bubble across the ridges of her left-open mouth, and busted when she made to speak again. "Ikenna, look at how you've already taken it. What do you think is the cause of all your misbehaviours if not because you believe your brothers will kill you? And now, you stand here, face me, and tell me you don't need prayers—that you don't need to be cleansed? Have the many years of training, and efforts by Eme and I taught neither of you nothing? *Ehh?*"

Mother shouted the last question with her hands thrust histrionically aloft. Yet, with a resolve that could have smashed gates of iron, Ikenna said: "I will not go is all I know." And apparently encouraged by Boja's support, he walked back to his room. Once he shut his room's door Boja rose and went in the opposite direction—to the room Obembe and I shared. Mother, wordless, sat back in the lounge and sank beneath the surface of the filled pot of her own thoughts, her arms clasped around her and her mouth moving as if she were saying something that had Ikenna's name in it, although inaudible. David threw a ball about with clattering steps, laughing aloud as he tried to make the sound of football stadium spectators all by himself. He was shouting when Obembe moved to sit with Mother.

"Mama, Ben and I will go with you," he said.

Mother looked up at him with eyes clouded with tears.

"Ikenna… and Boja… are strangers now," she stammered, shaking her head. Obembe drew closer to her and as he patted her shoulder with his thin long arms, she repeated: "Strangers, now."

For the rest of that day till when we left for the church, I sat thinking about it all, how this vision was the cause of everything Ikenna had done to himself and the rest of us. The encounter with Abulu was something I had forgotten, especially after it happened, when Boja warned that

Obembe and I should *never* mention it to anyone. When I asked Obembe once, why Ikenna no longer loved us, he had said it was because of the whipping Father gave us. And I had believed him, but now, it became very clear to me that I had been wrong.

Later, as I waited for Mother to dress and take us to the church, I cast my eyes on the columned shelf in the sitting room. My eyes then fell on the column that was covered in a quilt of dust, a cobweb strewn to the end of it. These were signs of Father's absence. When he was at home, we used to take weekly turns at cleaning the shelves. We stopped a few weeks after he left and Mother had not been able to effectively enforce it. In Father's absence, the perimeters of the house seemed to have magically widened as though invisible builders unclasped the walls, like they would a paper house, and expanded its size. When Father was around, even if his eyes were fastened to the pages of a newspaper or book, his presence alone was enough to enforce the strictest order and we maintained what he often referred to as "decorum" in the house. As I thought of my brothers' refusal to come with us to church to break what might be a spell, I craved for Father, and wished, strongly, that he would return.

That evening, Obembe and I followed Mother to our church, the Assemblies of God Church situated across the long road that stretched to the post office. Mother held David in one hand and fastened Nkem to her back with a *wrappa*. To prevent them from sweating and getting skin rashes, she'd powdered their necks so that they shone like masquerades. The church was a big hall with lights that hung in long lines from the four corners of its ceiling. At the pulpit, a young woman in a white gown, who was very much fairer than a typical African of these parts, sang "Amazing Grace" with a foreign accent. We sidled in between two rows of people, most of whom kept locking eyes with me until I got the feeling that we were being watched. My suspicion increased when Mother went up behind the pulpit where the Pastor and his wife and elders were seated, and whispered in the Pastor's ear. When the singer was done, the Pastor mounted the podium, dressed in a shirt and tie, his trousers strapped with suspenders.

"Men and brethren," he started in a voice so loud it made the speakers near our row go irrecoverably mute so that we had to pick up his voice from the speaker on the other side of the room. "Before I go ahead with the word of God tonight, let me say that I've just been told that the devil, in the form of Abulu, the demon-possessed, self-proclaimed prophet whom all of you know has caused so much damage to people's lives in this town, has been to the house of our dear brother James Agwu. You all know him, the husband of our dear sister here, sister Paulina Adaku Agwu. Some of you here know that he has many children, who, our sister told us, were caught fishing at the Omi-Ala at Alagbaka Street."

A faint murmur of surprise rang through the congregation.

"Abulu went to those children and told them lies," Pastor Collins continued, his voice rising as he spat his words furiously into the microphone. "Brethren, you all know that if a prophecy is not from God, it is of—"

"The devil!" the congregation shouted in unison.

"True. And if it is of the devil, then it has to be refuted."

"Yes!" they chorused.

"I didn't hear you," the Pastor spat into the microphone, shaking his fist. "I said if it is of the devil, then it MUST be—"

"Refuted!" the congregation yelled with so much vigour it seemed like a battle cry. From around the congregation, little children—including Nkem, perhaps frightened by the roar—burst out wailing.

"Are we ready to refute it?"

The congregation roared in agreement, with Mother's voice resounding above all, and trailing after the rest had stopped. I looked at her and saw that she'd begun to cry again.

"Then stand and refute that prophecy in the name of our Lord Jesus Christ."

The rows lifted as the people jumped to their feet and became caught up in a rapturous session of fierce prayers.

* * *

Mother's efforts to heal her son, Ikenna, were wasted on him. For the prophecy, like an angered beast, had gone berserk and was destroying his mind with the ferocity of madness, pulling down paintings, breaking walls, emptying cupboards, turning tables until all that he knew, all that was him, all that had become him was left in disarray. To my brother, Ikenna, the fear of death as prophesied by Abulu had become palpable, a caged world within which he was irretrievably trapped, and beyond which nothing else existed.

I once heard that when fear takes possession of the heart of a person, it diminishes them. This could be said of my brother, for when the fear took possession of his heart, it robbed him of many things—his peace, his well-being, his relationships, his health, and even his faith.

Ikenna began walking alone to the school he and Boja attended. He'd wake up as early as 7 a.m., skipping breakfast, to avoid going with Boja. He began skipping lunches and dinners when they were either eba or pounded yam, meals that were eaten together from the same bowl as his brothers. As a result, he started to emaciate until deep incurvatures were carved between his collarbones and his neck, and his cheekbones became visible. Then, in time, the whites of his eyes turned pale yellow.

Mother took notice. She protested, pleaded and threatened, but all to no avail. One morning towards the end of the school term in the first week of July, she locked the door and insisted Ikenna have breakfast before going to school. Ikenna was devastated because he was to have an exam that day. He pleaded with Mother to let him leave—"Is it not my body? What do you care if I eat or not? Leave me, why not let me be?"—he broke down and sobbed. But Mother held on until he finally resigned to eat. As he ate the bread and an omelette, he railed against her and all of us. He said everyone in our family hated him and vowed to leave the house someday soon, never to be seen again.

"You will see," he threatened, wiping his eyes with the back of his hand. "All of this will soon end and all of you will be free from me; you will see."

"But you know this is not true, Ikenna," Mother replied. "No one hates you; not me, not one of your brothers. You are doing all this to yourself because of your fear, a fear you have tilled and cultivated with your own hands,

Ikenna. Ikenna, you have chosen to believe the visions of a madman, a useless fellow, who is not even fit to be called a human being. Not even greater than—what should I compare him to?—the fish, no, the tadpoles you picked from that river? Tadpoles. A man who, just the other day, people in the market were talking about how he found a mallam's herd grazing in a field and calves suckling their mothers' udders, joined the cows and started sucking the udder of one of the cows!" Mother made a spitting sound to show disgust at the troubling image of a man sucking a cow. "How can you believe what a man who sucks cows' breasts says? No Ikenna, you have done this to yourself, eh? You have no one to blame. We've prayed for you even if you refused to pray for yourself. Don't blame anyone for continuing to live in useless fear."

Ikenna seemed to have listened to Mother, staring blankly at the wall before him. For a second, it appeared as if he'd realized his folly; that Mother's words had incised his tortured heart, causing the black blood of fear to leak it out. He ate his meal at the dining table for the first time in a long time in silence. And when he was finished, he murmured "Thank you" to Mother, the customary thanks we gave to our parents after every meal, which Ikenna had not said in weeks. He took the utensils to the kitchen and washed them as Mother had taught us to do rather than leave them on the table or in his room as he'd been doing for weeks. Then he left for school.

When he was gone, Boja, who'd just brushed his teeth and was waiting for Obembe to finish using the bathroom, came into the sitting room swaddled in the bath towel he shared with Ikenna.

"I'm afraid he will make good his threat and leave," he said to Mother.

Mother shook her head, her eyes focused on the fridge, which she'd begun cleaning with a rag. Then bending so that nothing but her legs alone became visible under the door of the refrigerator, she said: "He won't; where will he go?"

"I don't know," Boja replied, "but I fear."

"He won't; this fear will not last, it will leave him," Mother said in a voice that was assured, and I could tell at the time that she'd believed it.

Mother continued to strive to heal him and to protect him. I recall one Sunday afternoon when Iya Iyabo came in while we were eating black-eyed peas marinated in palm-oil sauce. I'd seen the commotion around the compound, but we'd been trained not to go out to watch such gatherings as other children of the town did. Someone could be armed, Father always warned, there could be gunshots, and you could be hit. So we stayed back in our rooms because Mother was at home and would have punished or reported an offender to Father. Boja had two tests the next day—on Social Science and History—two subjects he detested, and had grown prickly, cursing all the historical figures ("dead idiots") in the book. Not wanting to disturb him or be around him while in such a state of frustration, Obembe and I were in the sitting room with Mother when the woman knocked on the door.

"Ah, Iya Iyabo," Mother called, rising swiftly from her seat once the woman came in.

"Mama Ike," the woman, whom I still hated for telling on us, said.

"Come chop, we dey chop," Mother said.

Nkem threw her hands up from the table and reached for the woman who lifted her off her chair at once.

"What happened?" Mother said.

"Aderonke," the woman said. "Aderonke killed her husband today."

"*E-woh!*" Mother screamed.

"*Wo, bi o se, shele ni,*" the woman began. She often spoke Yoruba to Mother, who perfectly understood the language, although she never believed herself proficient in it and almost never spoke it otherwise, but would always have us talk with people on her behalf. "Biyi drunk again last night and came home naked," Iya Iyabo said, switching to pidgin English. She put her hands on her head and began to squirm plaintively.

"Please, Iya Iyabo, calm and tell me."

"Her pikin, Onyiladun, dey sick. As her husband come inside, she tell am make im give medicine money, but im start to beat-beat am and im pikin."

"*Chi-neke!*" Mother gasped, and covered her mouth with her hands.

"*Bee ni*—it is so," Iya Iyabo said. "Aderonke vex say im dey beat the sick pikin, and fear say because of im alcohol, say im go kill am, so she hit im husband with a chair."

"Eh, eh," Mother stammered.

"The man die," Iya Iyabo said. "Im die just like that."

The woman had sat on the floor, her head resting on the door, rocking and shaking her legs. Mother stood still with shock; seeming frightened, she hugged herself. The food I'd just scooped into my mouth was instantly forgotten at this news of Oga Biyi's death, for I knew the wasted man. He was like a goat. Although he was not mad, he snarled and plodded when in his usual state of drunkenness. In the mornings, we often saw him on the way to school, walking home, sober, but by evening you'd see him staggering about, drunk again.

"But you know," Mama Iyabo said, wiping her eyes, "I no think say she do am with clear eyes."

"Eh, how do you mean?" Mother said.

"Na that madman, Abulu cause am. Im tell Biyi say na the thing wey im treasure most go kill am. Now im wife don kill am."

Mother was stung. She glanced around at our faces—Boja, Obembe, and I—and took in our stares with her eyes. Someone stood up from a chair somewhere, not in the sitting room, and gently opened a door and appeared in the room. Although I did not look back to see him there, I knew. And it was clear that Mother, and everyone in the room knew, too, that it was Ikenna.

"No, no," Mother said loudly. "Iya Iyabo, I don't want you saying this nonsense, this thing here."

"Ah, what—"

"I said no!" Mother shouted. "How can you believe a mere madman could see the future? Just how?"

"But Mama Ike," the woman murmured, "Na so they say *im be*—"

"No," Mother said. "Where is Aderonke now?"

"Police station."

Mother shook her head.

"Them arrest her," Iya Iyabo said.

"Come make we go talk outside," Mother said.

The woman rose, and together, with Nkem following, they went out. After they left, Ikenna stood there, his eyes lifeless like those of a doll. Then, suddenly clutching his belly, he raced to the bathroom, making choking sounds as he retched into the sink. It was here that his illness began, when the fear robbed him of his health, for it seemed that the account of the man's death had established in him the unquestionable inescapability of Abulu's prescient powers, causing smoke to rise from things yet unburned.

A few days after that, a Saturday morning, we were all having breakfast at the dining table, fried yams and corn pap, when Ikenna, who had just taken his food and gone into his room, suddenly rushed out, a hand on his belly, grunting. Before we could make sense of what was going on, a cupful of disgorged food landed on the paved floor behind the blue lounge we'd named "Father's throne." Ikenna had been heading for the bathroom, but now, inhibited by the force he could only try to contain, he dropped to one knee on the floor, as he retched, partly disappearing behind the chair.

Calling, "Ikenna, Ikenna," Mother ran to him from the kitchen and tried to lift him, but he protested that he was fine, when in fact he looked pale and sickly.

"What is it, Ikenna? When did this begin?" Mother asked after he stopped, but he did not answer.

"Ikenna, why, why not even answer, why? Eh, why?"

"I don't know," he mumbled. "Let me go wash now, please."

Mother let go of his hand, and as he walked to the bathroom, Boja said, "Sorry, Ike." I said the same. So did Obembe. David did, too. Although Ikenna did not respond to any of these sympathies, he did not bang the door this time. He closed it and bolted it gently.

Once Ikenna was out of sight, Boja ran into the kitchen and returned with a broom—a stack of needle-thin sticks of raffia bound together with a tight cord—and a dust-pan. It was the quickness with which Boja had run to clean up the mess that had moved Mother.

"Ikenna, you live in fear that one of your brothers will kill you," she said aloud so Ikenna could hear her voice over the water, "but come and see—"

"No, no, no, Nne, no; don't say, please—" Boja pleaded effusively.

"Leave me, let me tell him," Mother said. "Ikenna come and see them, just come and—" Boja protested that Ikenna will not like to hear he was cleaning the vomit, but Mother was undeterred.

"See those same brothers of yours weeping for you," she continued. "See them cleaning up your vomit. Come out and see 'your enemies' caring for you, even against your wish."

Perhaps because of this, it took long for Ikenna to come out of the bath that day, but he did, eventually, swaddled in a towel. By that time, Boja had swept clean the spots and even mopped the floor and parts of the wall and the back of the lounge on which his vomit had caked. And Mother had sprinkled Dettol antiseptic everywhere. She would force Ikenna to go with her to the hospital afterwards by threatening that if he refused, she would phone Father. Ikenna knew Father took matters of health very seriously, so he caved.

To my consternation, Mother returned home alone hours later. Ikenna had typhoid and had been admitted at the hospital, receiving intravenous injections. When Obembe and I, gripped by fear, broke down, Mother comforted us saying assuredly he would be discharged the following day and that he would be fine.

But I had begun to fear that something bad was going to happen to Ikenna. I spoke little at school and fought when anyone provoked me until I was whipped by one of the disciplinary teachers. This too was rare; for I was an obedient child not only to my parents, but to my teachers as well. I dreaded corporal punishment and would do anything to prevent it. But the sadness I felt for my brother's deteriorating situation had inflamed a bitter resentment towards everything, especially school and all it contained.

The hope that my brother would be redeemed had been destroyed; I was afraid for him.

After his health and well-being, the venom next robbed Ikenna of his faith. He'd missed church for three consecutive Sundays, giving illness as an excuse—plus the one he could not attend because of the two nights he spent at the hospital. But on the morning of the next one, perhaps emboldened by the news that Father—who had travelled to Ghana on a three-month training course—would not be visiting Akure again until his return, Ikenna declared that he just didn't want to go to church.

"Did I hear you well, Ikenna?" Mother said.

"Yes, you did," Ikenna replied forcefully. "Listen, Mama, I'm a scientist, I no longer believe there's a God."

"What?" Mother cried, stepping backwards as if she'd stepped on a sharp thorn. "Ikenna, what did you say?"

He hesitated, a deep scowl on his face.

"I asked you: 'What did you say,' Ikenna?"

"I said I'm a scientist," he answered, with the word "scientist," which he had to say in English because there was no Igbo word for it, resonating with alarming defiance.

"And?" The silence she met would prompt her to say "Complete it Ikenna; complete this abominable thing you have said." Then, with her finger pointing to his face, charged, she said: "Ikenna, look here: one thing Eme and I cannot take, and will never accept, is an atheist of a child. Never!"

She tsked and snapped two fingers over her head to superstitiously stave off the possibility of that phenomenon. "So, Ikenna, if you still want to be a part of this family or eat any food in it, stand up from that bed of yours now, or else you and I will fit into the same trousers."

Ikenna was cowed by the threat; for Mother used that expression "fit into the same trousers" only when her anger had reached its peak. She went into her room and returned with one of Father's old leather belts wound halfway around her wrist, fully ready to flog him, something she almost never did. At the sight of it, Ikenna dragged himself to the bathroom to bathe and get ready for church.

On our way home after the service, Ikenna walked ahead of us, so Mother wouldn't pick issues with him in public and because Mother usually gave him the key so he could unlock the gate and the main door for us. She almost never went home directly after church; she always waited with the little ones for post-service women's meetings, or attended one visitation or the other. Once we were out of Mother's sight, Ikenna began quickening his steps. I and the rest followed him in silence. Ikenna, for some reason, took a longer route home through Ijoka Street, a street that was populated by the poor who lived in low-cost houses—mostly unvarnished—and in wooden shacks. Little children were playing in almost every corner of this dirty area. There were little girls jumping around within a big square of columns. A boy, not more than three, stooped over what appeared to be tawny ropes of excreta trailing down from him to form viscous pyramids. As this pyramid formed and polluted the air, the boy played on, marking the dirt with a stick, undisturbed by the league of flies that hovered around his fundament. My brothers and I spat into the dirt, and then by unquestioned instinct, immediately erased the spittle with the soles of our sandals as we passed, Boja cursing the little boy and the people of the neighbourhood—"pigs, pigs." Obembe, trying to cleanly erase his spittle, trailed behind momentarily. By spitting and erasing it, we were observing the superstition that if a pregnant woman stepped on saliva, the person who had spit—if male—would be rendered permanently impotent, which I understood at the time to mean that one's organ would magically disappear.

This was indeed a dirty street, the street in which Kayode, our friend, lived with his parents in an unfinished two-storeyed building whose floor alone had been paved. The house was in such a raw shape that masts of unshaped concrete and iron stretched from the attic, thrusting skeletal beams upwards. Unvarnished piles of blocks greening with moss were scattered around the entire compound. In the holes in the bricks and in its entire frame nested multitudes of lizards and skinks that scurried everywhere. Kayode once told us of how his mother found a lizard in the drum in their kitchen where they stored drinking water. The dead lizard lay atop the water for days unnoticed until the water acquired a sour taste. When his mother emptied the drum and the dead lizard slid to the ground in the pool of water, its head had swollen double, and *like all things that drown*, had started to decompose. At nearly every corner of the neighbourhood, heaps of trash ate into slabs and thrust into roadways. Some of the dirt piled in open sewers, brooding and choky like tumours, curved around pedestrian bridges like boas, nestled like bird nests between roadside kiosks, festered in small land cavities and peopled clearings. And all over the place, stale air hung, linking the buildings together with its invisible stench.

The sun was fierce in the sky, forcing trees to create dark awnings under their canopies. At one side of the road, a woman was frying fish in a pan on a hearth under a wooden shack. The billows of smoke rose steadily from both sides of the hearth, pooling towards us. We crossed to the other side between a parked truck and the balcony of a house whose interior I glimpsed briefly: two men seated on a brown couch, gesticulating while a roving standing fan slowly turned its head. A goat and her kids were squir-relled under a table in front of the balcony, surrounded by black pods of their own waste.

When we got to our compound, waiting for Ikenna to open the gate, Boja said: "I saw Abulu try to enter the church during the service today, but he was not allowed in because he was naked." Boja had joined a team of boys who played drums for our local church. The boys played by rotation and he'd played that day, and had thus sat at the front of the church near the altar—hence the reason why he'd been able to see Abulu come through the rear door of the church. Ikenna was fumbling in his pocket for the key, and had to turn the pocket inside out because the key had become tangled in a twine of the linen and unfurled fibres, wrapping itself out of his reach. The pocket was dirty: it was stained with ink, and small pieces of groundnut husks showered to the ground like dust when he thrust it out. When he tried to untangle the key without success, he tore it out with force, causing the pocket to spring a leak. He was starting to turn the key in the hole when Boja said, "Ike, I know you believe the prophecy, but you know we are children of God—"

"He is a prophet," Ikenna replied curtly.

He opened the door and as he extracted the key from the keyhole, Boja said, "Yes, but he is not of God."

"How did you know?" Ikenna snapped, turning to face Boja now. "I'm asking you; how did you know?"

"He isn't, Ike, I'm sure."

"What is your proof? Eh, what is your proof?"

Boja said nothing. Ikenna's eyes were raised upwards above our heads and we all followed, and saw the object of his view: a kite made of different polythene materials gliding aloft in the distance.

"But what he said cannot happen," Boja said. "Listen, he mentioned a red river. He said you will swim in a red river. How can a river be red?" He made a gesture that vocalized impossibility by spreading his hands, gazing at us as if asking for assurance that what he'd said was right. Obembe nodded in reply. "He is mad, Ike; he does not know what he says."

Boja drew closer to Ikenna and in an unexpected show of courage, put his hand on Ikenna's shoulder. "You have to believe me, Ike, you have to believe," he said, shaking Ikenna's shoulder as if he was attempting to demolish the mountain of fear deep within his brother.

Ikenna stood there, his eyes fixed on the floor—apparently moved by Boja's words. It was a moment of hope, one in which it seemed that we could restore him who was lost to us. Like Boja, I, too, wanted to tell Ikenna that I could not kill him, but it was Obembe who spoke next.

"He. Is. Right," Obembe stammered. "None of us will kill you. We are not—Ike—we are not even real fishermen. He said a fisherman will kill you, Ike, but we are not real fishermen."

Ikenna looked up at Obembe and his face wore the expression of one confounded by what he'd heard. Tears stood in his eyes. It was now my turn.

"We cannot kill you, Ike, you are strong, and bigger than us all," I said in a voice that was as collected as I could manage, having been nudged by the feeling that I, too, had something to say. But I did not know what gave me the audacity to take his hand and say: "Brother Ike, you said we hate you, but it is not true. We like you very much more than everyone."

Although at that point my throat became warm, I said with all the calm I could muster: "We like you even more than Daddy and Mama."

I stepped back from him and my eyes fell on Boja, who was nodding. For a moment, Ikenna seemed lost. Our words, it seemed, had had an impact on him, and for the first time in many weeks, my eyes and those of the others met his. His eyes were bloodshot and his face pale, but there was an expression on it that was so indescribable, so beyond recognition—as my memory at the time could afford—that it became the face that I now mostly remember of him.

A moment of great expectation followed, all of us waiting for what he would do next. As if nudged by a pat from a spirit, he turned and hurried into his room. Then from within it, he yelled: "I don't want anyone disturbing me from now on. All of you mind your business and leave me alone. I warn you, leave me alone!"

★   ★   ★

The fear, after destroying Ikenna's well-being, health and faith, destroyed his relationships, the closest of which was with us, his brothers. It seemed that he had fought the internal battle for too long, and now wanted to get it over with. As if to dare the prophecy to come true Ikenna began to do all he could to harm us. Two days after our attempt to persuade him, we woke to discover that Ikenna had destroyed our prized possession: a copy of the *Akure Herald* of June 15th, 1993. The newspaper had our photos on it; it had Ikenna's on the front page with the caption *Young Hero drives his younger brothers to safety*. The photos of Boja, Obembe and me were placed in a small rectangular box just over Ikenna's full image, under the title *Akure Herald*. The newspaper was priceless, our medal of honour even stronger than the M.K.O. calendar. At one time, Ikenna would have killed for it. The newspaper told the story of how he led us to safety during the internecine political riots, a seminal moment that changed everything in the life of Akure.

On that historic day, barely two months after we met M.K.O., we were in school when cars began honking interminably. I was in my class of mostly six-year-olds, unaware of the boiling unrest in Akure and around Nigeria. I'd heard of a war that had happened long before—a war Father often mentioned in passing. When he said the phrase "before the war," a sentence unconnected to the events of the war would often follow, and then sometimes end with "but all these were cut short by the war." There were times when, while chiding us for an act that smacked of laziness or weakness, he'd tell the story of his escapade as a ten-year-old boy during the war when he was left to cater for, hunt for, feed and protect his mother and younger sisters after they all took to the big Ogbuti forest to escape the invasion of our village by the Nigerian army. This was the only time he ever actually said anything that happened "during the war." Alternatively, the phrase would be "after the war." Then, a fresh sentence would take form, without any link to the war mentioned.

Our teacher disappeared early on when the commotion and the honking began. Once she'd left, my classroom emptied as children ran, crying for their mothers. The school was a three-storeyed building. The kindergarten and my nursery class were on the ground floor while the higher classes, the primary classes, started from the first floor up to the second. From the window of my class, I saw a mass of cars in different states—doors opened, driving off and some parking. I sat there, waiting for the moment when Father, like other fathers who had come to pick up their children, would come. But instead of him, Boja appeared at my classroom's door calling my name. I answered and took my school bag and my water bottle.

"Come, let's go home," he said, climbing up the desks towards me.

"Why, let us wait for Daddy," I said, looking around.

"Daddy isn't coming," he said, and put a forefinger across his lips to silence me.

He pulled my hand and led me out of the class. We ran between the scattered rows of wooden desks and chairs that had been uniformly arranged before the commotion began. Under an upturned chair lay a boy's broken food flask and its content—yellowed rice and fish—strewn over the floor. Outside, it was as if the world had been sawn in two and we were all teetering on the edge of the chasm. I removed my hand from Boja's grip. I wanted to return to my classroom and wait for Father.

"What are you doing, you fool!" Boja cried. "There's a riot; they are killing people, let's go home!"

"We should wait for Daddy," I said, following him with cautious steps.

"No, we can't," Boja objected. "If these men break in, they will recognize we are M.K.O.'s boys, 'Children of Hope '93', enemies, and, we'll be in greater danger than anyone else."

His words smashed my resilience into smithereens and frightened me. A crowd of mostly older pupils trying to get out had formed at the gate, but we did not head there. We crossed the fallen fence and began moving through a line of palm trees out of the school and joined Ikenna and Obembe, who were already waiting for us behind a tree in the bush, and together we ran.

The creepers crashed under our feet and a flood of air broke into my lungs. The bush spat us out into a small path that Obembe immediately identified as Isolo Street a few minutes later.

But the street was almost deserted. We ran past the timber market where, on normal days, we would have had to shield our ears because of the deafening noises of drilling machines. The many rickety trucks that transported heavy timber from the forests sat in front of a mountain of sawdust, but there was no one around them. From here, we saw the wide road split in two with a long rail the width of perhaps three of my feet placed in front of each other. It was the road to the Central Bank of Nigeria, the place Ikenna had suggested we go because it was the closest place protected by armed guards in which we could hide, because Father worked there. Ikenna insisted that if we did not go there, the junta's forces—bent on cracking down on supporters of M.K.O. in Akure, his home state—would kill us. The road was heavily littered that day with all sorts of things—personal effects that had dropped from people fleeing the carnage—making Akure appear as if an aircraft had thrown out belongings from a great height. When we crossed to a side of the road where there was a walled compound with many trees, a car filled with people raced down the road with hellish speed. Just as the distance swallowed it, a blue Mercedes Benz with one of my classmates, Mojisola, in the front seat, emerged from the road we had come from. She waved at me, and I waved back, but the car raced on.

"Let's go," Ikenna said, once the car was out of sight. "We could not have stayed back at school; they would have recognized we are M.K.O.'s boys and we would have been in danger. Let us go through that road." He pointed and glanced widely as though he had heard something we had not heard.

Every gripping detail of the riot my eyes saw, every smell of it, filled me with a concrete fear of death. We'd entered a bend when Ikenna cried: "No, no, let's stop. We shouldn't walk on the main road; it's not safe."

So we crossed to the other side, a major commercial lane, filled with shops that were all closed. The door of one of them was shattered, and pieces of broken wood, fecund with nails, dangled dangerously from the broken door. We were forced to halt somewhere in between a closed bar with crates of beer piled on each other and a truck littered with posters of Star Lager Beer, "33," Guinness and other brands. That instant, a loud cry for help, spoken in Yoruba, came from somewhere we could not immediately make out. A man emerged from one of the shops and ran towards the road to our school. Our fear of the palpable danger grew.

We crossed the dump into a street where we saw a house in flames. The corpse of a man lay on its veranda. Ikenna ducked behind the burning house and we followed, trembling. It was the first time I, and probably the rest of my brothers, had seen a dead man. My heart raced, and that moment I became conscious of a gradual warmth that began to slowly seep down the seat of my school shorts. When I looked at the ground beneath me, I realized that I had wetted my shorts and watched the last few drops slip to the ground, trembling. A group of men, armed with clubs and machetes, trooped past, casting furtive glances about and chanting, "Death to Babangida, Abiola must rule."

Squatted like frogs, we maintained a silence of stones for as long as this clique was in sight. Once they had passed, we crawled behind one of the houses and found a van with a dead man in it parked just across from the backyard, its front door left open.

We could tell from the man's attire—a long, flowing Senegalese robe—that he was a northerner: the main targets of the onslaught by M.K.O. Abiola supporters, who'd hijacked the riot as a struggle between his west, and the north, where the military president, General Babangida, belonged.

With a force no one thought he could muster, Ikenna hauled the dead man off the seat of the car. The man fell out of the car with a thud, blood spattering on the ground from his broken face. I screamed and began to cry.

"Keep quiet, Ben!" Boja cried, but I could not stop; I was very afraid.

Ikenna got in the driver's seat and Boja sat beside him, Obembe and me in the back seat.

"Let's go," said Ikenna. "Let's go to Daddy's office in this car. Close the doors quickly!" he cried.

With the key in the ignition beside the large wheel, Ikenna started the car and the engine roared and blared into life with a prolonged groan.

"Ike, can you drive?" Obembe asked, trembling.

"Yes," Ikenna said. "Daddy taught me how to some time ago."

He revved the engine, pushed the car backwards with a jerk, and it went dead. He was about to kick-start the car again when the sound of ammunition in the distance kept us at a standstill.

"Ikenna, please drive it," Obembe moaned, flapping his hands. Tears had begun to course down his face, too. "You asked us to leave the school, now we are going to die?"

There were bonfires and burning cars everywhere, for Akure was singed that day. We'd neared Oshinle Street on the east of the town when a military van filled with soldiers in full combat regalia sped past. One of them noticed it was a boy at the wheel of our car and tapped his friend, pointing in our direction, but the truck did not stop. Ikenna maintained a steady course, accelerating only when he saw the red clock-like arm of the speedometer move to a larger number, the way he'd always watched Father do it every time he sat with him in the front seat when he took us to school. We verged onto the road, staying close to its shoulder until Boja read out the sign *Oluwatuyi Street* and the small one beneath it with the inscription *Central Bank of Nigeria*. Then we knew we were safe and had escaped the 1993 election uprising in which more than a hundred people were killed in Akure. June the 12th became a seminal day in the history of Nigeria. Every year, as this day approached, it seemed as if a band of a thousand invisible surgeons, armed to the teeth with knives, trephines, needles and extraordinary anaesthetic materials, came with the influx of the north wind and settled in Akure. Then at night-time, while the people slept, they would commit frantic, temporal lobotomy of their souls in quick painless snatches, and vanish at dawn before the effects of the surgeries began to show. The people would wake with bodies sodden with anxiety, hearts pulsating with fear, heads drooping with the memory of loss, eyes dripping with tears, lips gyrating in solemn prayers, and bodies trembling with fright. They would all become like blurred pencil portraits in a child's wrinkled drawing book, waiting to be erased. In that grim condition, the city would retract inwards like a threatened snail. And by the dim squint of dawn's light, northern-born inhabitants would exit the town, shops would close and churches would convene for prayers of peace as the fragile old man that Akure often became in that month would wait for the passage of the day.

* * *

The destruction of that newspaper shook Boja greatly; he could not eat. Again and again he said to Obembe and me that Ikenna had to be stopped.

"This cannot continue," he repeated many times over. "Ikenna has lost his mind; he has gone mad." The following Tuesday morning, after a clear sky had bared its teeth, Obembe and I had slept late, having told stories into the rump of the night. Our door forcefully jerked open, rousing us to a swift awakening. It was Boja. He'd slept in the sitting room where he'd been sleeping since his first struggle with Ikenna. He came in looking sullen and cold, scratching every part of his body and grinding his teeth as he did.

"Mosquitoes nearly killed me last night," he said. "I'm tired of what Ikenna is doing to me. I'm really tired!"

He'd said it so loudly I feared Ikenna might have heard it from his room. My heart raced. I looked at Obembe, but his eyes were on the door. I sensed that, like me, he was looking to see what might come next through that door.

"I hate that he doesn't allow me into my own room," Boja went on. "Can you imagine? He doesn't let me into my own room." He beat his hand on his chest in a gesture of possession. "The room Daddy and Mama gave both of us."

He removed his shirt and pointed at places on his skin where he felt he'd been bitten. Although shorter than Ikenna, he closely followed him in maturity. Signs of hair growth had appeared on his chest, and actual hair now webbed his armpit. A dark shade trailed from under his navel down into his pants.

"Is the parlour so bad?" I asked in an effort to calm him, I did not want him to continue because I feared that Ikenna could hear it.

"It is!" he cried even louder. "I hate him for this, I hate him! No one can sleep there!"

Obembe cast a wary glance at me and I noticed that, like me, he was consumed with fear. Boja's words had dropped like a piece of chinaware, its pieces scattered about. Obembe and I knew something was coming, and it seemed Boja knew, too, for he sat down and placed his hand on his head. Within minutes, a door opened from within the house, creaking aloud, followed by footsteps. Ikenna entered the room.

"Did you say you hate me?" Ikenna said softly.

Boja did not reply, but kept his eyes fixed on the window. Ikenna, visibly stung (for I saw tears in his eyes), gently closed the door and moved further into the room. Then, casting a spear of a scornful glance at Boja, he took off his shirt, in the custom of the boys in the town when about to fight.

"Did you say it or not?" Ikenna shouted, but did not wait for a reply. He pushed Boja off the chair.

Boja let out a cry and rose to his feet almost immediately, panting furiously, shouting: "Yes, yes I hate you, Ike, I do."

Most times when I recall this event, I plead frantically for my memory to pity me and stop at this point, but it is always futile. I'd always see Ikenna stand still for a moment after Boja uttered those words, his lips moving for a long time before the words "You hate me, Boja" finally formed. But Ikenna uttered the words with so much power that his face seemed to lighten with relief. He smiled, nodded and blinked a tear.

"I knew it, I knew it; I have only been foolish all this while." He shook his head. "That was why you threw my passport into the well." A look of horror had appeared on Boja's face at those words, and he made to speak, but Ikenna spoke on in a louder voice, switching from Yoruba to Igbo. "Wait! Were it not for that malicious act, I would have been in Canada by now, living a better life." And as if every word Ikenna said—every complete sentence—struck him, Boja would gasp, mouth agape, and words would begin to form, but Ikenna's "Wait!" or "Listen!" would drown it out. And some strange dreams, Ikenna continued, had further confirmed his suspicions; in one of them, he'd seen Boja chasing him with a gun. Boja's face twitched at this, his face flushed with a mixture of shock and helplessness as Ikenna spoke. "So, I know, my spirit attests, to how much you hate me."

Boja walked springily to the door wanting to leave, but stopped when Ikenna spoke. "I knew," Ikenna was saying, "the moment Abulu saw that vision that you were the Fisherman he talked about. Nobody else."

Boja stood still and listened with his head bent, as if ashamed.

"That is why I'm not surprised when you now confess that you hate me; you always have. But you will not succeed," Ikenna said suddenly now, fiercely.

He made towards Boja and struck him on the face. Boja fell and hit his head on Obembe's iron box on the floor with a loud clang. He let out a jolting cry of pain, stamping his feet on the floor and screaming. Ikenna, shaken, took a step back as if teetering on the mouth of a chasm, and when he reached the door, he turned and ran out.

Obembe stepped forward towards Boja once Ikenna left the room. Then he halted suddenly and shouted, "Jesus!" At first, I did not see what Ikenna and Obembe had seen, but did that instant: the pool of blood that was filling the top of the box and trickling down to the floor.

In distress, Obembe ran out of the room and I followed. We found Mother at her garden in the backyard where, hoe in hand and a few tomatoes in her raffia basket, she was talking with Iya Iyabo, the neighbour who had reported our fishing, and we called out to them. When Mother came into our room with the woman, they were horrified by what they saw. Boja had stopped wailing, and now his body lay still, his face hidden in his bloodied hands, his body in a strange state of tranquillity as if he were dead. Beholding him lying there, Mother broke down and wept.

"Quickly, let us take him to Kunle's Clinic," Mama Iyabo called out to her.

Mother, agitated beyond measure, hurriedly changed into a blouse and a long skirt. With the help of the woman, she lifted Boja onto her shoulder. Boja remained calm, his eyes gazing vacantly, as he wept noiselessly.

"If anything happens to him now," Mother said to the woman, "what will Ikenna say? Will he say that he killed his own brother?"

"*Olohun maje!*—God forbid!" Iya Iyabo spat. "Mama Ike, how can you let such a thing into your head just because of this? They are growing boys and this is common with boys their age. Stop this; let's take him to a hospital."

Once they were gone, I became conscious of the steady sound of something trickling to the floor. I looked and saw it was the pool of blood. I sat in my bed, shaken by what my eyes had seen, but it was the memory Ikenna had conjured up that disturbed me. I remember that incident, although I was only about four at that time. Mr Bayo, Father's friend in Canada, was returning to Nigeria. Having promised to take Ikenna to Canada to live with him whenever he returned, Mr Bayo had got Ikenna a passport and a Canadian

visa. Then the morning Ikenna was to leave with Father
to Lagos, where he was to board the plane with Mr Bayo,
Ikenna could not find his passport. He'd kept the passport in
the breast pocket of his travelling jacket and hung it in the
wardrobe he shared with Boja. But it was no longer in that
jacket. They were running late and Father, furious, began
a frantic search for the passport, but they could not find it.
Afraid the plane would leave without Ikenna, as he would
need to go through a new process to get the passport and
travelling documents all over again, Father's anger escalated.
He was about to smack Ikenna for his carelessness, when
Boja, hiding behind Mother so Father wouldn't beat him,
confessed he'd stolen the passport. Why, Father asked, and
where was it? Boja, visibly shaken, said: "In the well." Then
he confessed to having thrown it there the previous night
because he didn't want Ikenna to leave him.

Father dashed for the well in delirious haste, but when
he looked, he saw pieces of the passport floating on the
surface of the water, damaged beyond repair. Father piled
his hands on his head, shaking. Then, as if suddenly possessed of a spirit, he reached for the tangerine tree, broke
off a stick, and ran back towards the house. He was about
to descend on Boja when Ikenna intervened. He'd arranged
for Boja to throw the passport in the well because he did not
want to leave without him; they would go together when

they were older. Although I'd come to understand later (and even our parents did so) that this was a lie, Father was overcome at the time by what Ikenna had deemed an act of love, which now, in this moment of his metamorphosis, had become to him an act of ultimate hatred.

When Mother and he returned from the clinic that afternoon, Boja appeared many miles from himself. Blood-stained gauze, with cotton wool underneath, covered the gash at the back of his head. My heart sank when I saw it and I wondered how much blood he'd lost and shuddered at the pain he must have endured. I tried to understand what had happened, what was going on but I could not; the reckoning of these things was not cheap.

Throughout the rest of that day, Mother was a mined road that exploded when anyone stepped within an inch of her. Later, while preparing eba for dinner, she began to soliloquize. She complained that she'd asked Father to request a transfer back to Akure or move us down with him, but that he hadn't. And now, she lamented, his children were splitting each other's heads. Ikenna, she continued, had turned into a stranger to her. Her mouth was still moving when she set dinner on the table, while each one of us pulled out the wooden dining chairs and sat on them. When she put out the last thing for dinner, the hand-washing bowl, she began to sob.

Silence and fear engulfed the house that night. Obembe and I retreated to our room early, and David, scared of being around Mother in her harsh mood, followed us. For long before I slept, I listened for any sign of Ikenna but heard none. Yet even as I waited, I secretly wished he would not come home until the next morning. One reason was my fear of Mother's fury, what she might do to him if he returned in this climate. The second was my fear of how, after they returned from the clinic, Boja had declared that enough was enough. "I promise," he'd said, licking the tip of his index finger in a gesture of oath-taking, "I will no longer be kept out of my room." And, to make good his threat, he'd retired to sleep there. I was afraid of the potential danger of Ikenna returning and finding him there and this filled me with the immense premonition that Boja would, someday, retaliate, for he'd been deeply wronged. And as my body yielded to the forceful closure of that day, I began to ponder how far the venom in Ikenna had travelled and feared where it would end.

8

THE LOCUSTS

Locusts were forerunners:

They swarmed Akure and most parts of Southern Nigeria at the beginning of rainy seasons. The winged insects, as small as the brown brush flies, would leap out of porous holes in the earth in a sudden invasion and converge wherever they saw light—it drew them magnetically. The people of Akure often rejoiced at the arrival of the locusts. For, rain healed the land after the dry seasons during which the inclement sun, aided by the Harmattan wind, tormented the land. The children would switch on bulbs or lanterns and hold bowls of water close so they could knock the insects into them or cause them to shed their wings and drown in the water. The people would gather and feast on the roasted remains of the locusts, rejoicing at the oncoming rain. But the rain would come down—usually on the day after the locust invasion—with a violent storm, plucking out roofs, destroying houses, drowning many and turning whole cities into strange rivers. It would transform the locusts from harbingers of good things into the heralds of evil. Such was the fate the week that followed Boja's head injury brought to the people of Akure, to all Nigerians, and to our family.

It was the week in August when Nigeria's Olympic "Dream Team" got to the final of the men's football. In the weeks before that, marketplaces, schools, offices had lit up with the name Chioma Ajunwa, who had won gold for the ramshackle country. And now, the men's team, having beaten Brazil in the semi-final, was in the final with Argentina. The country was mad with joy. As people waved the Nigerian flags in the summer heat in faraway Atlanta, Akure slowly drowned. Thick rain, armed with a fierce wind, which had left the town in a blackout, poured through the eve of the night of the final match between Nigeria's Dream Team and Argentina. The rain dragged into the morning of the match, the morning of August 3rd, and pummelled zinc and asbestos roofs until sunset when it weakened and ceased. No one went out of the house that day, including Ikenna, who spent most of the day confined to his room, silent except for times when his voice rose as he sang along to a tune on the portable radio cassette player that had become his main companion. His isolation had, by that week, become fully formed.

Mother had confronted him for the injury he'd inflicted on Boja, and he'd argued that he was right because Boja had threatened him first. "I could not have kept quiet and watched a little boy like him threaten me," he'd insisted, standing at the threshold of his room even though Mother had begged him to sit down in the sitting room and talk. Then, after he'd said that, he burst into tears. Perhaps ashamed of this outburst, he ran into his room and shut the door. Mother would say that day that she was *now* certain that Ikenna was obviously out of his mind, and that everyone should avoid him until Father returned to bring him back to his senses. But my fear of what Ikenna had become was already growing stronger by the day. Even Boja, despite his initial threat that he would no longer be cheated, complied with Mother's directions and stayed clear of Ikenna's way. He'd now fully recovered from his wound and the plaster had been taken off, revealing a curved dent where the stitch had been made.

The rain stopped in the evening, close to the time when the match was to begin. Once it drew near, Ikenna disappeared. We'd all waited for electricity to be restored in time to see the crucial match, but at eight in the evening, there was still a blackout. All day, Obembe and I sat in the sitting room, reading by the dim light of the grey sky. I was reading a paperback edition of a curious book, in which animals spoke and had human names and all of them were domesticated—dogs, pigs, hens, goats, etcetera. The book did not have the wild ones I liked in it, but I read on, drawn by the way the animals spoke and thought like humans. I was deep into the book when Boja, who had been sitting quietly all along, told Mother that he wanted to go see the match at La Room. Mother was seated in the sitting room playing with David and Nkem.

"Isn't it too late now—must you see the match?" Mother said.

"No, I will go; it is not too late—"

She seemed to ponder it a little while after which she looked up at us and said, "Okay, but be careful."

We took the torchlight from Mother's room and went out into the darkening street. All around there were pockets of buildings powered by generators that buzzed noisily, filling the neighbourhood with a confluence of white noises. People generally believed that in Akure, the rich bribed the National Electric Power Authority branch to interrupt power during big matches like this one so they could make money by setting up makeshift viewing centres. La Room was the most modern hotel in our district: a four-storeyed building, walled around with a high barbed-wire fence. At night, even in the absence of electricity, the bright fluorescent lamps stretching from within its walls cast a still pool of light over a stretch of the surroundings. La Room had that night, as on most nights when this power interruption occurred, turned its reception hall into a makeshift viewing centre. A big signboard outside the hotel attracted people with a coloured poster with the logo of the Olympic Games and the inscription: *Atlanta 1996*. And indeed, the hall was full when we got there. There were people in every corner of the hall, in different positions, trying to glean a view from the two fourteen-inch television sets placed opposite each other on two high tables. The viewers who had arrived the earliest had occupied the plastic seats closer to the television sets and a growing crowd now massed up behind them, watching.

Boja found a spot from which one of the televisions could be glimpsed and sneaked in between two men, leaving Obembe and me, but we, too, finally found a spot from where we could only see intermittently if we bent leftwards through a small space between two men whose shoes reeked like rotten pork. Obembe and I were submerged for the next fifteen minutes or so in a sickening claustrophobic sea of bodies that gave off the most profound smell of humanity. One man smelt of candle wax, another smelt of old

clothes, another of animal flesh and blood, another of dried
paint, another of petrol, and one, of sheet metal. When I
got tired of covering my nose with my hand, I whispered
into Obembe's ear that I wanted to go back home.

"Why?" he asked, as if surprised, although he too was
scared of the big-headed man behind him, and probably
wanted to leave as well. The man had eyes that stared
inwards at each other, the kind of eyes commonly known
as quarter-after-four eyes. Obembe was also afraid because
this scary-looking man had barked that he should "stand
properly," and rudely shoved Obembe's head with his dirty
hands. The man was a bat: ugly and terrible.

"We shouldn't go; Ikenna and Boja are here," he whispered back, stealing gazes at the man from the corner of
his eyes.

"Where?" I whispered back.

He let a good time pass, slowly tilting his head backwards
until he was able to whisper: "He's seated in front, I saw—"
But his voice was ferried away by the sudden uproar that
broke out. Frantic cries of "Amuneke!" and "Goal!" rent
the air, throwing the hall into a tumult of jubilation. The
bat-like man's companion elbowed Obembe in the head
while flailing his arms in the air, shouting. Obembe let
out a yelp that was absorbed by the riotous wail so that
it appeared as if he was rejoicing with the men. He fell

against me, cringing with pain. The man who'd hit him did not even notice, but went on shouting.

"Let's go home, this place is bad," I said to Obembe after I'd said a dozen "Sorry, Obe." But feeling this might not convince him, I said what Mother often said when we insisted on going out to see a football match: "We mustn't see this match. After all, should they win, the players aren't going to share the money with us."

This worked. He nodded in acceptance, stifling tears. I managed to edge forward and tapped Boja on the shoulder where he stood, sandwiched between two older boys.

"What?" he asked hurriedly.

"We're going."

"Why?"

I did not reply.

"Why?" he asked again, eager to return his eyes to the screen.

"Nothing," I said.

"Okay, see you then," he said, and swiftly turned back to the television.

Obembe asked for the torchlight but Boja did not hear the request.

"We don't need the torchlight," I said, as I struggled for space between two tall men. "We can walk slowly. God can guide us home safely."

We went out, his hand on the place the man had elbowed, perhaps feeling it to see if it had swollen. This night was dark—so dark we could barely see except for the light of cars and motorcycles intermittently passing on the road. But they were very few because everyone seemed to be somewhere, watching the Olympic match.

"That man's a wild animal, he couldn't even say sorry," I said, fighting the increasing urge to cry. It was as though I could feel Obembe's pain just as he did; the urge to cry overwhelmed me.

"Shhhh," Obembe said just then.

He pulled me into a corner close to a wooden kiosk. At first I did not see anything, and then I, too, saw what he'd seen. For there, standing by the palm tree outside our gate was Abulu the madman. The sight had come with such suddenness that it seemed unreal to me at first. I had not seen him since the day we encountered him at Omi-Ala, but in the days and weeks that passed, in absentia—or perhaps from a distance—he'd gradually filled my life, our lives, with his afflictive presence. I'd heard his story, been warned against him, had prayed against him. Yet I'd not seen him, and without knowing it, I'd been waiting to—even wanting to see him. And there he was, standing in front of our gate, staring intently into our compound, but seemingly not trying to enter it. Obembe and I stood there watching him as he gesticulated, waving his hand in the air as if in a conversation with someone he alone could see. Then, suddenly turning, he began walking towards us, whispering something as he went along. As he passed us, we heard—between muffled breaths—the whispering of something that I reckoned Obembe had heard distinctly, too; for he grabbed my hand and pulled me away from the madman's path. Panting, I watched him walk away into the outstretched darkness. A shadow of him created by the headlamps of our neighbour's truck loomed briefly over the street and then vanished as the truck drew closer.

"Did you hear what he was saying?" Obembe asked me once we lost sight of him.

I shook my head.

"Didn't you?" he breathed.

Just as I was about to answer, a man carrying a child on his shoulders waddled past. The child was mumbling a nursery rhyme:

> *Rain, rain, go away*
> *Come again another day*
> *Little children want to play…*

They were barely out of earshot when Obembe asked again.

I shook my head—to gesture that I hadn't, but it was a lie. Although not distinctly, I'd heard the word Abulu had repeated as he passed. It had sounded the same way it did the day the end of our peace was initiated: "*Ikena*."

* * *

A dubious joy swept through Nigeria, spreading from evening into morning the way locusts pour down at night, and vanish by sunrise, leaving their wings scattered through the town. Obembe, Boja and I rejoiced deep into the night, listening as Boja gave us a minute-by-minute commentary of the game, movie-like, so that Jay-Jay Okocha dribbled the opponents the way Superman delivered the kidnapped, and Emmanuel Amuneke had jet-balled his goal-scoring kick like a Power Ranger. Mother had to intervene around midnight, insisting that we retire to bed. When at last I slept, I had a million dreams and was asleep into the morning when Obembe tapped me forcefully, screaming "Wake up! Wake up, Ben—they are fighting!"

"Who, what?" I asked in confusion.

"They are fighting," he clattered. "Ikenna and Boja. It's a serious fight. Come." He moved in the ray of light like a disoriented moth and then, turning to see me still in the bed, cried: "Listen, listen—it is fierce. Come!"

Long before Obembe woke me, Boja had woken up, cursing. The rickety lorry of our cross-wall neighbours, the Agbatis, had torn through the thin layer that separated the dream world from the unconscious world with the sporadic buzz of *vroom! vroommm! vroommmmm!* Although the truck woke him, he'd wanted to wake early so he could go practise drum-beating with other boys of our church. He had a bath, ate his portion of the bread and butter Mother, who'd gone to her shop with David and Nkem, had left for us, but had to wait to change into a new shirt and trousers, because—although he had stopped sleeping in the room he shared with Ikenna—his possessions were still in his closet. Mother, the falconer, had repeatedly pleaded that he move in with Obembe and me, saying: "*Ha pu lu ekwensu ulo ya*—Leave the devil to his den." But Boja did not yield. He contended that the room was his as well as Ikenna's, and that he would not leave. And since Ikenna and he were not speaking, Boja had to often wait for Ikenna to wake and unlock the door without having to ask Ikenna to open it. Ikenna, however, had stayed out for most of that night to partake in the wild street celebrations that had swept through Nigeria, and remained in the room well into noon. Obembe would add, too, much later to me alone that Ikenna had returned home drunk. He'd said he'd perceived a strong smell of alcohol on Ikenna when

Obembe let him in through our shutters because Mother locked the main door and gate at midnight.

Boja waited restlessly with roiling anger. Then, close to eleven, his patience had all been used up, and he went to the door and knocked, first softly, then desperately. Obembe said Boja, in frustration, pressed his ear to the door as though it was a stranger's house and turned to him as if struck by lightning, and said: "I can't hear any sign of life. Are you sure Ikenna is still alive?"

Boja had asked this question, Obembe said, with genuine concern as if he was scared something evil had happened to Ikenna. Boja had then listened afresh for signs of life, before beginning to knock again, this time louder, calling on Ikenna to open the door.

When no response came, Boja began ramming his body against the door desperately. When he stopped, he stepped back, his eyes filled with relief and fresh fear.

"He is inside," he mumbled to Obembe as he moved away from the door. "I heard movements just now—he is alive."

"Who is the madman that was disturbing my peace?" Ikenna barked from the room.

Boja didn't speak at first. Then he shouted, "Ikenna, you are the madman not me. You'd better open the door right now; the room is mine, too."

A few hastened footfalls, and in a flash, Ikenna was out. He'd come out with such speed that Boja had not even seen the blow coming, he'd simply found himself on the ground.

"I heard all you said about me," Ikenna said as Boja attempted to rise back to his feet. "I heard it all—how you said I was dead and not alive. You, Boja, with all I've done for you, wish me dead, right? And, upon that, you even call me a madman. Me? I will show you today—"

He was still speaking when Boja, in a move as quick as lightning, scissored his legs, and sent him crashing against the door and into the room. Boja sprang up as Ikenna, grimacing in pain, swore and cursed.

"I am ready for you, too," Boja said from the threshold of the main door. "If this is what you want, come out to the open space in the backyard so we don't destroy anything in the house, so that Mama will not find out what happened."

Once he said that, he dashed out to the backyard, where the well and the garden were located, and Ikenna followed him.

* * *

The first thing I saw when I got to the backyard with Obembe was Boja trying to duck a blow from Ikenna's clenched fist, but failing so that the blow landed on his chest and sent him staggering backwards. As Boja tried to steady his feet, Ikenna pushed him down with his leg. He followed him to the ground as they tore at each other like gladiators of fisticuffs. I was gripped with indescribable horror. Obembe and I were transfixed in the doorway, unable to move, pleading with them to stop.

But they paid no heed, and we were soon distracted by the fierceness of the blows and stunned by the feral quickness of their legs as they swirled together. Obembe screamed when a blow hit one of them and gasped when either of them yelped in pain. I could not stand the scene either. I'd sometimes close my eyes when one of them made a violent move and open them when the move had been completed, my heart thumping. Obembe resumed pleading again when Boja started bleeding from a cut above his right eye. But Ikenna chewed him out.

"Shut up," he snarled, spitting into the dirt. "If you don't shut up, now, both of you will join him. Idiots. Didn't you see when he talked to me the way he did? I'm not to be blamed. He started this and—"

Boja cut him off with a ferocious punch to his back, grappling for Ikenna's waist; they crashed onto the earth, raising a fume of dust. They fought on with fierceness uncommon when boys of that age engage their siblings in a fight. Ikenna punched with a zeal that was far greater than he'd punched the chicken-selling boy at the Isolo market who called Mother an *ashewo*—a whore, when she refused to buy his chicken one Yuletide season. We'd cheered him and even Mother, who detested every form of violence, had said—after the boy got back on his feet, picked up his portable raffia-plaited poultry cage and took flight—that the boy had deserved the beating. Yet, Ikenna's blows this time were far harder—far weightier—far stronger than ever before. Boja too kicked and lunged with more daring than he did when he fought the boys who'd threatened to stop us from fishing at Omi-Ala one Saturday. This fight was different. It was as though their hands were controlled by a force that possessed every bit of their beings, even down to the smallest plasma of their blood, and it was perhaps this force—and not their conscious beings—that caused them to deploy such heavy-handed tactics against each other. As I watched them fight, I was seized by the presentiment that things would not remain the same after this. I feared that every blow was imbued with an impregnable power of destruction that cannot be stayed, contained or reverted. As these feelings seized me, my mind—like a whirlwind gathering dirt into its concentric fold—went into a mad spin of frenzied thoughts, the most dominant of which was the strange and unfamiliar thought that overpowered all else: the thought of death.

Ikenna broke Boja's nose. Blood gushed out in spurts and dripped down from his jaw to the dirt. In visible pain, Boja sank to the ground, weeping and dabbing his bloodied nose with the rags his shirt had become. Obembe and I, at the sight of Boja's bloodied nose, began to cry. I knew that the fight was long from being over. Boja would avenge this terrible blow, for he was never one to chicken out. When I saw him beginning to creep towards the garden, attempting to rise, an idea came to me. I turned to Obembe and told him we should get a grown-up to separate them.

"Yes," he agreed, tears trickling down his cheeks.

We dashed off at once into the next house, but there was a padlock on the gate. We'd forgotten that the family had travelled out of town two days before and would not return until later that evening. As we made off from here, we saw Pastor Collins—the pastor of our church—driving past in his van. We waved at him frantically, but he did not see us. He drove on, bobbing his head to some music on the car's stereo. We hopped an open sewer in which was the mangled body of a dead snake, one that appeared to be growing into a python, smashed dead with stones and pelts.

The man we found at last was Mr Bode, the motor mechanic, who lived three blocks from our house in a chain of unpainted and unvarnished bungalows. It was a half-completed building with pieces of wood and small heaps of sand lying about. Mr Bode had a military appearance: a towering height, heavy biceps, and a face that was as stern as the cavernous bark of an iroko tree. He'd just returned from his workshop to relieve himself at the latrine he shared with the other occupiers of the five rooms of the bungalow when we found him. His trousers were still unbuckled, his boxers pulled up to his waist as he washed his hands at the long-necked tap that sprouted out from the ground near the wall, humming a tune.

"Good afternoon, sir," Obembe greeted.

"My boys," he replied and raised his head to look at us. "How are you?"

"We are fine, sir," we chorused.

"What is it, boys?" he asked, wiping his hand against his trousers, which was black with grime and car oil.

"Yes, sir," Obembe replied. "Our brothers are fighting and we—we—"

"They are bleeding, *eje ti o po*—much blood," I said, seeing that Obembe could not continue. "Please come and help us."

The man's face contracted as he gazed on at our tearful faces as if attacked by a sudden stroke. "What kind of thing is this?" he said, waving his wet hands to dry them. "Why are they fighting?"

"We don't know, sir," was Obembe's curt riposte. "Please come help."

"Okay, let's go," Mr Bode said.

He darted back towards the house as if going for something, but stopped short and gesturing forward, said: "Let's go." Once on the way, my brother and I began to run but stopped so Mr Bode could catch up.

"We have to be quick, sir," I begged.

At this, Mr Bode began running, too, barefooted. Close to home, two women blocked the edge of the sidewalk. They were dressed in cheap grime-tainted gowns, and each bore a sack laden with corn on her head. Obembe brushed past one of them and two small cobs fell from a hole in the sack. The woman swore as we raced away.

The first thing we saw when we got to our compound was the pregnant goat with a bloated belly and sagging udders, owned by our neighbours. It crouched near the gate, bleating with its tongue unfurled from its mouth like adhesive tape unrolled from its spool. All around its dark, heavy and reeking body were small black pods of its faeces, some squashed into brown pus-like paste and others coagulated in twos, threes and multiples. The only sound I could hear from the compound was the *huee, huee* sound of the goat's heavy breathing. We ran to the backyard, but all we saw were pieces of rags from what had been their clothes, bloodstains streaked into the dirt, and a palimpsest of rich dirt defaced with their footprints. It was impossible to have imagined they could have ended the fight without mediation. Where had they gone? Who'd intervened?

"Where did you say they were fighting?" Mr Bode asked, bemused.

"Here, on this spot," Obembe replied, pointing to the dirt, tears welling in his eyes.

"Are you sure?"

"Yes, sir," Obembe said, "here, right here is where we left them. Here." Mr Bode looked at me and I said, "Here, they were fighting here. See the blood." I pointed to the spot where blood had mixed with earth and formed into a lump, and another spot where there was a wet, rounded, dark patch the shape of a half-closed eye.

Mr Bode gazed on in confusion and said: "Then where might they be?" He began looking about him again and as he did, I wiped my eyes and blew my nose into the dirt. A low-flying bird, a pigeon, perched on the fence by my right hand, fluttering its wings rapidly. As though threatened, the bird leapt off, and glided over the well to the fence. I looked up to see if Igbafe's grandfather was still where I'd seen him seated during the fight. But he, too, was no longer there. A plastic cup was on the chair where he'd sat only a while ago.

"Okay, let us go look inside the house," I heard Mr Bode say. "It is well, let's go. Maybe they stopped fighting and went back inside."

Obembe nodded and led the way while I remained in the backyard. The goat came doddering towards me, bleating. I made a move to deter it, but it merely halted, raised its horned head and bleated like a speechless creature that, having witnessed something terrible, was mustering all its strength to force out a sensible speech to report it. But even in its best effort, the best it could only come up with was a deafening bleat of *mbreeeeeeeeeeeh!*—a bleat which, looking back now, I recognize must have been a plea in hircine-speak.

I left the goat and headed for the garden. Obembe and Mr Bode went inside the house, calling my brothers' names. I was negotiating my way through the heads of corn that had started thriving in the soft rain of August and had almost reached the end of it—where the old asbestos sheets lay piled against the wall—when I heard a sharp cry from the direction of our kitchen. At once, I made a mad rush towards there. I found the kitchen in disarray.

The top shelves were opened and inside them was an empty bottle of Horlicks, a can of yellow custard and old coffee tins that sat atop each other. Lying by the door, broken at the arm, and pointing its soot-black feet upwards, was Mother's plastic kitchen chair. A pool of reddish palm oil mapped across the top of the board beside the sink filled with unwashed plates, dripping down its edge to the floor. The blue cask in which the oil had been stored now lay on the ground on its side, blackened at the dregs, the last of the oil still in it. A fork lay like a dead fish, still, in the pool of red oil.

Obembe was not alone in the kitchen. Mr Bode stood beside him, his hands on his head, gnashing his teeth. Yet, there was a third person, who, however, had become a lesser creature than the fish and tadpoles we caught at Omi-Ala. This person lay facing the refrigerator, his wide-opened eyes still and fixed in one place. It was obvious these eyes could not glimpse a thing. His tongue was stuck out of his mouth from which a pool of white foam had trailed down to the floor, and his hands were splayed wide apart as though nailed to an invisible cross. Half-buried in his belly was the wooden end of Mother's kitchen knife, its sharp blade deep in his flesh. The floor was drenched in his blood: a living, moving blood that slowly journeyed under the refrigerator, and, uncannily—like the rivers Niger and Benue whose confluence at Lokoja birthed a broken and mucky nation—joined with the palm oil, forming an unearthly pool of bleached red, like puddles that form in small cavities on dirt roads. The sight of this pool caused Obembe, as if possessed of a prating demon, to continue to utter with quivering lips the refrain "River of red, river of red, river of red."

It was all he could do, for the hawk had taken flight, soaring on an unapproachable thermal. All that there was to do was scream and wail, scream and wail. I, like Obembe, stung to stillness by the sight, cried out the name, but my tongue became lost to Abulu's so that the name came out corrupted, slashed, wounded, subtracted from within, dead and vanishing: *Ikena*.

9

THE SPARROW

Ikenna was a sparrow:

A thing with wings, able to fly out of sight in the blink of an eye. His life had already gone by the time Obembe and I returned to our compound with Mr Bode, and what we found on the floor in a pool of blood was his empty, bloodied and mangled body. Then, not long after we found it, it disappeared in an ambulance from the General Hospital, returning to our compound in a wooden coffin on the back of a pickup four days later. Obembe and I still did not see him then; our ears merely picked up allusions to "his body in the coffin." We swallowed the many words people said to us to comfort us like bitter pills with the power to heal us: "*E jo, ema se sukun mo, oma ma'a da*—do not weep, it will be well." They did not mention that Ikenna had become a traveller overnight, a curious traveller that journeys out of his own body, leaving the rest of himself lying empty like the twin husks of a groundnut capped together after its content had been extracted. Although I knew he had died, it felt improbable to me at that time. And although he was in the ambulance outside the house, it was hard to imagine he would never again stand up and walk into the house.

Father knew too, for he returned two days after Ikenna died. It was drizzling, wet and slightly cold. I saw his car drive into the compound through the arc formed from wiping the sheet of fog off the louvres in the sitting room where I'd passed the night. It was his first visit since the morning he had called us his fishermen. He returned with all his things, with no intention of leaving again. He'd tried repeatedly but unsuccessfully to get permission to leave the three-month training course in Ghana for a few days to visit Akure when Mother began telling him about Ikenna's changing behaviour. Then, when Mother made the distress call hours after Ikenna was found dead—a call in which the only words she'd said were: "Eme, Ikenna *anaaaa!*" before throwing herself back to the floor—Father scribbled his resignation letter and submitted it to a colleague at the training-course centre in Ghana. Once he arrived back in Nigeria, he took a night bus to Yola, packed his things into his car and drove back to Akure.

Ikenna was buried four days after Father returned—with Boja's whereabouts still unknown. Although the news of the tragedy had spread across the district and neighbours were thronging our house to offer what they'd heard or seen, no one knew where he was. A neighbour, a pregnant woman who lived in a house across the road from ours, said she'd heard a loud cry at about the time Ikenna died. It had woken her from sleep. Another, a university doctorate student, whom everyone called "Prof," an elusive figure who was almost never in his home—the small one-bedroom bungalow beside Igbafe's house—had, while studying, heard the bang of a metal object around that time. But it was Igbafe's mother who—having brought the message from her father, Igbafe's grandfather—gave details close to what might have happened. One of them (Boja, apparently) had staggered up from the ground and rather than continue the fight, had gone towards the kitchen in blind fury and agony, the other trailing. At that point, the man, horrified and thinking the fight had ended, had left his seat and entered the house. He could not tell where Boja had gone.

Like a miracle, a host of people, almost all of whom were relatives, *Nde Iku na' ibe*, some of whom I'd seen before and others whose faces merely peopled the many daguerreotypes and fading photographs tucked away in our family albums, arrived at the house within two days. They had all come from the village, Amano, a place I barely knew. We'd visited it only once, during the burial ceremony of Yee Keneolisa, an old immobile man, who was Father's uncle. We'd travelled through a seemingly interminable road sewn between two vast stretches of thick forests until we reached a place where the great jungle shrank into a few trees and cultivated heaps and a distributed army of scarecrows. Soon, as Father's Peugeot negotiated the sand-filled tracks, jerking furiously, we began to meet people who knew him. These people greeted our parents and us with a boisterous effulgence of geniality. Later, dressed in black clothes with a host of others, we'd marched down in a procession to the funeral, no one speaking, but merely crying as if we had been transformed from creatures capable of making speech to ones that could only wail; this had amazed me beyond words.

These people arrived now exactly the way I last saw them: wearing black clothes. Ikenna was, in fact, the only one dressed differently at his funeral. The sparkling white shirt and trousers he wore gave him the appearance of an angel who—caught unawares during a physical manifestation on earth—had his bones broken to prevent him from returning back to heaven. Everyone else was dressed in black and cloaked in different shades of grief at the ceremony except for Obembe and me: we alone did not cry. Through the days that had collected like bad blood in a boil since Ikenna died, Obembe and I had refused to cry except for initial tears we'd shed in the kitchen when we saw his lifeless body. Even Father had wept a few times: once, while pasting Ikenna's obituary poster on the wall of our house, and again while talking with Pastor Collins during the latter's first condolence visit. Although I cannot rationalize my decision not to shed a tear, I'd held it so strongly—and it seemed Obembe held it, too—that rather than weep, I fixed my eyes instead on Ikenna's face, which I feared would soon be lost. His face had been washed and oiled with olive oil so that it gleamed with unearthly radiance. Although the tear on his lip and the scar across his eyebrows were still visible, his face wore an uncanny peace as if he were not real, as if I and the rest of the mourners had simply dreamt him up. It was as he lay there that I first saw what Obembe had long seen and known—that Ikenna had grown a beard. It seemed to have sprouted overnight and now lined beneath his jaw like a delicately inscribed sketch.

In the coffin, Ikenna's body—his head facing up, cotton wool plugs blocking his nostrils and ears, hands clinging to his sides, legs tagged together—had the shape of a prolate spheroid; an ovoid, the shape of a bird. This was because he was, in fact, a sparrow; a fragile thing who did not design his own fate. It was designed for him. His *chi*, the personal god the Igbos believe everyone had, was weak. His was the *efulefu* kind: the irresponsible sentinel that sometimes abandoned its subject and went on far journeys or errands, leaving them unprotected. This was the reason why, by the time he became a teenager, he'd already had his fill of sinister events and personal tragedies, for he was a mere sparrow who lived in a world of black storms.

When he was six, a boy kicked him in the crotch while they were playing football, sending one of his testes out of his scrotal sac into his body. He was rushed to a hospital where doctors scrambled to carry out a testicular transplant; while in a room in the same hospital they struggled to revive Mother, who had fainted upon hearing of Ikenna's injury. By the morning of the following day, both of them were alive—Mother with relief in place of the grief of the past day when she'd greatly feared he would die, and Ikenna with a small pebble in his scrotum in place of his lost testes. He did not play football for three years. Even when he began playing again, he often grabbed his crotch with his hand to protect it whenever the ball was kicked in his direction. Two years after that, at age eight, he was stung by a scorpion while sitting under a tree in his school. Again, he survived the sting; but his right leg became permanently impaired, shrunken to a smaller size than the other one.

The funeral was held at St. Andrew's Cemetery, a walled field full of gravestones and a few trees. It was filled with posters that were made for the burial. Some of the obituary posters printed on white A4 papers were pasted on the buses that conveyed members of our church and other guests to the funeral, and some on the wind-shield and rear window of Father's car. One was on the exterior part of the wall of our house, just by the postal number, which was written in a circle with charcoal chalk by census workers during the 1991 national census. One was pasted on the rounded electric pole outside the gate of our compound and another on the noticeboards of the church. They pasted one on the gate of my school—where Ikenna was once a pupil—and Aquinas College, Akure, the junior secondary school he and Boja attended. Father had decided they should only be pasted where necessary, "just to let our family and friends know what has happened." The posters were headlined with the word "obituary" printed in ink that spilled at the head of the *b*, and at the tails of the *a* and *r*. In almost all of them, the whiteness of the paper seemed to blur out Ikenna's photo and make him look like one who existed in the nineteenth century. Under the photo was the inscription *Although you left us too early, we love you dearly. We hope we will meet again when the time comes.* And this below:

IKENNA A. AGWU (1981 — 1996),
survived by his parents,
Mr and Mrs Agwu and his siblings,
Boja, Obembe, Benjamin, David and Nkem Agwu.

* * *

At the funeral, before Ikenna was obliterated by sand-fill, Pastor Collins requested that members of our family gather round him while the others stepped back. "Step back *a bit*, please," he said in English cadenced with a thick Igbo accent. "Oh, thank you, thank you. The Lord bless you. A little bit more please. The Lord bless you."

My close family and our relatives surrounded the grave. There were faces I hadn't seen since I was born. After nearly all had surrounded the grave, the Pastor asked that eyes be closed for prayers, but Mother burst into a piercing cry of anguish, sending a terrible wave of sorrow down the line. Pastor Collins ignored her and prayed on, his voice shimmying. Although his words—*that you forgive and receive his soul in your kingdom… we know that in the same way you gave, you have taken… the fortitude to bear the loss… thank you Lord Jesus for we know you have heard us*—seemed to me to have little meaning, all the people hummed a high-sounding "amen" at the end of them. Then one after the other, they scooped earth with a single shovel, threw it into the grave, and passed the shovel on to the next person in the ring. While waiting my turn, I looked up and noticed the horizon had become filled with wool-shaped clouds, so thickly ashen that I thought even white egrets would have been mocked into greyness were they to fly past at that very hour. I was lost in this observation when I heard my name. I dropped my eyes and saw Obembe tearfully muttering something inaudible as he held the shovel towards me with trembling hands. The shovel was big and heavy in my hands, weightier because of the patch of earth that clung to the back of it like a hunch. It was cold, too. My feet sank into the heap of sand when I dug the shovel into the earth and lifted some of it. I then threw it into the grave, and passed the shovel to Father. He took it, dug up a mighty heap of sand and threw it into the grave. Because he was the last person, he dropped the shovel and put his hand on my shoulder.

Then, as if someone had signalled him, the Pastor cleared his throat again, and attempted to move forward but dangled delicately over the edge of the grave, inadvertently pushing sand into it as he struggled to hold himself from falling. A man helped him regain balance and then he moved back a little more.

"It is now time to read briefly from the word of God," the Pastor began when he'd steadied himself. He spoke in spurts as if his words were tropical grasshoppers that flew out of his mouth and paused, the way a grasshopper perches and hops off, again and again and again until he completed his speech. And as he spoke, his Adam's apple bobbed up and down in his throat. "Let us read from the book of Hebrews; Paul's letter to the Hebrews. Let's read from the first verse of chapter eleven." He raised his head, and held the entire group of mourners in one stern stare. Then bowing slightly, he began to read: "Now faith is the substance of things hoped for, the evidence of things not seen…"

While the Pastor read, I felt an incredible urge to watch Obembe, to gauge his feelings at the time. When I looked at him, memories of my lost brothers filled me, for it seemed the past suddenly exploded and fragments of the past began floating freely in his eyes like confetti in an air-filled balloon. First, I saw Ikenna, face funnelled, dim-eyed and angry, standing over Obembe and me who were kneeling on the ground. This was near the esan bush, on our way to Omi-Ala just after Obembe had mocked the white garment church, when he'd ordered us to kneel in punishment for "disrespecting other people's faith." Next, I saw Ikenna and myself sitting in the crook of the tangerine tree in our compound, both of us theatrical Commando and Rambo, lying in wait for Obembe and Boja. They were Hulk Hogan and Chuck Norris respectively and were hiding at the veranda of our bungalow. They emerged every now and then, pointing their toy guns at us, making gun-battle sounds—*drirididi* or *ti-ti-ti-ti-ti*. When they jumped or screamed, we responded with the din of a bomb blast—*gbum!*

I saw Ikenna, dressed in his red vest, standing across the white chalk line drawn on the dirt pitch of the sports ground of our primary school. It is 1991 and I'd just finished the kindergarten race in the colours of the blue team and had emerged as the second from the rear—after I'd managed to edge out the runner for the White House. I'm now in Mother's arms, standing with Obembe and Boja behind the long rope fastened to poles at both ends, which cordoned off the spectators from the track field. We are cheering for Ikenna from this sideline, Boja and Obembe clapping intermittently. A whistle goes off at some point and Ikenna—who is on the same par as four others in colours: green, blue, white and yellow—bends one knee to the ground as the voice of Mr Lawrence, the jack-of-all-trades teacher who also happened to be the sports master, cries: "On your mark!" He pauses as all the runners raise one leg with their fingers pointing to the ground like kangaroos. "Set!" Mr Lawrence cries next. When he cries "Go!" it seems that although the athletes had apparently begun running, the boys are still on the same line—standing shoulder-to-shoulder. Then, one after the other, they disengage. The colours of their shirts appear like a momentary vision, and then disappear only for others to take their various places. Then, the Green House runner trips, and falls, fanning dust into the air. The boys seemed to be engulfed in smoke, but then Boja sees Ikenna raise his arm in celebration at the other end of the finish line; then I see it too. In a breath of a moment, he is surrounded by a flock of Red Vest wearers shouting: "Up Red House! Up Red House!" Mother leaps for joy with me in her hands and then suddenly stops. I see why: Boja, having crawled under the barricading rope, is racing towards the finish line crying "Ike, winner! Ike, winner!" Behind him, in hot pursuit and with a long cane, is the teacher guarding the barricade.

When my attention returned to the funeral, the Pastor had reached the thirty-fifth verse, his voice louder, incantatory, so that every verse he read hung on the mind's fish hook, pulsing like captured fish. The Pastor closed the dog-eared Bible and put it under his armpit. With an already damp handkerchief he wiped his brow.

"Let us now share the grace," he said.

In response, everyone at the funeral massed into a forceful fellowship of noisy throats. I recited as loud as I could with my eyes firmly closed: "May the grace of our Lord Jesus Christ, the love of God and the sweet fellowship of the Holy Spirit, be with us now and forever. Amen."

The amen died off slowly, carried along the rows of the massive graveyard whose language was silence. The Pastor signalled the grave-diggers. They immediately returned from where they had sat talking and laughing during the funeral. These curious men began pulling the heap back in haste, quickening Ikenna's obliteration, as if they were oblivious of the fact that once they covered him, no one would ever see him again. As chunks of earth fell on him, a fresh outbreak of grief erupted and nearly everyone at the funeral cracked open like small pod-producing ifoka nuts. Although I did not cry there, I felt strongly the real palpable reach of loss. With a bewildering air of apathy, the diggers dug on, quicker, one of them briefly stopping to remove a flattened earth-covered water bottle half-buried in the mound of sand that now partly concealed Ikenna's body. As I watched the men throw more earth into the grave, I dug into the cold soil of my own mind, and it became suddenly clear—the way things always become clearer only after they have happened—that Ikenna was a fragile delicate bird; he was a sparrow.

Little things could unbridle his soul. Wistful thoughts often combed his melancholic spirit in search of craters to be filled with sorrow. As a younger boy, he often sat in the backyard, brooding and contemplative, his arms clasped over his knees. He was highly critical of things, a part of him that greatly resembled Father. He nailed small things to big crosses and would ponder for long on a wrong word he said to someone; he greatly dreaded the reproof of others. He had no place for ironies or satires; they troubled him.

Like sparrows—which we believed had no homes—Ikenna's heart had no home, no fixed allegiances. He loved the far and the near, the small and the big, the strange and the familiar. But it was the little things that drew and consumed his compassion, the most memorable of which was a small bird he owned for a few days in 1992. He was sitting out in the corridor of the house alone one Christmas Eve while the others were inside dancing and singing carols, eating, and drinking, when a bird fell to the dirt in front of him. Ikenna bent low and inched towards it in the dark and then wrapped his hands around its feathery body. It was a badly deplumed sparrow that had been caught by someone and had escaped, a strand of twine still wound around its leg. Ikenna's soul cleaved to the sparrow, and he guarded it jealously for three days, feeding it with whatever he could find. Mother asked him to let it go, but he refused. Then, one morning, he lifted the bird's lifeless body in his hand and dug a hole in the backyard; his heart was broken. He and Boja covered the sparrow with sand until the bird was buried under the earth. This was exactly how Ikenna vanished, too. First, the earth poured by the mourners and the undertakers covered his white-shrouded trunk, then his legs, arms, face and everything, until he was obliterated forever from our eyes.

10

THE FUNGUS

Boja was a fungus:

His body was filled with fungi. His heart pumped blood filled with fungi. His tongue was infected with fungi, and, perhaps, so were most organs of his body. It was because his kidneys were filled with fungi that he could not stop bed-wetting till he was twelve. Mother became worried he was under a bed-wetting spell. After taking him for sessions of prayers, she began marking the edges of his bed with anointed oil—small-bottled olive oil on which prayers had been made—every night before he slept. Yet, Boja could not stop, even when he had to endure the shame of taking out his mattress—often spotted with urine patches of different shapes and sizes—every morning to dry in the sun, risking being seen by kids in the neighbour-hood, especially Igbafe and his cousin Tobi, who could see into our compound from their storeyed building. It was because Father had mocked him for bed-wetting that he caused a stir in our school in the eventful morning of that day in 1993, in which we met M.K.O.

Just as a fungus hides in the body of an ignorant host, Boja lived on unseen in our compound for four days after Ikenna's death, without us knowing it. He was there—silent, hidden away, refusing to speak, while the entire district and even the town desperately searched for him. He did not suggest a clue to the Nigerian police that he was within reach. He did not even try to restrain mourners who swooped on our house like bees around a keg of honey. He did not mind that his photo—printed on a poster with fading ink—was floating like an outbreak of influenza around the town—spotting bus stops, motor parks, motels and driveways, and that his name was on the lips of the people of the town.

Bojanonimeokpu "Boja" Agwu, 14, was last seen at his house at No. 21 Akure High School Road, Araromi Street on August 4, 1996. He wore a faded blue T-shirt with a portrait of Bahamas beach. The shirt was blood-stained and torn the last time he was seen. Please, if seen, kindly report to your nearest police station or call 04-8904872.

He did not cry out when his photo streamed non-stop across the screens of televisions in Akure, taking up considerable airtime on OSRC and NTA channels. Instead of making himself known, or even just his whereabouts, he decided to appear in our dreams at night-time and in figments of Mother's troubled visions. So he sat in the big lounge in our sitting room in Obembe's dream—the night before Ikenna was buried—laughing at Mr Bean's tricks on television. Mother often reported sighting him in the sitting room, aproned in the dark, vanishing whenever she raised an alarm and turned on the bulb or lantern. Yet, Boja was not just a mere fungus; he embodied a wide variety of his species. He was a destructive fungus: a man of force, who forced himself into the world, and forced himself out of it. He forced himself out of Mother's womb while she was in bed about to have a nap in 1982. A sudden labour took her unawares like a strong enema-induced bowel passage. The first nudge was a bullet of pain that overwhelmed her. The pain pulled her down and she, unable to move her body, crawled atop her bed, screaming. The landlady of the house where our parents lived at the time heard her cry and came to her aid. Seeing that there was no time to take Mother to a hospital, the woman shut the door, took a piece of cloth and wrapped it around Mother's legs. Then, with the woman blowing on and fanning Mother's private place with all the energy she could muster, Mother gave birth on the bed she shared with Father. She often recalled, years later, how so much blood had leaked through the mattress that it formed a huge permanent stain on the floor beneath the bed.

He destroyed our peace and set us all on edge. Father hardly sat for a minute during those days. Less than two hours after we returned from Ikenna's burial, he announced that he was going to the police station to find out what progress had been made in the search for Boja. He said this while we were seated in the sitting room, all of us. I could not tell what it was that sent me out running after him calling "Daddy, Daddy!"

"What, Ben?" he asked, turning, his bunch of keys hanging from his index finger. I noticed that the zipper of his trousers was open, I pointed at it before replying. "What is it?" he asked again after looking at his zipper.

"I want to come with you."

He zipped his trousers, gazing at me as if I were a suspicious object lying in his path. Perhaps he noticed that I had not shed a single tear since he'd returned. The police station was built along the old rail track that encircled a bend and veered left into a heavily pockmarked road that was filled with muddy water. The station was a large compound with a few wagons painted black—the colour of the Nigerian police—parked under a fabric awning whose pillars were cast in irons ballasted into the paved floors. A few young men, all of them naked to the waist, were arguing loudly somewhere under a torn fabric awning, while police officers listened. We walked straight to the reception: a huge wooden barricade. An officer was seated behind it on what must have been an elevated stool. Father asked him if he could see the Deputy Police Officer.

"Can you identify yourself, sir?" the constable at the desk replied with an unsmiling face, yawning as he spoke, dragging the last word, "sir," so that it sounded like the final word of a dirge.

"I'm Mr James Agwu, a staff member of the Central Bank of Nigeria," Father said.

Father reached into his breast pocket and showed the man a red ID card. The constable examined it. His face contorted, and then brightened. The man handed back the card with a full-faced smile, rubbing his hand around his temple.

"Oga, will you do us well?" the man said. "You know say na you be, oga."

The man's subtle request for a bribe irked Father, who was an ardent hater of all forms of corruption plaguing the Nigerian nation; he would often rail against it.

"I don't have time for this," Father said. "My child is missing."

"Ah!" the officer cried, as though suddenly faced with a grim epiphany. "So you are the father of those boys?" he asked reflexively. Then, as if suddenly realizing what he'd said, "Sorry for that, sir. Please wait, sir."

The officer called at someone and another officer emerged from the passageway, stamping his feet in an awkward way. He stamped to a halt, raised his hand to the side of his lean, swarthy face, held his fingers straight above his ear and dropped the hand against the side of his leg.

"Take him to Oga DPO's office," the first officer ordered in English.

"Yes, sir!" the junior officer cried and stamped his feet on the floor again.

The officer, who seemed oddly familiar, came forward towards us, his countenance fallen.

"I'm sorry, sir, but we will be conducting a brief search on you before you go in," he said.

He passed his hand over Father's body, up to his trouser pockets, frisking. He stared at me, seeming to scan me with his eyes for a while and then he asked if I had anything in my pocket. I shook my head. Convinced, he turned away from me and repeated the salute with his hand cupped above his ear again and cried "All correct, sir!" to the other officer.

The latter gave a curt nod and, gesturing that we follow him, ushered us into the hall.

The Deputy was a slender and very tall man with a striking facial structure. He had a broad forehead that seemed to spread wide like a slate over his face. His eyes were deep-set and his brows bulged as if swollen. He swiftly rose to his feet when we entered.

"Mr Agwu, right?" he said, stretching his hand to shake Father's.

"Yes and my son, Benjamin," Father muttered.

"Right, you're welcome. Please, sit down."

Father sat on the only chair in front of his desk and motioned that I sit on the other one by the side of the wall close to the door. The office was old-fashioned. All three cupboards in the room were filled with stacks of books and folders. A bright rod of daylight pierced through the aperture between the brown curtains in the absence of electricity. The air smelt of lavender—a smell that reminded me of my visits to Father's office when he was still working in the Akure branch of the Central Bank.

Once we'd sat, the man placed his elbows on the table, clasped his hands together and said: "Erm, Mr Agwu, I regret to say that we are yet to have a word on the location of your son." He adjusted himself in his chair, unclasped his hands and quickly put in, "But we have been making progress. We questioned someone in your neighbourhood who confirmed she saw the boy somewhere across the street that afternoon; the description she gave matched yours—the boy she saw wore blood-stained clothes."

"Which direction did she say he went?" Father asked in a flustered hurry.

"We don't know for now, but we are investigating thoroughly. Members of our team—" the Deputy began saying before breaking off to cough into his hand, slightly quivering as he did.

Father muttered "Sorry," and the man thanked him.

"I mean our team has been conducting the search," he continued after spitting into a handkerchief. "But, you know, even that will be futile if we don't attach a ransom soon. I mean to involve the people of this town to assist us." He opened a hardcover book before him and seemed to peruse it while he spoke. "With money on the ground, I am sure people will respond. If not, I mean, our efforts will be akin to sweeping the streets with a broom at night, I mean, by the dim squint of moonlight."

"I understand what you are saying, DPO," Father said after a while. "But I want to trust my instincts in this matter, and wait for your preliminary search to be completed before I go on with any personal plans of mine."

The DPO nodded rapidly.

"Something tells me he is safe somewhere," Father went on. "Perhaps he is merely hiding because of what he did."

"Yes, that might be it," the DPO said in a slightly raised voice. He seemed to be uneasy in his seat: he adjusted the chair by the hook under it, put his hands on the table and began mechanically picking sheets of paper scattered all over his table as he spoke. "You know a child and even adults—having done such a terrible thing... I mean, after killing his blood brother—would be afraid. He might be afraid of us the police, or even you his parents, of the future—of everything. There's even a chance he may have left the town entirely."

"Yes," Father said in a mournful tone, shaking his head.

"That reminds me," the policeman said with a snap of his finger. "Have you tried to reach any of your relatives in nearby places to ask—"

"Yes, but I don't think this is likely, though. My sons have rarely visited our relatives except for when they were quite small, and never once without me or their mother. And, most of our relatives are here, none of them have seen him. They came for his brother's funeral which we just concluded a few hours ago."

The DPO's eyes caught mine at that moment when I was staring at him, pondering on the heavy resemblance I thought he bore to the dark-spectacled military man in the portrait behind him—the Nigerian dictator, General Sani Abacha.

"I understand your point. We will do our best, but we hope he returns by himself—in his own time."

"We hope, too," Father said repeatedly in muffling tones. "Thank you for your efforts, sir."

The man asked Father something I did not catch, for I'd gone blank again, an image of Ikenna with the knife in his belly hovering in my mind. Father and the man stood up and shook hands, and we left the office.

* * *

Boja was also a self-revealing fungus. After four torturous days in which no one had the faintest idea of what happened to him or where he was, he showed himself. He took pity on Mother, who was almost dying of grief, or perhaps he knew Father had become worn down by it all, and could not sit in the house because Mother swore at him and blamed him incessantly. When Father drove into the compound the morning after Ikenna died, she'd run up to him, opened the door of his car, and dragged him out of the car into the rain, screaming, strangling him by the collar in the rain.

"Did I not tell you?" she cried. "Didn't I tell you they were fast slipping from my grip? Didn't I, Didn't I? Eme, did you not know that if a wall does not open its mouth by cracking, lizards cannot enter through it. Eme, didn't you?" She did not let go of him, even when Mrs Agbati, awakened by the noise, ran into the compound, pleading with Mother to let Father go inside. "I won't, no," Mother resisted, sobbing even more. "Look at us, just look, look. We opened our mouths, Eme, we opened them wide and now we have swallowed a multitude of them."

I cannot forget how Father, pressed for breath and soaking in the rain, kept the sort of calm I'd swear he was incapable of until Mother was wrested off him. Many times in the past four days, she'd tried to attack him, and was often held back by people who had come to console us. Perhaps too, Boja might have looked upon Nkem who followed Father about, wailing incessantly because Mother could not nurse her. Obembe mostly tended to David, who also cried for no reason sometimes and got hit by Mother once when he pestered her. Perhaps, Boja saw all this and pitied her and the rest of us, too. Or, perhaps he was merely forced to reveal himself because he could no longer hide. No one will ever know.

He revealed himself not long after Father and I returned from the police station. His photo, the one in which he crouched with his hand to the photographer as if he was going to knock the man over, had just popped up on the OSRC News commercials with the heading *Missing Person* immediately after a clip of the Nigerian Olympic Dream Team being mobbed as they arrived in Lagos from the United States with the men's football Olympic gold. We were eating yam and palm-oil sauce—Obembe, Father, David and me. Mother lay on the carpet in the other part of the sitting room, still dressed in all black. Nkem was in the hands of Mama Bose, the pharmacist. One of our aunties, the last of the mourners still left, but who would take the night bus back to Aba that same day, sat beside Mama Bose and Mother. Mother was talking to the two women about peace of mind, and of how people had responded to our family's grief so far while my eyes were focused on the television, where the Dream Team's Austin Jay-Jay Okocha was now shaking hands with General Abacha in Aso Rock when Mrs Agbati, a next-door neighbour, ran to our main door, screaming. She'd come to fetch water from our well, an eleven-foot well, believed to be one of the deepest in the district. Our neighbours, especially the Agbatis, often used it when their own wells dried or had insufficient water.

She threw herself at the threshold of our storm door, crying, "Ewooooh! *Ewooooh!!*"

"Bolanle, what is it?" Father asked. He'd sprung up at the woman's shout.

"He is... in the well oooooo, *Ewoooh*," Mrs Agbati managed to say between wailing and mournful wriggling on the floor.

"Who?" Father asked aloud, "what, who is in the well?"

"There, there, in the well!" the woman, whom Boja disliked and often called an *ashewo* because he said he once saw her going into the La Room motel, repeated.

"I said, who?" But as he asked, he'd begun to run out of the house. I followed, Obembe behind me.

The well, with its slightly torn metal lid, was filled with water to a level above eight feet. The neighbour's plastic bucket lay at the foot of the silt around the mouth of the well. Boja's body was floating atop the water, his clothing formed a parachute behind him, bloated like a full balloon. One of his eyes was open and could be seen beneath the surface of the clear water. The other was closed and swollen. His head was held half above the water, resting against the fading bricks of the well, while his light-skinned hands lingered on top of the water as though he was locked in an embrace with another who no one else but he could see.

This well in which he had hidden and then revealed himself had always been a part of his history, though. Two years earlier, a mother hawk—probably blind or deformed in some way—fell into the open well and drowned. The bird, like Boja, was not discovered until after many days, and so it simply lay beneath the water at first, quietly, like venom in a bloodstream. Then when its time was due, it spawned and swam upstream, but by that time, *it had started to decompose*. That incident happened around the time Boja was converted at the Great Gospel Crusade organized by the international German preacher, Evangelist Reinhard Bonnke, in 1994. After the bird was removed from the well, persuaded that if he prayed over it, it could not harm him, Boja announced he would pray over the water and drink it. He put his faith in the scripture passage "Behold, I give unto you power to tread on serpents and scorpions, and over all the power of the enemy: and nothing shall by any means hurt you." While we were waiting for the Ministry of Water Affairs officers Father had summoned to come purify the water, Boja drank a cup of it. Fearing he would die, Ikenna let the cat out of the bag, throwing our parents into a panic. Swearing he would whip Boja thoroughly afterwards, Father took him to the hospital. It was a great relief when test results showed that he was safe. So at the time, Boja conquered the well, but years later, the well conquered him. It killed him.

His form was inconceivably altered when he was pulled out. Obembe stood staring at me in horror as a mob gathered from every part of our district. In small communities in West Africa in those days, a tragic occurrence such as this travelled like a forest fire in the Harmattan. Once the woman cried out, people—both familiar and unfamiliar—started pouring into our compound until they crowded it. Unlike at the scene of Ikenna's death, neither Obembe nor I tried to stop Boja from being taken away. Obembe did not act the same way he did when, after recovering from his enchanted intoning of "river of red, river of red, river of red," he held Ikenna's head and frantically tried to pump oxygen into his mouth, beckoning, "Ike wake up, please wake up, Ike" until Mr Bode pulled him off Ikenna. This time around, with our parents present, we watched from our balcony.

There were so many people that we could barely see the unfolding scene, for the people of Akure and most small towns in West Africa were pigeons: passive creatures that grazed lazily about in marketplaces or in playgrounds waddling as if waiting for a piece of rumour or news, congregating wherever a handful of grain is poured on the ground. Everyone knew you; you knew everyone. Everyone was your brother; you were everyone's brother. It was hard to be somewhere and not see someone who knew your mother or brother. This was true of all our neighbours. Mr Agbati came wearing just a white singlet and brown shorts. Igbafe's father and mother came in same-coloured traditional attire, having just arrived from some event and not having had the chance to change clothes. There were other people, including Mr Bode. It was he who entered the well and brought Boja out. I would gather from the commentaries of the people there that he'd first climbed in with a ladder passed down and tried to pull Boja out with one hand, but Boja's dead weight refused to *come forth*. Mr Bode put his hand on the side of the well and pulled Boja up again. This time, Boja's shirt snapped under the arm, and the ladder sank lower into the well. At the sight of that, the men at the lip of the well pulled tightly at him to prevent him from sliding in. Three men held on to the last man's legs and waist. But when Mr Bode tried again, descending down the rungs of the ladder a bit lower, he pulled him out from the watery tomb in which he'd been dead for days. And like the scene when Lazarus was raised, the mob roared in approval.

But his appearance was not like that of a resurrected body, it was the unforgettable frightening image of a bloated dead. To prevent this image from imprinting on our minds, Father forced Obembe and me into the house.

"You both—sit here," he said, panting, his countenance like I had never seen it before. Sudden wrinkles had appeared on his face, and his eyes were bloodshot. He knelt down when we sat, and placing his hands on both of our thighs, said: "From this moment on, both of you will be strong men. You will be men who will look into the eyes of the world and order your ways and paths through it... with... with the sort of courage your brothers had. Do you understand?"

We nodded.

"Good," he said, nodding repeatedly and absent-mindedly.

He bowed his head and put his face between his palms. I could hear his teeth gritting in his mouth as he sustained a mechanical muttering, the only word of which we could hear being "Jesus." When he lowered his head, I saw the middle of his scalp where his baldness, unlike Grandfather's, had stopped its spurn as a mere arc of hairless portion hidden away in the midst of a ring of hair.

"Remember what you said some years ago, Obembe?" Father said, facing up again.

Obembe shook his head.

"You have forgotten,"—a wounded smile flashed across his face and wilted away—"what you said when your brother, Ike, drove the car to my office during the M.K.O. riots? Right there at the dining table," he pointed to the table which had been left in a raucous state of unfinished meals on which flies were now perching, half-drained glasses of water and a jug of warm water from which, unaware of the absence of its drinkers, vapour had continued to rise. "You asked what you would do should they die."

Obembe nodded now—like me, he'd remembered that night of June 12, 1993, when, after Father drove us home in his own car, we'd all begun in turns to tell stories of the riot at dinner. Mother told of how she and her friends ran into the nearby military barracks as the pro-M.K.O. rioters razed the market, killing anyone they thought was a northerner. When all finished, Obembe said: "What will happen to Ben and me when Ikenna and Boja grow old and die?"

Everyone burst into laughter except the little ones, Obembe and me. Although I had not thought of the possibilities till then, I considered the question a valid inquiry.

"Obembe, you will have grown old, too, by then; they are not much older than you," Father replied, squeaking with laughter.

"Okay." Obembe wavered, albeit for a moment. He kept his eyes on them, questions crowding his mind like an unbearable urge. "But what if they died?"

"Will you shut up?" Mother yelled at him. "Dear God! How can you ever allow such a thought into your head? Your brothers will not die, you hear me?" She held the lobe of her ear, and Obembe—pumped with fear—nodded affirmatively.

"Good, now eat your food!" Mother thundered.

Dejected, Obembe would drop his head and continue his meal in silence.

★ ★ ★

"Yes, now that this has happened," Father continued after our nods. "Obembe, you have to drive yourself and your younger brothers, Ben, here, and David. They will be looking up to you as their elder brother."

Obembe nodded.

"I'm not saying you should drive them in a car, no." Father shook his head. "I mean, you just lead them."

Obembe seconded his initial nod.

"Lead them," Father mumbled.

"Okay, Daddy," Obembe replied.

Father stood up and wiped his nose with his hand. The mess slid down the back of his hand, its colour like Vaseline. As I watched him, I remembered that I'd once read in the *Animal Atlas* that most eagles lay only two eggs. And that the eaglets, once hatched from the eggs, are often killed by the older chicks—especially during times of food shortages in what the book termed "the Cain and Abel syndrome." Despite their might and strength, I'd read, eagles do nothing to stop these fratricides. Perhaps these killings happen when the eagles are away from the eyrie, or when they travel camel distances to get food for the household. Then when they pick the squirrel or mouse and mount the clouds in hasty flight to their eyrie, they return only to find the eaglets—perhaps two eaglets—dead: one bloodied inside the eyrie, its dark red blood leaking through the nest, and the other swollen double, bloated and floating on a nearby pool.

"You both stay here," Father said, cutting into my thoughts. "Don't come out of here until I tell you to. Okay?"

"Yes, Daddy," we chorused.

He rose to leave, but turned slowly. I believe he started a sentence, perhaps a plea: "Please I beg you—" but that was it. He went out and left us there, both of us startled.

It was after Father left that it struck me that Boja was also a self-destructive fungus: one who inhabited the body of an organism and gradually effected its destruction. This was what he did to Ikenna. First, he sank Ikenna's spirit and then he banished his soul by making a deadly perforation through which Ikenna's blood emptied from his body and formed a red river below him. After this, like his kind, he turned against himself and killed himself.

It was Obembe who first told me that Boja killed himself. Obembe gathered from the people who'd congregated in the compound that this must have been the case, and had waited to tell me about it. And once Father left the room, he turned to me and said, "Do you know what Boja did?"

This stung me deep.

"Do you know that we drank the blood from his wound?" Obembe continued. I shook my head.

"Listen, you don't know anything. Do you not know that there was a big hole in his head? I—saw—it! And we made tea with this well water this morning, and we all drank from it."

I could not understand this, I could not understand how he might have been there all along. "If he was there, there all the time, there—" I began to say but stopped.

"Go on," Obembe said.

"If he was there all this while, there—there," I stammered.

"Go on?" he said.

"Okay, if he was there how didn't we see him in the well when we fetched water this morning?"

"Because when something drowns, they don't come up immediately. Listen, remember the lizard that fell into Kayode's water drum?"

I nodded.

"And the bird that fell into the well two years ago?"

I nodded again.

"Yes, like these; it happens that way." He gestured wearily towards the window and repeated, "Like that—it happens that way."

He stood from the chair and lay on the bed and covered himself with the *wrappa* Mother had given us, the one with the portraits of a tiger etched all over it. I watched the movement of his head as the sound of suppressed sobs came from under the covering. I sat still, glued to where I was but conscious of a gradual eruption in my bowel, where something that felt like a miniature hare was gnawing inside it. The gnawing continued until, suddenly feeling a vinegary taste in my mouth, I vomited a lump of moist food in soupy pastry on the floor. The outburst was followed by bouts of coughing. I bent to the floor and coughed out more.

Obembe jumped out of his bed towards me. "What? What happened to you?"

I tried to answer, but could not; the hare had continued scratching deeper into my bones. I gasped for breath.

"Eh, water," he said. "Let me get you some water."

I nodded.

He brought water, and sprinkled it on my face, but it felt as if I was immersed in water, as if I were drowning. I gasped as the beads trickled down my face, and frantically wiped them off.

"Are you all right?" he asked.

I nodded and mumbled: "Yes."

"You should drink some water."

He left and returned with water in a cup.

"Take, drink," he said. "And don't be afraid anymore."

When he said that, I remembered how, once, before we began fishing, while we were coming back from the football pitch, a dog leapt out of one of the skeletal rooms of an uncompleted building, and started barking at us. This dog was a lean thing, so thin its ribs could easily be numbered. Spots and fresh wounds covered its body like freckles on a pineapple. The poor beast came towards us in intermittent steps, belligerently, as though it wanted to attack. Although I loved animals, I was scared of dogs, lions, tigers and all those in the cat family, for I had read so much about how they tore people and other animals to pieces. I screamed at the sight of the dog and clasped to Boja. To quench my fear, Boja picked a stone and aimed at the dog. The stone missed the dog, but scared it so much that the dog woofed on, jutting mechanically, wagging its thin tail as it went away, marking its footprints in the dirt. Then, turning to me, he said: "The dog is gone, Ben; don't be afraid anymore." And that instant, my fear was gone.

As I drank the water Obembe had brought, I became conscious of the sudden surge in the pandemonium outside. A siren was blaring at a close distance. As the peal grew louder, voices shouted orders for people to allow "them" to come in. An ambulance had apparently arrived. A tumult overwhelmed our compound as men bore Boja's swollen body to the ambulance. Obembe rushed to watch them load Boja's corpse into the ambulance from the window of our sitting room, making sure Father did not see him and trying to keep an eye on me at the same time. He returned to me when the sirens began blaring again, this time deafeningly. I'd drunk the water and had stopped vomiting, but my mind could not stop spinning.

I thought of what Obembe had told me on the day Ikenna pushed Boja against the metal box. He'd sat quietly in a corner of our room, hugging himself as if he'd caught a cold. Then he asked if I saw what was in the pocket of Ikenna's shorts when he came into the room earlier.

"No, what was it?" I had asked him, but he merely gazed, dazed, his mouth hardly closing, so that his large incisors appeared bigger than they actually were. He went to the window, his face still filled with that look. He set his eyes outside where a long cavalcade of soldier ants was making a procession along the fence, which was still wet from the long days of rain. A piece of rag was stuck to it, dripping water in a long line that slowly slid down to the foot of the wall. A cumulus cloud hung in the horizon above the walls.

I had waited patiently for Obembe's answer, but when it became a long time coming, I asked him again.

"Ikenna had a knife—in his pocket," he answered, without turning to look at me.

I sat up and raced to him as though a beast had rammed through the wall into the room to devour me. "A knife?" I asked.

"Yes," he said, nodding. "I saw it, it was Mama's cooking knife, the one with which Boja killed the cock." He shook his head again. "I saw it," he repeated, gazing first at the ceiling—as if something there had nodded in the affirmative to confirm that he was right. "He had a knife." With his face contorting now and his voice falling, he said: "Perhaps, he wanted to kill Boja."

The ambulance's siren began to wail again, and the noise of the mob rose to a deafening pitch. Obembe withdrew from the window and came towards me.

"They have taken him," Obembe said presently in a husky voice. He repeated it as he took my hand and gently laid me down. My legs had, by that time, weakened from squatting to retch on the floor.

"Thank you," I said.

He nodded.

"I'll clean this and come lie with you, just lie there," he said and made towards the door but, as if on second thought, stopped and smiled, two blinking pearls stuck to the pupil of both eyes.

"Ben," he called.

"Eh."

"Ike and Boja are dead." His jaw wobbled, his lower lip pouted as the two pearls slid down, marking their trails with twin liquid lines.

Because I did not know what to make of what he said, I nodded. He turned and left the room.

I closed my eyes while he packed the mess with the dustpan, my mind filled with the imagination of how Boja had died, of how—according to what they said—he'd killed himself. I imagined him standing over Ikenna's corpse after the stabbing, wailing, having suddenly realized that by that singular action, he had plundered his own life in one single haul like a cave of ancient riches. He must have seen it, must have thought about what the future held in stock for him and dreaded it. It must have been these thoughts that birthed the heinous courage that administered the suicidal idea like morphine into his mind's vein, starting off its slow death. With his mind dead, it must have been easy to move his legs, carry his body, fear and uncertainty sewing his mind thread-by-thread, the bulge thickening, the loom pilling until he made the plunge—head first, like a diver, the way he always dived into the river, the Omi-Ala. At once, he must have felt a rush of air flood his eyes as he dipped, quietly, without a slight moan or a word spoken. There must have been no increased throbbing and no increased pulse in his heart as he dipped; rather, he must have maintained a curious calm and tranquillity. In that state of mind, he must have glimpsed an illusory epiphany, a montage of images of his past that must have consisted of still images of a five-year-old Boja mounted on the high branch of the tangerine tree in our compound, singing Baltimora's "Tarzan Boy"; five-year-old Boja with a bowl of excreta in his pants when he was asked to stand before the entire school morning assembly and lead the school in the Lord's Prayer; ten-year-old Boja who acted as Joseph the Carpenter, husband of Mary the mother of Jesus in our church's Christmas play of 1992 and said: "Mary, I will not marry you because you're an *ashewo*!" to the astonishment of all; Boja, who was told by M.K.O. never to fight, *don't ever!*; and Boja who, earlier in the year, was a zealous Fisherman. These images may have assembled in his mind like a swarm of bees in a hive as he dipped lower until he hit the bottom of the well. The contact dashed the hive and scattered the images.

The plunge, I pictured, must have been quick. As his head sank, it must have first hit the rock that protruded from the side of the well. This contact must have then been followed in succession by the sound of bursting, of crashing skull, of breaking bones, of blood purling, then spilling and swirling in his head. His brain must have scattered into smithereens, the veins that connected it to other parts of his head uncoupling. His tongue must have thrust out of his mouth at the moment of the contact, tearing his eardrums apart like an antique veil, and pouring a tenth of his teeth into the floor of his mouth like a pack of dice. A synchrony of noiseless reactions must have followed this. For a short time, his mouth must have kept uttering something inaudible, like a pot of boiling water bubbling as his body convulsed. This must have been the peak of it all. The convulsion must have started to gradually let go of him, calm returning to his bones. Then a peace not of this world must have descended on him, calming him to deadly stillness.

11

THE SPIDERS

When a mother is hungry, she says:
"Roast something for my children that they may eat."

ASHANTI PROVERB

Spiders were beasts of grief:

Creatures whom the Igbo believes nest in the houses of the aggrieved, spinning more webs and weaving noiselessly, achingly, until their yarns bulged and covered vast spaces. They appeared as one of the many things that changed in this world after my brothers died. In the first week after their deaths, I went about with the feeling that a fabric awning or an umbrella under which we'd sheltered all along was torn apart, leaving me exposed. I began to remember my brothers, to think of minute details of their lives, as if through the telescope of hindsight that magnified every detail, every little act, every event. But it was not my world alone that was changed after the incidents. We all—Father, Mother, Obembe, me, David and even Nkem—suffered differently, but in the first few weeks after their deaths, Mother emerged as the greatest sufferer.

Spiders built temporary shelters and nested in our home as the Igbo people believe they do when people mourn, but they took their invasion a step further and invaded our mother's mind. Mother was the first to notice the spiders and the bulging orbs clipped by thread-like fangs to the roof; but that was not all. She began seeing Ikenna spying on us from the carapace of the spiders hanging in the orbs, or saw his eyes looking through the spirals. She complained about them: *Ndi ajo ife*—These beastly, scaly, terrifying creatures. They scared her. They made her weep, pointing at the spiders, until Father—in a bid to soothe her, and having been mightily pressed by Mama Bose, a pharmacist, and Iya Iyabo to hearken to the voice of a grieving woman no matter how absurd he might consider her request—dislodged every webbed abode in the house and smashed several spiders dead against the walls. Then, he also drove out wall geckos, and drew battle lines against cockroaches, whose proliferation was fast becoming a menace. Only then was peace restored; but it was a peace with swollen feet and a limp in its gait.

For soon after the spiders left, Mother began to hear voices from the edge. She suddenly became conscious of the perpetual manoeuvres of an army of biting termites that she perceived had infested her brain and had begun gnawing at the grey matter. She told people who came to comfort her that Boja had forewarned her in a dream that he would die. She frequently recounted the strange dream she had the morning Ikenna and Boja died to the neighbours and church members who swarmed like bees to our home in the days succeeding the deaths, pegging the dreams to the tragedy because the people of that area, and even all of Africa, very strongly believed that when the fruit of a woman's womb—her child—dies, or is about to, she somehow obtains prescient knowledge of it.

The first day I heard Mother recount this experience— on the eve of Ikenna's funeral—the reaction that followed it had moved me. Mama Bose, the pharmacist, threw herself on the floor in a loud wail. "Ohhh, that must have been God warning you," she moaned as she rolled from one end of the floor to the other. "It must have been God warning you it was going to happen, *ooooo, eeeyyyy*." Her ejaculation of pain and sorrow was uttered in wordless groans that consisted of jarred vowels stretched to precipitous levels—sometimes totally meaningless, but the nuance of which everyone there perfectly understood. What gripped those who were there even more was what Mother did after telling the story. She stood near the Central Bank calendar that hung on the wall still open to the eagle's page—to May—because no one had remembered to change it during the terrible weeks of Ikenna's metamorphosis. Raising both hands up, Mother cried: "*Elu na ala*—Heaven-and-earth, look at my hands and see that they are clean. Look, look at the scar of their birth, it has not yet healed and now they are dead." When she said this, she raised her blouse and pointed below her navel. "Look at the breasts they sucked; they are still full, but they are no more." She pulled up her blouse—apparently to show her breasts—but one of the women rushed forward spryly to pull it back down. Too late, for almost everyone in the room had already seen it: the two vein-strewn breasts with prominent nipples—in broad daylight.

The first time I heard Mother tell this account, I'd felt a gripping fear that I might have received a clearer warning in the dream of the bridge if only I'd known dreams could be warnings. I told my brother the dream after Mother recounted hers, and he said it was a warning. Mother recounted that dream again to the pastor of our church, Pastor Collins, and his wife a week or so after that. Father was not home at the time. He'd gone to buy petrol at the filling station on the outskirts of the town.

The government had increased fuel price the week Boja was found from twelve naira to twenty-one naira, sending filling stations to hoard petrol and resulting in long, endless queues at stations all over the country. Father stayed in one of them from afternoon until early evening before returning with his car tank full, a cask full of kerosene in the trunk. Tired, he made straight for one of the lounges, his "throne" one, and sank into it. He was still removing his sweaty shirt when Mother began telling him about all the people that had called that day. Although she sat beside him, she was oblivious of the strong odour of palm wine that had returned with him like flies trailing a cow with a fresh wound. She spoke on for a long time until he cried out "Enough!"

"I said enough!" he repeated, already on his feet, his bare arms bursting with sinews as he stood over Mother, who had stiffened and clasped her hands on her thighs. "What is this rubbish you are even telling me, eh, *my friend*? Has my house now become a stray zoo for every kind of living thing in this town? How many people will come to commiserate? The dogs will soon come, then the goats, the frogs, and even the puffy-cheeked cats. Do you not know that some of these people are simply nothing but mourners who cry louder than the bereaved? Will there be no limit?"

Mother did not answer him. She dropped her eyes to her thigh that was covered in a faded *wrappa*, shaking her head as she stared at it. By the light of the kerosene lantern on the table in front of them, I saw her eyes filling up with tears. I have come to believe that that confrontation was the needle that poked her psychic wound and it started bleeding from that day. She stopped talking, and the silence that would numb her entire world began. From then on, she sat in the house, silent, staring wildly at nothing in particular. Most times when Father spoke to her, she stared merely at him as if she had heard nothing at all. This tongue, which was now frozen, used to produce words as fungi produced spores. When agitated, words often sprang like tigers from her mouth, and poured like leaks from a broken pipe when sober. But from that night onwards, words pooled in her brain but only very little leaked out; they congealed in her mind. But when Father—fretting over the silence—pestered her daily, she broke the regime of silence and complained frequently about a presence she perceived to be that of Boja's restless spirit. By the last few days of September, the complaints had become a daily nagging that Father could no longer take.

"How can a city woman be this superstitious?" he burst out one morning after Mother had told him she'd felt Boja standing in the kitchen while she was cooking. "Just how, *my friend*?"

Mother's ire was sparked profoundly; she went into a fury. "How dare you tell me this, Eme?" she screamed back at him. "How dare you? Am I not the mother of these kids? Can I not know when their spirits disturb me?"

She wiped her wet hands on her *wrappa* as Father, grinding his teeth, grabbed the remote control, and amped the volume of the television until the voice of the Yoruba actor's incantations threatened to drown out Mother's voice.

"You can pretend you are not listening to me," she taunted, slapping her hands together. "But you cannot pretend our children died the way they should have. Eme, you and I know they didn't! Just go out and see. *A na eme ye eme*—it isn't the norm, anywhere. Parents should not bury their own kids; it should be the other way around!"

Although the television was still on and a movie effect was blaring like a siren from the screen, Mother's words wrapped the room with a quilt of silence. Outside, the horizon was covered with a grey mist of heavy clouds. Just as Mother sank into one of the lounges, after she finished speaking, blasts of thunder ripped through the sky, sending a whoosh of rain-soaked wind that slammed the kitchen door shut. Power vanished in an instant, throwing the room into near darkness. Father closed the windows, but left the curtain for the light that still could be got from outside. He returned to his seat, silent, surrounded by legions bred by Mother's words.

* * *

Mother's space in the room of existence gradually shrank as days passed. She became encircled by ordinary words, common tropes, familiar songs, all of which transformed into fiends whose sole purpose was the obliteration of her being. Nkem's familiar body, long arms and long plaited hair—all of which she used to adore—suddenly became abhorrent. And once, when Nkem attempted to sit on her lap, she called her "this thing trying to mount my lap," scaring away the little girl. Father, who was fixed in the world of the *Guardian* at the time, was alarmed.

"Gracious me! Are you serious, Adaku?" he asked in horror. "Was it Nkem you treated that way?"

Father's words caused a drastic change in Mother's countenance. As if she'd been blind and had suddenly regained her sight, she gazed at Nkem with weedy scrutiny, her mouth agape. Then, glancing from Nkem to Father and back again, she mumbled "Nkem" with her tongue darting about in her mouth as if it were unhinged. She looked up again, and said: "This is Nkem, my daughter" in a way that seemed as if she were—all at once—making a statement while asking and suggesting it at the same time.

Father stood there as if both his feet were nailed to the ground. Although his mouth opened, he did not speak.

When Mother again said: "I did not know it was her," all he did was nod, and, lifting Nkem, who was wailing and sucking her thumb to his chest, quietly walked out of the house.

In reply, Mother began to cry.

"I did not know it was her," she said.

The next day, Father made breakfast while Mother, dressed in sweaters as if sick with a cold, sobbed on her bed and refused to rise. She lay there all day until nightfall, when she emerged from her room while we were all seated, watching television with Father.

"Eme, do you see the white cow grazing here?" she asked, pointing around the room.

"What, what cow?"

She threw her head backwards and laughed throatily. Her lips were dry and cracked.

"Can't you see the cow eating the grass there?" she demanded, opening her palm.

"Which cow, *my friend*?" She'd said it with so much conviction in her eyes that Father, for a moment, looked around the room as though he expected that a cow might actually be in it.

"Eme, have you gone blind? Is it that you can't see that shiny white cow?"

She pointed at me seated on a lone chair with its cushion on my lap. I could not believe it. I was so surprised that when she pointed, I'd turned back to see—as if it was possible—if a cow was behind the chair in which I sat; then I realized that Mother had actually pointed at me.

"Look at one there, and one there"—she went on, pointing at Obembe and David—"and one is eating outside while one is in this room—they are grazing everywhere. Eme, why can't you see them?"

"Will you shut up?" Father roared. "What are you talking about? Good gracious! When did your children become cows grazing in our house?"

He grabbed her and shoved her towards the master bedroom. She staggered, her braided hair pouring over her face, and her massive breasts dancing in her ash-coloured sweater.

"Leave me, leave me, let me watch the shiny white cows," she shouted as they struggled.

"Shut up!" Father cried in response every time she spoke.

Her voice shrieked awkwardly as Father pushed her forwards. Nkem broke into a wail at the sight of their struggle. Obembe reached for her and carried Nkem, but her legs danced against him, as she wailed even louder for Mother. Father dragged Mother to their room and locked the door. They stayed there for a long time, their voices intermittently audible. Finally, Father came out and asked us to go to our room. He asked David and Nkem to stay with us a bit while he went to get us bread. It was about six in the evening. They agreed, but once we locked our door, we heard the prolonged sound of feet shuffling, the door slamming against the wall, the frantic cry of "Eme, leave me alone, leave me, where are you taking me to?" and the sound of Father's laboured breathing. Then the main door shut with a loud bang.

Mother vanished for two weeks. She was, as I would find out later, in a psychiatric hospital, tucked away as if she were a dangerous explosive material. There had been a cataclysmic explosion of her mind, and her perception of the known world had been blasted into smithereens. Her senses became imbued with extraordinary sensitivity so that to her ears the sound of the clock in her ward became noisier than the din of a drilling machine. The sound of a rat came to her as the peal of many bells.

She developed a destructive nyctophobia, so that every night became a pregnant mother that birthed litters of terrors that haunted her. Big things shrunk to incredible smallness while small things bulged, bloated, and turned monstrous. Animated Achara leaves with long, giant prickly stalks—and with the preternatural power to grow by the minute—suddenly surrounded her, and began to slowly squeeze her out of existence. As visions of this plant—and of the forest she became persuaded she was in—tormented her, she began to see more things. Her father, who was blasted to bits by artillery fire while fighting on the Biafran Front during the civil war in 1969, came frequently to dance in the centre of the hospital room. Most times, he danced with two hands in the air—his before-the-war body. And at other times—the times she screamed the loudest—he came to dance in his during/after-the-war body, with one movable hand and the other, a stump of bloodied flesh. Sometimes, he lured her, with endearments, to join him. But of all these, the visions of invasive spiders ruled supreme. And by the end of her second week at the institution, every speck of spider web had been removed from the vicinity and every spider smashed to bits. And it seemed that with every spider smashed, by every inky smear on the wall, she drew closer to healing.

The days she was away were difficult. Nkem cried almost perpetually, refusing to be pacified. I tried many times to sing her songs—lullabies that Mother often sang to her, but she would have none of them. My brother's attempts were also mere Sisyphean rituals. When Father returned one morning and saw Nkem in this state of helpless grief, he announced that he would take us to see Mother. Nkem's wailing instantly ceased. Before we left, Father, who had been making all the meals since the morning Mother left, made breakfast—bread and fried eggs. After breakfast, Obembe followed him to Igbafe's compound to fetch buckets of water—our well was still locked up since Boja was dragged out of it. Then one after the other, we bathed and dressed. Father wore a big white T-shirt with a neck that had yellowed from washing. He'd grown an unusual amount of beard, completely changing his appearance. We all followed him to the car, Obembe sat in front with him, and David, Nkem and I, in the back seat. He did not say anything; he merely locked the door, wound down the window and started the ignition.

He drove in silence through the street that was, on that morning, alive and bustling. We took the road around the big stadium from which the floodlights and innumerable Nigerian flags were flying. The great statue of Okwaraji which had always inspired awe in me loomed above this part of the town. As I gazed at it, I noticed a huge slate-black bird resembling a vulture, perched on top of its head. We drove up the right side of the two-way lane leading out of our street until we reached the small open market on the clearing beyond the shoulder of the road. The car slowed down, negotiating the unpaved stretch of road littered with dirt. The carcass of a hen lay on one side of the lane, flattened against the asphalt, its feathers scattered about. A few metres away from there I saw a dog dining on the contents of a split-open bag of trash, its head lost in the bag. From here, the car moved carefully between heavy-duty trucks and semis wedged on both sides of the road. Beggars holding up placards advertising their plights—*I am blind, please help me*, or, *Lawrence Ojo, a burn victim needs your assistance*—stood like guards of honour on both sides of the open-market pathway. One of them, a man I recognized by virtue of having seen him everywhere in our street—by the church, around the post office, near my school, and even in the market—crawled by on a small slate with rollers, his hands gloved with shrunken flip-flops. Passing the Ondo State Radio Station, we merged awkwardly into the round traffic circle in the centre of Akure, in the midst of which were statues of three men beating traditional talking drums. Around the concrete platter under the statutes were cacti striving with small weeds.

Father parked in front of the yellow building, and sat a moment in the car as though he'd just realized he had made a mistake. Just then, I noticed why Father had made this diversion. Alighting from a car just in front of us was a group of people surrounding a middle-aged man who was laughing crazily and dangling his large penis that stuck out from between his zippers. This man would have passed for Abulu were he not fairer in complexion and better looking. Once Father saw the man, he turned to us at once and said aloud, "Ngwa, close your eyes and let us pray for Mama—quickly!"

He turned back at once and saw me still gazing at the man.

"All of you close your eyes now!" he barked. He watched to ensure we'd all complied and then said, "Benjamin, lead us in prayer."

"Yes, Daddy," I replied, clearing my throat, and began praying in English, the only language in which I knew how to pray. "In Jesus' name, Lord God, I ask that you help us... bless us, oh God, please heal Mama, you who healed the sick, Lazarus and all, let her stop talking like a madwoman in Jesus' name we have prayed."

The rest chorused "Amen!"

By the time we opened our eyes, the group had reached the entrance of the hospital, but still visible was the dust-caked fundament of the deranged man as he was being forced into the hospital. Father came to the back-seat door and opened it from where I sat, Nkem sandwiched between David and me.

"Listen, *my friends*," he began, his bloodshot eyes peering down into our faces. "Number one: your mother is not a madwoman. Listen, all of you, when you enter there, do not look left or right; just face straight ahead of you. Whatever you see within these halls will remain in your mind. I will give anyone who misbehaves a Guerdon once we get home."

We all nodded in agreement. Then, one after the other, we alighted with Obembe leading, Father beside him, I at the back. We walked through the long line of flowers to the entrance of the big building whose floors were fully tiled and smelt of lavender. We entered a large hall full of people chattering. I tried not to look, so as not to get whipped, but I could not resist. So when I thought Father was not looking, I diverged to the left, my eyes falling on a pale girl with a thin long neck that moved mechanically as though she were a robot. Her tongue stuck halfway almost interminably out of her mouth and her hair was so thin and pale her scalp could be glimpsed. I was horrified. When I turned back to Father, he was taking a blue tag from the white-uniformed woman across the counter and saying: "Yes, they are all her children, they shall come with me."

When he said this, the woman behind the glass counter rose to her feet and looked at us.

"Her children," Father mumbled.

"Are you sure they can see her in this condition?" the woman asked.

She was light-complexioned, clothed in a white pinafore. Her nursing cap sat solidly on her beautifully oiled hair and the clipped tag on the top of her breast read: *Nkechi Daniel*.

"I believe it will be okay," Father mumbled. "I have carefully weighed the consequences and believe I can manage it."

Not satisfied, the woman shook her head.

"We have regulations here, sir," she said. "But please give me one minute, let me ask my boss."

"All right," Father agreed.

While we waited there, clustered around Father, I could not let go of the feeling that the eyes of the pale girl were set on me. In turn, I tried to focus on a calendar on the wooden wall of the small room behind the counter, and on the many photos of medicine and medical instructions. One of them was the silhouetted portrait of a pregnant woman with a child on her back and two toddlers on both sides of her. A little distance in front of her was a man who was apparently her husband. He had a child sitting on his shoulder and one about my height was before them carrying a raffia basket. I could not see the writing below it, but I could guess what it was—one of the numerous ads in the aggressive government campaign for birth control.

The nurse returned and said, "Okay, you may all go in, Mr Agwu; ward thirty-two. *Chukwu che be unu.*"

"*Da-alu*—Thank you, nurse," Father said in reply to her Igbo, bowing slightly.

The Mother we saw in ward thirty-two was vacant-eyed, and sat in an emaciated body that was packed into a black blouse she had been wearing since the day Ikenna died. She'd become so frail and pale that I almost cried out in shock. I wondered, at the sight of her, if this horrible place sucked out the flesh of human beings and deflated large buttocks. That her hair was messy and dirty, her lips flaking and dried, and that she looked so changed, greatly horrified me. Father went to her, as Nkem cried out, "Mama, Mama."

"Adaku," he said, putting his arms around her, but Mother did not even turn. She kept staring at the naked ceiling, at the unmoving ceiling fan in the centre of it, and at the corners of the walls. As she stared, she whispered in silent, cautious, knowing tones "*Umu ugeredide, umu ugeredide*—the spiders, the spiders."

"Nwuyem, which spiders again, have they not all been removed?" He looked around at the edges of the ceiling. "Where did you find them now?"

She continued her whispering, her hands clasped to her chest as though she did not hear him.

"Why are you doing this to us—your children and me?" Father said as Nkem's wailing soared. Obembe lifted her but she struggled with him, kicking wildly at his knees until he dropped her.

Father made to sit beside Mother on the bed, but she pulled away, crying "Leave me! Go away! Leave me alone!"

"I should leave you, eh?" Father asked, rising to his feet. His face had turned colourless and the veins at the side of his head had become deeply pronounced. "Look at you, look at the way you're pining away before the eyes of the rest of your children. Ada, do you not know that there is nothing the eye can see that can make it shed the tears of blood? Do you not know that there is no loss we cannot overcome?" He gestured at her with a splayed-out palm rising from her head to her feet.

"Pine away, go on and pine away."

I noticed then that David was standing there beside me, his hand on my shirt. When I looked, I saw that he was about to cry. I felt a sudden need to hold him to stop his tears. I pulled him closer and held him. I sniffed the olive oil with which I'd oiled his head that morning and thought of how Ikenna used to bathe me when I was a little boy and hold me by the hand on the way to our primary school. I was a shy child, who was very scared of the teachers because of their canes, and would not raise my hand when pressed to say: "Excuse me, ma, I want to go and *pupu*." I would rather raise my voice instead and cry as loud as I could in Igbo so that Boja, whose classroom was partitioned from mine by just a wooden wall, could hear me say: "Brother Boja, *achoro mi iyun insi*." Boja would rush out of his class, and take me to the latrine while his classmates and mine were thrown into a fit of laughter. He would wait for me to finish, clean me up and return me to the class, where most of those times, I would be asked to stretch my palms out in front of everyone and the teacher would whip me on them for disrupting the class. This happened many times, and in all of those times, Boja did not once complain.

★ ★ ★

Father did not let Obembe and me return to the hospital. He sometimes took Nkem and David along with him to see Mother only after they'd disturbed him beyond what he could bear. She was tucked away for three more weeks. Those days were cold and unnatural, even the wind that blew every night seemed to croon like a dying animal. Then, in late October, the Harmattan—a season when the dry dusty wind from the Sahara desert of northern Nigeria travelled south and covered most of sub-Saharan

Africa—seemed to have appeared overnight, leaving a thick, heavy fog to hang suspended in patches of cumulus awnings over Akure like a spectral presence even into sunrise. Father drove into the compound with Mother at his side in the car. She'd been away for five weeks, and had doubly shrunk. Her fair colour had darkened as though she had tanned without ceasing for innumerable days. Her hands had become spotted with scars from intravenous punctures, and on one of her thumbs was a plaster stuffed with much cotton wool. While it was obvious that she would not be the same again, it was hard to comprehend the enormity of what had happened to her.

Father guarded her like the egg of a rare bird and would often shoo us—David mostly—away from her as if we were gnats. Only Nkem was allowed to hover around her. He relayed messages from her to us and hurried her off to their room when people came to visit. He'd kept her condition secret from people except his closest friends, and lied to neighbours most of the time that she had travelled to our village near Umuahia to stay with her family to regain strength from the loss of her children. He'd warned us in the strictest terms, and with his hands pulling at the lobes of his ears, not to mention Mother's illness to anyone. "Even the mosquito singing beside your ear must not hear it," he'd warned. He continued to cook all the meals afterwards, serving her first and then us. He ran the home alone.

Then, almost one week after her return, we caught phrases from what seemed to have been an intense argument carried out in whispers and behind closed doors. Obembe and I had gone to the cinema near the post office earlier, and when we returned, we found Father carrying out cartons in which Ikenna had stored many of his books and drawings. At the place where we played football, most of our brothers' belongings were already stacked in a growing heap. When Obembe asked him why he wanted to burn them, Father replied that Mother had insisted that their things be burned. She did not want the curse on them—Abulu's curse—to be transferred to the rest of us via contact with their possessions. He did not turn to look at us while he explained, and when he finished, he shook his head and went back to the house to take more things until the room was emptied. Ikenna's study table had been pushed against the purple wall that was covered with pencil sketches and watercolour paintings. His bent chair was placed on the top of it. Father went out with the last of Boja's bags, and poured out their contents into the heap. He kicked in Ikenna's old guitar, which had been given to him by a Rastafarian musician who used to entertain people on the street when Ikenna was a child.

That man, with dreadlocks that stretched to his chest, would often render Lucky Dube and Bob Marley, drawing a large audience from neighbourhood kids and adults. He often sang under the coconut tree in front of our gate and Ikenna would—against our parents' warning—dance to entertain the audience. He would become known as "Rasta Boy," a designation that Father exorcised by the power of a smarting Guerdon.

We watched as Father sprinkled kerosene on the heap from the red can, every drop we had left in the house. Then, with a few glances at Mother, he struck the match. The heap lighted and a burst of smoke exploded into the air. As the fire gnawed the belongings of Ikenna and Boja and the things they had touched while on earth, the sense of their end filled my body with a thousand tacks. Vividly do I recall how one of Boja's favourite garments, a kaftan, struggled with the fire. It first spread out from its compressed state when the fire caught it as if it were a living thing struggling for life, then it slowly began to tilt backwards, wilting, as it dissolved into black ash. I heard Mother's sobs, and looked back. I saw she had come out of the room and was now sitting on the ground a few metres from the heap with Nkem squatted beside her. Father stood for long beside the heap, the empty can of kerosene in his hand, wiping his rheumy eyes and his dirtied face.

Obembe and I stood beside him. When he noticed Mother, he dropped the can and went to her.

"Nwuyem," he said, "I told you this grief will pass— eh. We cannot continue to grieve forever. I've told you that we cannot flip precedence. We cannot bring forward what is behind, nor can we bring what is forward back. It is enough, Adaku, I beg you. I'm here now, we will get through this together."

A flock of birds, barely visible in the approaching darkness, had begun to circle the skyward smoke. The sky above us had now become the colour of bright fire, and the trees, now turned into mere silhouettes, appeared like uncanny witnesses of the burning as the ashes of Ikenna's briefcase, Boja's bags, their clothes, their shoes, Ikenna's bad guitar, their M.K.O. writing books, their photographs, notebooks with sketches of Yoyodon, tadpoles, the Omi-Ala River, their fishing clothes, one of the tins we'd hoped to store fish in but never used, their toy guns, their alarm clock, their drawing books, their matchboxes, their underpants, their shirts, their trousers—all the things they once had or touched—rose in a cloud of smoke, and vanished into the sky.

THE SEARCHDOG

O bembe was a searchdog:
The one who first discovered things, who knew things and who, after discovering them, examined them. He was perpetually pregnant with ideas, and in the fullness of time, delivered them as creatures equipped with wings—able to fly.

It was he who first found that there was a loaded pistol behind the sitting-room shelf two years after we moved into our house in Akure. He'd found the gun while chasing a small housefly around our room. The fly had droned over him, and escaped two frantic blows with the *Simple Algebra* textbook Obembe swiftly employed for the purpose of killing it. The fly leapt up after the last miss and glided into the space on the shelf where the television, VHS and radio were set in their various columns. When he chased the fly there, he let out a scream, dropping the book. We had just moved into the house and no one had looked behind the shelf to see the barrel of the pistol slightly sticking out from under it. Father would pick the pistol up and take it to the police station, petrified as all of us were, but thankful that it was not found by one of the younger children, David or Nkem.

Obembe's eyes were a searchdog's.

Eyes that noticed little things, negligible details others overlooked. I have come to believe he had an inkling that Boja was in the well long before Mrs Agbati found him there. For the morning she found Boja, Obembe had discovered that the water from the well was greasy, and had a foul odour. He'd fetched it to bathe and had noticed a slick on the surface of the water in the bucket. He called me to see it and when I scooped the water in my hand, I spat and threw away the water. I'd perceived the smell, too—the smell of rot, or of dead matter—but had not been able to tell what it was.

It was he who unravelled the mystery about what happened to Boja's corpse, since we did not attend his burial. There were no posters, no visits, not a single sign of his funeral. I'd wondered and asked my brother when it would be done, but he did not know and did not want to question our parents, the two ventricles of our home.

Although he did not raise any alarm at the time or push further, were it not for him, I would never have known what became of Boja's body after his death. On the first Saturday of November, a week after Mother returned from the psychiatric hospital, he found something I had not noticed before although it had been on the top shelf in the sitting room, behind a framed portrait of our parents on their wedding day in 1979, all along. Obembe showed me a small transparent jar that sat on that shelf. In it was a polythene bag containing something ash-coloured and grey like loamy sand dug from under dead logs of wood and dried in the sun to fine grains the size of salt. I noticed, just as I reached for it, that it was tagged: *Boja Agwu (1982—1996)*.

When we confronted Father a few days afterwards, Obembe saying he knew the strange substance was Boja's ashes in the jar, Father, staggered, gave up. He and Mother, he revealed, had been warned strictly by clansmen and relatives that Boja should not be buried. It was a sacrilege to Ani, goddess of the earth, for a person who committed suicide or fratricide to be interred in the earth. Although Christianity had almost cleanly swept through Igbo land, crumbs and pieces of the African traditional religion had eluded the broom. Stories came from time to time from our village and from clansmen in diasporas, about mysterious mishaps—even deaths, owing to punishments from the gods of the clan. Father, who did not believe a goddess would punish him or that such a contraption "by illiterate minds" existed, decided not to bury him just for Mother's sake, and because he'd already had a dose of tragedies. They did not say a word to my brother and me, and we did not know about this, until Obembe, the searchdog, found out.

*   *   *

Obembe's mind was a searchdog's: a restless mind that was always engaged in the search for knowledge. He was a question-asking person—an inquirer, who read widely to feed his mind. The lantern, the tool with which he read, was his greatest companion. Before my brothers died, we had three kerosene lanterns in the house. A sprocket-controlled wick dipped into their small fuel tanks to absorb the kerosene. Because there was a perennially erratic power supply in Akure in those days, Obembe read with one of the three lanterns every night. After the death of our brothers, he began to read as if his life depended on it. Like an omnivorous animal, he stored the information he garnered from these books in his mind. Then, after he had processed and pruned it down to the essentials, he passed it on to me in the form of stories he told me every night before we slept.

Before our brothers died, he told me the story of a princess who followed a perfect gentleman of great beauty to the heart of a forest insisting she'd marry him only to discover the man was merely a skull who'd borrowed the flesh and body parts of others. That story, as all good stories, planted a seed in my soul and never left me. During the days Ikenna was a python, Obembe told me of Odysseus, king of Ithaca, from the simplified copy of the Odyssey of Homer, forever inscribing in my mind images of the Poseidon seas and the deathless gods. He mostly told me the stories at night-time, in the near darkness of the room, and I gradually burrowed into the world his words created.

Two nights after Mother returned from hospital, we were seated on the bed in our room, our backs against the wall, drifting off to sleep. Suddenly, my brother said: "Ben, I know why our brothers died." He snapped his fingers and rose up, clutching his head. "Listen, I just—I just discovered."

He sat down again and began telling me a long story he once read in a book whose title he could not recall, but which, he was sure, had been written by an Igbo. I listened as my brother's voice soared above the rattling ceiling fan. When he finished, he fell silent, while I tried to process the story of the strong man, Okonkwo, who was reduced to committing suicide by the wiles of the white man.

"You see, Ben," he said, "the people of Umuofia were conquered because they were not united."

"It's true," I said.

"The white men were a common enemy that would have been easily conquered if the tribe had fought as one. Do you know why our brothers died?"

I shook my head.

"The same way—because there was a division between them."

"Yes," I muttered.

"But do you know why Ike and Boja were divided?" He suspected I didn't have an answer, so he did not wait long; he went on. "Abulu's prophecy; they died because of Abulu's prophecy."

He put his fingers on the back of his left hand and scratched absent-mindedly, not seeing the white lines that had formed on his dry skin. We sat in silence for a while afterwards, my mind drifting backwards as though I were skating a sharp steep slope.

"Abulu killed our brothers. He is our enemy."

His voice seemed to have cracked and his words came forth like a whisper from the end of a cave. Although I knew Ikenna was transformed by Abulu's curse, I had not thought he was directly involved the way my brother now phrased it. I had never thought the madman could be blamed directly even when I could see signs that it was he who planted the fear in my brother. But when my brother now said it, it occurred to me that it was true. As I pondered this, Obembe lifted his legs to his chest to hug them, dragging off the bed sheet so that a part of the mattress became exposed. Then, turning to me and planting one hand on the bed so that it sank down to the springboard, he slugged his fist into the air and said: "I will kill Abulu."

"Why would you do that?" I gasped.

He let his eyes, which were fast clouding with tears, navigate my face for a little and said: "I will do it for them because he killed our brothers. I will do it for them."

Dumbfounded, I watched him go to lock the door first, then to the window. He dipped his hand in his short pocket. Then came flashes of two attempts to light a match. The third time, it clicked and a small light sparked and disappeared. I was shocked. In its wake, the silhouetted form of him put a cigarette in his mouth, smoke wafting upwards and out into the dark night. I nearly jumped out of bed. I had not known, could not have imagined, could not tell how or what had happened. "A cigare——" I quavered.

"Yes, but shut up, it is nothing to you."

In a flip, his silhouette had become a force that massed before me by the bed, the smoke from his cigarette rising steadily over his head.

"If you tell them," he said, his eyes filled with so much darkness, "you will only increase their pain."

He blew the smoke out of the window as I watched in horror at the sight of my brother, only two years older than me, smoking and sobbing like a child.

★ ★ ★

The things my brother read shaped him; they became his visions. He believed in them. I have now come to know that what one believes often becomes permanent, and what becomes permanent can be indestructible. This was the case with my brother. After he broke his plan to me, he detached from me and developed his ideas every day, smoking at night. He read more, sometimes up in the tangerine tree in the backyard. He rejected my inability to be brave for my brothers, and complained that I was not willing to learn from *Things Fall Apart* and fight against our common enemy: Abulu the madman.

Even though our father tried to restore us back to the days before he moved out of Akure—the egg-white days of our lives—my brother remained unmoved. He was not endeared by the new movies Father brought home—new Chuck Norris movies, a new James Bond movie, one titled *Waterworld*, and even a movie played by Nigerians, *Living in Bondage*.

Because he read somewhere that if someone drew a sketch of any problem and visualized its complete make-up, they could solve that problem, he spent most of the day drawing matchstick men portraits of his plans to avenge our brothers, while I sat and read. I stumbled on them one day, about a week after our altercation, and was frightened. In the first, drawn with sharpened pencil, Obembe hurls stones at Abulu, who then falls and dies.

In another, set in the area outside the escarpment where Abulu's truck sat, Obembe brandishes a knife, his matchstick legs captioned in the motion of walking with me following him. There are distant trees and pigs brooding nearby. Then in the truck, through the transparent capture of the goings-on inside it, his own matchstick man portrait decapitates Abulu—*like Okonkwo killed the court messenger.*

NIGHT.

ME WITH KNIFE. THE DECREPIT TRUCK. THE PIG MIRE

I KILL HIM, AND CUT OFF HIS HEAD LIKE OKONKWO KILLED THE COURT MESSENGER.

The sketches terrified me. I held the paper and examined it, my hands trembling, when he came in from the toilet after having been gone for about ten minutes.

"Why are you looking at that?" he cried in fury. He pushed me and I fell into the bed with the paper still in my hand.

"Give that to me," he raged.

I threw the paper at him and he took it from the floor.

"Don't ever touch anything on this table again," he roared. "Do you hear me, you blockhead?"

I lay in the bed, shielding my face with my hand from fear that he might hit me, but he merely put the papers in his closet and covered them with his clothes. Then he went to the window and stood there. Outside, in the next house hidden by a high fence, the voices of children playing reached our ears. We knew most of the children. Igbafe, one of the boys who fished the river with us, was one of them. His voice intermittently rose above those of the others: "Yes, yes, give me the ball, shoot! Shoot!! Shoot!!! Ah, what did you do?" Then laughter, the sound of children running and panting. I sat up in bed.

"Obe," I called to my brother as calmly as I could.

He did not answer, he was humming a tune.

"Obe," I called out again, almost with a cry. "But why must you try to kill the madman?" I asked.

"It is simple, Ben," he said with such a collected calm that I was thrown off my nerves. "I want to kill him because he killed my brothers, and so does not deserve to live."

The first time he'd said it, after he told me the story of *Things Fall Apart*, I'd thought he was merely broken and had said he would do it because of anger; but now, hearing the way he said it with grave determination and seeing these drawings, I began to fear he meant what he'd said.

"Why, why do you—you want to kill a person?"

"You see?" he said, diminishing the alarm that had leaked into my words and had caused me to shout the word "kill" rather than plainly say it. "You don't even know why because you have forgotten our brothers so soon."

"I haven't," I protested.

"You have, if not, you would not sit here, and watch Abulu continuing to live when he killed our brothers."

"But must we try to kill the demon-man? Is there no other way, Obe?"

"No," he said, shaking his head. "Listen, Ben, if you and I were not too scared to interfere when they were fighting until they killed each other, we must not be afraid to avenge them now. We must kill Abulu or else we cannot have peace; I cannot have peace; Daddy and Mama cannot have peace. Mama was driven crazy because of that madman. There's a wound he has inflicted on us that would never ever heal. If we do not kill this madman, nothing will ever be the same."

I sat there, frozen under the power of his words, unable to say anything. I could see that an indestructible plan had been formed within him, and night after night, he sat on the pane of the shutters and smoked, naked to the waist most times—because he did not want to trap the cigarette smell in his shirt. He would smoke and cough and spit, slapping himself on the skin frequently to swat mosquitoes. When Nkem toddled to the door and began banging on it, babbling that dinner was ready, he opened the door, and just as light flashed in, he closed it and darkness returned.

When weeks passed and he was still not able to convince me to join in his mission, he moved away, determined to carry out his task alone.

★ ★ ★

Towards the middle of November, when the dry Harmattan breeze turned people's skin ashen white, our family emerged like a mouse—the first sign of life from the rubble of a burnt-out world. Father opened a bookshop. With the savings he had, and generous support from his friends— most especially Mr Bayo in Canada, who had announced that he would be visiting Nigeria to see us and whose visit we were eagerly awaiting—he rented a one-room shop just about two kilometres from the Akure monarch's palace. A local carpenter constructed a large wooden signboard with the words *Ikeboja Bookshop* engraved in red paint on its white background. The signboard was then nailed to the lintel of the bookshop. Father took us all to see it the day he opened it. He'd arranged most of the books on the wooden shelves—all of them smelling of wood-spray. He told us he'd got four thousand books for a start and that it would take days to load them onto the shelves. Sacks and cartons of books were packed in an unlit room he said would serve as the store. A rat darted out of the door of the store the moment he opened it, and Mother laughed a long throaty laugh—her first since our brothers died.

"His first customers," she said, as Father chased the rat that was ten times swifter than he, until it was out the door, while we laughed. Father, gasping for breath, then told us about the strange case of one of his colleagues in Yola, whose house was invaded by rats. The man had endured the presence of the legion for very long, fighting only with mousetraps because he did not want them to die in a place he couldn't easily locate so they wouldn't begin to decay before their corpses were discovered. Every other measure had been futile in the past. But when two rats appeared in broad daylight while he was entertaining two of his colleagues, embarrassing him, he decided to end the ordeal. He evacuated all the members of his family to a hotel for one week, and then lined every nook and cranny of the house with *Ota-pia-pia*. By the time they returned, there was a dead rat in almost every corner of the house, even in shoes.

Father's office table and chair were placed at the centre of the bookshop, facing the doorway. There was a flower vase on the top of the table and a glass atlas David would have knocked over had Father not made quickly to save it. When we stepped outside the shop, we saw a tumult just across the road from the bookshop. Two men were fighting, and a mob had gathered there. Father, ignoring them, pointed at the big signboard by the side of the road that read *Ikeboja Bookshop*. It was David alone who had to be told that the name was a combination of our brothers' names. Father drove us from there down to the big Tesco supermarket to buy cakes, and while returning, he took the route through the street at the haunch of our district, through the small road from which we could see the stretch of esan bush that hid the Omi-Ala River. On the way we passed a group of dancers playing music from a truck loaded with boomboxes. The street was filled with wooden testers and fabric awnings under which women sold petty items. Others lined tubers of yam stacked on thread sacks, rice in basins, even baskets, and many other wares on the roadside. Motorcycles laden with passengers thrust dangerously in-between cars—for it would be only a matter of time before some of their heads would be crushed on the road. The statue of Samuel Okwaraji, the erstwhile Nigerian football player who died on the field of play in 1989, loomed over the buildings from where it stood in the stadium with a ball hanging interminably still on his foot and his finger pointing perpetually towards an unseen teammate. His dreadlocks were caked with dust, and threads of metals, which had loosened from the sculpture, were hanging awkwardly from his buttocks. Across the road from the stadium, people were gathered under tarpaulins, dressed in traditional clothes. They were seated on plastic chairs, a few tables filled with wine and other drinks in front of them. Two men, bowed over, were beating a tune on hourglass-shaped talking drums, while a man wearing an *agbada* and long trousers of the same fabric, danced acrobatically about, flapping his flowing robe.

We had barely reached the detour from which a leftward track led straight to our house when we saw Abulu. It was the first time since our brothers died. Before now, he'd disappeared like he never existed; as if he entered into our house, kindled a small fire and vanished. He was rarely mentioned at all by our parents after Mother returned except for when she brought a piece of news about him. He'd gone away, bereft of any burden hanging around his neck, the way the people of Akure had always allowed it to be.

Abulu was standing by the roadside looking in the distance when he saw our car slowly slaloming towards him because of the speed breakers. He dashed forward towards the car, waving and smiling. There was a gap in his upper dentition where it seemed one of the upper teeth had fallen out. Under his raised arm was a long fresh scar, still red and bloody. He was swaddled in a *wrappa*, one that had flowery designs all over it. I saw him cross onto the sidewalk, swaggering and gesticulating as if he had a companion. Then, as we closed in, to allow a Bedford truck filled with building materials to drive past on the narrow road, he stopped, and began examining something on the ground with keen interest. Father continued driving as though he did not see him, but Mother uttered a prolonged hiss and murmured "Evil man" under her breath, snapping her fingers over her head. "You will die a cruel death," Mother continued in English as if the madman could hear her, "you surely will. *Ka eme sia.*"

A van towing a damaged car trudged noisily down the road, honking erratically. In the side mirror where I'd fixed my eyes to keep Abulu in sight, the madman receded like a fighter jet. After he vanished from view, I kept my gaze on the mirror, on the inscription: *Caution: objects in the mirror are closer than they appear.* I thought then of how Abulu had been close to our car and I imagined he had touched it. This set off an avalanche chain of thoughts in my mind. First, I pondered Mother's reaction to the sight of the madman: the possibility of his death, and concluded it would not be possible. Who, I wondered, could kill him? Who could go close and put a knife in his stomach? Would the madman not see it coming and even kill the person first? Would most of the people of this town not have killed off this man if they could? Had they not chosen instead to swivel in concentric circles and to run dazed in pulsating rings? Had they not always turned into pillars of salt at the gate of reckoning as though Abulu was beyond harm?

Obembe had given me a questioning look upon Mother's outburst, and when I turned now from the mirror, his eyes trapped me in the netting that was the question "Can you see what I have been telling you?" It triggered an epiphany. I saw, at once, that Abulu was indeed the designer of our grief. As we drove past Argentina, the cross-wall neighbour's rickety lorry, its exhaust pumping billows of black smoke, it struck me that it was Abulu who had wounded us. Although I had not supported my brother's idea to punish the madman, seeing Abulu that day changed me. I was moved, too, by Mother's reaction, her curse, and the tears that began coursing down her cheeks at the sight of him. I felt a numbing ripple through my body when Nkem, in her sing-song voice, said: "Daddy, Mama is crying."

"Yes, I know," Father said, looking in the overhead mirror. "Tell her to stop crying."

When Nkem repeated "Mama, Daddy said I should tell you to stop crying," my heart burst like a dam and the flood of the wrongs this man had done to us broke out.

1. It was he who took away our brothers.
2. It was he who deposited the poisonous venom in the hot blood of our brotherhood.
3. It was he who took away Father's job.

4. It was he who caused Obembe and me to miss a school term.
5. It was he who almost drove Mother insane.
6. It was he who caused all of my brothers' possessions to be burned.
7. It was he who caused Boja's body to be burned like trash.
8. It was he who caused Ikenna to be obliterated by landfill.
9. It was he who caused Boja to be bloated like a balloon.
10. It was he who caused Boja to float around the town as a "missing person."

The list of his evils was endless. I stopped counting, and it continued running on and on and on like a left-open tap. I was appalled by the thought that despite all he'd done to us; despite how much he'd put upon this family; despite the torture he'd inflicted upon my mother; despite the way he'd broken us—this madman did not appear to be remotely aware of what he'd caused. His life had simply gone on, unscathed, untouched.

11. He destroyed Father's map of dreams.
12. He birthed the spiders that invaded our house.

13. It was he, not Boja, who planted the knife in Ikenna's belly.

By the time Father switched off the engine, the golem that this new discovery had created in me had risen to its feet, and shaken off the extra layers of earth from its creation. The verdict was now inscribed on its forehead: Abulu was our enemy.

When we got to our room, I told Obembe, while he was slipping his short trousers over his naked waist, that I wanted to kill Abulu too. He froze, and gazed at me. Then, he moved forward and threw his arms around me.

That night, in the dark, he told me a story, something he hadn't done in a long time.

13

THE LEECH

Hatred is a leech:

The thing that sticks to a person's skin; that feeds off them and drains the sap out of one's spirit. It changes a person, and does not leave until it has sucked the last drop of peace from them. It clings to one's skin, the way a leech does, burrowing deeper and deeper into the epidermis, so that to pull the parasite off the skin is to tear out that part of the flesh, and to kill it is self-flagellating. People once used fire, a hot rod, and when they burned the leech, they left the skin singed. This, too, was the case of my brother's hatred for Abulu; it was deep under his skin. For from the night I joined him, my brother and I put our door on near perpetual lock and convened daily to plan our mission, while our parents went to their workplaces: Mother to her shop and Father to the bookshop.

"First," my brother said one morning, "we must conquer him here in our room." He raised the papers on which he'd sketched his plans as matchstick men fighting and killing the madman. "In our minds, then on our papers before we can conquer him in the flesh. Haven't you heard Pastor Collins say, many times, that whatever happens in the physical already has happened in the spiritual?" It was not a question to which he expected an answer, so he went on: "So, before we leave this room in search of Abulu, we must first kill him here."

At first, we considered the five sketches of Abulu's moment of destruction, the possibility of achieving them. The first one he referred to as "The David and Goliath Plan"; he hurls stones at Abulu and Abulu dies.

I questioned the possibility of the design succeeding. I reasoned that since we were neither servants of God as David was, nor were we destined to be a king like David, we might not be able to hit his forehead. It was a full sun-out moment of the day when I said this, and Obembe had turned on the ceiling fan. From somewhere in the neighbourhood, I heard a man hawking rubber sandals, crying his wares: "Rubber, rubber—hereeeeeee!" My brother sat in his chair, his hand on his chin, pondering what I'd said.

"Listen, I understand your fears," he said finally. "You may be right, but I have always thought we could kill him by stoning, but how do we stone him? Where, at what time of the day can we do it without being caught in the act? Those are the real problems with that idea, not about being a king like David."

I nodded in agreement.

"If we stone him when people can see, we can't tell what might happen, and what if we aim wrong and hit someone else in the process?"

"You are right," I said, nodding.

Next he placed the one in which Abulu was stabbed to death with a knife, just the way Ikenna was killed. He'd marked it "The Okonkwo Plan," after the story of *Things Fall Apart*. The image scared me.

"What if he fights or stabs you first?" I said. "He is very wicked, you know?" I asked.

This possibility troubled my brother. He took a pencil and crossed out the sketch.

Then one after the other, we propped up an idea from a sketching, sank our teeth into it, and after we found it untenable, crossed it out. After we'd torn up all of them, we began weaving a set of imagined incidents, most of which we withdrew and discarded before they were fully formed. In one, we chased Abulu down the road on a windy evening and he fell into a running car, which knocked him to the ground and spilled the content of his head on the tarred road. I wove this fictional reality, my imagination spotted with pieces of the madman's crushed body on the asphalt like one of the various road kills—chickens, goats, dogs, rabbits—I'd seen. My brother sat for a while, his eyes closed while his mind was at work on this. The rubber-sandals hawker had returned to the neighbourhood, this time crying even louder "Rubber, rubber—heeeee! Rubberrrrr sandals hereeee!" The hawker's voice seemed to draw closer to our compound now, and was getting so loud that I did not realize my brother had started to speak. "—Good idea," I heard him say, "but you know those ignorant fools, *kowordly* people who don't know what that madman had done to our family, would try to stop us."

Again, as always, I agreed that he was right. He tore it up and poured the pieces angrily on the floor.

The leech that was my brother's resolve to avenge our brothers was so deeply embedded it could not be destroyed by anything, not even fire. Over the following days, once our parents left home, we went off to find the madman. We went in late mornings, between ten in the morning and two in the afternoon. Although the new term had begun, we were not enrolled. Father had written to the headmistress of our school to allow us a term off to recover because we were not fit to resume school just yet, since the deaths of our brothers were still fresh in our minds.

So to avoid meeting classmates or kids we knew around the streets and district, we trod covert paths. Over the following days of the first week of December, we combed the district for any sign of the madman, but found none. He was not at his truck, not around the street; he was not close to the river. We could not ask anyone about him, as people in the district knew so much about us and would often put on sympathetic faces when they met us as if we bore an insignia of the tragedy of our brothers' deaths on our foreheads.

These failures did not deter my brother, not even what we heard about the madman that week, an incident that killed all the courage I had gathered when I pledged to join him in his quest. The madman had been elusive for many days—never once spotted around the district. So we began asking people we felt didn't know us if they'd seen him. This way, we reached the end of our district to the north, near the big petrol station with the huge complex that had a motley-garbed human-shaped balloon that constantly bowed, tilted sideways, and waved its hands as the wind blew at it. There we found Nonso, Ikenna's old classmate. He sat on a wooden stool on the side of a main road, newspapers and magazines spread on flat raffia sacks before him. He told us after shaking our hands with slaps, that he was the chief vendor of our district.

"Haven't you heard of me?" he asked, with a voice that was cracked as though he was high on some drug, his eyes darting between our faces.

His earring glistened in the sun and his punk—a brush of equal hair in the centre of his head—was dark and polished. He'd heard of Ikenna's death, how his "younger dude" stabbed him in the belly. He'd always hated Boja. "Anyway, may their souls rest in peace," he said.

A man, who had been reading a copy of the *Guardian*, stood up, dropped the paper and gave Nonso some coins. When he put the paper on the table, I saw the slain Kudirat Abiola, wife of the 1993 presidential election winner on its front page. He gestured that we take the man's seat on a bench just under a fabric awning. I thought of the day we encountered M.K.O.; she'd stood beside us, and had scratched my head with her ringed fingers. I remembered how her voice had carried equal measures of authority and humility when she asked the crowd to step back. In the photo on the cover of the newspaper, her eyes were shut and her face was lifeless—devoid of all hue.

"It is M.K.O.'s wife, don't you know?" Obembe said, taking the paper from me.

I nodded. I recalled how, long after we'd met M.K.O., I'd longed to see the woman again. I'd thought, at the time, that I'd loved her. She was the first person I'd thought of as a wife. Every other woman was either a woman or someone's mother or a girl, but she was *a wife*.

My brother asked Nonso if he had seen Abulu recently.

"That demon?" Nonso said. "I saw him two days ago—right here. On this main road just by the filling station, beside the corpse—"

He pointed to the dirt track by the side of the long main road that connected to a highway leading to Benin.

"What corpse?" My brother asked.

Nonso shook his head, took a small towel he habitually hung on his shoulder, and wiped ripples of sweat from his neck so that it glistened in the sun. "What, haven't you heard?"

Abulu, he said, had found the body of a young woman killed early that morning—probably at dawn. Owing to the typical slow response of the traffic police in that part of Nigeria, the body had been allowed to remain on the spot for long, even until midday so that people who'd come that way had often stopped to see the body. When it was almost past noon, the corpse had begun to attract less attention when another mob started gathering around it, this time with an unruly cacophony. Nonso looked down the road but the mob blocked the view of what was going on at the centre.

His curiosity piqued to the extreme, he'd crossed the road to the gathering, abandoning his newspapers. When he got to the mob and negotiated his view, he saw the corpse of a woman, whose head lay on a nimbus formed by the blackened patch of her blood. Her hands were thrown sideways like he'd seen before, a ring glimmering on one of the fingers—the blood-soaked hair sticky and uneven in shape. But this time, it was naked, her breasts unclothed, and Abulu was on top of her, thrusting into her as the mob watched in horror. Some of them were arguing whether it was right to let him defile the dead while others held that the woman was already dead and that it was no harm; others claimed he should be stopped but those people were few. When he'd relieved himself, he fell asleep, clinging to the dead woman as if she was his wife until the police took her away from him.

My brother and I were so shaken by this story that we did not go out on any other reconnaissance mission that day. A shawl of dread of the madman fell over me and I could see that even Obembe, my brother, was afraid. He sat in the sitting room for long, silent until he fell asleep, his head against the top of the chair. I had started to dread the madman, to wish my brother would give it up, but could not face him to say it. I feared he would be angry or even hate me, but towards the end of that week, providence intervened—as I have now understood, now that things in the past are clearer—to save us from what was to come. Father announced that his friend, Mr Bayo, who moved to Canada when I was just three, had arrived in Lagos. It was over breakfast, and the news came like a flash of thunder. Mr Bayo, Father continued, had promised to take my brother and me with him to Canada. The news exploded over the table like a grenade, scattering shrapnel of joy all across the room. Mother shouted "Hallelujah!" and, rising from her chair, burst into singing.

I, too, was elated and my body was suddenly charged with wanton joy. But when I glanced at my brother, I saw that the expression on his face had not changed. A shade stood on his face as he ate. Had he not heard? It didn't seem so, for he was bent over the table, eating as if he hadn't.

"What about me?" David asked, tearfully.

"You?" Father asked, laughing. "You will go, too. How can a chief like you be left here? You will go; in fact, you will be the first on the plane."

I was still wondering what my brother was thinking when he said: "What about our school?"

"You will get a better one in Canada," Father replied.

My brother nodded and continued his meal; I was surprised by his lack of enthusiasm at what seemed the best news of our lives. We ate on while Father narrated the story of how Canada developed over a short period to surpass other countries, including Britain, from which it had emerged. Then he brought the talk down to Nigeria, down to the corruption that had eaten the entrails of the nation and finally, as usual, he berated Gowon, a man we had grown to hate, the man he'd repeatedly accused of bombing our village several times—the man who killed very many women during the Nigerian civil war. "That idiot," he snapped, his Adam's apple bobbing up and down in his throat, his neck taut with sinews, "is the greatest enemy of Nigeria."

After Father went to the bookstore and Mother left with David and Nkem, I went to my brother, who was fetching water from the well to fill the drum in the bathroom, a chore Ikenna and Boja used to do exclusively because he and I were thought to be too small to use the well. It was the first time anyone had fetched from it since August.

"If it is true that we are going to Canada soon," he said, "then we have to kill that madman as soon as possible. We have to find him quickly."

Before now, this would have excited me, but this time, I wanted to tell him to let us forget the madman and go and start a new life in Canada. But I could not. Instead, I found myself saying: "Yes, yes, Obe—we must."

"We have to kill him soon."

My brother was so worried by what should have been good news that he did not eat that night. He sat sketching and erasing and tearing, his temper burning until his pencil was reduced to a size of his finger and the table was filled with shredded paper. He'd told me at the well, shortly after our parents left for their workplaces that we must act quickly. He'd said it fiercely, pointing to the well: "Boja, our brother, decomposed here like—like a mere lizard in this place because of that madman. We must avenge or else; I'm not going to any Canada without doing that."

He'd licked his thumb to accentuate his vow, to make me see that it was a vow. He was determined. He'd lifted the buckets of water he'd fetched and gone into the house, leaving me standing there, beginning to wonder—as he always left me to do—if I missed my brothers, Ikenna and Boja, just as he did. Then I would comfort myself with the conviction that I did, but was merely scared of the madman. I could not kill, either. It is evil, and how might I, only a child, do it? But my brother had said he would carry out the plan with all the powers of persuasion, determined that he would succeed, for his desire had become an indestructible leech.

14

THE LEVIATHAN

But Abulu was a leviathan:

An undying whale that could not be easily killed by a band of valiant sailors. He could not die as easily as other men of flesh and blood. Although he was no different from other people of his kind—the insane vagabond who wallowed, by reason of his mental condition, in the lowest level of privation possible and was thus exposed to extreme dangers—he'd probably had closer shaves with death than any one of them. It was known too well that he mainly fed on filth—filth from dumps. Because he had no house, he fed from whatever he chanced upon—leftover meat scattered around the open-pavilioned abattoirs, crumbs of food from dumps, fruits dropped from trees. To have fed from there, for so long, one would expect him to have long contracted some infirmity. But he lived, hale and healthy, his belly bulging into a paunch. When he walked on a bed of shattered glass and bled out, people thought that was it, but he showed up again within days. Yet, these were only little stories of what should have killed the madman; there were many more.

Solomon had told us, when we convened at the Omi-Ala the day after the encounter with Abulu, that the reason he'd warned us sternly not to listen to Abulu's prophecy was because he believed Abulu was an evil spirit manifesting in bodily form. To buttress this point, he told us of something he'd witnessed many months earlier. Abulu was walking by a roadside when he suddenly stopped. It was drizzling, and the rain was making him wet. Facing the road, the madman began calling to his mother who he believed was standing in the centre of the road, pleading with her to forgive him for all he did to her. As he pleaded, apparently conversing with her, he saw a car racing down from the other side of the road. Frightened, he began shouting to his mother to leave the road, but the apparition, who the madman was convinced was real, stood firm in the heart of the road. Abulu dashed onto the road just in the moment the car reached where he thought his mother had stood, to save her. The car swiftly pushed him to a grassy shoulder of the road, and slightly skidded off the road into the nearby bush before pulling to a halt. It was said that Abulu, thought to have immediately died, lay still for a while where the car had left him. Then he scrambled to his feet, bloodied all over, a gape on his forehead. When he stood, he began flapping his drenched clothes as though the car had merely blown a cloud of dust on him. He would limp away, frequently turning to the way the car had gone and saying: "Do you want to kill someone, eh? Can't you stop when you see a woman on the road? Do you want to kill a person?" He limped on, asking innumerable questions as he went away, sometimes stopping to take a backward glance with his hand on the lobe of his ear to admonish the driver to drive slowly next time: "You hear, you hear?"

The day after Father announced our potential immigration to Canada, my brother shoved a sketch into my hand, and I sat gazing at it while he spoke.

"We could kill him with *Ota-pia-pia*. We could buy one and put it in bread or something, and give the madman, since he eats from everywhere and just about anything."

"Yes," I agreed, "he even feeds from gutters."

"That's true," he said, and nodded. "But have you thought of why those years of feeding from these things haven't killed him? Isn't it from dumps and trash heaps he feeds? Why hasn't he died?"

He expected an answer, but I said nothing.

"You remember the story Solomon told us about why he was really scared of him and wouldn't want to have anything to do with him?"

I nodded.

"You see, then? Listen, while we must not give up, we must know that this man is strange. These stupid people"—the way he now referred to the people of Akure town because they allowed the madman to remain alive—"believe he is a kind of supernatural being who cannot be physically killed because; you know, they foolishly think his years of living outside the realm of human reasoning have altered his humanity, and hence he is no longer a mortal man."

"Is this true?" I asked.

"If we feed him poisoned bread, people will think he died from something he ate by himself from some garbage dump." I did not ask him how he'd found this out because he was the keeper of secret knowledge whom I unquestioningly believed. So, a while later, we went out with the front pockets of my brother's shorts swollen with shredded pieces of bread marinated with rodenticide packed in a small sack. He'd got the bread by slicing out a piece from his breakfast the previous day. My brother had brought out the shrivelled crumbs and laced them some more with the poisoned mixture, filling the room with the piquant odour. He'd said that he wanted us to go out on "this mission" just once, and that would be it—just once. Armed with these, we went to the truck where Abulu lived, but he was not there. Although we'd heard that its door could still open and close, the truck was left almost perpetually opened. There were the rickety seats that were shrunken to their wooden bones, their flesh—the leather coverings—torn or worn off. Its rusted roof had holes through which rain entered. The seats were filled with various waste materials: a used blue curtain, which reached from the seat to the floor of the truck; the frame of an old kerosene lantern with its glass tube missing; a stick; papers; wrecked shoes; tins; and many other items picked from some trash.

"Perhaps it is not yet time," my brother said. "Let's return home and come back in the afternoon; perhaps we will find him then."

We went home, and returned later that afternoon, after Mother had briefly come home to boil yams for lunch and gone back to her shop. When we got there, the madman was there all right, but nothing had prepared us for what we'd encounter. He was bent over a wok set on two big stones, and was emptying the liquid content of a water bottle. Pieces of wood—apparently intended as firewood—were piled between the stones, but they were unlit. After draining off the content of the bottle into the earthenware, the madman took up a beverage can whose content we could not easily decipher, turned it into the wok, and began painstakingly emptying its content into it. He would shake the tin, peer into it microscopically, and scratch out its content into the wok until, satisfied he'd emptied it, he placed the tin delicately on a small stool on which was a pile of assorted things. Then, dashing into his truck, he returned with what appeared to be a pack of leaves, some bones, a spherical object, a white powder that must have been salt or sugar. He poured these things into the wok and stepped back with a jolt as if he'd encountered the inflammable effect of plunging things into heated oil. It became clear, to my utter bemusement, that the madman was—or thought he was—cooking a gallimaufry of filth and waste materials. For a moment, we abandoned our quest and stood watching the scenario in disbelief until two men stopped by to join us as spectators of Abulu in his kitchen.

The men were dressed in cheap long-sleeved shirts tucked into soft-fabric trousers—one wore black trousers and the other one green. They held hardback books that we immediately knew were bibles; they had just left some church.

"Perhaps, we could pray for him," one of the men—swarthy, with a balding that had stopped in the middle of his head—suggested.

"We have been fasting and praying for three weeks now," the other said, "asking God for power. Isn't it time to use it?"

The first man nodded sheepishly. And before he could respond, someone else said, "It surely isn't."

It was my brother; the two men turned to him.

"This man, here," my brother continued with a countenance masked with fear, "is a fake. This is all pretence. He is a sane man. He is a well-known trickster who pretends to be like this to beg for alms, dancing on the roadsides, storefronts, or marketplaces, but he is sane. He has children." My brother looked at me, although he was addressing the men. "He is our father."

"What?" the balding man exclaimed.

"Yes," my brother continued to my complete shock, "Paul, here"—he pointed at me—"and I have been sent by our mother to bring him back home, that it is enough for today, but he has refused to return home with us."

He made a gesture of entreaty to the madman who was looking around the stool and the ground as though searching for a missing object, and did not seem to notice my brother.

"This is unbelievable," the swarthy man said. "There's nothing we won't hear or see in this world—a man pretending to be insane just to earn a living? Unbelievable."

Shaking their heads repeatedly, the men took their leave, bidding us to pray for God to touch him, and convict him of his greed. "God can do anything," the swarthy one said, "if you ask in faith."

My brother agreed and thanked them. When the men were gone out of earshot, I asked my brother what that was all about.

"Shh," he said, grinning. "Listen, I was scared those men had some power. You never know: they have fasted for three weeks? Phew! What if they had power like Reinhard Bonnke, Kumuyi or Benny Hinn, and they could pray and get him healed? I don't want that to happen. If he is well, he won't roam about anymore, maybe he would even leave this town—who knows? You know what that means don't you? That this man will escape, go scot-free after what he did? No, no, I won't let that happen—over my dead bo—"

My brother was forced to truncate his speech by what we now saw: a man, his wife and son about my age had stopped to watch the madman, who was chuckling. Obembe was saddened by this, as these people would again delay us till the madman left the spot. Discouraged, he concluded it was too open a place to use the poison, so we went home.

★ ★ ★

Abulu was not in his truck when we went to search for him the following day, but we found him near the small primary school with a high fence. From inside the compound, we could hear the uniform voices of children reciting poems and of their teacher breaking in, and sporadically asking them to give themselves a round of applause. The madman soon rose, and began walking majestically, his hands curved around him like the CEO of an oil company. Lying open, just a close distance from him was an umbrella with its skeletal ribs unclipped from its cleated battered tarpaulin. With his eyes fixed on a ring on one of his fingers, Abulu stamped about, chanting a string of words: "Wife," "Now wed," "Love," "Marry," "Beautiful ring," "Now wed," "You," "Father," "Marry"…

Obembe would tell me—after the madman and his gibberish had petered out of sight—that he was mimicking a Christian wedding procession. We followed him from a distance, slowly. We passed the place where Ikenna had pulled a dead man from a car in 1993. As we went, I thought of the potency of the rat poison we carried and my fear soared and again I began to feel pity for the madman, who seemed to be living just like a stray dog feeding everywhere. He often stopped, turned back, and posed like a model on a runway, stretching the hand that had the ring on it. We'd never been to this street before. Abulu made towards three women at a balcony, in front of a bungalow, plaiting the hair of one seated on a stool. Two of them gave him a chase, picking up stones and throwing them in his direction to scare him away.

Long after the women had retreated—they'd barely moved, and had only screamed at him to get his filthy self away—the madman was still running, looking back intermittently, the lascivious smile still on his face. The dirt track, as we would find out just shortly afterwards, was hardly used by cars because it ended with a wooden bridge about two hundred metres long over one part of the Omi-Ala. This made it easy for some street children to convert the track, only a few metres long, into a playground. The children lined four big rocks on both ends of the road, with spaces between them; the stones were the goal posts. They played football here, shouting and raising dust. Abulu watched them, his face filled with smiles.

Then, positioning himself this and that way—with an invisible ball in his hand—he kicked wildly into the air, almost falling in the act. He shouted, thrusting his hands in the air with flourish, "Goaaaal! It. Is. A goalllll!"

When we caught up with him, we saw that Igbafe and his brother were among the boys. The moment we stepped on the bridge, I remembered the dream of the footbridge I'd seen around the time Ikenna was undergoing his metamorphosis. The familiar smell of the river, the sight of multi-coloured fish similar to the ones we used to catch, swimming at the edges of the waters, the sound of invisible croaking toads and chirping crickets and even the smell of dead river matter, all reminded me of our fishing days. I watched the fish closely because I'd not seen them swimming in a long time. I used to wish I was a fish, and that all my brothers were fish too. And that all we did, all day, every day, was swim forever and ever and ever.

As expected, Abulu began walking towards the bridge, his eyes fixed on the horizon, until he reached its foot. When he climbed, we felt his weight bear down on the wooden slab from the other end of the bridge where we were standing.

"We'll run away, fast, once we feed it to him," my brother said as the madman drew nigh. "He could fall into the water and die there; no one will see him die."

Although I was afraid of this plan, I merely nodded in
agreement. When Abulu climbed the bridge, he immediately went close to the railing and holding on to it, began
urinating into the river. We watched until he finished,
and his penis reclined like an elastic string relapsing to the
centre of his waist, spitting a few last drops on the footbridge. My brother looked around to be sure no one was
watching and brought out the poisoned bread and made
for the madman as he went.

Now up close and certain he would soon die, I let my
eyes take an inventory of the madman. He appeared like
a mighty man of old when men shredded everything they
grasped with bare hands. His face was fecund with a beard
that stretched from the side of his face down to his jaw.
His moustache stood over his mouth as though it had been
applied there by fine brush strokes of charcoal paint. His
hair was dirty, long, and tangled. Thick foliations of hair
also covered a large part of his chest, his wrinkled and
swarthy face, the centre of his pelvis, and encircled his
penis. The matrixes of his fingernails were long and taut,
and in the bed beneath each plate were masses of grime
and dirt.

I observed that he carried on his body a variety of
odours, the most noticeable of which was a faecal smell
that wafted at me like a drone of flies when I drew closer to

him. This smell, I thought, might have been a result of his going for long without cleaning his anus after excretion. He reeked of sweat accumulated inside the dense growth of hair around his pubic regions and armpits. He smelt of rotten food, and unhealed wounds and pus, and of bodily fluids and wastes. He was redolent of rusting metals, putrefying matter, old clothes, ditched underwear he sometimes wore. He smelt, too, of leaves, creepers, decaying mangoes by the Omi-Ala, the sand of the riverbank, and even of the water itself. He had the smell of banana trees and guava trees, of the Harmattan dust, of trashed clothes in the large bin behind the tailor's shop, of leftover meat at the open abattoir in the town, of leftover things devoured by vultures, of used condoms from the La Room motel, of sewage water and filth, of semen from the ejaculations he'd spilled on himself every time he'd masturbated, of vaginal fluids, of dried mucus. But these were not all; he smelt of immaterial things. He smelt of the broken lives of others, and of the stillness in their souls. He smelt of unknown things, of strange elements, and of fearsome and forgotten things. He smelt of death.

Obembe held out some bread for the madman, and he took it when he reached us. He seemed not to recognize us at all, as though we were not the same people he'd prophesied about.

"Food!" he said, sticking out his tongue. He then broke out into a monotonous chorus of words: "Eat, rice, beans, eat, bread, eat, that, manna, maize, eba, yam, egg, eat." He bumped his knuckle into the palm of his other hand, and continued his rhythmic chant, which had been ignited by the word "food."

"Food, food, *ajankro ba*, f-f-f-f-food! Eat this." He bulked a space between his palms, imitating the shape of a pot. "Eat, food, eat, eat—"

"This is good food," Obembe stuttered. "Bread, eat, eat, Abulu."

Abulu rolled his eyes, now, with such dexterity that would have put the best eye-rollers to shame. He took a piece of the bread from Obembe, chuckled, and yawned as though it was a punctuation of some sort, and therefore part of the language he had just spoken. Once he took the bread, Obembe glared at me, drew back until, reaching a safe distance, we picked up speed. We'd run down another street before we thought to stop. In the distance, a wild motoring road undulated on a swathe of dirt road.

"Let's not go too far away from him," my brother said, panting, holding my shoulder for support.

"Yes," I mumbled, trying to catch my breath.

"He will soon fall," my brother purred, his eyes a horizon accommodating a single, radiant star of joy, but my eyes were filled with the rapid waters of ripping pity. The story Mother told of how Abulu sucked a cow's teats had come to my mind just then, and so did the feeling that it was privation and destitution that had driven him to such desperation. In our fridge were cans of milk, Cowbell, Peak, all with pictures of cows. Perhaps, I'd thought, he could not afford any of these. He had no money, no clothes, no parents, no house. He was like the pigeons in the Sunday-school song we sang: "Look at the Pigeons, They Have No Clothes." They have no gardens, yet God watches them. I thought that Abulu was like the pigeons, and for this I pitied the madman, as I sometimes found myself doing.

"He will soon die," my brother said, cutting off my thoughts.

We'd stopped in front of a shed where a woman sold petty things. The shed was covered on the grille by netting under which a cashier-like space opened for interaction with customers. Hanging from the top of the grille were various sachets of beverage, powdered milk, biscuits, sweets, and other food. As we waited here, I imagined Abulu falling and dying away on the bridge. We'd seen him put the poisoned bread in his mouth, his moustached mouth shaking as he chewed. We saw him now, still holding the nylon, peering into the river. A few men passed him, one of them turning back to look at him. My heart skipped.

"He is dying," my brother whispered, "Look, he is probably trembling now, and that is why the men are looking at him. They say when the effect begins, the body first starts to tremble."

As if to confirm our suspicion, Abulu bent downwards to the bridge and appeared to be spitting onto it. My brother was right, I thought. We'd seen so many movies in which people coughed and foamed at the mouth after consuming poison, and then fell and died.

"We did it, we did it," he cried. "We avenged Ike and Boja. I told you we will. I said it."

Elated, my brother began talking about how we would now have peace, and how the madman would no longer bother people. He stopped talking when he saw Abulu starting to walk towards us, dancing and clapping as he went. This miracle came towards us dancing and singing rhapsodies of a saviour on whose palms nine-inch nails were driven and who would someday return to the earth. His psalmody whooped the darkening evening into an eso-teric realm as we followed, shocked that he was still alive. We trudged along past the long road, past shops closing until Obembe, short of words, stopped, and turned back towards home. I knew that he, like me, had come to spot the difference between an unhurt thumb blood-covered from being dipped into a pool of blood, and a thumb robed in blood from a gash. He'd understood that the poison would not kill Abulu.

* * *

While the leech that infested my brother and me pasteurized our grief and kept our wound fresh, our parents healed. Mother cast away her mourning clothes towards the end of December and returned to normal life. She no longer burst out in sudden rage nor plunged into sudden declivities of grief, and it seemed the spiders had gone extinct. Because of her recovery, the valedictory service for Ikenna and Boja, which had been postponed for many weeks due to Mother's illness, was held the following Saturday—five days after our first failed attempt on Abulu's life. That morning, all of us in black dress, including David and Nkem, packed into Father's car, which had had to be repaired the previous day by Mr Bode. His role in that tragedy had brought him closer to our family, and he'd visited many times, once with his betrothed, a girl whose set of protruding dentition made it hard for her to firmly close her mouth. Father had now called him "my brother."

The service was composed of songs of valediction, a brief history of "the boys" rendered by Father, and a short sermon by Pastor Collins, who wore a gauze on his head that day. He'd had an accident a few days before on a motorcycle taxi. The auditorium was full of familiar faces from our neighbourhood, most of whom were members of other churches. In his speech, Father said Ikenna was a great man—Obembe cast a lingering stare at me when he said that—a man who would have led men if he'd lived.

"I will not say much about him, but Ikenna was a fine child," he said. "A child who knew a lot of hardships. I mean, the devil tried to steal him, many times, but God was faithful. A scorpion stung him at age six—" Father was interrupted by a muted gasp of horror that ran through the congregation upon this revelation.

"Yes, at Yola," he continued. "And just a few years later, one of his testicles was kicked into his body. I will spare you the rest of the details about that incident, but please know that God was with him. His brother, Boja—" and then the kind of silence I'd never experienced before in my life descended on the congregation. For, still at the podium, in front of the church, Father—our father, the man who knew all things, the brave man, the strong man, the Generalissimo, the commander of the forces of corporal discipline, the intellectual, the eagle—had begun to sob. A feeling of shame seized me at the sight of my father openly weeping, I bent my head and fixed my eyes on my shoe while Father continued; albeit, this time, his word—like an overloaded lumber truck caught in Lagos traffic—slalomed through the pockmarked dirt of his moving speech, halting and jerking and slumping.

"He would, have been great, too. He… he was a gifted, child. He, if you knew him, he… was a good child. Thank you all for coming."

After the long applause when Father's hurried speech ended, the hymns began. Mother cried softly through it, dabbing her eyes with a handkerchief. A small knife of grief sliced slowly through my heart as I wept for my brothers.

The congregation was singing "It Is Well with My Soul," when I noticed unusual movements. In a moment, heads began turning and eyes diverting towards the back. I did not want to turn because Father was seated beside us, next to Obembe. But just as I was wondering, Obembe tilted his head towards me, and whispered: "Abulu is here."

I turned at once and saw Abulu, dressed in a muddied brown shirt with a large circle of sweat and grime, standing somewhere among the congregation. Father cast a glance at me, his eyes ordering me to focus. Abulu had attended the church many times before. The first time, he came in the middle of a sermon, walked past the ushers at the door, and sat down on a bench in the women's row. Although the congregants instantly became aware that something unusual was happening, the Pastor preached on while the ushers, young men who kept watch at the doors, kept a close watch on him. But he maintained an unusual composure throughout the sermon, and when it was time for the closing prayer and hymn, he indulged in both as if he was not who everyone knew him to be. When the assembly was dismissed, he went out quietly leaving a stir in his wake. He attended a couple more times afterwards, mostly sitting in the women's row, triggering a hot debate between those who felt his nudity was unwelcome because of the women and the children, and those who felt the house of God was meant for anyone who wished to come in, naked/clothed, poor/rich, sane/insane and to whom identity was of no importance. Finally, the church decided to stop him from attending services, and the ushers chased him with sticks whenever he came near the premises.

But on that day of my brothers' valediction service, he took everyone by surprise. He'd slipped in when no one was watching, and was already inside when they noticed him. And because of the sensitive nature of the service, the officials let him stay. Later, after the church had closed and he'd left, the woman beside whom he'd sat recalled how he cried during the service. She said he asked her if she knew the boy, and went on to say he knew him. The woman, with a shake of her head in the manner of one who had seen a ghost in broad daylight, said Abulu had repeatedly mentioned Ikenna's name.

I did not know what my parents made of Abulu's attendance at the valediction service of their sons, whose deaths he caused, but I could tell, from the grave silence that enshrouded us all the way home, that they'd been shaken by it. No one said a word except for David who, enthralled by one of the songs we'd sung in the service, hummed or tried to sing it. It was about midday and most churches in this predominantly Christian town now closed, vehicles filled the roads. As we motored through the clogging traffic, David's soulful song—a miraculous creation rendered in palatal babble and mispronunciations, half-slit words, upturned connotations, and strangled meanings—filled the car with a sedating atmosphere, so that the silence became palpable, as if two more persons—who could not be seen by mere eyes—were seated there with us, and were, like all of us, sedated.

> *Whe pis lak' a rifa ateent ma so*
> *Whe so ow lak sea billows roooooo*
> *What eefa my Lord, if at cos me to say*
> *It is weh, (it is weh) with ma so*
> *It is weh, (it is weh) with ma so, (with ma so)*
> *It is weh, (it is weh) with ma so.*

Shortly after we got home, Father went out and did not return for the rest of the day. As time slipped past midnight, Mother's fear was piqued to curious levels. She darted like a

frenzied cat about the house, then to the neighbours, raising alarm that she did not know the whereabouts of her
husband. Her anxiety was such that a sizeable number of
our neighbours gathered at our house, counselling her to
be patient, to wait a bit more—till the next day at least—
before going to the police. Although Mother took counsel,
she was in a delirious state of anxiety when Father returned.
The rest of the children, even Obembe, had slept at that
time except me. He did not answer Mother's pleas to give
an account of where he'd been and why he had a bandage on
one of his eyes. He merely dragged his feet into his room.
When Obembe asked him the next morning, he merely
said: "I had a cataract operation. No more questions."

I swallowed saliva that had formed a lump in my throat
as I tried to restrain more questions from pouring out.

"You couldn't see?" I asked, after a while.

"I said. No. More. Questions!" he barked.

But I could tell, from the mere fact that neither he
nor Mother had gone to work that something was truly
wrong with him. Father, who'd been greatly changed by
the tragedies and his job, was never the same again. Even
after the bandage was removed—the lid of that one eye
could no longer close completely like the other.

Obembe and I did not go out to hunt Abulu that entire
week, because Father stayed home throughout, listening

to the radio, watching television or reading. My brother repeatedly cursed the sickness, the "cataract" that caused Father to stay at home. Once, when Father was watching television, his eyes fixed on the prime-time news being read by Cyril Stober, Obembe asked him when we were to go to Canada. "Early next year," Father replied phlegmatically. On the screen before him was a scene of fire, frantic pandemonium, and then blackened bodies in different shades of cremation, lying about in a scorched field from where black smoke was rising. Obembe was about to say something else, but Father raised his five splayed fingers to stop him as the TV said: "Due to this unfortunate sabotage, the nation's daily output has now been cut by fifteen thousand barrels a day. Hence, the government of General Sani Abacha urges the citizenry to express caution even as the queues at the petrol stations return, knowing that it will be temporary. However, the government will duly punish any miscreants."

We waited patiently, so as not to distract him until a man brushing his teeth from up-to-down came on the screen.

"In January?" My brother quickly said once the man came on the screen.

"I said 'early next year,'" Father mumbled, lowering his eyes, the affected one half-closed. I wondered what truly was wrong with Father's eyes. I'd overheard him arguing with Mother who'd accused him of lying, that he had no "katacat." Perhaps, I thought some insect had got into his eyes. It pained me that I could come up with nothing, and I came down with the feeling that were Ikenna and Boja still alive they could—by virtue of their superior wisdom—have provided an answer.

"Early next year," Obembe mumbled when we returned to our room. Then, his voice lowering like a camel reclining, repeated it: "Early. Next. Year."

"It must be in January?" I suggested, inwardly delighted.

"Yes, January, but that means we don't have much time—in fact, we don't have time at all. We don't have much time." He shook his head. "I won't be happy in Canada, or wherever, if that madman still walks about freely."

Although I was very wary of inflaming my brother's ire, I could not help but say: "But, we have tried, he just isn't dying. You said it; he is like the whale—"

"Lie!" he cried, a single tear rolling down his reddened eye. "He is a human being; he too can die. We've only made one attempt, just one attempt for Ike and Boja. But I swear, I will avenge my brothers."

Father called out at that time and asked us to go clean his car.

"I will do it," my brother whispered again.

He wiped his eyes with a cloth until they were dry. Later, after he'd cleaned the car with a towel he soaked in a bucket of water, he told me we should try "The Knife Plan". This was how it should go: we should steal out of the room in the dead of the night and find the madman in his truck, then stab him to death and run away. What he described frightened me, but my brother, this small man of sorrow, having locked the door, lit a cigarette for the first time in a long time. Even though there was electricity he'd turned off the light so our parents could think we were asleep. And although the night was a little cold, he left the window open as he blew out the smoke. Then when he was done, he turned to me, and whispered: "It shall be this night."

My heart skipped. I heard a familiar Christmas carol playing from somewhere in the neighbourhood. It dawned on me, suddenly, that that night was December 23rd, and the next day would be Christmas Eve. I was struck by how different that Christmas season had been: bleak and uneventful compared to the others. It came as always with befogged mornings that when cleared, left sagging clouds of dust in the air. People filled their houses with decorations, with the radio and television stations rolling out carols after carols. Sometimes, the statue of the Madonna at the gate of the big cathedral, the new one they erected after Abulu desecrated the first, shone with colourful decorations, attracting many as the highlight of the Yuletide celebrations in our district. People's faces would beam with smiles even as prices of commodities—predominantly of live cocks, turkey, rice, and all the fancy Christmas recipes—soared beyond the reach of the common man. None of these things had happened—at least not in our house. No decorations. No preparations. Whatever we had in the natural way of living, it seemed, had been mauled by the monstrous termite of grief that had attacked us. And our family had become a shadow of what we once were.

"This night," my brother said after a while, his eyes on mine, the rest of his face, silhouetted. "I have the knife ready. Once we are sure Daddy and Mama are asleep, we will leave through the window."

Then, as if he'd projected the words through the rising indistinct body of smoke, said, "Will I be going alone?"

"No, I will come with you," I stammered.

"Good," he said.

Although I badly wanted my brother's love and did not want to disappoint him again, I could not bring myself to go hunt the madman at midnight. Akure was dangerous at night; even adults were careful where they went after dark. Just towards the end of the school term, before Ikenna and Boja died, it was reported at the morning assembly that

Irebami Ojo, one of my classmates who lived on our street, had lost his father to armed robbers. I wondered why my brother, who was only a child, was not afraid of the night. Did he not know, had he not heard these things? And the madman, the demon, perhaps he knew we would come and would lie in wait. I pictured Abulu grabbing the knife and stabbing us. This filled me with terror.

I rose from the bed and said I wanted to go drink some water. I went to the sitting room where Father was still seated, his hands folded across his chest, watching the television. I fetched water in a cup from the cask in the kitchen and drank. Then, I sat in the lounge close to Father, who barely acknowledged my presence with a nod, and asked if his eye was okay. "Yes," he said and turned back to the television. Two men dressed in suits were debating and in the background was a poster that said *Economic Matters*. I'd thought of an idea, a way to escape going out with my brother. So, I took one of the newspapers from Father's side and began reading. Father loved this; he enjoyed every effort made to acquire knowledge. As I scanned through the paper, I asked Father questions to which he merely provided short answers, but I wanted him to talk for long. So I asked him about the day he said his uncle went to fight in the war. Father nodded and began, but he was sleepy, yawning again and again, so he made it short.

Yet his story was the same as he'd recollected it: his uncle hiding in trees along the highway to lay ambush for a convoy of Nigerian soldiers. His uncle and the men opening a barrel of fire on the soldiers who, not knowing the direction from which the bullets were coming, shot frantically into the empty forest until they were all killed. "All of them," Father would enunciate. "Not one of them escaped."

I planted my eyes back on the newspaper and began reading and praying Father would not leave anytime soon. We'd been talking for an hour and it was almost ten. I wondered what my brother was doing, if he would come for me. Then Father began to sleep. I switched off the light and curved into the lounge.

It must have been less than an hour later that I heard a door open and a movement in the sitting room. I felt the movement reach behind my chair, then, I felt his hand shake me, first slowly, then forcefully, but I did not even stir. I tried to make faint noises with my throat, but as I was starting, Father moved and there was a sharp movement behind my chair—perhaps my brother ducking. Then I felt him crawl slowly back to our room. I waited a while, and then opened my eyes. Father's posture struck me. He was asleep, his head tilted sideways against the chair, and his arms hanging loosely by his sides. A steady stream of light from the bright yellow bulb from our neighbour's house, which often shone into our house from above our fence, rested on a fraction of his face through the parted curtain, giving him the appearance of someone wearing a double-sided mask—one black, one white. I watched Father's face for a while until, convinced my brother had gone, I tried to sleep.

When I woke the next morning, I told my brother I'd gone to drink water and Father had started talking to me, that I did not know when I fell asleep. My brother did not say a word in reply. He sat where he was, looking at the cover of a book that had a ship at sea and mountains, his head leaning on his hand.

"Did you kill him?" I asked after a long silence.

"The idiot wasn't there," he said, to my surprise. I'd not expected it, but it seemed my brother had believed me, that my trick had worked. I'd never thought I could play a trick on him—ever. But he told me now, of how he'd gone out alone after I failed to come with him, armed with the knife. He'd slowly walked—there was no one, no one at all on the streets at that time of the night—to the madman's truck, but the madman was not in his truck! My brother was outraged.

I lay in bed, my mind wandering across a vast territory of the past. I remembered the day we caught so many fish, so many that Ikenna complained his back ached, when we sat by the river and sang the fishermen's song as if it was some freedom song, so much that our voices cracked. All we did for the rest of that evening was sing, the dying sun pitched in a corner of the sky as faint as a nipple on the chest of a teenage girl a distance away.

★ ★ ★

My brother was wrapped in his own skin for many days afterwards, broken by our successive failures. On Christmas Day, he stared out of the window at lunch, while Father talked about the money he'd sent to his friend for our journey. The word "Toronto" danced around the table like a fairy, often filling Mother with profound joy. It seemed that Father—with one eye that closed halfway—mentioned it frequently for her sake. On New Year's Eve, while the claps of firecrackers boomed around the town despite the ban placed on them by the military governor, Captain Anthony Onyearugbulem, my brother and I stayed in our room, silent and brooding. In the past, we and our elder brothers blasted firecrackers across the street, sometimes joining the street kids in mock warfare using the crackers. But not that New Year.

It was tradition to pass into the New Year in a church service, so we all packed into Father's car and joined the church, which was filled with people that night, so full that people stood at the threshold; everyone went to church on the eves, even atheists. That night was rife with superstition, with fears of the vicious, malicious spirit of the "ber" months that fought tooth-and-nail to prevent people from passing into the New Year. It was generally believed that more deaths were recorded in those months—September, October, November and December—than in all the other months of the year combined, and afraid of the grim-reaping spirit prowling across the land for last-minute harvests, the church was thrown into a claustrophobic cacophony at twelve midnight when the Pastor announced that we were now officially in 1997, shouts of "Happy New Year, hallelujah! Happy New Year, hallelujah!" renting the air as people jumped and threw themselves into each other's arms, unknown people, shaking, whistling, cooing, singing and shouting. Outside the church, fireworks—harmless rockets of strobe lights and man-made lightning—tore into the sky from the palace of the monarch of Akure, the Oba. This was the way things have always been, the way of the world that had continued on in spite of the things that had happened.

In the spirit of Yuletide, no sorrow was allowed to stay in the minds of the people. But like a curtain merely swiped to a corner for light to illuminate a room during the day, it would stand, patiently waiting for the time when night would descend, and the curtain would be swiped back to its place. It was always this way. We would return home from church, have pepper soup and sponge cakes and soft drinks and just as in past years, Father would play a video of Ras Kimono for the New Year dance.

David, Nkem and I would take to the floor with my brother, who, having forgotten our failures and even the mission, stamped his feet in rhythm at the staccato beat of Ras Kimono's reggae. Mother cheered and shouted "*Onye no chie, Onye no chie*" as Obembe, my veritable brother, danced in the light. Like most people, on that day, he sought transitory relief so much that his sorrow may have sunk into the ground, allowing him in this circus of bliss. And by dawn, when the town had reclined to sleep and calm had returned to the streets and the sky was quiet and the church was empty and deserted and the fish in the river had slept and a mumbling wind riffled through the furred night and Father was asleep in the big lounge and Mother in her room with the kids, my brother stepped back out beyond the gate, and the curtain returned to its position, closing behind him. Then dawn, like an infernal broom, swept the detritus of the festival—the peace that had come with it, the relief and even the unfeigned love—like confetti scattered on a floor after the end of a party.

15

THE TADPOLE

H ope was a tadpole:

The thing you caught and brought home with you in a can, but which, despite being kept in the right water, soon died. Father's hope that we would grow up into many great people, his map of dreams, soon died despite how much he guarded it. My hope that my brothers would always be there, that we'd all give birth to children and have a clan, even though we nurtured it in the most primal of waters, also died. So did the hope of our immigration to Canada, just as it was close to being fulfilled.

That hope came with the New Year, bringing in a new spirit, and a peace that belied the sadness of the past year. It seemed that sadness would not return to our home. Father repainted his car a shiny navy blue and talked often, even incessantly, of Mr Bayo's coming and of our potential immigration to Canada. He started to call us pet names again: Mother, *Omalicha*, the beautiful; David, *Onye-Eze*, the king; Nkem, *Nnem*, his mother. He prefixed Obembe's name and mine with "fisherman." Mother, too, recovered her weight. My brother was, however, untouched by this change. Nothing appealed to him. No news, no matter how big, pleased him. He was not moved by the idea of flying in an airplane or living in a city where we could ride through the streets on bicycles and skateboards like Mr Bayo's children. When Father first announced the possibility of this, the news had come to me as big, the animal equivalent of a cow or an elephant, but to my brother, a mere ant. And when he and I went into our room later, he pinched the ant-sized promise of a better future between his fingers and threw it out of the window, and said, "I must avenge our brothers."

But Father was determined. He woke us in the morning of January 5th—the same way he'd come into our room exactly a year before, to announce that he was moving to Yola—to announce that he was travelling to Lagos, filling me with a déjà vu. I'd heard someone say that the end of most things often bears a resemblance—even if faint—to their beginnings. This was true of us.

"I'm leaving for Lagos right now," he announced. He wore his usual spectacles, his eyes hidden behind them, and was dressed in an old short-sleeved shirt on whose front pocket was a badge of the Central Bank of Nigeria.

"I am taking your photographs with me to apply for your travel passports. Bayo will have arrived in Nigeria by the time I return and then we will all go together to Lagos for your Canadian visa."

Obembe and I had had our heads shaved two days before, and then followed Father to "our photographer," Mr Little, as we called him, who operated Little-by-Little Photos. Mr Little had made us sit in soft-cushioned chairs over which was a large fabric awning with a shiny fluorescent bulb hanging above it. Behind the chairs was a white piece of cloth that covered a third of the wall. He'd flashed a blinding light, thumped his finger and asked my brother to take the seat.

Now, Father brought out two fifty-naira notes, and put them on the table. "Be careful," he mouthed. Then turning, just like the morning he moved to Yola, he was gone.

After a breakfast of cornflakes and fried potatoes, while fetching water from the well to fill the drums, my brother announced it was time for "the final attempts."

"We will go find him once Mama and the kids are gone," he said.

"Where?" I asked.

"The River," he said without turning to look at me. "To kill him like fish, with hooked fishing lines."

I nodded.

"I have traced him two times now to the river. He seems to go there every evening."

"He does?" I asked.

"Yes," he said and nodded.

For the first few days of the New Year he did not talk about the mission, but brooded and stayed aloof, often sneaking out of the house especially in the evenings. He'd return and write things down in a notebook, and then make matchstick sketches of things. I did not ask him where he went at any time, and he did not tell me either.

"I have been monitoring him for some time now. He goes there every evening," my brother said. "He goes there almost every day and bathes there, then he sits under the mango tree where we saw him. If we kill him there," he paused as if a contradictory thought had suddenly flashed across his mind, "no one will find out."

"When shall we go?" I mumbled, nodding.

"He goes there at sunset."

Later, after Mother and the kids had gone and we were left alone, my brother pointed towards our bed and said: "We have the fishing lines here."

He dragged the long staffs from under the bed. They were long barbed sticks with sickle-like hooks attached to their ends. The lines had been shortened so much that it seemed the hooks were pinned directly to the long sticks, making them unrecognizable. I knew it was my brother who had transformed this fishing equipment into a weapon. This thought froze me.

"I brought them here after I traced him to the river yesterday," he said. "I'm now ready."

He must have fashioned the weapons during the times he disappeared from sight without telling me. I'd become suddenly filled with fear and a pond of dark imaginations. I'd searched for him frantically all over the compound wondering, feverishly, where he was, until a stubborn thought gripped me and wouldn't let me go. In response, I hurried to the well, breathing heavily until I prised the well's lid open, but it fell from my hand and slammed shut as if in protest. The noise scared a bird in the tangerine tree and it leapt up with a loud call. I waited while the dust that was raised from the splintered concrete—made by the force of the closure—blew past. Then I opened the well again and peered into it. All I could see was the sun shining from behind me into the water's top, revealing the fine sand at the bottom of it and a small plastic bucket half-buried in the clay bed beneath. I looked closely, shading my eyes until I became convinced he was not there. Then I closed the well, panting, disappointed at my own grim imagination.

The sight of the weapons made the mission real and concrete to me, as if I'd just been told about it for the first time. As my brother placed them back under the bed, I remembered all that Father had said that morning. I remembered the school we'd go to, with white people, to get the best Western education Father had always talked about as if it was a sliver of paradise which, in some way, had eluded even him. But it was abundant in Canada like leaves in a forest. I wanted to go there, and I wanted my brother to come with me. He was still talking about the river, how we were to position ourselves unseen at the banks and wait for the madman when I burst out with a cry of "No, Obe!"

He was startled.

"No, Obe, let's not do it. Look, we are going to Canada, we are going to live there." I continued, taking advantage of his silence, tasting the sap of my own courage. "Let us not do it. Let us go, we could grow up and become like Chuck Norris or Commando and come here and shoot him, even—"

I stopped abruptly because he'd begun to shake his head. Then, just then, I saw the fury in his tearful eyes.

"What, what is it?" I stammered.

"You are a fool!" he shouted. "You don't know what you are saying. You want us to run away, run away to Canada? Where is Ikenna? Where, I ask you, is Boja?"

The beautiful streets of Canada were blurring out of my mind now as he spoke.

"You don't know," he said. "But I know. I know, too, where they are now. You may leave; I don't need your help. I will do it all by myself."

At once, the images of children riding on bicycles faded from my mind and a sudden desperation to please him seized me. "No, no, Obe," I said, "I will go with you."

"You won't!" he cried, and then stormed out.

I sat still for a while, then, too afraid to remain in the room and fearing my dead brothers may have heard I did not want to avenge them as my brother had said they could, I went to the balcony and sat there.

My brother was away for a long time, gone to a place I would never know. After I'd stayed on the balcony for a while, I went to the backyard where one of Mother's multi-coloured *wrappas* hung on the ropes on which we dried our laundry. Using a low branch, I climbed up the tangerine tree and sat there thinking of everything.

When Obembe came back later, he headed straight to our room. I climbed down from the tree and followed him in, got on my knees and began pleading that I wanted to join him.

"Don't you want to go to Canada anymore?" he asked.

"Not without you," I replied.

For a moment he stood still, then, walking to the other side of the room, said: "Stand up."

I did.

"Listen, I want to go to Canada, too. That's exactly why I want us to do this quickly and pack our things. Don't you know that Father has gone to get the visas?"

I nodded.

"Listen, we will be unhappy if we leave Nigeria without doing it. Listen, let me tell you," he said, drawing nearer. "I am older than you and I know much more than you do."

I agreed with a nod.

"So, I am telling you, now listen, if we go to Canada without doing this, we will hate it there. We will not be happy. Do you want to be unhappy?"

"No."

"Me neither," he said.

"Let us go," I said, sufficiently convinced. "I want to do it."

But he hesitated. "Is that the truth?"

"The truth."

He searched my face with his eyes. "The truth?"

"Yes, the truth," I said, nodding again and again.

"Okay, let us go then."

It was late in the afternoon, and shadows had appeared like dark frescoes everywhere. My brother had put the weapons outside behind the shutters, covered with an old *wrappa*. That way, Mother would not see them. I waited for him to go behind our window and bring the fishing lines. He handed me a torchlight he'd also brought.

"In case we have to wait till it gets dark," he mumbled as I took it. "It is the best time now, we will surely find him there."

* * *

We went out into the evening like the fishermen we once were, carrying hooked fishing lines concealed in old *wrappas*. The appearance of the horizon evoked a strong feeling of déjà vu in me. Its face was rouged, the sun a hanging orb of red. As we went towards Abulu's truck, I noticed that the wooden pole of the street had been knocked down, the craning lamp smashed into bits, and the cables that held the bulbs in the lamp head unfurled so that the fluorescent core had snapped and now sagged low. We avoided places where we might be seen by the street people, who already knew our stories and who would gaze at us with sympathy or even with suspicion as we went by. We'd planned to lie in wait for the madman at the path between the esan bushes leading to the river.

As we waited, my brother told me how he'd found some men at the Omi-Ala before in a strange posture, as if worshipping some deity, and hoped they wouldn't be there this time. He was still speaking when we heard Abulu's voice approaching the river, singing happily. The madman stopped in front of a bungalow where two men, naked to the waist, sat across from each other on a wooden bench, playing Ludo. There was a glass rectangular slate with the photo of a white woman model on it. Following a marked track, the men rolled the dice around the board until they reached the prize lines. Abulu knelt across from them, vigorously babbling and shaking his head. This was dusk, the time of the day when he usually transformed into Abulu the extraordinary, and his eyes became that of a spirit and not of a man. His prayers were deep, a sort of groaning in front of the men who kept on playing their games as though they were oblivious that he was praying for them, as though one of them was not Mr Kingsley and the other, a Yoruba name ending with *ke*. I grasped the end of the prophecy: "… when this child of yours, Mr Kingsley, said he was ready to sacrifice his own daughter for money ritual. He will be shot to death by armed robbers, and his blood will be splashed on the window of his car. Lord of hosts, The Sower of Green Things, says he will be—"

He was still speaking when the man Abulu had called "Mr Kingsley," jumped to his feet and dashed into the bungalow in fury. He emerged brandishing a machete, spitting murderous curses as he chased Abulu down to where a path carved itself out between the esan and stopped. The man returned to his house, warning that he would kill Abulu if he came near his house again.

We edged away from there and made towards the river after Abulu. I followed my brother like a child who was being dragged to the scaffold of corporal punishment, dreading the whip but unable to turn away. At first we walked slowly, Obembe holding the wrapped lines, and I the torch, so as not to arouse suspicion from people around, but once we entered the area where the Celestial Church blocked the street from sight, we picked up speed. A small goat lay on its belly across from their door, a map of yellow urine beside it. An old piece of newspaper, apparently ferried by wind, stuck halfway to the door of the house like a poster, while the rest of it lay open on the dirt.

"Let us wait here," my brother said, trying to catch his breath.

We were almost at the end of the path leading to the bank. I could see that he, too, was afraid, and that, like me, the udder of courage from which we'd drunk our fill had been drained, and was now shrunken like a crone's breast. He spat and wiped it into the earth with his canvas shoe. I saw that we were close enough now, for we could hear Abulu singing and clapping from the direction of the river.

"He is there, let us attack him now," I said, my heartbeat quickening again.

"No," he whispered wagging his head, "we have to wait a bit to make sure no one is coming. Then we will go and kill him."

"But it is getting dark?"

"Don't worry," he said. He looked around, craning his head into the distance. "Let's just be sure the men are not here when we do it—the two men."

I noticed his voice was now cracked, like one who'd been crying. I imagined us turning into the ferocious matchstick men he'd drawn—those fearless ones who were capable of killing the madman, but I feared that I was not poised to be as brave as the fictitious boys who'd finished the madman with stones, knives and hooked fishing lines. I was absorbed in these thoughts when my brother unwrapped the weapons and gave me one. The sticks were very long, taller than both of us when we held them to the ground like spears of warriors of old. Then as we waited, hearing a spontaneous splash of water and the singing and clapping, my brother threw a glance at me and I heard an unsaid *Ready*? And every time I heard it, my heartbeat would pause, and then pick up again as I waited anxiously for my brother's order.

"Ben, are you afraid?" he asked me after he gave me the hooked fishing line and tossed the *wrappa* into the thickets. "Tell me, are you?"

"Yes, I am."

"Why then are you afraid? We are about to avenge our brothers, Ikenna and Boja." He wiped his brow, dropped his line into the bed of grass and placed his hand on my shoulder.

He moved closer, and raising his hooked fishing line so that the *wrappa* fell off, embraced me.

"Listen, do not be afraid," he whispered into my ear. "We are doing the right thing and God knows. We will be free."

Too scared to tell him what I really wanted to say—that he should return and let us go back home; that I was afraid he could get hurt—I muttered the verbal smokescreen: "Let's do it quickly."

He looked at me, and his face lit slowly like a lantern's light coming on. And I could tell, in that memorable moment, that the tender hands turning up the light were those of my dead brothers.

"We will!" my brother cried into the darkness.

He waited, then he rushed forward in the direction of the river, and I followed.

Later, after we got to the riverbank, I could not tell exactly why we had cried loudly as we lunged at Abulu.

Perhaps it was because my heart stopped beating the moment I sprang to my feet and I wanted to stir it back to life, or perhaps it was because my brother had begun to sob as we made forward like soldiers of old or because my spirit had rolled before me like a ball across a pitch of muck. Abulu was lying on his back, facing the sky, singing aloud when we reached the shore. The river stretched out behind, its waters covered in a quilt of darkness. The madman's eyes were closed and even though we'd lunged forward with a frantic cry spilling from the deep of our souls, he did not notice we were upon him. The djinn that seemed to suddenly possess us that moment leapt to the fore of my mind and tore every bit of my senses to shreds. We jabbed the hook of our lines blindly at his chest, his face, his hand, his head, his neck and everywhere we could, crying and weeping. The madman was frantic, mad, dazed. He flung his arms aloft to shield himself, running backwards, shouting and screaming. The blows perforated his flesh, boring bleeding holes and ripping out chunks of his flesh every time we pulled out the hooks. Although my eyes were mainly closed, when I opened them in flashes, I saw pieces of flesh unbuckling from his body, blood dripping from everywhere. His helpless cries shook the core of my being. But persistently, like caged birds, we flung our anger wild at him, leaping from bar to bar of the cage, from the roof to the floor. The madman jabbered about, his voice deafening, his body in flustered panic. We kept hitting, pulling, striking, screaming, crying, and sobbing until weakened, covered in blood, and wailing like a child, Abulu fell backwards into the water in a wild splash. I'd once been told that if a man wanted something he did not have, no matter how elusive that thing was, if his feet do not restrain him from chasing it, he would eventually grab it. This was our case.

As we watched his body being ferried away spouting blood on the darkening waters, like a wounded leviathan, we heard voices behind us, speaking aloud in Hausa. We turned in frenzy and saw the silhouettes of two men running towards us, torches flashing. Before we could lift our legs, one of them was upon me, holding my trousers from behind. The smell of alcohol was heavy around him and domineering. He wrestled me to the ground, speaking a rushed, smattering language I could not understand. I saw my brother running along the trees, calling my name aloud as the other man, drunk, too, stumbled after him. The man held my left arm in a vice-like grip, and it seemed that if I pulled harder, my arm would rip out. As I struggled to wrestle myself free, I grabbed the hooked fishing line and hit the man with the hooked end with all the courage I could muster. He cried out and stamped about in searing pain. His torch fell down and showered a momentary flash on his boot. I knew at once that he was one of the soldiers we'd seen at the river the other day.

A dust devil of fear swallowed me. In frenzy, I ran away as fast as I could, between houses, bush paths, until I was close to Abulu's decrepit truck. Then I stopped, dropped my hands to my knees and gasped for life, for air, for peace—all at once. As I stooped there on the ground, I saw the soldier, who had chased my brother, now running back towards the river. I crouched down behind Abulu's truck to duck, my heart racing, afraid the man might have seen me while walking past. I waited, still, imagining the man would come up and drag me from behind the truck, but as I waited, I became reassured by the thought that he could not have seen me since there were no street lights around the truck, and the closest one in the distance had been broken, bent from its ballast, flies nestling around it like vultures congregating on carrion. Then, I crawled for a distance through the small patch of foliage between the truck and the escarpment behind our compound and ran home.

Because I knew Mother must have closed up and returned home, I took the backyard route, through the pig mire. A distant moon illuminated the night so the trees looked scary—like still monsters with dark, indecipherable heads. A bat flew past as I neared our compound's fence, and I followed it with my eyes as it glided towards Igbafe's house. I remembered his grandfather, the only person who may have seen Boja fall into the well. He'd died at a hospital outside the city in September. He was eighty-four. I was climbing the fence when I heard a whispering. There was Obembe, standing inside the compound, beside the well, waiting for me.

"Ben!" he whispered aloud, rising swiftly from the neck of the well.

"Obe," I called out as I climbed.

"Where's your line?" he asked, trying hard to catch his breath.

"I… left it there," I stammered.

"Why?!"

"It stuck in the man's hand."

"It did?"

I nodded. "He almost caught me, the soldier. So I hit him with it."

My brother did not seem to have understood, so as he led me to the tomato garden at the back of the compound, I told him how it had happened. We then removed our blood-stained shirts and flung them over the fence like kites into the bush behind our compound. My brother took up his hooked fishing line to hide it behind the garden. But when he flashed the torchlight, I saw a patina of Abulu's bloodied flesh impaled on the hook. While he knocked the hook against the wall to remove it, I crouched beside the wall and retched into the dirt.

"Don't worry," he said, the chirping of the night crickets punctuating his speech. "It is finished."

"It is finished," a voice repeated in my ears. I nodded and my brother, dropping the line, inched forward and embraced me.

16

THE ROOSTERS

My brother and I were roosters:

The creatures that crow to wake people, announcing the end of nights like natural alarm clocks, but who, in return for their services, must be slain for man's consumption. We became roosters after we killed Abulu. But the process that transformed us into roosters really began moments after we left the garden and entered the house to find the pastor of our church, Pastor Collins, who seemed to appear almost every time something happened, concluding a visit to our home. He was still wearing a plaster over the wound on his head. He was seated in the lounge chair in the sitting room by the window, his legs sprawled out so that Nkem sat between them, playing and chattering away. He hollered at us in his deep, sonorous voice when we came in. Mother, who had grown apprehensive of our whereabouts and would have pummelled us with questions if the Pastor were not there, threw a curious glance and a sigh at us when we entered.

"The Fishermen," Pastor Collins cried once he saw us, thrusting his hands in the air.

"Sir," Obembe and I chorused in unison. "Welcome, Pastor."

"*Ehen*, my children. Come and greet me."

He stood slightly to shake our hands. He had the habit of shaking hands with everyone he met—even little children—with certain unusual reverence and humility. Ikenna once said that he was not a foolish man for his meekness, but that he was humble because he was "born again". He was a few years older than Father, but was short and solidly built.

"Pastor, when did you come?" Obembe said, flashing a smile, standing beside him, and although we'd thrown our shirts away into the dump behind our fence, he smelt of the esan grass, sweat, and of something else. The Pastor's face brightened at the question.

"I have been here a while," he replied. He peered with a squint into the watch that had slid from his arm to his wrist. "I think I have been here since six; no, say, since quarter to six."

"Where are your shirts?" Mother asked, perplexed.

I was startled. We had not planned a defence, not even thought about what it would be and had merely thrown the shirts because Abulu's blood had stained them, and entered the house with our shorts and canvas shoes.

"The heat Mama," Obembe said after a pause, "we were soaked in sweat."

"And," she continued, rising to her feet, her eyes scanning us closely. "And look at you, Benjamin, your head all covered in mud?"

All eyes fell on me.

"Tell me, where did you go?"

"We've been playing football at a pitch near the public high school," Obembe replied.

"Oh dear!" Pastor Collins cried. "These street football people."

David began to remove his shirt, distracting Mother. "What for?" Mother inquired.

"Heat, heat, Mama, I'm feeling hot, too," he said.

"Eh, you feel hot?"

He nodded.

"Ben, put on the fan for him," Mother ordered while the Pastor chuckled. "And go right away, both of you, into the bathroom and clean up!"

"No, no, let me do it," David cried. He hurriedly carried a stool to the switch box pinned to the wall, mounted it and wound the knob clockwise. The fan came to life, swirling noisily.

David had saved us, for while they were at it, my brother and I slipped away to our room and locked it. Although we'd worn our shorts inside out to conceal the bloodstains, I feared that Mother, who often found out what we did, would discover everything if we'd stood there a moment more.

The watt bulb caused me to squint for a moment when my brother turned it on when we entered the room.

"Ben," he said, his eyes filling with joy again. "We did it. We avenged them—Ike and Boja."

He locked me in a warm embrace again, and when I rested my head on his shoulder, I felt the urge to cry.

"Do you know what it means?" he said now, detaching from me, but holding my hands.

"*Esan*—reckoning," he said. "I've read a lot and know that without it, our brothers would never forgive us, and we could never be free."

He gazed away from me now to the floor. I followed his eyes and saw bloodstains on the back of his left leg. I closed my eyes, nodding in acceptance.

We huddled into the bathroom afterwards and he bathed from a bucket he placed in a corner of the bathtub, scooping water sporadically with a big jug, and pouring it on his body to wash off suds from a bar of soap. The soap had been left in a small pool of water, which had dissolved it into half its original size. To use the soap judiciously, he'd first rubbed it on his hair to lather. Then, pouring water on his head, he rubbed himself with his hands as the water and suds swam down his body. He wrapped himself with the large towel both of us shared, still smiling. When I took over at the bathtub, my hands were shaking. Winged insects that had flocked in from the tear in the netting behind the louvres of the small bathroom window to congregate around the light bulb, crawled about the walls of the bathroom while the ones that had shed their wings formed insect goo around it. I tried to focus on the insects to steady my mind, but I could not. A feeling of some great terror hung about me, and as I tried to pour water on my body, the plastic jug fell from my hand and broke.

"Ah Ben, Ben," Obembe called, dashing forward. He steadied my shoulders with his hands, "Ben, look me in the eyes," he said.

I could not so he raised his hands to my head, moved my head to focus on him.

"Are you afraid?" he asked.

I nodded.

"Why Ben, why? *Ati gba esan*—We have achieved reckoning. Why, why, Fisherman Ben, are you afraid?"

"The soldiers," I mustered. "I'm afraid of them."

"Why, what will they do?"

"I'm afraid the soldiers will come for us and kill us—all of us."

"Shh, put your voice down," he said. I had not realized that I had spoken aloud. "Listen, Ben, the soldiers won't. They don't know us; they won't. Don't even think of that. They don't know where we are or who we are. They didn't see you come here, did they?"

I shook my head.

"So, why then do you fear? There is nothing to be afraid of. Listen, days decay, like food, like fish, like dead bodies. This night will decay, too and you will forget. Listen, we will forget. Nothing"—he shook his head vigorously— "nothing will happen to us. No one will touch us. Father will come back tomorrow and take us to Mr Bayo and we will go to Canada."

He shook me to get an approval and I believed—at the time—that he easily knew when he'd convinced me, when he'd totally upturned a belief of mine or a piece of inferior knowledge as one would upturn a cup. And there were times when I needed him to do it, when I deeply craved his words of wisdom, which often moved me.

"You see it?" he asked, shaking me now.

"Tell me," I said, "what about Daddy and Mama; will the soldiers not touch them either?"

"No, they won't," he said, punching his left fist into his right palm. "They will be just fine, happy and will always come to Canada to see us."

I nodded, was silent a while before another question—like a tiger—sprang out of the cage of my thoughts. "Tell," I said softly, "what—what about you, Obe?"

"Me?" he asked. "Me?" He wiped his face with his hand, shaking his head. "Ben, I said, I said: I. Will. Be. Fine. You. Will. Be. Fine. Daddy, will be fine. Mama, will be fine. Eh, all—everything."

I nodded. I could see that he'd become frustrated with my questions.

He took a smaller jug from inside the big black drum and began washing me. The drum reminded me of how Boja, after he got saved at a Reinhard Bonnke evangelical convention, persuaded us to be baptized else we'd all go to hell. Then one after the other, he coaxed us into repentance and baptized us in the drum. I was six at the time, and Obembe, eight, and because we were much smaller, we both had to stand on empty Pepsi crates to be able to dip into the water. Then one after the other, Boja bent our heads into the water until we began to cough. Then he would lift our heads, his face gleaming, hug us and declare us free.

* * *

We were dressing when Mother called out that we should hurry up, because Pastor Collins wanted to pray for us before he left. Later, when the Pastor asked my brother and me to kneel, David insisted he would join us.

"No! Get up!" Mother barked. But David made a face, ready to cry. "If you cry, if you try that, I will flog you."

"Oh, no, Paulina," the Pastor said, laughing. "Dave, please don't worry, you will kneel after I finish with them."

David agreed. Placing his hands on our heads, the Pastor began praying, occasionally splashing spittle on our heads. I felt it on my scalp as he prayed from deep down in his soul, that God should protect us from the evil one. Midway through the prayers, he began talking about the promises of God concerning His children as if delivering a homily. When he'd finished this, he asked that these things might be "our portion" in Jesus's name. He then begged for God's mercy on our family—"I ask, oh heavenly Father that you help these kids move on after the tragic events of last year. Help them to succeed in their quest to travel overseas and bless them both. Make the officials at the Canadian embassy grant them the visas, oh God, for thou art able to make all things right; Thou art able." Mother had been interjecting a loud "amen" all along—followed closely by Nkem and David, and the muffled ones from my brother and me. She joined the

Pastor, who suddenly broke into singing, interspersing the song with hisses and clicks.

> *He is able/ abundantly able/ to deliver/ and to save/*
> *He is able/ abundantly able/ to deliver/ those who trust in Him.*

After the third round of the same tune, the Pastor returned to the prayers, this time more spiritedly. He delved into the issue of the papers needed for the visas, the funds, and then for our father. Then he prayed for Mother—"you know oh God, how this woman has suffered, so much; so much for the kids. You know all things, oh Lord."

He raised his voice louder as the sound of Mother's stifling sobs made its way into the prayers. "Wipe her tears, Lord," and then, he continued in Igbo, "Wipe her tears, Jesus. Heal her mind forever. Let her not have any cause to ever cry over her children again." After the entreaties, he thanked God, many times, for having answered the prayers, and then, requesting that we shout a "thunderous amen," he ended the prayers.

We all thanked him and shook his hands again. Mother left with him and Nkem to walk him to the gate.

★　★　★

I had lightened up after the prayers and the burden I'd brought home had felt slightly lifted. It was perhaps the assurance Obembe had given me, or the prayers; I did not know. I knew, though, that something had lifted my spirit from the pit. David informed us "our beans" were in the kitchen. So, my brother and I were eating when Mother returned from walking the Pastor, singing and dancing.

"My God has finally vanquished my enemies," she sang, lifting her hands. "*Chineke na' eme nma, ime la eke le diri gi…*"

"Mama, what is it, what?" my brother said, but she ignored him and trailed into another round of singing while we waited impatiently to know what had happened. She sang one more song, her eyes on the ceiling, before turning to us and with tear-filled eyes, said: "Abulu, *Onye Ojo a wungo*—Abulu, the evil one is dead."

My spoon, as if pushed out of my hand, fell to the floor, throwing mashed beans about. But Mother did not seem to notice. She told us what she'd heard: that "some boys" had murdered Abulu, the madman. She'd met the neighbour who found Boja's body in the well on her way from walking the Pastor. The woman was exultant and was coming to our house to break the news to her.

"They said he was killed near Omi-Ala," Mother said, tightening her *wrappa* around her waist after it came slightly undone when Nkem tugged at her legs. "You see, it was my God that kept you safe when you were going to that place every evening to fish. Although it still caused a major damage in the end, but at least none of you was hurt there. That river is such a place of evil and horror. Imagine the body of that evil man lying there?" she said, pointing at the door.

"You see, my Chi is alive and has finally avenged me. Abulu lashed my children with his tongue and now that tongue will rot in his mouth."

Mother carried on her celebration while Obembe and I tried to understand what we had brought on ourselves. But we could not, for if one attempted to look into the future one would see nothing; it was like peeping into a person's earhole. It was hard for me to believe that knowledge of a deed carried out in the cover of darkness had spread so widely; Obembe and I had not expected this to happen. We wanted to kill the madman and let him die off by the river shore with his body only discovered after it had begun to decompose—just like Boja.

My brother and I retired into our room after dinner to sleep in silence, with my head filled with images of the last minutes of Abulu's life. I was thinking about the strange force that'd possessed me in that moment, for my hands had moved with such precision, such pressure that every blow had cut deep into Abulu's flesh. I was think-ing of his body on the river, of the fish crowding it when my brother, who, like me, was unable to sleep and was oblivious that I too was awake, suddenly rose from the bed and burst into tears.

"I didn't know… I did it for you, we, Ben and I, we did it for you; both of you," he sobbed. "I'm sorry for this Mama and Daddy. I'm sorry, we did it so you may not suffer anymore, but—" The words went inaudible, drowned in a storm of jerking sobs.

I watched him discreetly, my mind tormented by the fear of a future I thought was nearer than we could imagine—a future that was the next day. I prayed then, quietly, in the faintest whispers possible, that the day might not come, that the bones of its legs be broken.

★ ★ ★

I did not know when I'd slept, but I was awoken by the voice of a distant muezzin calling the faithful to prayer. It was at the neck of the morning, and early sunlight had percolated into the room through the window my brother had left open. I could not tell if he'd slept at all, but he was seated at his study table, reading a dog-eared book with yellowed pages. I knew it was the book about the German man who walked from Siberia to Germany, the title of which I'd forgotten. He was nude to the waist, his collarbones prominent. He'd lost a considerable amount of weight over the weeks of deliberation and planning of our now accomplished mission.

"Obe," I called out at him. He was startled. He rose briskly to his feet and came to the bed.

"Are you afraid?" he asked.

"No," I said at first, but then said, "But I still fear those soldiers might find us."

"No, no, they won't," he said, shaking his head. "We have to stay inside, though, till Father comes, and Mr Bayo takes us to Canada. Don't worry, we will leave this country and all of it behind."

"When are they coming?"

"Today," he said. "Father is coming today, and we might leave for Canada next week. Possible."

I nodded.

"Listen, I don't want you to be afraid," he said again.

My brother stared blankly on, lost in thoughts. Then, collecting himself and thinking it might have worried me, said, "Should I tell you a story?"

I said yes. Again he was lost for a moment; his lips seemed to move but articulated no words. Then, again calling himself to order, he began the story of Clemens Forell who escaped from Russian imprisonment in Siberia and journeyed to Germany. He was still telling the story when we began to hear loud voices in the neighbourhood.

We knew it must be from a mob gathering somewhere. My brother stopped telling the story and fixed his eyes on mine. Together, we went out to the sitting room where Mother was preparing to leave for her shop, dressing up Nkem. It was long into the morning, about nine and the room smelt of fried food. There was a plate of leftover fried eggs between the prongs of a dinner fork, and a piece of fried yam on the table beside the plate.

We sat in the lounges with her and Obembe asked her what the noise was about.

"Abulu," she said, as she changed Nkem's diapers. "They are taking his body away in a truck and they say that soldiers are going about searching for the boys who killed him. I don't understand these people really," she said in English. "Why can't someone kill that useless person? Why shouldn't the boys kill him? What if he'd put some stark fear in their minds that some evil will befall them? Who should blame them? Anyway, they said the boys fought the soldiers, too."

"Do the soldiers want to kill them?" I said.

Mother looked up at me and her eyes betrayed surprise at my question. "No, I don't know if they will kill them." She shrugged her shoulders. "Anyway, both of you should stay indoors—no going out until this has cooled. You know that already you are connected to that madman in some way, so I don't want you to witness any of this.

None of you is getting involved with that creature again ever, whether in life or in death."

My brother said: "Yes Mama" and I followed in a broken voice. Then Mother, with David repeating every word of the order, asked that we come and lock up the gate and the main door as they left for work. I rose to go lock the gate.

"Be sure to open the gate for Eme when he returns," she said. "He will come in the afternoon."

I nodded and hurriedly locked the gate after them, afraid someone outside might see me.

My brother charged at me when I got back into the house, and pushed me against the storm door, sending my heart out of my body.

"Why did you say that in Mama's presence, eh? Are you stupid? Do you want her to fall sick again? Do you want to destroy us again?"

I shouted "No!" to every question, shaking my head.

"Listen," he said, panting. "They must not find out. You hear?"

I nodded, my eyes on the floor, wetting. Then it seemed that he pitied me. He softened and put his hand on my shoulder as he had always done.

"Listen, Ben, I didn't mean to hurt you," he said. "I'm sorry."

I nodded.

"Don't worry, if they come here, we will not open for them. They will think the house is unoccupied and go away. We will be safe."

He closed every curtain in the house and locked the doors, and then went into Ikenna and Boja's now empty room. I followed him and we sat on the new mattress Father had bought—the only thing in the room. Even though it was empty, signs of my brothers were everywhere, like indelible stains. I could see the shinier portion of the wall where the M.K.O. calendar had been yanked off, and the various graffiti and matchstick man portraits. Then I gazed at the ceiling that was full of cobwebs and spiders, indications that time had passed since they died.

I was watching the outline of a gecko climbing up the thin transparent curtain on which the sun was shining while my brother sat as quiet as the dead when we heard loud banging at our gate. My brother dragged me frantically under the bed with him, and we rolled into the dark enclave as the banging continued, attended by cries of "Open the gate! Anyone in there, open the gate!" Obembe pulled the bed sheet so that it sagged downward, covering us up. I accidentally pushed an empty lidless tin close to my side; it was filled with a gossamer film of web through which the tin's interior—which was black as tar—could be seen. It must have been one of the tins we had gathered for the storage of fish and tadpoles, one that had escaped Father's eyes when he emptied the room.

The banging at the gate stopped shortly after we got under the bed, but we remained, in the darkness, breathless, my head throbbing.

"They are gone," I said to my brother after a while.

"Yes," he replied. "But we must remain here till we are sure they won't return. What if they are going to climb the fence and come in, or if they—" He discontinued, staring blankly as if he could hear something suspicious. Then, he said: "Let's wait here."

We remained there, me holding back an unbearable urge to urinate. I did not want to give him any cause to be afraid or sad.

* * *

The next knock on the gate came some hour or so after the first one. It was soft and was followed by the familiar voice of Father calling out our names, asking if we were at home. We emerged from under the bed and began wiping the dust off our clothes and bodies.

"Hurry, hurry, open for him," my brother said as he ran to the bathroom to wash his eyes.

Father was beaming with smiles when I opened the gate. He wore a cap and his spectacles.

"Were you both asleep?" he asked.

"Yes, Daddy," I said.

"Oh, good gracious! My boys are now idle men. Well, all that is about to change," he chattered as he entered.

"Why are you locking it when we are in?"

"There's been a robbery today," I said.

"What, in broad daylight?"

"Yes, Daddy."

He was in the sitting room, his briefcase on a chair beside him, talking with my brother, who stood behind the chairs, while Father removed his shoes. As I entered the house, I heard my brother say "How was your journey?"

"Great, just great," Father said, smiling, as I had not seen him do in a long time. "Ben said there was a robbery here today?"

My brother shot a look at me before nodding his head.

"Wow," Father said. "Well, anyway, I have good news for both of you my sons, but first, any idea if your mother left food in the house?"

"She fried yams this morning, and I think some are still left—"

"She left some for you in your chinaware," my brother said, completing what I'd begun to say.

My voice shook as I spoke because a siren, wailing somewhere in the street, had engulfed me with fresh fear of the soldiers. Father noticed. He glanced from face to face searching for what he did not know. "Are you all right, both of you?"

"We remembered Ike and Boja," my brother said. He burst into tears.

Father gazed emptily at the wall for a moment, then raising his head, said: "Listen, I want both of you to put all that behind you from now on. It is why I'm doing all this—borrowing, running here and there and doing everything—to get you into a new environment where you'd not see anything that can remind you of them. Look at your mother, look at what happened to her." He pointed towards the blank wall as if Mother was there. "That woman has suffered a lot. Why? Because of the love she has for her children. The love, I mean, for you—all of you." Father shook his head rapidly.

"Now, I am telling both of you, henceforth, before you do anything, anything at all, think first of her, of what it might do to her—only and only then should you make your decision. I'm not even asking you to think of me; think of her. Do you hear me?"

We both nodded.

"Good, now, someone should get me the food; I will eat it, even if cold."

I went into the kitchen with the words he'd said in

my head. I carried the plate of food—fried yam and fried eggs—to him, with a fork. The big smile had returned to his face, and as he ate, he told us about how he'd procured our travel passports from the immigration office in Lagos. He did not imagine, even remotely, that his ship had sunk, and his life's worth of goods—his map of dreams (Ikenna=pilot, Boja=lawyer, Obembe=doctor, I=professor)—was gone.

He brought out cakes wrapped in shiny wrappers and tossed two of them to each of us.

"And you know what is more?" he said, still rummaging in his bag. "Bayo is now in Nigeria. I called Atinuke yesterday, and spoke with him. He will be here next week to take you to Lagos for your visas."

Next week.

These words brought the possibility of Canada so close again that I was broken by it. The time Father had said— "next week"—seemed too far. I wished that we would make it there. I thought we could pack our things and go to Ibadan to stay away at Mr Bayo's house, and when our visas were ready, we could go from there. No one would trace us to Ibadan. I yearned to suggest this to Father, but was afraid about how Obembe might take it. But later, after Father had eaten and fallen asleep, I said this idea to my brother.

"That would mean giving ourselves away," he replied without raising his head from the book he was reading.

I struggled to give an answer, but couldn't.

He shook his head. "Listen, Ben, don't try it; not at all. Don't worry, I have a plan."

When Mother returned that evening and told Father of the searching, and of what she'd heard in the streets that the kids killed the madman with fishing hooks, Father wondered why we hadn't mentioned it.

"I thought the robbery was more important," I said.

"Did they come here?" he asked, his eyes stern under his eyeglasses.

"No," my brother replied. "I was mostly awake while Ben slept, and I did not hear anything except for when you came."

Father nodded.

"Perhaps he'd tried to prophesy to the kids and they'd fought him, fearing it would come to reality," he said. "It's a shame that such spirit possessed that man."

"It might have been so," Mother agreed.

Our parents spent the rest of the night talking about Canada. Father recounted his errand to Mother with the same measure of joy, while my head ached badly, and by the time I retired to bed—earlier than anyone else—I was feeling so ill I feared I would die. The longing to move to Canada had become, by this time, so strong that I wanted badly to do it, even if without Obembe. This continued long into the night, after Father had dozed off in the lounge, his throat buzzing with loud snorts. Then the calm and assurance took flight and a chilling fear, as strong as a cold, flushed into me. I began to fear that something I could not yet see, but could smell—could tell was coming—would come before *next week*. I sprang from the bed and tapped my brother who was under a *wrappa*. I could tell he was not asleep.

"Obe, we should tell them what we have done so Father can take us—run away—to Ibadan to meet Mr Bayo. So we can travel to Canada next week."

I'd rushed the words as if I'd memorized them. My brother emerged from under the *wrappa* and sat up.

"Next week," I muttered to him, my breath catching.

But my brother did not respond. He looked at me in a way that made it seem as though he couldn't see me. Then he returned under the *wrappa* and disappeared.

★   ★   ★

It must have been in the dead of the night when, panting and covered in sweat, and my head still aching, I began hearing "Ben wake up, wake up," as a hand shook me.

"Obe," I gasped.

But he was not visible for the first few moments after I opened my eyes. Then, I saw him throwing out clothes from his closet and packing things into a bag, dashing about.

"Come, stand up, we have to leave this night," he said, gesturing.

"What, leave home?"

"Yes, right now," he broke off from his packing, and hissed to me. "Listen, I have realized the possibilities—the soldiers can find us. I saw the old priest of that church while I was running away from the soldier, and he recognized me. I almost knocked him down."

My brother could see the horror that filled my eyes at this revelation. Why, I wondered, didn't he tell me this before?

"I have been afraid that he would tell them it was us. So, let us leave, now. They could still come this night, and they, too, might identify us. I've been awake and I've heard noises outside all night. If they don't, they will surely come in the morning or anytime. We'll go to prison if they find us."

"So, what should we do?"

"We must leave, leave: that's the only way. It is the only way we can protect ourselves and our parents—Mama."

"Where would we go?"

"Anywhere," he said, starting to cry. "Listen, don't you know they will find us by morning?"

I wanted to say something, but no words came. He turned back and started unzipping a bag.

"Won't you move from there now?" he said when he looked up again and saw me still standing there.

"No," I said. "Where shall we go?"

"They will search here in the morning, once the sky clears." His voice broke. "And they will find us." He paused and sat on the edge of the bed for less than a second and stood again. "They'll find us." He shook his head gravely.

"But I'm afraid, Obe. We should not have killed him."

"Don't say this. He killed our brothers; he deserved to die."

"Father will get us a lawyer, we shouldn't leave, Obe," I said emptily, sobs choking my words. "Don't let us go."

"Listen, don't be stupid. The soldiers will kill us! We wounded their man, they will shoot us, like Gideon Orkar, don't you know?" He paused to drive his question home. "Imagine what will happen to Mama. This is a military regime, Abacha's soldiers. Let's go somewhere, maybe to our village for a while then write to them from there. They can then arrange to meet us, take us to Ibadan, and then Canada."

The last words temporarily submerged my fears.

"Okay," I declared.

"Then pack, quick, quick."

He waited for me to put my things in the bag.

"Quick, quick. I can hear Mother's voice, she is praying; she might come in here to see us."

He craned his ear to the door for any sound whatsoever as I pooled all my clothes into my rucksack and packed our shoes into another. Then, before I knew what was happening, he jumped out of the shutters with his bag and the shoes and became a silhouette whose arms I could barely see.

"Throw yours!" he whispered from below the window.

I threw my rucksack and jumped after him, falling. My brother hoisted me up and we started off across the road that led to our church, passing houses that were dead in sleep. The night was dimly lit by the bulbs on the verandas of houses and a few street lamps. My brother would wait for me, run and wait, whispering "come" or "run" every time he paused. As we ran, my fear increased. Strange visions encumbered my movement as memories rose from their tombs; now and again I glanced backwards to the direction of our home, until I could no longer see it. Behind us, the moonlight percolated across the night sky and cast a grey hue around the way we'd come and over the town that lay asleep. Somewhere, the sound of singing voices, supported by drumming and bell-ringing, steadily reached us even louder than the distant noise.

We'd covered a good distance, and although it was difficult to make out in the darkness, I reckon we were about to reach the district centre when Father's words—"henceforth, before you do anything, think first of her, of what it might do to her, and then make your decision"—pierced me sharply, sending a stray rod into my track. I lost balance like derailing boxcars, my heart tooting, and found myself on the ground.

"What happened?" he asked, turning back.

"I want to go back," I said.

"What? Benjamin, are you mad?"

"I want to go back."

When he moved towards me, afraid he'd try to drag me along, I cried: "No, no, don't come, don't come. Just let me go back."

He made forward again, but I started to my feet and staggered off. My knees had been bruised and I could tell they were bleeding.

"Wait! Wait!" he cried.

I stopped.

"I won't touch you," he said, lifting his hands in surrender.

He unclasped his rucksack, laid it on the ground and walked to me. He made to hug me, but once his hands were around my neck, he tried to pull me forward, but I put my leg between his like Boja was adept at doing and scissored his legs. We both fell sprawling together. While we struggled, he kept insisting we had to go together, while I pleaded with him to let me return to our parents—that I didn't want them to miss us both. I extricated myself in the end, leaving with my shirt partly ripped.

"Ben!" he cried when I ran a distance from him.

I'd begun to sob freely, too. He gazed at me, his mouth open. He could now see that I was determined to go back, for my brother knew things.

"If you won't come with me, then tell them," he said in a shaky voice. "Tell Daddy and Mama that I… ran away."

He could barely speak, his heart was now bursting with grief.

"Tell them that we—you, me—did it for them."

In a flash, I was back to him—clasped to his body. He held me closer and put his hand behind my head, to the oblong side of my scalp. For a long time Obembe sobbed against my shoulder, then he disentangled from me, and moved backwards without turning away from me. He raced a distance away. There he stopped, and cried: "I will write to you!"

Then, the darkness swallowed him. I lunged forward and cried: "No, don't go Obe, don't go, don't leave me." But there was nothing; no trace of him in the darkness.

"Obe!" I called aloud, making a frantic dash forward. But he did not stop, did not seem to hear. I tripped, fell and struggled up. "Obe!" I called even louder, more desperately into the night as I entered the road. To my left, to my right, forward, backwards—no trace of him. No sound, no one about. He was gone.

I sank to the ground and began to wail anew.

THE MOTH

I, Benjamin, was a moth:

The fragile thing with wings, who basks in light, but who soon loses its wings and falls to the ground. When my brothers, Ikenna and Boja, died, I felt like a fabric awning that had always sheltered me was torn off from over my head, but when Obembe ran away, I fell from space, like a moth whose wings were plucked off its body while in flight, and became a being that could no longer fly but crawl.

I had never lived without my brothers. I'd grown up watching them while I merely followed their lead, living a version of their early lives. I'd never done anything without them—especially without Obembe who, having absorbed much wisdom from the older two and distilled broader knowledge through books, had left me totally dependent. I had lived with them, relied on them so much that no concrete thought ever took shape in my mind without first floating through their heads. And even after Ikenna and Boja died, I'd lived on as if unaffected because Obembe had closed in on their absence, proffering answers to my questions. But he, too, was now gone, leaving me at the threshold of a door I shuddered to enter. Not that I feared to think or live for myself, I did not know how, had not prepared for it.

When I returned, our room was dead, empty and dark. I lay on the floor weeping as my brother ran, his rucksack on his back, his small Ghana-must-go bag in his hand. As the darkness gradually lifted over Akure, he ran on, panting, sweating. He must have run—perhaps spurred by the story of Clemens Forell—as Far As His Feet Would Carry Him. He must have trod along the silent, dark street and reached its end. He may have stopped there a while to look up at the swathe of plain tracks, unable to decide, for a moment, which way to go. But like Forell, he must have been subdued by the fear of capture, and the fear must have powered his mind like a turbine, spinning out ideas. He must have stumbled many times as he ran or fell into potholes, or was tripped by tangled foliage. He must have got tired along the way and become thirsty, needing water. He must have been drenched in sweat, becoming dirty. He must have raced on, carrying the black banner of fear in his heart, perhaps the fear of what would become of me, his brother, with whom he had attempted to put out the fire that had engulfed our household. And that fire had, in return, threatened to consume us.

My brother was probably still running when the horizon cleared and our street woke with the tremor of voices, loud cries and gunshots as if under an invasion by an enemy army. Voices barked orders and howled, arms banged on doors, feet stamped the ground with feral intensity and hands brandished guns and cowhides. They collected into a whole—half a dozen soldiers—and began banging on our gate. Then, once Father opened, they shoved him away, barking like wounded dogs: "Where are they? Where are those juvenile delinquents?"

"Murderers!" another spat.

As the tumult erupted, Nkem cried out as Mother rushed to the door of my room and banged repeatedly, calling, "Obembe, Benjamin, wake! Wake!" But while she spoke, the boots stamped in and the voices closed in on hers. There was an outcry, a shriek and the sound of one falling to the ground.

"Please, please officers, they are innocent, they are innocent."

"Shut up! Where are those boys?"

Then the ferocious knocking and booting on the door began.

"Will you boys open now or I will blast your heads."

I unlatched the door.

★ ★ ★

The next time I came home was three weeks after they took me away, long after my entrance into the new and frightening world devoid of my brothers. I had returned to have a bath. On Mr Bayo's persistence, our lawyer, Barrister Biodun, had persuaded the judge to allow me to be brought here to have a bath at least. Not a bail, they'd maintained, but a reprieve. Father told me Mother had worried I had not had a bath in three weeks. At the time, whenever he told me something she'd said, I imagined as hard as I could, how she'd said it because, for all those three weeks, I'd hardly seen her speak. She'd relapsed into what she became after my brothers died—afflicted by invisible spiders of grief. But although she wasn't speaking, her every gaze, every movement of her hand seemed to contain a thousand words. I avoided her, wounded by her grief. I'd once heard someone say—when Ikenna and Boja died—that a mother who loses a child loses a part of herself. When she put a bottle of Fanta in my mouth just before the second court session, I wanted to reach to her and tell her something, but I could not. Twice during the trial she lost control and screamed or cried out. One such time was after the prosecutors, led by a very dark man whose appearance in black apparel gave him the look of a movie demon, argued that Obembe and I were guilty of manslaughter.

On the day before my first trial when he'd visited me, Barrister Biodun had counselled me to just focus on something else, the window, the railing—anything. The wardens, men in brown khaki uniforms, had brought me out to meet him, my lawyer and Father's old friend. He'd always come with smiles and a certain confidence that sometimes annoyed me. He and my father had come into the small room where I received visitors while a junior warden started a stopwatch. The place had a pungent smell that often reminded me of my school latrine—the smell of stale shit. Barrister Biodun had told me not to worry, that we would win the case. He'd said, too, that justice was going to be manipulated because we'd injured one of the soldiers. He was always confident. But Barrister Biodun, on this last day of my expedited trial, was not full of smiles. He was sullen and sober. The map of emotion splayed over his face was grainy and unintelligible. When he came to where Father and I stood at a corner of the courtroom, where he'd revealed the mystery about his eye to me, he'd said: "We will do our best and leave the rest in God's hands."

We returned home in Pastor Collins's van. He'd come to pick me up with Father and Mr Bayo, who'd almost totally abandoned his own family in Ibadan, returning to Akure every now and then with the hope that they would secure my release and he would take me with him to Canada, where he lived with his children. I almost could not recognize him. He was now much different than the man I last saw when I was four or so. He was much lighter in complexion and tints of grey hair creased the sides of his head. He seemed to pause between speeches in the way a driver would pull the brake, slow down and ramp up again.

We drove in the van, the one with the name of the church, *Assemblies of God Church, Araromi, Akure Branch* and its motto, *Come as you are, but leave as new*, boldly inscribed on it. They spoke little to me because I'd barely answered questions, only nodding. Since the day I was first taken to the prison, I'd begun avoiding talking to my parents and Mr Bayo. I could not bear to face them. The salvation I had thrashed—the prospect of a new life in Canada—had hit Father so hard that I often wondered how he still kept on a calm veneer as if unfazed. I confided mostly in the lawyer, a man whose voice was thin like a woman's and who often assured me, beyond every other person, that I would soon be released, with the refrain "in a short time."

But as we drove home, unable to hold back the question that had been throbbing in my brain, I said: "Has Obembe returned?"

"No," Mr Bayo said, "but he will soon return." Father was about to say something, but Mr Bayo put it off by adding: "We have sent for him. He will come."

I wanted to ask where they found him, but Father said: "Yes, true." I waited, and then I asked Father where his car was.

"Bode has taken it for repairs," was his curt riposte. He turned back and met my eyes, but I quickly looked away. "It's got a 'plug' problem," Father said. "Bad plug."

He'd said this in English because Mr Bayo, a Yoruba, did not know Igbo. I nodded. We'd set into a road that was so beat-up and potholed that Pastor Collins, like other commuters, had to veer to the shoulder to escape the gaping maws. As he negotiated the boundary of a stretch of bush, a school of copse—mostly elephant grasses—rapped against the body of the van.

"Are they treating you well?" Mr Bayo asked.

He was sitting with me in the back seat, the space between us filled with tracts, Christian books and church advert bills, most of which featured the same images of Pastor Collins, holding a microphone.

"Yes," I said.

Although I'd not been beaten or bullied, I felt I'd lied. For there had been threats and verbal slurs. The first day in the prison, amidst the inconsolable tears and frantic beating of my heart, one of the wardens had called me a "little murderer." But the man had disappeared soon after they kept me in the empty, windowless cell with bars through which I could see nothing but other cells with men in them, sitting like caged animals. Some of the rooms were empty, except for the prisoners. Mine had a worn-out mat, a bucket with a lid into which I defecated and a water cask that was refilled once a week. The cell that faced mine was occupied by a fair-skinned man, whose face and body were covered with wounds, scars and dirt, giving him a horrible appearance. He sat at one corner of his cage, staring blankly at the wall, his expression vacant—catatonic. This man would later become my friend.

"Ben, do you mean you have not been beaten or hit at all?" Pastor Collins asked after I said yes to the first question from Mr Bayo.

"No, sir," I said.

"Ben, tell us the truth," Father said. He glanced back. "Please, tell the truth."

I met his eyes again, and this time, I could not look away. Instead of speaking, I began to cry.

Mr Bayo reached for my hand, and began squeezing, saying: "Sorry, sorry. *Ma su ku mo*—stop crying." He revelled in speaking Yoruba to my brothers and me. The last time he visited Nigeria, in 1991, he'd often joked about how my brothers and I, mere children, had learned Yoruba, the language of Akure, better than our parents.

"Ben," Pastor Collins called in his tender voice as the van neared our district.

"Sir," I answered.

"You are and will be a great man." He raised one hand from the wheel. "Even if they end up putting you there—I hope not, and that won't be the case in Jesus's name—"

"Yes, amen," Father interrupted.

"But should that happen, know that there will be nothing greater, nothing grander than that you will be suffering for your brothers. No! There will be nothing greater. Our Lord Jesus says: 'For there's no greater love than for a man to suffer for his friends.'"

"Yes! Very true," Father yodelled, nodding fiercely.

"Should they put you there, you will not be suffering for mere friends, but for your brothers." This one was answered by a clash between Father's booming "Yes" and

Mr Bayo's foreign-accented vociferation of "Absolutely, absolutely, Pastor."

"Nothing," the Pastor repeated.

Father's yodelling of "yes" took a turn for the worse at this, it even silenced the Pastor. When Father finished, he thanked the Pastor, heartily, gravely. Then, for the rest of the journey, we drove in silence. Although my fear of incarceration was now increased, the thought that whatever I faced, I would be facing it for my brothers, comforted me. It was a strange feeling.

I was broken earthenware filled with dust by the time we got home. David lingered around me, watching me from a distance but avoiding my eyes and darting backwards whenever I inched closer to take his hand. I moved around the house like a wretched stranger who'd suddenly found himself in the court of a monarch. I trod the ground with caution and did not enter my room. Every step I took brought the past to me with gripping palpability. I was little bothered by the days I'd spent on the unpaved floor of the cage-like room where I'd been confined for many days, with only a book to keep me company. I was bothered by the effect of the confinement on my parents, especially on Mother, and by the whereabouts of my brother. I thought, as I bathed, about what Father had revealed to me in the court the previous week, when, before a session, he'd drawn me to a corner of the court and said: "There's something I must let you know" in a grave voice. I noticed he was crying. When we'd gone out of earshot of anyone else, he nodded and suppressed a grin in an attempt to conceal his grief. He raised his head again to look at me and moved his finger to the end of his eyes to wipe the tears. He removed his spectacles and stared at me with his bad eye. He hardly removed the spectacles since that day he returned home with a plaster around his eye, a scar on the left side of his face. He tilted his head forwards, held my hand and whispered.

"*Ge nti*, Azikiwe," he said in a subtle Igbo. "What you have done is great. *Ge nti, eh*. Do not regret it, but your mother must never hear a word of what I tell you here now."

I nodded.

"Good," he said in English, his voice diminishing. "She must never. See, this thing in my eye is not a cataract, it was—" He stopped, gazing fixedly at me. "The madman you killed did it to me."

"Eh!" I cried out, drawing attention from the surroundings. Even Mother looked up from where she was beside David, her hands encamped around her frail body.

"I told you not to shout," Father said like a scared child, his eyes in Mother's direction. "You see, after that madman came to your brothers' service of songs, I was very hurt. I felt ashamed and I felt he'd smitten us enough. I wanted to kill him with my own hands, since neither these people nor this government would do it for me. I went with a knife but just as I advanced on him, he threw the content of a bowl in my face. That man you killed almost blinded me."

He folded his hands together as I tried to make sense of what he'd told me, the image of the day he returned as poignant in my mind as the present. He rose and walked across the hall, while I found myself thinking of how fish in the Omi-Ala swam and how they were suspended and held up against the currents.

When I finished my bath, I wiped my body with Father's towel and then wrapped it around me; I replayed what Father had told me earlier, before we came home.

"Bayo got both of you Canadian visas. If this hadn't happened, you both would have been on your way there by now."

I began to grieve again, and returned to the sitting room after my bath in tears. Mr Bayo was seated across from Father, his hands resting on both knees, his eyes completely focused on Father's face.

"Take your seat," Mr Bayo said. "Benny, when you go there today, don't be afraid. Don't be at all. You're a child and the man you killed was not just a madman, but one that had wronged you. It will be wrong to jail you for this. Go there, say what you did and they will free you." He paused. "Oh no, stop crying."

"Azikiwe, I have told you not to do this," Father said.

"No, Eme, don't; he is but a child," Mr Bayo said. "They will free you and I will take you to Canada the next day. It is why I'm still here—waiting for you. You hear?"

I nodded.

"Then, please wipe your eyes."

His mention of Canada skewered my heart again. The thought that I had been close enough to going to the places in the photos he sent us or living in a house made of wood, the leafless trees under which his daughters, Kemi and Shayo, posed atop bicycles. I thought of "Western education," this phenomenon that I'd craved so badly, the only thing I'd grown up thinking could ever make Father happy, slipping beyond my grasp. This feeling of lost opportunity so strongly overwhelmed me that, without a thought, I sank to my knees, clasped his legs and began saying, "Please Mr Bayo, take me now, why not take me now?"

For a moment he and Father exchanged glances, short of words.

"Daddy, please tell him to take me now," I pleaded, rubbing my palms together. "Tell him to take me now, please, Daddy."

In reply, Father sank his head down to his palms, weeping. It dawned on me for the first time that Father, our father, the strong man, could not help me; he'd become a tamed eagle with broken claws and a crooked beak.

"Ben, listen," Mr Bayo began but I was not listening. I was thinking of flying in an actual plane, soaring like a bird in the sky. It would be long after he'd spoken that I would recall he'd said: "I cannot take you now because, you know, they will arrest your father. We need to face them first. Don't worry, they will free you. They have no other choice."

He reached for my hand and slipped a handkerchief in it, saying: "Wipe your tears, please."

I buried my head in the handkerchief so that I could recline away—even if for a moment—from a world that had now become a pool of fire threatening to obliterate me, a mere little moth.

18

THE EGRETS

David and Nkem were egrets:

The wool-white birds that appear in flocks after a storm, their wings unspotted, their lives unscathed. Although they became egrets in the midst of the storm, they emerged, wings afloat in the air, at the end of it, when everything as I knew it had changed.

The first was Father: the next time I saw him he had grown a grey beard. It was on the day of my release and I had not seen him and the rest of my family in six years. When they finally came, I noticed they had all changed beyond recognition. I was saddened by what Father had become—a gaunt, wiry man whom life, like a blacksmith, had beaten into the shape of a sickle. Even his voice had accrued a certain rancour as though the detritus of words long left unsaid inside the cave of his mouth had become rusty and scattered in tiny bits on the top of his tongue whenever he opened his mouth to speak. Although I could tell he had undergone many medical procedures over the past years, the changes were difficult to fully describe.

Mother had got much older, too. Like Father, a certain weight had gathered like a lump behind her voice, making her words come forth as if bogged down, the way obesity affects a person's gait, causing them to lumber. While we sat on a wooden bench inside the prison house awaiting the final signature of the head warden, Father had told me about how the spiders returned to her vision after Obembe and I left home, but that she soon recovered. As he spoke, I looked at the opposite wall that was littered with different portraits of hateful men in uniforms and obituaries printed on cheap posters. The blue paint was weak, faded and mildewed from humidity. I let my eyes focus on the clock on the wall because I hadn't seen one in a long while. The time was forty-two minutes after five and the little hand was moving towards the six.

But of all of them, it was the change that I noticed in David that surprised me the most. When I saw him, it struck me how he'd taken up Boja's exact body. There was almost no difference in him except that, while Boja was characteristically spirited, David came across as shy and somewhat restrained. The first time he said anything after

the initial pleasantries we shared at the prison compound
was when we drove close to the heart of the town. He
was ten. This was the same child, I recalled, for whom, in
the memorable months leading to his birth (and Nkem's),
Mother would often break into a song she believed gave
the unborn child joy, and we all believed this back then.
My brothers and I would gather when she began singing
and dancing, for her voice was enthralling. Ikenna would
become a drummer, and would drum with spoons on the
table. Boja would become a flautist, and he would make
flute sounds with his mouth. Obembe would become a
whistler, and he would blow whistles to the tune. I would
become a cheerer, clapping to the beats while Mother
repeated the refrain:

Iyoghogho Iyogho Iyoghogho,

Ka'nyi je na nke Bishopu	Let us go to the Bishop's,
na five akwola	it is five o'clock
Ihe ne ewe m'iwe bun	I'm only sad because
a efe'm akorako	my laundry is still wet
Nwa'm bun a-afo	But I'm relieved to know that
na'ewe ahuli	the child in my womb is happy

A strong urge to draw David to myself and embrace him
had seized me, when Father suddenly said: "Demolitions,"
as if I had asked him. "Everywhere."

He'd seen a crane somewhere in the distance pulling down a house, people gathered around it. I had seen a similar scene somewhere earlier, near an abandoned public toilet.

"Why?" I asked.

"They want to make this place a city," David said without looking at me. "The new Governor has asked that most of those houses be brought down."

A preacher, the only person allowed to see me, had told me about the change in government. Because of my age at the time, the judge had deemed me unworthy of a life imprisonment or capital punishment. And, also, I was not worthy of juvenile prison because I'd committed murder. Hence, they decided that I serve an eight-year incarceration without visits or contact with my family. That session, all of it, had been stored in a sealed bottle, and many nights in the cell, while mosquitoes buzzed around my ears, I'd catch sudden glimpses of the courthouse, green curtain waving, and the judge seated across on the elevated podium, his voice deep and guttural:

...*you will be there till society deems you an adult, able to conduct yourself in a civilized way acceptable to the society and mankind. In light of this, and by the powers conferred in me by the Federal Justice System of the Federal Republic of Nigeria, and by the recommendations of the jury that justice be tempered with mercy—for the sake of your parents, Mr and Mrs Agwu, I hereby sentence you,*

Benjamin Azikiwe Agwu, to eight years' confinement without familial contacts—until you, now ten, shall reach societal-proved maturity age of eighteen. The court is hereby dismissed.

Then I would see how, in the immediate fear that seized me, I shot a glance at my father and saw a smile hop to his forehead like a praying mantis as Mother, with an outcry, and hands that helicoptered over her head, pleaded with God who lived there that He couldn't afford to be silent when all this was happening to her, *not this time*. Then when the wardens handcuffed me, and began pushing me towards the back exit, my understanding of things suddenly shrunk to that of an unformed child—a foetus, as if everyone there were visitors who'd come to see me in my own world and were now about to leave—as if it wasn't me, but them that were being taken away.

* * *

The prison, by policy, allowed a preacher to visit the inmates. One of them, Evangelist Ajayi, came every fortnight or so, and it was through him I kept abreast of the happenings in the outside world. He'd said, a week before I was told that I was to be released, that in the spirit of the first ever transition from military to civilian rule in Nigeria, Olusegun Agagu, the governor of the state of Ondo whose capital was Akure, had decided to free some prisoners. Father said my name had topped the list. And that sweltering day of May 21st, 2003 was fixed as the day of our release. But not all prisoners had been lucky. A year after I got into prison, in 1998, Evangelist Ajayi brought news that General Abacha, the dictator, died frothing at the mouth, and news floated that a poisoned apple had killed him. Then, exactly one month later, as he was about to be released, Abacha's prime prisoner and arch enemy, M.K.O. died much the same way—after drinking a cup of tea.

M.K.O.'s afflictions had begun a few months after we met, when the 1993 election he was believed to have won was annulled, setting off a chain of events that put Nigeria's politics on an unprecedented slide for the mud. One day in the following year, while gathered in the sitting room to watch the NTA national network news, we saw M.K.O. rounded up in his house in Lagos by a convoy of about two hundred heavily armed soldiers in armoured tanks and military vehicles, and then led off in a Black Maria; he'd been accused of treason and his long incarceration had begun. But although I had been aware of M.K.O.'s troubles, the news of his death came to me with the force of a blow from a weighted fist. I recall how I hardly slept that night, how I lay on the mattress, covered in the *wrappa* Mother gave me, and thought of how much that man had meant to my brothers and me.

We crossed a portion of the Omi-Ala, the largest in the town and I caught sight of men paddling the mud-coloured water, a fisherman casting a fishnet into the waters. A long line of street-lamp poles ballasted into the concrete lane divider tracked along the road. As we drove towards home, forgotten details of Akure began to open their dead eyes. I noticed that the road had changed a great deal, and that a lot had changed in six years in this city where I was born, in whose soil my feet had been planted. The roads had widened so that the sellers got pushed back many metres from the jumbled roadways, which often filled with cars and trucks. An overhead bridge had been constructed over the road on two sides. Everywhere, the cacophony of vendors crying their wares roused the silent creatures that had crept into my soul. A man dressed in a faded Manchester United jersey ran along as we stopped in the middle of the clogged traffic, banging on the car, as he attempted to shove a loaf of bread through the window near Mother's side. She wound up the glass. In the distance beyond the nearly thousand cars that were honking and raving with impatience was a mighty semi making a slow U-turn under the overhead pedestrian bridge. It was this vehicular dinosaur that had brought the entire traffic to a halt.

Everything that moved around me now was in strong

contrast to the years in prison—when all I did was read, gaze, pray, cry, soliloquize, hope, sleep, eat and think.

"Many things have changed," I said.

"Yes," Mother said. She smiled now and I remembered, in flashes, how spiders had tormented her.

I returned my eyes to the streets. As we drew near home, I heard my own voice say "Daddy, do you mean Obembe has not returned at all, all these years?"

"No, not even once," Father answered sharply, shaking his head.

I wanted to catch Mother's eyes when he said this, but she was staring out of the window and instead, my father's eyes met mine from the overhead mirror. I felt like telling them Obembe wrote to me a few times from Benin, that he said he was now living with a woman who loved him, and adopted him as a son. He'd entered a bus from Akure and travelled to the city of Benin the morning after he left home. He said he'd simply thought of Benin because of the story of the great Oba Ovonramwen of Benin who defied the British imperial rule and decided to go there. When he arrived at the city, he saw a woman coming out of a car and walked up bravely to her and told her he had nowhere to sleep. She took pity on him and took him to her house where she lived alone. He wrote that there were things that would sadden me if he told me and some things he thought I was too young to hear and may not understand, but he promised he would tell them later. The few things he said I should know, for now, were these: the woman was a widow who lived alone, and that he had become a man. He said, in that same letter, that he'd calculated the exact date of my release—February 10th, 2005—and that he would return to Akure that same day. He said Igbafe would keep him abreast of developments, and that way, he would know what happens to me.

Igbafe delivered his letters to me. My brother first met Igbafe when, once—after the first six months in exile—he tried to return home. He'd made the journey, but had been too afraid to enter our compound. He'd sought out Igbafe instead who told him everything and promised to deliver letters to me. He wrote almost every month over the next two years, through Igbafe, who would then give the letters to a junior warden to pass to me—usually with a bribe to persuade them. I often replied to the letters while Igbafe waited outside. But after the first three years, Igbafe suddenly stopped coming, and I never found out why or what became of Obembe. I waited for days and months and then years but nothing. Then all I got was the occasional letter from Father and once, from David. I began to read and reread the letters, about sixteen of them, that Obembe

had sent me until the entire content of the last one he
dated November 14th, 2000—it became stored in my
head like water in a coconut:

> *Listen, Ben,*
>
> *I can't face our parents now and alone. I can't. I'm
> to blame for everything that happened, everything. It
> was I who told Ike what Abulu said when the plane
> flew past—I'm to be blamed. I was so stupid, so stupid.
> Listen, Ben, even you have suffered because of me. I want
> to go to them, but, I can't face them alone. I will come
> the day they release you so we can meet them together
> and beg them forgiveness for all we've done. I need you
> to be there when I come.*
>
> Obembe

As I thought of the letter, it struck me to ask about Igbafe.
I thought I could perhaps find out from him why my
brother had stopped writing. When I asked if Igbafe was
still living in Akure, Mother gazed at me with a startling
measure of surprise.

"The neighbour?" she said.

"Yes, the neighbour."

She shook her head.

"He's dead," she said.

"What?" I gasped.

She nodded. Igbafe had become a truck driver like his father, ferrying timber from forests to Ibadan for two years. He died in an accident when his truck skidded off the road into a deathly crater carved by devastating erosion.

I held my breath when she relayed this. I'd grown up playing with this boy; he'd been there from the beginning and had fished the Omi-Ala with my brothers and me. It was terrible.

"How long ago was this?"

"Two years or so ago," Mother said.

"Incorrect!—two and a half," David interjected.

I looked up when he said this, seized by a strong feeling of déjà vu. I thought for a moment that this was 1992 or 1993 or 1994 or 1995 or 1996 and that it was Boja correcting Mother in that exact way. But this was not Boja, it was his much younger brother.

"Yes," Mother said with half a smile, "two and a half years."

Igbafe's death shocked me even more because I had not contemplated, at the time, the possibility that anyone I knew could have died while I was in prison, but many had. Mr Bode, the motor mechanic, was one of them. He was killed in a road accident, too. Father had written this in a letter, one in which I could almost feel his anger. The last three lines of that letter, charged and powerful, would stand strong in my memory for many years:

Young men are killed on rutted and dilapidated highway "death traps" called roads every day. Yet, these idiots at Aso Rock claim this country will survive. There lies the issue, their lies is the issue.

A pregnant woman rushed carelessly into the road and Father pulled to an abrupt halt. The woman waved in apology as she crossed. We soon entered where I reckoned was the beginning of our street. The streets from here had been cleaned up and new structures had been erected everywhere. It was as though everything had become new, as though the world itself had been born again. Familiar houses popped into sight like vistas rising from a fresh battleground. I saw the spot where Abulu's old decrepit truck used to stand. All that was left was a few pieces of metal, like fallen trees, tangled in a garden of esan grass. A chicken and its chicks were grazing there, dipping their beaks mechanically into the soil. I was amazed at this sight, and I wondered what had happened to the truck, who had removed it. I began to think of Obembe again.

The more we drew near home, the more I thought of him and these thoughts threatened my infant joy. I began to feel that thoughts of a sun-splashed tomorrow—if Obembe did not return—would not breathe for too long. It would slump and die like a man staggering on with bullet holes. Father had told me that Mother had believed Obembe was dead. He said she buried a photo of him four years ago just after she returned from her year-long institutionalization at the Bishop Hughes Memorial Psychiatric Hospital. She said she had dreamt that Abulu killed Obembe like he killed his brother, impaled him with a spear to a wall. She'd tried pulling him off the wall, but he'd died slowly before her eyes. Convinced the dream was real, she began to mourn Obembe, wailing, refusing to be pacified. Father, who believed otherwise, felt it was best to agree with her for the sake of her healing. His friend, Henry Obialor, had advised him to let her get away with it as it was not wise to argue with her. David and Nkem had refused to allow it at first, citing that Abulu, being dead, could not have killed Obembe. But Father cautioned them, and allowed the belief to stay. He followed her to where she'd buried him beside Ikenna in a session she'd forced him to attend, threatening to take her own life if he didn't. But what she buried was not him; it was a photo of him.

Father had changed so much that when he talked, he no longer made eye contact. I'd observed this in the prison reception hall where he'd told me about Mother. He used to be a stronger man; an impregnable man who defended fathering so many children by saying he wanted us to be many so that there could be diversity of success in the family. "My children will be great men," he'd say. "They will be lawyers, doctors, engineers—and see, our Obembe, has become a soldier." And for many years, he'd carried this bag of dreams. He did not know that what he bore all those days was a bag of maggoty dreams; long decayed, and which, now, had become a dead weight.

It was almost dark by the time we got home. A girl I immediately—but not without troubles—recognized to be Nkem opened the gates. She had Mother's exact face and was much taller than a seven-year-old. She wore long braids that stretched down her back. When I saw her, I realized, at once, that she and David were egrets: the snow-white dove-like birds that appear after a storm, flying in groups. Although both of them had been born before the storm that shook our family, they did not experience it. Like a man asleep in the midst of a violent storm, they'd slept through it. And even when—during Mother's first medical exile—they'd felt a touch of it, it had merely been a whimper, not loud enough to have awakened them.

But the egrets were also known for something else: they were often signs or harbingers of good times. They were believed to cleanse the fingernail better than the best nail files. Whenever we and the children of Akure saw them flying in the sky, we rushed out and flapped our fingers after the low-flying white flock travelling overhead, repeating the one-line saying: "Egrets, egrets, perch on me."

The harder you flapped your fingers, the faster you sang; the harder and the faster you flapped your fingers and sang, the whiter and cleaner and brighter your nails became. I was thinking of these when my sister ran into my arms, and gave me a warm embrace, bursting into sobs while saying "Welcome home, brother, Ben" repeatedly.

Her voice sounded like music to my ears. My parents and brother, David, stood behind us, by the car, watching us. I was holding her, muttering that I was happy to be back when I heard someone toot aloud twice. I raised my head and saw, in that moment, the shadowy reflection of a person move across the fence of the compound near the well where many years ago, Boja had been pulled out. The sight startled me.

"There's someone there," I said, pointing towards the near darkness.

But no one moved; it was as if they had not heard me. They all stood there, watching, Father's arms around Mother and a bright smile splayed on David's face. It was as if they asked me, with their eyes, to find out what it was, or that they thought I was wrong. But as I looked in the direction where years ago, my brothers had fought, I saw the reflection of two legs climbing up the fence. I inched closer, the frenzied tom-toms of my heart roused to a fresh awakening.

"Who is there?" I asked aloud.

At first, there was no word, no movement, nothing. I turned back to my family behind me to ask who was there, but they were all fixed in one spot, staring at me, still unwilling to say a word. The darkness had enraptured them and they'd formed a backcloth of silhouettes. I turned again to the spot and saw the shadow rise against the wall and then stand still.

"Who is there?" I said again.

Then, the figure answered and I heard it loud and clear—as if no cause, no bars, no hands, no cuffs, no barriers, no years, no distance, no time had come between the time I last heard his voice and now; as if all the years that had passed were nothing but distance between when a cry was let out and the time it tapered off. That is: the time I realized it was him and the time I heard him say "It is me, Obe, your brother."

For a moment, I stood still as his form began to move towards me. My heart leapt like a free bird at the thought that it was him, my veritable brother, that had now appeared as real as he once was, like an egret after my storm. As he came towards me, I remembered how in court, on the final day of my judgment, I'd seen what seemed like a vision of his return. Before I mounted the stand that day, Father had noticed that I had begun to cry again and pulled me aside to a corner of the courtroom, close to the massive aquamarine wall.

"This is not the time for this, Ben," he whispered once we got there. "There isn't—"

"I know, Daddy, I'm only sad for Mama," I replied. "Please tell her we're sorry."

"No, Azikiwe, listen," he said. "You will go there like the man I've trained you to be. You will go like the man you were when you took up arms to avenge your brothers." A tear dropped down his nose as he carved the invisible torso of a huge man with his hands. "You will tell them how it all happened, you will say it all like the man I brought you up to be—menacing, juggernauts. Like—remember, like—"

He paused, his stray fingers on his shaven head, searching his mind for a word that appeared to have fallen to the back of his mind.

"Like the Fisherman you once were," his quivering lips uttered finally. "Do you hear me?" He shook me. "I said do you hear me?"

I did not answer. I could not, even though I noticed that the commotion outside had increased and the wardens, who held me before, were now approaching. More people were trooping into the court, some of them newsmen with cameras. Father saw them and his voice soared with urgency. "Benjamin, you will not fail me."

I was crying freely now, my heart pounding.

"Do you hear me?"

I nodded.

Later, after the court had been seated and my accuser—a hyena—had described details of Abulu's wounds ("...multiple holes from a fish hook found on the body of the victim, a bust in the head, a punctured vascular tube on the chest..."), the judge asked to hear my defence.

As I made to speak, Father's words—"menacing, juggernauts"—began to repeat themselves in my head. I turned and looked at my parents, who were seated together, and David beside them. Father caught my eyes and nodded. Then he moved his mouth in a way that made me reply with a nod. And once he saw me nod, he smiled. It was then that I let the words pour out, my voice soaring over the arctic silence of the courthouse as I began the way I had always wanted to begin.

"We were fishermen. My brothers and I became—"

Mother let out a loud piercing cry that startled the court, throwing the session into a tumult. Father struggled to cover her mouth with his hand, his whispered entreaties that she be mum, breaking out aloud. All attention went to them as Father's voice leapt from communal apology: "I'm deeply sorry, your Lordship," to *"Nne, biko, ebezina, eme na'ife a*—Do not cry, don't do this." But I did not look at them. I kept my eyes on the green curtains that covered the heavily panelled and dust-covered louvres high above the level of the seats. A strong push of wind flayed them gently so that they looked for a moment like green waving flags. I closed my eyes while the commotion lasted and reclined into an encompassing darkness. In the darkness I saw the silhouette of a man with a rucksack walking back home the same way he'd left. He was almost home, almost within reach when the judge knocked his staff on the table three times and bellowed: "You may now proceed."

I opened my eyes, cleared my throat, and started all over again.

Acknowledgements

Although it carries only my name, *The Fishermen* was produced through the efforts of many:

Unsal Ozunlu, great teacher and early reader—my Turkish father; Behbud Mohammadzadeh, my best friend, inestimable brother; Stavroula, who saw me through most parts of this; Nicholas Delbanco, helper, the shepherd, teacher of good habits; Eileen Pollack, eagle-eyed reader, who scraped the edges of the pages with a red pen; Christina, whose feedback turned the tide; Andrea Beauchamp, the kind helper; Lorna Goodison, the supplier of peace and love...

Jessica Craig, first-rate agent, tour guide, and friend in whose hands I feel at ease; Elena Lappin, the acquirer and editor, the invisible hand behind every page, the great believer; Judy Clain, bringer of joy, editor; Adam Freudenheim, publisher extraordinaire, who, even when bowled over, would not let go; Helen Zell, supplier of abundance and gift to writers...

Bill Clegg, early cheerer, a harbinger of good things; Peter Steinberg, who first sent word out; Amanda Brower, the swift one; Linda Shaughnessy, agent who flung the book far and wide; Peter Ho Davies, the deft trumpeter; Emeka Okafor; Berna Sari; Agnes Krup, DW Gibson and the wonderful people of Ledig House (Amanda Curtin, Francisco Haghenbeck, Marc Pastor, Saskya Jain, Eva Bonne and all); my wonderful fiction cohort and the great writers and faculty of the Helen Zell Writers' program at the University of Michigan who go blue with their pens…

Daddy, the father of many; Nnem, the mother of a crowd; Aunty, the historian; Sisters—Maria, Joy, Kelechi, Peace; my brothers—Mike, Chinaza, Chuwkwuma, Charles, Psalm, Lucky, Chidiebere, this one is for you, a tribute…

To all whom I couldn't, due to space constraints, mention, you know your hands were here, and I thank you as much as those listed here. And to my readers, a hundred times more.

AN IMPRINT OF PUSHKIN PRESS

ONE, an imprint of Pushkin Press, publishes one exceptional fiction or non-fiction title a season. Its list is commissioned and edited by the writer and editor Elena Lappin, who selects the best writing by authors whose extraordinary voices, talent and vision deserve a wide readership and media focus.

THREE GRAVES FULL
Jamie Mason

"Incredibly entertaining and suspenseful... brilliant" *The Times*

A SENSE OF DIRECTION
PILGRIMAGE FOR THE RESTLESS AND THE HOPEFUL
Gideon Lewis-Kraus

"A winning blend of earnestness, wit and high-octane intellect" *Observer*

A REPLACEMENT LIFE
Boris Fishman

"Piercing, witty and enviably well written" *New Statesman*

THE FISHERMEN

Chigozie Obioma

"Striking, controlled and masterfully taut… timeless" *Financial Times*

WHISPERS THROUGH A MEGAPHONE

Rachel Elliott

"Sharp, realistic… charming" *Daily Mail*

THE MINOR OUTSIDER

Ted McDermott

"A spirited, audacious, and drolly funny debut" Patrick deWitt, author of *Undermajordomo Minor*

DAREDEVILS

Shawn Vestal

"Electrifying… a major new voice in fiction" Jess Walter, author of *Beautiful Ruins*

DON'T LET MY BABY DO RODEO

Boris Fishman

www.pushkinpress.com/one